A B... THE ...

ENJOYING THE
GOOD LIFE
IN MALLORCA

ANNA NICHOLAS

A BULL ON THE BEACH

Summersdale Publishers Ltd
46 West Street
Chichester
West Sussex
PO19 1RP
UK

www.summersdale.com

Printed and bound in the UK by CPI Group (UK) Ltd, Croydon, CR0 4YY

ISBN: 978-1-84953-263-1

For Sari and Tomeu, and their daughters, Isabel and Catalina,
whose friendship has been an enduring factor of Sóller Valley life

CONTENTS

ACKNOWLEDGEMENTS

Many kind souls have aided me on this latest adventure exploring the many wonderful aspects of Mallorcan rural life and, more importantly, island sustainability. Some of those who have gone the extra mile include my dear friends Ignacio and Cristina Recalde, Barbara Mesquida of Jaume Mesquida wines, Cristina Alcover, sheep farmer Jaume Jaume and Manuel Romero of Angus Mayol.

It would be unforgiveable of me not to acknowledge the enduring support of Roger Katz, Maggie Tyler, Pere and Margarita Serra, Ignacio Vasallo and Enrique Ruiz of Turespaña, Jason Moore, editor of the *Majorca Daily Bulletin*, Lluc Garcia, editor of the *Sóller* newspaper and Biel Aguareles, editor of the *Veu de Sóller*. I would like to thank Sven Gevers, director of La Residencia in Deia for his support of my books and for his excellent advice about Catalan caviar, and Mariló Ribes for introducing me to a wealth of ecological producers across the island.

I much appreciate the continuing generosity of Jumeirah Hotels, one of whose flagship properties now adorns Sóller Port, and also the new Corinthia Hotel London. As before I would like to give a special mention to Jennifer Barclay, commissioning editor of Summersdale Publishers for her continuing friendship, and to the company's editorial and publicity teams.

And finally I would like to offer a well-deserved *abraçada* to Alan and Ollie for their unstinting good humour and patience, and extend my sincerest thanks to the Sóller community for its warm friendship and to my readers for having so loyally supported my work.

ABOUT THE AUTHOR

As a freelance journalist, Anna Nicholas has contributed to titles such as *The Telegraph, Financial Times, The Independent, Tatler, Daily Mail, Daily Express UltraTravel* and the *Evening Standard*. She contributes a twice-weekly 'Majorcan Pearls' blog to *The Telegraph Expat* and a weekly column to the *Majorca Daily Bulletin*. She is a fellow of the Royal Geographical Society and has been an international adjudicator for *The Guinness Book of Records*. Together with explorer Colonel John Blashford-Snell she has also organised an expedition to carry a grand piano to the remote Wai Wai tribe in South America, which was the subject of a BBC TV documentary. Her author website is at www.anna-nicholas.com.

AUTHOR'S NOTE

Most of the local vernacular used in this book is in the Mallorcan dialect. Although Mallorcan is derived from Catalan and is believed to have been spoken for more than five or six centuries, it varies greatly when written. During the Franco era, Mallorcan was forbidden in Balearic schools and this has made it an oral language, reliant on Catalan when transcribed to print because no dictionary in Mallorcan exists. Today, Catalan is the main language used in Mallorcan schools with the Mallorcan dialect being spoken in the street and in the home. The vocabulary and spelling often varies greatly from village to village in Mallorca. I have taken advice from local language experts and so hope to have accurately transcribed the Mallorcan language to print. However, I apologise unreservedly to any fervent linguists who may care to differ!

One

THE NAKED TRUTH

Something is sizzling in the sun. Not a sausage, but what appears to be a naked human form smothered in a deep, coppery-hued oil and sporting swimming goggles. I stop on the track to catch my breath, rubbing my eyes hard to dispel the bizarre mirage shimmering before me in the fierce late summer heat. When I look up, it's still there, lying corpse-like on the cement surface of my neighbour Rafael's squat *cisterna*, his decrepit old water tank that stands a few feet from the track. What to do? There's nothing for it. I decide to jog casually by in my well-worn, dusty trainers, directing my gaze to the distant, verdant flanks of the Tramuntana mountains where hopefully I might see nothing more surprising than a frisky *cabra Mallorquina*, the island's famed goat, or possibly a hunter setting off home in the early morning with a cache of rabbits.

As I reach Rafael's front yard, there's a flicker of movement from the *cisterna* and the strange bronzed creature rises up onto its feet, grasps a small towel to cover its modesty and yells out to me.

'Hey, running woman! You don't say *hola* to your neighbours any more?'

I turn round, wincing under the white glare of the sun. 'Rafael, please tell me that's not you.'

He raises the goggles carefully up onto his head displaying two ludicrously white circles around his brown eyes. 'Of course it's me! I am sunbathing, how you say, *au naturel*. Is the same in English?'

'We have many expressions, but I rather like "in your birthday suit".'

'But I can sunbathe in my birthday suit even when is not my birthday? And why say "suit" when I wear nothing at all?'

'"Suit" just refers to the naked state you were in on the day you were born. It's just a funny expression.'

He claps his hands together enthusiastically. 'OK, so today I shall wear my birthday suit until the sun goes down!'

'Well, I wish you wouldn't. You're frightening the chickens.'

Indeed Rafael's brood of histrionic scrawny hens and cockerels, which are forever wandering freely on the track in kamikaze fashion, are now flapping about his feet and squawking in evident shock and disdain. He shows me a set of gleaming teeth and does a little jiggle.

'My friend bring me this special tanning oil from Hungary, but he tell me to wear tight goggles because if it runs in your eye, the pain is very bad.'

'And what's with the swimming cap?'

'*Hombre*! I don't want this stuff in my hair. My friend say in one week I go as brown as rum.'

'But you are already.'

'Yes but not...' he pauses with a meaningful glint in his eye. '... everywhere. Here I show you...' The towel edge flickers.

'I can use my imagination, thank you, Rafael.'

He giggles inanely. 'I only joking. Come on, don't act like my *madre*. So you all ready for the Cologne marathon? Your ankle OK now?'

My seventh marathon attempt is only a month away and my training schedule has recently gone to pot since I began to feel a niggling pain in my left ankle while hill running. I'm off to see a traumatologist – about the swelling in my foot, not because I'm having a trauma – although seeing Rafael in the buff could induce one.

He shoos a hen out of his way to inspect my ankle a little more closely.

'Swelling? That's not good. It could mean blood clots, poisoning or some infection. Maybe you need surgery.'

'You really are a great comfort, Rafael. Now, I'd better get home before Catalina arrives.'

He smiles gallantly as I start jogging off up the track playing hopscotch with his stray hens and chicks.

'Hey wait a minute!' he calls after me, and in reaching up to a nearby fig tree to pluck me some fruit, promptly loses his towel altogether.

As I near my front gate I stop to listen to the loud rhythmic song of the cicada that, like the frantic clicking of a thousand knitting needles, fills the valley. From the courtyard and front garden I can hear a different sound – that of my musical frogs. Unlike British frogs, the Mallorcan variety quack rather than croak, their raucous voices at times deafening in the stillness of the balmy night. For a glorious moment in the still, warm air I turn to admire the jagged peaks of the Tramuntanas that embrace the valley like a greeny-grey crown, their flinty tips sparkling under the rays of the sun. My reverie is suddenly interrupted when someone begins calling my name from the lemon orchard above. I squint up to see Fernando, a relatively new arrival in our neighbourhood, peering down at me from behind a high wire fence in the manner of a caged prisoner. After exchanging pleasantries he waggles a sheet of paper at me.

'My mother's doctor has recommended some pills for her *nervios* but the instructions are all in English. What use is that? Could you translate them for me?'

I reach up to take the page of printed matter he's wafting at me, noting that it's been issued by an American drug manufacturer and that the typeface is tiny.

'It seems odd that your mother's doctor should prescribe American drugs. What exactly is wrong with her?'

He shrugs. 'Old age maybe. She gets herself in a state over nothing and has been suffering from some strange hallucinations.'

'Really?'

He laughs. 'Take the other night; she was convinced she saw a rat on the kitchen table munching on some olives.'

'Maybe she did.'

'Ah, but it was wearing a tuxedo and white gloves and had a napkin tied around its neck. That's not normal.'

'No, indeed. I've never seen such a display of manners from any of the rats in our orchard.'

I wander into the courtyard, wondering whether the unremitting sunshine is having an adverse effect on the fragile minds of my neighbours. There hasn't been the tiniest drop of rain for months, and even the normally robust and cheerful crimson bougainvillea running along the front wall of the courtyard is lethargic and limp. Silvery-grey lavender spills from the borders in messy clumps like dry, tangled hair and our once-flourishing bushes of smoky-green thyme have all but shed their leaves, instead displaying spindly bald sprigs that poke forlornly from the soil. It's not just Pepita, Fernando's mother, who's suffering from hallucinations. Often in the night I've convinced myself that I can hear torrential rain pounding on the cobbles below only to awake with a start in the morning to find the sun leering in at the window, and the upper terraces as cracked and raw as chapped lips.

Leaning against one of the pillars of the porch, I stretch out my stiff legs and calculate that I've run at least ten miles. It's not a bad effort, but hardly sufficient to calm my own *nervios* about the forthcoming marathon. The door springs open and Alan, my husband – the Scotsman as he is known – strides out onto the porch, a trug of scrawny, sorry-looking lemons tucked under one arm.

'You'll never believe it. Now there's not even a drop of water in the *acequia*. How am I supposed to keep the vegetables going? I'll have to talk to Arturo.'

Wiping the perspiration from my face, I begin doing a bandy stork impression, pulling one leg up behind me in a stretch while wobbling precariously on the other. The *acequia*, or *siquia* as it's known in Mallorquin, is our water irrigation channel that runs through the orchard and field. It has been a lifeline during the arid summer but perhaps even the mountain springs that supply it have given up the ghost. Poor Arturo, the local *síquier*, who keeps an eye on all the channels in the valley, closes off the sluices when water is running precariously low and has to cope with grumbles and complaints from all and sundry.

'Hopefully it's only a temporary thing. Arturo wouldn't stop the supply unless it was absolutely necessary. Now, more importantly, I have to tell you about Rafael. He's taken to sunbathing naked on top of his *cisterna*. It gave me quite a turn this morning.'

He raises an eyebrow. 'What, you mean completely starkers?'

'Well, that all depends whether you consider swimming goggles to be an item of modesty.'

He's about to respond when a car, horn blasting wildly, appears on the track and rumbles across the gravel into the courtyard. My irrepressible friend Catalina throws open the driver's door and offers a cursory glance in our direction.

'Hey, you won't believe what we just seen!'

'A naked man covered in brown oil?' I proffer.

Miquela, who assists Catalina in her local cleaning business, has already jumped out of the passenger seat and joined us on the porch.

'*Que susto!*' she cries. What a fright. 'We were driving up the track and all of a sudden we caught sight of him by Rafael's chicken shed, singing and wearing nothing but goggles and a swimming cap. Catalina put her foot down, I can tell you.'

'It's only Rafael trying out a new fast-tanning method.'

Catalina barges past us into the *entrada* and shakes her head. 'He should be careful. Someone might report him to the Guardia Civil.'

Somehow I can't imagine the local military police being too fussed about a bakery owner tanning himself in the buff on his own land. All the same, in future he would be wise to avoid the communal track. We traipse after Catalina into the wide hallway where I throw off my trainers, delighting in the cool of the marble floor. She regards me with some disdain.

'Take your smelly shoes upstairs and have a shower, then you can make me a coffee.'

'OK, commandant.'

I head up the stairs, grateful to leave behind the cacophony of Miquela and Catalina doing battle with pots and pans, ironing boards, brooms, buckets and mops. Ever since moving to rural Mallorca, Catalina has been a constant in my life, although our friendship began in England when, in her late teens, she au-paired for my sister, Cecilia. It was Catalina who first urged the Scotsman and me to holiday in the rugged north-west of the island; where by chance in the Sóller Valley we discovered a dilapidated *finca*, an old country farmhouse, in need of love and renovation. Continuing to work flat out in London where we ran a busy public relations consultancy, we gradually made the house habitable with the help of local builders until we were able to up sticks completely nine years ago and make Mallorca our home. Now every week Catalina and Miquela sweep by like a dynamic Batman and Robin attacking dust and cobwebs and polishing off our mountain of ironing.

I pull off my running gear and take a shower, watched over by a voyeuristic Moorish gecko that observes me upside down from the ceiling with a troubled expression. A splash of water reaches him and in a flash he's disappeared into a tiny crevice above the window frame.

In the kitchen I find Catalina hovering over the ironing board while white steam hisses and swirls about her fingers. She sets down the iron.

'You know what happened at the *correbou* yesterday?'

'I will if you tell me,' I reply, filling the coffee machine with fresh water.

The *correbou* held annually in Fornalutx village as part of the Mare de Déu fiesta is the only bull-running event still tolerated in Mallorca, and has become a controversial affair increasingly attracting animal activists. Some years ago, I attended the event and was pained to see the fear in the young bull's eyes as it was heckled and paraded around the village square. However, unlike such affairs on the mainland, the bull is not chased around the streets by hysterical youths because it is bound by heavy ropes, and once, as custom dictates, it has been crowned with a laurel wreath, it is slaughtered humanely and parcels of its flesh distributed to every member of the village community. While I continue to eat meat, and enjoy the hospitality of the islanders, I feel it is not my place to pass criticism on an age-old tradition.

Catalina gives a loud tut. 'These animal protesters turned up and began jumping about on the floor pretending to be bulls. How silly is that?'

'How did the villagers react?'

'What do you think? We all ignored them and carried on with the event. The mayor told us not to let them provoke us after what happened last time.'

I think Juan, the village mayor, did the right thing. The previous year there had been a scuffle when locals clashed with protestors, and the police were forced to step in.

'So, what happened?' I ask, placing a cup of coffee at her side.

'*Pues*, the protesters were all kept on the local football pitch while we did the bull run and afterwards they left.'

'No confrontation, then?'

She stops her ironing to take a sip of coffee. 'No, but it was still annoying. The thing is, this is a local village event that has been going for many years. We don't want trouble and we don't want to hurt the bull. We are nice people.'

And indeed the villagers of Fornalutx are good people, but times are changing and such traditions are being reassessed and judged according to modern attitudes.

'You know that Catalonia has just announced that it's banning all bullfights in the region?'

She yawns. 'But it has little to do with animal rights and everything to do with politics.'

Catalina has a point. The Catalan nationalists are keen to distance themselves from any tradition supported by the conservative elements of Spanish society, of which bullfighting is one.

'Well, at least with the fiesta over you can get back to the diet.'

She pounds a sheet with the iron. 'No chance! It's Mallorca Day celebrations soon, and then there's the Sóller music fiesta and the Bunyola fiesta. Ramon's family will expect us over there. And before you know it, it'll be Christmas!'

'So you'll have one of my raspberry muffins then?'

She gives me a wink. '*Pues*, if you insist.'

An hour later I am in Ollie's bedroom trying to make sense of the jumble of clothes, books, files, bubblegum wrappers and random dead ants and flies that seem to have swallowed up the wooden floor. Under his bed I discover a discarded can of Bitter Kas – his favourite local tipple that tastes like Campari but without the alcohol – some dusty firecrackers, two video games and a pile of empty chocolate bar wrappers. Curiously the story of *Chicken Licken*, one of his favourite childhood books is lying with its pages flung open in the middle of the chaos. A wave of nostalgia hits me and pulling it closer, I sit back on my knees and begin reading the first page. Irksomely Catalina is suddenly bearing down on me with a distinct glimmer of disapproval in her eyes and a duster in her hand.

'Since you give up all this flying back and forth to London, you start wasting your time. Leave all this for me and get on with your work.'

The whole point though was that I could play truant more often in Mallorca. Since merging my London public relations consultancy with Dynamite PR, I have subsequently been balancing my days between freelance consultancy work for Dynamite and a few former clients, book writing and journalism, with a small dollop of time-wasting thrown in. Catalina has other ideas. I slope upstairs to the office and glimpse the emails littering my inbox. Rachel, my former super-efficient, no-nonsense managing director, is now on the board of Dynamite PR and is already calling the shots, which doesn't surprise me in the least. I read her email and guffaw. She has taken on a new client, a state-of-the-art men's health and virility clinic in Harley Street called All Man – oh purleese – and wonders whether I could cast an eye over a proposal for its launch. I give her a call.

'Love the sound of your new client.'

'Oh be quiet!' Her voice ripples with laughter. 'The clinic's big on Viagra and testosterone testing so I'm just the girl for the job – I don't think. Mind you Raisa Ripov will test my mettle.'

'Sorry?'

'Didn't you get my email about her yesterday?'

Somewhat guiltily I see that I have left the email unopened, probably because I had something far more pressing to do – a hen to feed, or a tray of salted tomatoes to leave out in the sun.

'So who is Raisa Ripov, a Russian cartoon character?'

'You're not far off the mark. She's a seventy-year-old Russian–Czech who's opening a new day spa and aesthetics centre in Mayfair called Radiance. A bit cheesy, but it could be worse.'

'Please tell me Ripov isn't her real name.'

'Afraid so.'

'I thought Russian women added an *a* at the end of their surnames, so shouldn't it be Ripova?'

'God knows. Anyway her father's a Czech. She's a bit of a diva so I'd rather not start questioning her about her name.'

'Oh, not another one. I've got enough on my hands with Dannie Popescu-Miller at the moment.'

Dannie is a long-standing American client of Rumanian ancestry who runs her Miller Magic interior design business from Trump Tower in New York, and claims to be a descendant of Vlad the Impaler. When I merged my agency, Dannie was one of three clients whose PR needs I agreed to handle on a private basis.

'How's Dannie doing?' asks Rachel.

'She's found a site for a new store in St Petersburg, so we're meeting in London next month to talk through launch plans.'

'Is everything else OK? Missing the office banter?'

'Remember I have my frogs. And don't forget Johnny.'

She groans. 'Good to know you're still insane. Catch up later. Oh, and remember to send me your thoughts on the All Man launch.'

I stand up and lean out of the office window which overlooks the front lawn, noting that the arthritic old olive tree is in need of a bit of attention. Our latest addition to the feline family, Doughnut – whom the Scotsman has rechristened DO NOT – has taken to blunting his claws on the bark every morning and it seems to be taking its toll. The frogs are aimlessly cluttered about the rocks and rushes in the pond, chirruping loudly while Johnny, my beloved toad, is nowhere to be seen. Next month they will all hop off on their annual five-month amphibian holiday, though the location is a closely guarded secret. Come October, on the same day throughout the valley, the frogs and toads simply disappear. I've tried asking Johnny where they go to but he remains tight-lipped. I like to imagine them playing leapfrog and Twister in some Florida aqua park, but they could just as easily be hanging out in the Tramuntana mountains, striding forth with miniature hiking poles and singing 'A frog he would a-wooing go' at the top of their voices. Alan potters on to the patio below and begins inspecting the pond. There's a series of loud plops as the frogs leap into the murky depths.

'You've disturbed their sunbathing.'

He looks up at me. 'We're going to have to dredge this pond. The bulrushes have completely taken over.'

'But we'll have to wait for the frogs to leave first.'

He puffs out his cheeks. 'I'd rather do it sooner than later. They'll just have to find another pond somewhere until October.'

'But we can't make them homeless. I insist we wait until they've gone.'

He raises an eyebrow and mutters something under his breath which fortunately I don't hear, and plods off to examine the olive tree. The telephone rings.

'Guv, it's me.'

Uh-oh. It's Greedy George on the line, my irreverent and thoroughly mischievous, though ingenious, client who runs Havana Leather, a luxury goods business just off Piccadilly.

'How's life in London?'

'Remember what Oscar Wilde said, guv? "When a man gets bored of London, he's bored of life".'

'Actually you've got it completely wrong. It was Samuel Johnson who said "When a man is tired of London, he is tired of life", and anyway, you can't say bored *of*, it's bored *with*.'

'And that, guv, is why you're such a pain in the neck. Always nitpicking. So what's new?'

'Let me think. Well, we've just had a bumper crop of aubergines and the hens are laying at least three eggs between them a day...'

'STOP! I can't keep my eyes open. Your life's just too scintillating.'

'You did ask. Anyway, you're supposed to be on holiday.'

'Yeah, me and the missus are off tomorrow so I thought I'd touch base. Any tips?'

'Don't upset anyone and if you go to the Sagrada Familia, don't wear shorts.'

He yawns heavily. 'Nah, I'm not going to Barcelona for culture or religion. We're only there a week. I'm planning on finding a nice nudist beach so I can watch the girls and hang out in some groovy bars in the evening.'

'You're revolting.'

'Cheers, guv. Have you heard of Mar Bella beach? It's supposed to be for naturists.'

'Fortunately not. And is Bianca excited about the trip?'

A deep rumble of laughter fills the line. 'Bianca doesn't get excited about anything apart from the odd lettuce leaf and Ayurvedic massage. She's hacked off because we're not going back to the villa in Tuscany, but Italy's really getting a bit passé. Anyway, I've found her a detox clinic off the Ramblas so that'll cheer her up.'

'Is your housekeeper looking after Harris?'

'Consuela? God no, they eat dogs in the Philippines, guv. Best not to put temptation her way. I don't want to find Harris hotdogs in the freezer when we get back.'

I finally get him off the line and begin wading through a screenful of emails. After editing an article for an in-flight magazine I add some thoughts to Rachel's proposal for the All Man Clinic and polish off one of the weekly blogs that I write for a national newspaper's 'Expat' section. A pang of hunger begins gnawing at me like a persistent mouse, so I potter downstairs in search of food only to find the fridge empty. In truth, it does contain food but nothing particularly tempting, or rather of a comforting calorific nature. Aubergines and lemons are cluttering up the sink and work surfaces where the Scotsman has helpfully dumped them after evidently having had a good forage in the orchard and vegetable patch, but the cupboards are bare. There are two forlorn raspberry muffins left in a tin, but I feel I should leave them for Ollie's return from school. There's no alternative. I will have to do battle with the local supermarket. Catalina walks in from the garden with a basket of sheets newly plucked from the washing line, and grins.

'Just in time to help me fold them.'

'I might just find the energy before collapsing with hunger.'

She laughs and shakes a crumpled white corner in my direction. Together we begin our weekly ritual of pulling and folding the cotton sheets into submission before she thumps them down on to the ironing board. I inspect the fridge once more in the foolish belief that I might find an egg.

'We need some more chickens,' I announce.

'Why, the hens not laying enough?'

'About half a dozen a week, but we could do with more. Besides, I think Salvador needs a bit of excitement. Goneril and Regan are always pecking at him and Cordelia's become a bit of a drag, always moping in the corner of the corral.'

'Ramon will go with you to Santa Maria market. His friend is selling the best layers there now. I'll get him to call you.'

Ramon, Catalina's husband, tends a healthy brood of hens that live on a parcel of land in Fornalutx village. Like ours, they are the traditional Mallorcan breed with bronze and white plumage and wary, startled green eyes. Adding three more females to the melee will certainly keep Salvador on his toes.

'We could do with a larger henhouse and corral too. And then we need a new donkey hut and to repair the fence by the stream, and the pond's in a complete mess.'

Catalina smiles. 'Buy the chickens and then you can worry about everything else later. *Poc a poc.*'

Little by little. Nine years down the line and I'm still kidding myself with the soothing Mallorcan mantra that in time everything will get done.

I turn to Catalina. 'If you say that fast enough, you can sound just like a hen. *Poc a poc, poc a poc, poc a poc...*'

Alan pops his head round the open kitchen door. 'Good impression of a demented chicken. Talking of which, Cordelia's left you a present.'

He holds out a warm egg which I take gleefully in my hand. A tiny brown feather is still attached to the tip, giving it a rather jaunty look. I regret my earlier hasty comments about poor old Cordelia. She's really not such a bad egg after all.

Two

A SIGHT FOR SORE EYES

When Catalina and Miquela have finally departed I return to the squeaky clean kitchen to admire the freshly mopped floor and sparkling windows. A minute later the Scotsman appears in his clodhopper gardening boots, scattering mud everywhere.

'Well done. You've just ruined Catalina's spotless floor. We could have eaten our lunch off it.'

He offers me a concerned look. 'Why on earth would we have wanted to do that?'

I sit down at the kitchen table with my aunt's old pickle and preserving bible that was written in the sixties, and indicate that he should take a seat.

'Now, I've been thinking...'

'Oh dear,' he interjects. 'That spells trouble.'

'... we keep talking about becoming self-sufficient here, but have we gone far enough?'

His brow furrows. 'Well, we're not doing badly. We grow most of our own veg and fruit, and what we don't grow we buy from Això és Vida.'

It's true that we have become increasingly independent over the years, to the extent that our vegetable patch is thriving and our fruit trees are well-developed. All the same, we like to support small organic farms and producers of authentic local cheeses and meat, firmly believing that aside from tourism this is where the island's future lies. We have recently been supporting an ecological cooperative of young Mallorcan farmers and smallholders called Això és Vida, meaning 'that's life'. Every fortnight this group delivers pre-ordered boxes of assorted fresh produce to customers across the island. In Sóller, it supplies a new group initiative to which we belong called Almaeco, meaning 'soul of eco', that also supports a number of other independent eco-producers. So every two weeks cheery Teo Nogara, one of Això és Vida's representatives, arrives in a small van which he unloads at the Red Cross offices off the town's square. It's become quite a social gathering and other organic produce is exchanged among the group – honey, eggs, stoneground flour, chick peas, goat and sheep cheese, fresh lamb and beef from a herd of Angus cattle reared near Valldemossa.

Alan continues. 'And we've got the hens and the wormery and the compost heap…'

'I know all that, but we could do more.'

'Such as? I mean Pep and I are starting to cultivate our own wine, and soon we're going to get cracking on making limoncello.'

'Hmm. What I'm talking about is making sure we do things in a more organised manner, according to the seasons. We waste a lot of fruit and veg because we don't bottle it in time and we buy too much from the supermarket. I want to do all my own pesto and pickles and jams and jellies.'

He nods. 'I'm all for that, but we need to buy new bottling jars and seals, and maybe we should devote whole mornings or days to the task.'

'Now you're talking. I mean, I do a lot of small production runs on my own but it would be quicker if we did it together.'

'I'm game, but you'll have to teach me how to sterilise the jars and I've no idea how you make those Moroccan lemons.'

'That's all easy-peasy,' I say, warming to my theme, 'it's just a question of getting our ducks in a row and using a bit of logic. Then there's the whole waste issue. I was reading in one of the local papers that the average person in the Balearics generates two kilos of rubbish a day.'

He shakes his head. 'That's incredible. So, how can we improve on that front?'

'Take our vegetable scraps bucket, for example. We should have separate ones for compost and the chickens instead of one big mess.'

'That's easily remedied. While we're on the subject, we should create another for waste paper and cardboard. We can use most of it on the fire.'

'And we should be recycling things more,' I reply. 'We give clothes that Ollie's outgrown to Catalina to distribute to hard-up families in the valley but that rule should apply to everything. Even old sheets and tea towels.'

'My mother used to make them into dusters.'

'Precisely. We just get used to throwing things away that could be put to good use.'

'You mean because of planned obsolescence?'

'That's only partly to blame. Take buttons.'

'Buttons?' he quizzes.

'Yes, lazily I forget to take them off old garments that are too ancient and threadbare to give away. Do you remember it cost me a fiver for a replacement plastic button for my coat? The store assistant told me that no one sewed any more, so the price of buttons was soaring because of low production.'

'Madness.'

'Exactly. Anyway, it got me thinking that we must change the way we do things. We've got to be less wasteful.'

'So, where do we begin?'

'How about we bottle all those aubergines together? I've got a great recipe.'

He walks over to the sink and rolls up his sleeves. 'What do we have to do with them?'

'Peel and cut them into slices, cover them in salt and let them rest for several hours.'

'Then what?'

'The rest is fairly straightforward. We rinse and squeeze the water out of them and place the slices in sterilised jars in layers with garlic cloves, basil leaves, peppercorns and a little red wine vinegar. When that's all done, we cover the whole lot in olive oil.'

He sighs. 'So it's quite time-consuming?'

I shrug. 'If we make sharp work of it, we should have them all salted and ready to bottle this evening. And another thing.'

He winces. 'Yes?'

'I want to create a garden gym with logs and branches and rocks as weights, a kind of fitness arena without having to go to a stuffy gym.'

'But you don't go anyway.'

'I know, but it would be a great way to get fitter. Running and gardening's OK as far as it goes, but heaving a few logs before breakfast would liven us up.'

'And where are we going to get all the logs?'

'From Llorenç of course. He's delivering some wood soon, so I'll ask him to cut some logs of different sizes. We could do with a skipping rope, maybe some kettle bells and one of those wobbly boards.'

'This is worse than a Gulag camp.'

'I know,' I say, squeezing his arm. 'We're going to create our very own boot camp. How thrilling is that?'

Ollie and I are ambling along a mountain track in the fading sunlight. It's only just gone seven but he is yawning heavily, probably in anticipation of the pile of homework awaiting him back at the house. Now that he's become a teenager, he's developed a slouch and has started a trend for wearing mismatched socks and sneakers with brightly coloured laces. His Spanish friends seem to deem this the height of coolness. Having a few hours earlier picked him up from school I had lured him, with the promise of a Bitter Kas and an ice cream, to take a stroll with me in the hills. There is nothing better than walking in the early evening when the scent of rosemary and lavender hangs heavy in the air, and the sun begins to melt like honey on the horizon. Our peace is rudely interrupted by the sound of boots on crunching gravel, and we turn to see a phalanx of male and female hikers carrying walking poles and rucksacks. I do a double take, because aside from beanie hats, socks and boots they're wearing little else. Ollie blinks hard and turns his head away, a rosy hue creeping up his cheeks. The male leader smiles and yells a cheerful German greeting in our direction and, without the slightest embarrassment, leads his naked troop of all shapes and sizes down into the car parking area and on to an awaiting minibus. Ollie and I gawp at each other.

He begins chortling. 'What the hell?!'

I turn to him. 'How extraordinary. Have you ever witnessed such a sight?'

Ollie grabs my arm. 'Best to stay here until they've gone. It wasn't a pretty sight. Have you ever heard of Stephen Gough?'

'No.'

'He's a bit of a legend. An ex-military guy known as the naked rambler. He was arrested when he walked from Land's End to John o'Groats in 2003. He's always in prison for hiking naked. He's pretty sick.'

'No wonder. It must be freezing walking without clothes in British weather.'

He gives me an old-fashioned look. 'You really are sad. I meant he's cool, you know, sick?'

'How can it be cool to be sick? And I'm not remotely sad.'

'Time for you to return to the mothership.'

Since turning thirteen, my son has adopted a new cyberspeak, a kind of gobbledygook vernacular often transmitted in the form of texts to his friends which his father and I find totally unintelligible. When I fail to grasp teen-speak, cannot identify a supposedly hot new musical talent on the radio or recognise a self-styled celebrity in a magazine, he is wont to gasp, 'What planet are you on?' Of late he has reached the certainty that I must be of an alien species. Perhaps he knows something I don't.

I'm intrigued that my son seems to be an authority on naked rambling. I learn something new about him every day. 'So, if it's illegal to hike nude in the UK, why isn't it here?'

Ollie shrugs. 'We're in Mallorca. As if anyone would give two hoots!'

He watches as the hikers drive off in their old tour bus, a balloon of grey dust gently rising up in their wake, and begins jogging down the steep, stony slope to the car park. Once in the car, I notice Fernando's medical instruction sheet peeping out of my handbag and pass it to Ollie.

'Fernando's mother has been given some new pills, but the instructions are all in Americanese. Would you mind translating them for him?'

'Why can't you do it?'

'My Spanish isn't as good as yours.'

He grunts. 'Practice makes perfect, mother. All right, here's the deal. If I do this you let me go on the PlayStation after dinner.'

I start up the engine and smile in agreement. Sometimes it's better to give in gracefully to filial demands, especially when the payback involves a translation of tedious and tricky Spanish terminology in impossibly small print.

It's late morning and the Scotsman is pottering around the vegetable patch tending his tomatoes and aubergines. He hasn't spied me yet, otherwise he wouldn't be puffing with quite so much gusto on one of his beloved *puros*, a cigar with the girth of a Swiss roll. Much as Ollie and I try by devious means to curb his tobacco vice, not least hiding packets of cigars in imaginative nooks and crannies around the *finca*, he resolutely puffs on, secreting his stash in his *abajo*, his potting shed-cum-lair, in the orchard. Often in the late evening when he thinks I'm curled up in bed with a book, I tiptoe to the window and see a tiny luminescent dot, like that of a glow-worm doing cartwheels in the still night air, a sure sign that he's taking his *puro* for a late night walk around the terraces.

A flycatcher flitters by and a fat blackbird swoops down on some old crumbs I've left on the kitchen windowsill. Standing out on the back terrace I look beyond the pool, to the field and orchard. The hens are strutting around their corral just in front of the *abajo*, and far beyond, obscured by chubby palm trees, is the donkey den where Minny and Della, a docile mother and daughter, normally graze under the shadow of the Tramuntanas. For now, they are back with Jacinto who originally sold them to us, while we make their plot of land more secure and build a new donkey shelter, offering better protection from the weather. In a sheltered area to the left of the field we created a site for a small cattery, which we had to put on hold when new regional planning laws came into force. The simple wooden structure will be reintroduced once we receive permission from the local council to progress with our plans. The regional elections will be happening soon enough and we are confident that if the town's vet is elected mayor, we will be given the green light. The orchard to the far right, normally a fiery tableau, is lacking its citrus guests. The lemons are all but past their best and our oranges and tangerines are a sickly green. It'll be December before they return to their full splendour. The Scotsman catches sight of me and quickly drops his cigar to the ground, stubbing it out underfoot. I watch as he makes his way across the field and over to the flight of stone stairs. When he reaches the top step, he stops to catch his breath. 'It's getting a bit cooler. Should be rain soon.'

'Dream on...'

He looks up into the blue cloudless sky and sighs. 'By the way, I popped up to Fernando's house and gave him Ollie's translation. Did you know that he'd drawn a large skull and crossbones at the top of the page? Thankfully Fernando found it funny.'

'That lad is a wag. Maybe I should have done it after all, but the bits Ollie read out to me seemed OK. He said that the medication warned of a lot of side effects.'

'Sometimes it really doesn't pay to read the small print. Fancy a coffee?'

We enter the kitchen to find Doughnut and Minky wrestling on the tiled floor while Tiger, our German neighbours' cat, has somehow managed to ascend the fridge freezer and is glaring down on the others like a vengeful Zeus. We shoo them out into the sunshine.

The Scotsman suddenly beams. 'Guess what? I've got a little surprise for you. I've had a go at making sun-dried tomatoes. Wait here.'

He leaves the kitchen and potters back in with one of my metal muffin trays. He sets it proudly on the table and is slightly put out when I shake my head in dismay.

'What's up? I cut them vertically and sprinkled them with sea salt just like you do, and stuck them out in the sun.'

I pick up one of the tomato halves and show him how the sea salt and acidic juice has eaten through the non-stick coating of the muffin tin.

He pulls a face. 'Oh dear.'

'Lesson number one is always to lay them out on a non-metallic tray or dish, and you have to keep an eye on them in case insects settle on them, as they have done on yours. See these ants? That's why it's best to cover them with a light muslin cloth.'

He gives me a hangdog look. 'And I thought I was doing so well.'

'At least we've got heaps more tomatoes, so it's not the end of the world.'

'How long should you leave them out in the sun, anyway?'

'About two or three days, depending on how strong the sun is. They should feel spongy and free of moisture when they're ready for bottling.'

He frowns at the muffin tray. 'I'm sorry about that. I suppose it's a write-off?'

I give him a wink 'Actually, I've had my eye on some of those new silicone muffin moulds, so perhaps you've done me a favour.'

'Well, it's our twentieth wedding anniversary coming up soon. They could make the perfect gift.'

I give him a nudge. 'You won't get off the hook that lightly.'

He laughs. 'No, I suppose not.'

'Actually, maybe we should mark the occasion with something special. A sort of joint gift to ourselves?'

'Such as?' he asks.

'Maybe a new chicken house?'

He puffs out his bottom lip. 'Not very romantic, but on the other hand...'

He gives a start when the buzzer goes at the gate and moments later, Stefan, our builder and two of his Bolivian workers, Rudi and Jaime arrive. Stefan is Catalina's younger brother and it's thanks to him that our house is now habitable. It was Stefan who nearly a decade ago worked tirelessly with his fellow local artisans to turn it from a ruin into a family home. He stands grinning in the wide *entrada*.

'So what shall we do first? Clear the pond or set to work on the fence down by the stream?'

I'm acutely aware that the frogs are still happily frolicking around in the pond and that Johnny will be furious if uprooted from his favourite slimy rock prior to his amphibian getaway.

'Let's concentrate on the fence first, Stefan.'

He nods. 'Fine by us.'

The Scotsman is chuntering over the coffee machine. 'This contraption is enough to drive a man to drink.'

'Still bothering you?' says Stefan sympathetically at the same time slipping me a wink. Alan's ineptitude in operating what has to be the simplest coffee machine in the world is legendary.

'Let me do it.' I grab some cups and begin handing round espressos and a sugar bowl.

'I hear you're off with Ramon to buy new hens,' says Stefan.

'We could do with a few more.'

He drains his cup. 'A new larger chicken house wouldn't go amiss and you could do with expanding the corral.'

The Scotsman and I look at one another. Although we've already discussed the purchase of a better chicken house, we also need to build a new donkey shelter and we still have a multitude of gardening projects to get started.

'What came first, the chicken or the egg?' asks the Scotsman mysteriously to which Stefan shrugs, and replies, 'Always the chicken, Alan. You can be sure of that.'

It is Friday evening and we're off for supper to Es Turo, one of our favourite local restaurants in Fornalutx. The marbled sky is sullen and threaded with slate-hued clouds. Ollie sits in the back of the Mini sending text messages to his legion of cyberfriends as we rattle along the stony track. Helge and Wolfgang's house, which is closest to ours, is in darkness and will remain so until they return in the spring, but delicious cooking smells waft from the kitchen of Rafael's *finca*, a sure sign that his new girlfriend will be popping round for supper. At the mouth of the track, we wave to Silvia who is sitting in her mahogany rocking chair out on the patio, while her husband Pedro leans over a newspaper at a table, illuminated by the light of an ancient standard lamp. Across from their home is the white chalet once occupied by Margalida, the elderly mother of Silvia, who until she died was one of my cherished friends. In the neat front garden her favourite jacaranda tree continues to thrive, its delicate, lacy green mane rippling in the light breeze. Most days and come all weathers Tomeu, her old tabby cat, loyally stands guard at its base as if expecting his mistress's imminent return. As we're about to turn on to the road, someone raps on the back of the car and a second later Fernando's face appears at my open window. He's out of breath.

'I just wanted to thank you for translating those medical instructions for my mother.'

He looks over at Ollie and smiles. 'I liked the skull and cross bones warning. How right you were!'

'What do you mean?' I ask.

'*Pues,*' he says, shaking his head. 'They seem to have made her worse than ever. We'll have to tell her doctor.'

'I'm sorry to hear that,' chips in the Scotsman.

Fernando gives a little whinny. 'I shouldn't laugh, but this afternoon she told us she'd looked down from our terrace and seen a naked man on your track covered in mud and wearing goggles. Imagine!'

There's an unearthly groan from the heavens and water begins tumbling from the sky. 'Rain!' shrieks the Scotsman with elation. 'At last, wonderful rain!'

I'm about to reply to Fernando, but he's already dashed from the car with a backward wave and has begun scrambling up the path to his land. I close the window and smile up at the sodden sky. Every cloud has a silver lining. If the rainy season is now upon us, it should put a stop to Rafael prancing about in his birthday suit for quite some time.

Three

HEN PARTY

I awaken in the sultry early morning light to hear Salvador trumpeting madly from the orchard. It's not a half-hearted, effeminate cock-a-doodle-doo, the hallmark of Rafael's four puny cockerels, but a full-bodied, deep and macho roar that echoes around the still Tramuntana mountains awakening every living beast within our small enclave of the valley. Donkeys bray, sheep bleat, birds chatter and neighbours' dogs bark excitedly as Salvador welcomes in the new day. I turn to my bedside clock and see that it is 6.00 a.m. Time for an early shower, even if it is Sunday morning. Ramon will be here in less than an hour to accompany us on our hen-buying mission to Santa Maria market. I attempt to jolt the Scotsman awake but he fixes me with a resentful and bleary eye.

'Someone kill the cockerel,' he murmurs, and falls back to sleep.

I get ready and pop downstairs to wake Ollie. To my amazement he's already up and about, hair wet from the shower, and wearing his favourite grey jeans and turquoise sneakers. These days my son is a veritable fashion statement of cool brands, always sweet-smelling and scrubbed to within an inch of his life with all sorts of mysterious lotions and potions cluttering up his bathroom shelf. Suddenly hot water and soap have become fashionable, girls are no longer the enemy, texting has replaced speech, clothes need ironing and books collect dust on shelves.

'Would you like some tea?'

He rubs his eyes and yawns. 'Whatever.'

Outside the kitchen door, five anxious faces greet me. There's Inko, disdainful queen of the group, our part-Siamese cat with the quirky apology for a tail, smoky-grey twins Minky and Orlando, tabby and tubby Doughnut and Bat Cat, previously known as Damian. Why Bat Cat has morphed into a bat can only be explained by his exceptionally large ears and the fact that his pelt is the colour of liquorice. Scraggy, also known as Fagin for his habit of luring young abandoned kittens to join his hunting and begging forays on the communal track, is nowhere to be seen. He is ownerless but falls upon my charity every morning. I fill their food bowls, and watch as the cats shoot into the kitchen to take their allocated places. The sound of their collar bells chinking against the metallic bowls reminds me of the demure murmur of cutlery against porcelain and for a moment I imagine myself transported to a rather genteel guesthouse where breakfast is consumed politely and wordlessly by the assembled eclectic throng.

When I arrive at the corral with the customary bowl of warm oat, raisin, corn and bread mush, Goneril and Regan begin pecking excitedly at my plimsolls. Between them they manage to undo both laces, no doubt imagining that they are grappling with two particularly tough and flavourless worms. Salvador and Cordelia stand aloof by the gate, eyeing up the food but waiting until I have filled the water trough and exited the corral. Tentatively they step closer, eventually elbowing the greedy sisters out of the way, and in a matter of minutes the bowl is empty. As I jog up the steps from the orchard I hear a car engine and see

Ramon waving from the driver's window. In the kitchen I press the button that operates the electronic gate and his battered old white van rumbles into the courtyard. He jumps out, kisses me on both cheeks and follows me into the warm kitchen.

'Time for a coffee?'

He tuts and shakes his head. 'We can do that later. Best to get to the market early before all the best chickens have gone.'

He peers at the row of jars lined up on the kitchen table and picks one up to inspect it.

'Are these aubergines?'

'Yes, bottled in olive oil and garlic. Do you want a jar?'

He smiles, 'If one's going.'

'Leave them for a month and then serve them up as antipasti with *jamon Serrano* or salami and goat's cheese. Delicious.'

'*Graciès*. Catalina will love them. Now where's my favourite *chico*?'

Ollie sidles into the kitchen and they exchange fist punches on the arm, a distinctly male greeting which seems to amuse them no end. The Scotsman, now wide awake, appears on the porch and looks at his watch.

'Good grief, Ramon. It's not even seven. We should get the pick of the bunch.'

Ramon laughs. 'Just wait and see. The place will be packed by the time we arrive.'

We pile into his van and off we go, bouncing along the quiet track and through winding narrow streets until we are on the main Palma road. A few early birds sit outside cafes with coffees and newspapers but there is little traffic until, some twenty minutes later, we reach the village of Santa Maria. In the twinkling of an eye, the streets become clogged with cars, vans, *motos* – the popular local pop-pop bikes – and swarms of shoppers. Finding somewhere to leave the car is nigh impossible until Ramon swings into a makeshift car park on rough, sandy terrain a hop, skip and a jump from the market. The attendant slaps Ramon on the arm and pleasantries are exchanged. I notice that Ramon leaves the windows wound down and doesn't lock the car doors.

'Will it be safe?'

He grins. 'What's there to steal?'

Walking up the busy market aisles bulging with fresh produce, I find myself wanting to buy everything in sight.

We arrive at a stand selling huge chunks of warm, stoneground bread, straight from the oven. The aroma is utterly tantalising and as I stop to admire the olive, walnut and herb varieties, the owner pats my arm and reminds me that we met at a Sóller food fair the year before when I apparently cleaned out her stall. The boys wait patiently while we chatter away and finally I make my selection, handing the bulging paper carrier bag to Ollie. He takes it willingly, but only so that he can surreptitiously nibble at the fresh bread as we stroll along. At the far end of the market are some of the farmers from Això és Vida who greet us like old friends. I promise to visit Llorenç Payeras at his farm, Can Morey, in Lloseta in the next few weeks. He is one of the few producers of traditional Mallorcan *cabra*, goat and *oveja roja* sheep cheese still operating on the island.

Finally we reach the livestock part of the market where Ramon's friend, Tofol, offers us a cheery wave. When he learns that we need some good layers, he begins sifting through his startled stock that's flapping about in the pens and wire coops. Rather romantically I envisage choosing my three girls carefully according to their looks, apparent temperament and demeanour, but Tofol's having none of that. He shoves his hand into one of the larger coops, deftly threading the combined feet of three chickens through his fingers and presents them to us upside down in a cacophony of wide-open beaks, fluttering wings and claws. A moment later to indignant cries from the russet-feathered birds he thrusts them into a cardboard box and bangs down the lid, tightly securing it with a piece of old string.

'How about some baby ducks?' he beams.

Ollie and I look into a box full of bright-yellow fluffy ducklings and, just as I'm happily imagining them waddling about the terrain, the Scotsman shakes his head and laughs.

'Not today, *gracias*!'

But Tofol doesn't give up easily, having noticed the yearning in my eye to adopt all things feathery, fluffy or woolly.

'Do you like baby goats?'

I coo over the little white creature in a pen that is plaintively maaaa-ing and rubbing against my hand. It allows me to fondle its long ears while it eyes up my wicker basket. I think back to Bill, our little fawn and white goat whom we gave on loan to some friends a few years ago. He was a gift from my client, Greedy George, and was a perky little chap. The problem was that he didn't have a proper penned-off area and began to eat everything in sight. I have every intention of getting him back once we organise the land more sensibly and create a specially protected area that will prevent him wandering at will and demolishing half the vegetable patch.

'How about a rabbit?' proffers Tofol.

It is Ollie this time who raises an eyebrow and steers me gently away from the hutch.

'Listen mother, you're not Old MacDonald for heaven's sake. We haven't got anywhere to put one at the moment. Besides, a genet would eat it and you'd end up in tears.'

He's right about the genets. We have already witnessed one of these glorious, yet lethal, animals with its spotted grey coat and long, stripy tail stalking our feathery friends late one night. Only keeping them secure in the henhouse as soon as the sky darkens has put paid to any predator's plans.

'What about a few ducks?'

My son sighs heavily. 'Alan's already said no to the ducklings, so why would he agree to ducks? Anyway, we'd need a pond and they can't use the one up by the front lawn because the frogs would object. And what would Johnny say?' He curses under his breath. 'There, you're even turning me mad. I'm beginning to talk about your old toad as if he really can speak.'

'Well, he talks to me,' I reply.

'There, there, mother, keep taking the tablets.' He pats me on the head and pulls a face at Ramon, screwing a finger into the side of his head to indicate my pottiness.

'Once you get the land in order, you can increase your livestock,' smiles Ramon. 'As we say here, *poc a poc...*' Ah, that handy little refrain again.

My mobile, or rather my little silver spy nicknamed Judas, is howling in my basket. With relief I hear Catalina's voice. I had dreaded that it might be a client. Manuel and Dannie never think twice about ringing me on a Sunday with some trifle or other.

'I've just woken up. The girls have gone off with some friends for the day so I wondered if I could pop over for breakfast?'

'We'll be back in under an hour. Fancy fresh eggs for breakfast?'

'Now that's an offer I can't refuse.'

We trundle back to the van, Ramon gripping the cardboard box tightly as the hens flap about inside. The vehicle is still there where we left it, windows open, doors unlocked.

Ramon nudges me. 'See, what did I tell you? Sometimes all you need in life is a little faith.'

Pep and the Scotsman are standing in the kitchen – *my* kitchen – creating mayhem. For the last few months, these two overgrown school boys have turned winemakers, gathering ruby grapes from the vines hanging in heavy clusters from the pergola just outside our kitchen door. It was decided between them that all production would be carried out at our *finca*, with Pep providing a large aluminium drum for grape-crushing and a small oak cask for fermenting and storing the wine. In June he drove down to the house in his dusty blue truck with a whole load of ancient winemaking paraphernalia which was disgorged on to the drive and secreted in the Scotsman's Tardis-like *abajo*. Pep is one of the Scotsman's best buddies and they are forever dreaming up absurd money-making schemes which inevitably run out of steam when they hit on yet another great idea. The truth is, they just like having fun together whether Juana, Pep's wife, or I, like it or not.

Today, I return from dropping Ollie off at school in heavy rain to find Pep stomping up and down inside a cumbersome aluminium vessel about four feet high right in the middle of the kitchen. The Scotsman is sifting through piles of black grapes which are strewn all over the old oak table while Pep, whom I assume is bare-footed, attempts to tread those that have already been sorted inside the container. I throw the car keys on the lid of the piano in the *entrada*, and take a deep breath. I am not amused.

'Pep, what did I say about bringing that treading bin into the house?'

'*Bon dia* to you too, *cariño*!' he yells chirpily. 'Perhaps you haven't noticed that it is pouring outside.'

The Scotsman stifles a grin and gets up hastily to make me a coffee. Just the thought of him bumbling around the machine for the next five minutes, cursing loudly, has me shooing him back to his chair.

I wipe the damp hair from my face, and make sure the coffee machine is topped up with water. 'I know it's raining, Pep, but that is not my problem. You should have waited until it stopped, but if you're both so impatient to strut your stuff, go onto the porch.'

'*Per favor*! It's not very cosy out there,' he whines.

I pour myself a coffee and add a sugar. 'No indeed, but I'd rather you weren't clogging up my kitchen.'

'You see how women take ownership, Alan? *My* kitchen? It's as if you don't exist!'

Alan suddenly jumps up and begins shaking his jumper. 'Look, I'm covered in ants. They're all over the vines. Absolute menaces.'

To my dismay I see battalions of ants forming expeditionary parties, some descending the table legs, others milling about the surface of the table.

'Didn't it cross your mind to wash the grapes in the sink first?' I ask in frustration.

He looks genuinely surprised. 'That is a good idea.'

'A little late in the day now. You'd better clear them up.'

The Scotsman steals a glance at his partner in crime and they both assure me that they'll clean up after them.

'Right, I'm going up to my office to kill off some work, and then by midday I want the kitchen spick and span, so that I can bottle the sun-dried tomatoes. *Entens?*'

Pep smiles ingratiatingly. '*No problema.* I'll just finish trampling the grapes and then we'll leave the juice to ferment.'

'Well make it snappy.'

The Scotsman tuts. 'Pep's got to take his time or he could crush the seeds and release some undesirable tannin. We wouldn't want that.'

'It's slow work,' Pep adds, 'but more effective than a stepper machine. See how fit I'm getting with all this exercise.'

'It's just like the *Verbena de la Vermada* wine-treading competition in Binissalem, isn't it?' says the Scotsman. 'All those locals getting stuck in.'

Pep claps his hands together. 'But the battle of the *uvas* is the best. Remember we were all dripping in grape juice when we took part last year?'

'Isn't it this month?' asks the Scotsman.

'End of September. Maybe we could do it again?' suggests Pep.

'No way! One battle of the grapes is enough for a lifetime,' I reply. 'Anyway, I just hope you washed your feet before getting into the barrel.'

Pep shoots me a wounded look. 'What do you think I am, a savage?'

Upstairs I set to work on an article. I've been commissioned to write a piece for a lifestyle magazine about celebrities buying real estate on the island and the most likely place to spot a famous face. I find it galling that the island's celebrity culture is gobbled up so voraciously by the press these days, when the richer and more valuable aspects of island life are often neglected – mountain life, rural traditions, natural history, gastronomy and culture. My mobile phone bleeps and I notice a message from my traumatologist's secretary, reminding me of my appointment in the morning. What a way to spend my twentieth wedding anniversary. The Scotsman and I have already decided to mark the occasion with a dinner at Agapanto, one of our favourite restaurants in the port of Sóller, but haven't any other plans save browsing for a new chicken house. Over the years we've reached the conclusion that anniversaries offer a good excuse to enjoy a delicious dinner *à deux* at a favoured gastronomic den, but we don't make a big hullabaloo about the occasion. Twenty years is of course quite a major milestone – or should that be millstone? – but we intend to treat it pretty much as any other day. Sometime later I finish the article and glance at my watch. It's only 11.30 a.m., time maybe for a cup of Darjeeling. As I stand up and stretch at my desk I hear an almighty crash from below.

I rush down the staircase. Sprawling in a sea of red juice on the kitchen floor, Pep looks up at me with a face full of astonishment as rivulets of dark fluid mingled with pips and mangled grape skins course across the marble tiles of the *entrada* and form tiny puddles by the stone fireplace. A convincing Laurel and Hardy double act, the Scotsman bites his lip and attempts to pull the writhing Pep to his feet while accidentally kicking the aluminium bin into the fridge.

'It all happened so quickly,' says the Scotsman. 'One minute Pep was reaching for his coffee cup, the next he went over like a ninepin.'

Orlando wanders into the kitchen eyeing the mess warily, and takes a lick of the juice before recoiling and beating a hasty retreat to the garden.

I turn to address the two culprits. 'Now, I don't care how you do it or how long it takes, but I want this mess cleaned up and my kitchen restored to order before I return to make myself a cup of tea.'

Pep is now on his feet, his white shirt and shorts saturated in red juice, and his face covered in sticky grape residue. I note that a twig sporting a few mashed grapes protrudes from his wet, wavy grey hair so that he resembles a slapstick version of Carmen Miranda.

'But where are you going?' he blurts.

'You can't just leave us like this,' adds the Scotsman.

I fix them with a rictus smile as I head for the stairs. 'Just watch me.'

Johnny is puffing out his chest in feigned indignation while chewing on a grub or perhaps it's a stick of gum. He blinks coldly at me from his favourite rock.

'So, let me get this right. When these builder guys finish in the field they're going to dredge the pond, rip out all the bulrushes and make us homeless?'

'You're being a little overdramatic. We won't start work until you and the frogs have gone off for the winter.'

'You're all heart. And what about the fish?'

'Well, we'll just have to keep them in fresh water until we've resealed the pond and cleaned it out properly.'

His tongue flickers. 'Thinking about it, I haven't seen those fat carps for a while. Always barging around as if they own the place. Good riddance, I say.'

I peer into the murky depths, trying to make out the orange forms that glide like mini-submarines under the water's surface. It's impossible to see very much and the bulrushes are now so dense that even the frogs elude me.

'I hope they're OK.'

He begins chortling. 'As if you care! Can't wait till we're all gone. And I'll tell you something for nothing, you've got water snakes, lady. So watch out!'

He leaps off his rock into the water with a sizeable plop. Did he really say that? In fact, the Scotsman and Ollie would kindly remind me that my toad with an American twang didn't say anything at all. They grow weary of what they term my imaginary conversations with Johnny, but of course I know better. I rise to my feet and make for the porch just in time to greet Jorge the postman. He thumps down his bright-yellow postbag on the front steps and mops his brow. Today he has tied back his mane of golden-brown hair with a thick blue ribbon.

'Talking to your friendly toad again?' he laughs.

'Well, he's not being very friendly today. He says we might have water snakes.'

He plays along. 'Better listen to him then. If you've got snakes you won't have fish for much longer.'

He hands me a package. 'Another book? When do you find time to read?'

'In bed. It's my nightly treat.'

He exhales deeply. 'I'm afraid I don't read any more. Once I get home, Beatriz and I have supper and then watch a bit of television, after I've finished a few chores.'

'Why not read a book instead of watching TV?'

He looks horrified. 'But it's how I catch up with the news and get to relax.'

I shrug. 'Well you could always buy a newspaper or read news online instead.'

He pulls the bag over his shoulder and winks. 'Too much effort. I'm a simple man.'

I watch as he strides through the gate, his bronzed face breaking into a smile as he waves back at me along the track. Alan plods out of the house and gives me a hug.

'Time for the traumatologist, *chérie*. What a fun way to spend our wedding anniversary.'

'Well, that shouldn't take too long. Afterwards we can set off on our chicken house hunt,' I reply.

'As long as you're happy with that. Actually, isn't china associated with twentieth anniversaries?'

'I don't want a bowl or an egg cup, thank you. Mind you, a trip to Shanghai would be nice.'

'Sorry, haven't got the budget today. Let's stick to finding a new chicken house.'

'A china one?'

'Not the best idea. What about wood?'

'Excellent. But where shall we find one?'

'Let's just potter and see where the road takes us.'

And so a little later we are driving through Binissalem and on the country road towards Inca without a thought for where we are heading. A determined sun has cleared away the brooding, grey rain clouds that were littering the sky, and a smear of blue now appears on the anaemic horizon. My appointment with the traumatologist passed without incident although he has asked that I have a full ankle and foot scan in a few days' time. Reluctantly, I agreed. With the marathon so close I'd rather not face bad news. On our quest to find a new chicken shed we have visited various gardening centres and builders' merchants without much luck. Stopping in Santa Maria for some tapas and a glass of wine, we decided to continue our search in the cheerful belief that, as Wilkins Micawber once put it, something would turn up when least expected. And indeed it does. As we tootle along, cooing over the pasture land, so very different from the hilly terrain of Sóller, and discussing the merits of Sardinian warblers over greenfinches at this time of the year, I suddenly catch sight of a wooden hut in a field and get the Scotsman to take a sharp right. We pull into a muddy yard and find ourselves surrounded by wooden sheds and rustic benches, horse boxes, kennels and pergolas of every shape and size. It's not the usual, predictable array of outdoor furniture churned out by factories for urban garden centres. No, this is the real McCoy, the bee's knees, the cat's whiskers. A humble sign, with the words 'Can Just' hangs over the door of a sizeable workshop ahead of us. Alan looks at me.

'Well, what do you make of this?'

I turn with a squeal of excitement. 'I've just seen a chicken shed!'

He turns off the ignition. 'Where?'

Jumping out of the car, I point across to a traditional wooden structure standing alone on the edge of a field. It has our name firmly written on it – if not literally, metaphorically. It is constructed of hardy slats of dark-blond timber with wire meshing panels at the sides and at the front, where there is also a door and a tinier squat version for the chickens' access. The interior includes two nesting boxes and a roosting shelf and a wide, wooden ladder on which hens can presumably perch. It is exactly as I had envisaged it and, by the smile on the Scotsman's face, is just what he had in mind too. We wander over to examine it, our delight palpable. A door opens from the side of the workshop and a dog comes bounding over to us, quickly followed by its elderly owner whom we discover is Tomeu, the foreman. He regards us with an air of amusement as we stand smiling inanely and wordlessly at the prize before us.

'Are you after a chicken house?' he asks.

'We want this one. It's perfect,' I reply.

He chuckles. 'We do have other models and bigger ones too. This would suit about six hens.'

The Scotsman nods. 'That's just about right, if you don't count Salvador.'

'Who's Salvador?' the man asks a tad warily, perhaps imagining that we force a small boy to bunk down with the hens.

'He's our *gallo*,' I explain. 'He keeps the girls in order.'

He breaks into giggles and slaps his thigh. 'You call your cockerel Salvador? That's the funniest thing.'

'Really?'

'*Hombre*! Who'd ever call their cockerel Salvador?'

'What sort of names do they usually have?'

'That's the point, they don't have names!'

After another burst of unashamed laughter, he wipes his eyes and leads us to his workshop, which is attached to a large room with a lofty ceiling like that of an aeroplane hangar. It's a hive of activity with men sawing, drilling and polishing while various dogs waft round barking and wagging their tails.

'I love my dogs,' he says as he gets to work on some paperwork. 'So how did you hear about us?'

'We didn't. We just found you by luck,' says the Scotsman.

'It's our twentieth anniversary present to ourselves,' I offer as some kind of explanation.

He grins. '*Enhorabuena.*' Congratulations. 'It'll certainly be a gift to remember. All our henhouses are one-offs and made to order, but if you wanted the one on show, we could deliver it immediately.'

He pulls out a price sheet and, when we discover that the cost is well within our budget, we agree the purchase.

'Have much problem with rats and genets?' he asks casually.

'Not really,' replies the Scotsman. 'We lock up the hens at night.'

He nods sagely. 'All the same, I'd get your builder to do a concrete base, and you might want to add some traditional tiles to the roof to keep the hens cool in the summer and snug in the winter.'

We shake hands and promise to agree a delivery date as soon as we discuss the matter with Stefan. With our mission accomplished we set off back to Sóller in high spirits. Who would have thought that a henhouse could create such a feeling of inexplicable joy?

Stefan looks up at the fiery sun and wipes beads of sweat from his brow. It's early evening and the aquamarine sky is cloudless.

'Who'd believe that it's nearly October?'

We stand in the field admiring his handiwork. The new henhouse with its roof of traditional Mallorcan terracotta tiles sits in an enhanced corral and, most importantly, faces the mountains. It caused Stefan and his builders, Rudi and Jaime, no end of mirth when I insisted that the chickens wake up to *una buena vista* each day. Salvador and the girls had previously looked on to Alan's *abajo*, not the most salubrious aspect, rather like being given the dud room at an urban hotel with views over the municipal car park. Now they would awaken to scenes of untold splendour: mysterious swirling mists engulfing the higher ridges of the grizzled Tramuntanas at dawn, orchards brimming with olives and citrus fruits, and in the distance Sóller town with its grand Gaudi-styled church and roofs the colour of sun-dried tomatoes. Salvador raises his handsome head with its formidable crimson cock's comb and surveys the mountains imperiously from the door of the henhouse. The sun catches his extraordinarily beautiful multicolored coat, an artist's palette of crimson, grey, blue, black, white, honey and bronze. His tail feather, an exotic pearlescent black plume that was wont to rise up like a jet of dark water, sadly wilted and dropped off during the fierce August heat and his sense of loss is palpable. I hope like a gecko's tail, it will reappear in the cooler weather.

'They should be here soon.' I say, flicking a glance in the direction of the courtyard.

'We're in Mallorca, remember,' warns the Scotsman.

As if to prove him wrong, Llorenç's white van swerves into the courtyard. He strides over the gravel and looks down at us from the terrace above. His pewter locks are cropped close and his sinewy bare arms as brown as toast.

'Shall I unload your wood first?'

I beckon to him. 'No, come down and see the henhouse. Have you seen Neus and Bernat?'

'They're walking along the track. Refused to have a lift. You know how stubborn old people can be!'

He jogs down the stone steps to the field and walks across the gravel path towards us.

'They have to be the most spoilt hens on the planet! What is this, a henhouse or a palace?'

Llorenç, one of the main suppliers of kindling and logs in the valley, has a *finca* high in the mountains and is completely self-sufficient, keeping a large brood of hens, sheep and goats and growing an impressive variety of vegetables and fruit all year round. When he telephoned to arrange a delivery of logs for the autumn, I suggested he join us for the inauguration of the henhouse. He didn't demur, having long grown used to my eccentricities. My dear old friend Neus who lives nearby, and her fiancé, Bernat, promised to pop by on their way to a Mass, and Juana and Pep will be coming for supper. Catalina has already paid her respects on the way to pick up her twin girls from school.

Ollie strolls forward to shake hands with Llorenç, who in turn gives him the customary punch on the arm.

'*Va bé*? Everything good at school?'

They talk quickly in Mallorquin, reminding me once again that my grasp of the local dialect is still not up to scratch. I can read the local *Veu de Sóller* and *Sóller* newspapers without much difficulty and even conduct simple conversations, but I am often thrown by the complex seven vowel sounds in Mallorquin – popularly identified in the word *deu*, which is pronounced in varying ways. There's *deu* denoting the number ten, *déu* meaning God, and *deu* from the verb *deure*, which is translated as must, duty or debt. I've also come across *deu*, denoting a natural spring. In every town across the island, the pronunciation of the Mallorquí language, a dialect of Catalan, is quite unique. Sóllerics, as the people of Sóller are known, are renowned for using closed vowel sounds; so for example with the word *cotxe*, meaning car, they will pronounce it as *cotchoo*, rather than the usual *cotcher*. Of course, now on the island things are very muddled idiomatically and the language has sadly become a rather political issue with Catalan being enforced in schools as the main language, Castilian Spanish playing second fiddle and the rather charming dialect of Mallorquí being relegated to third place, a street language for oral use only. This is a shame in some ways, because Mallorquí is actually a very pretty language on the ear and has many interesting, wholly unique words in its vocabulary, which one hopes will not be lost with the predominance of Catalan.

'*Idò!*' says Llorenç. That's that. He slaps his hands together. 'So what was the result of your ankle scan? All fit for the marathon?'

'Well, it wasn't the best news. I've got two extended ligaments and tendonitis apparently. The traumatologist wants me to do at least fifteen sessions of rehab before the marathon.'

'*Joder*! But it's next week!'

'I know, so I'll just have to do my best. That reminds me. I'm going to create an open-air gym in the field and I need some big logs and branches.'

He gives a hearty cough. 'You are joking?'

'Of course not. It'll be a great way to keep fit in the mountain air and all for free.'

'So, let me guess. You want me to bring you the wood?'

'*Exacto*, but they have to be cut to the right size. I've got a fitness book which recommends certain measurements.'

He laughs. 'OK, just ring me with the sizes you want, but I won't be able to do it for a while because I'm flat out with pre-winter orders.'

'*No problema*. Now can I get you a beer?'

He looks at his watch and shrugs. '*M'es igual.*' It's all the same to me.

This is another Mallorcan idiosyncrasy that still foxes me. When offering a Mallorcan a drink or something to eat, it is nigh impossible to receive a straight answer. I put it down to a natural politeness and reserve and possibly a get-out clause in case the offer turns out not to be to their liking. I head up the steps to the patio and reach the kitchen just as Neus and Bernat burst into the *entrada*.

'*Uep!*' Bernat calls out in surprise when I bang open the kitchen door. '*Com anam?*'

'I'm fine, and you?'

We exchange kisses. I notice that Bernat is wheezing from the exertion of walking up the track, his long fingers gripping a wooden stick with the tenacity of a leech. He sits down on the piano stool and passes a huge white cotton handkerchief over his rather gaunt face, carefully pulling off a pair of wire-rimmed glasses to mop at his eyes. Neus fusses over him like an old hen, holding his stick patiently while his breathing steadies.

'What can I get you both to drink?'

'Water is perfect,' says Neus.

Bernat exclaims loudly, '*Que va*! A small glass of red wine for me, please.'

She pushes a fretful hand through her wiry hair. 'Maybe a very small one.'

'So how are things, Neus?'

'*Va bé*, although the new English woman renting the house next door is a nuisance. She's told me she's got all sorts of allergies and can't be near animals or trees.'

'So why has she moved here?'

She laughs. '*Exacto*! Bernat said the very same thing. She gets hysterical when the cats go into her garden but what am I to do? I can't lock them up all day.'

'She doesn't sound like a lot of fun. I'd just ignore her, Neus.'

Bernat nods his head rigorously. '*Si*, that kind of person is just an attention seeker. Besides, she's only rented the *finca* for six months.'

'It's long enough,' grumbles Neus.

A few minutes later we make our way to the henhouse, with Neus and Bernat following behind me as I carefully balance a large tray of assorted drinks and snacks. The Scotsman offers them a hearty greeting and Llorenç decides to show them around the corral. When Neus and Bernat examine the interior of the henhouse they both begin chortling.

'Whatever next!' Neus exclaims.

Bernat shakes his head. 'It might be the cleanest henhouse in the world today, but give those hens a few hours and they'll turn it into a pigsty. They're the filthiest creatures.'

'Close your ears,' I shout over to Cordelia who turns her head huffily away.

Ollie takes a sip of his Bitter Kas and chinks glasses with Llorenç.

'So have you given the new hens any names?'

'My potty mother has christened them Carmen Miranda, Barney and Lucky Clucky,' Ollie replies.

'Lucky is *sort, si*?'

Ollie nods. 'It'll need to be lucky living in this madhouse.'

Neus, Bernat and the Scotsman discuss the benefits of *guano* or *gallinassa*, bird excrement, as a fertiliser. Llorenç tuts and joins in the discussion.

'*Cuidado*.' Be careful. 'That stuff can be very acidic. You should use it sparingly on plants or it can kill them off.'

The Scotsman nods his head thoughtfully.

Llorenç stares out across the field. 'And another thing, are those your peacocks?'

The two elegant *pavos reales* that stalk regally about our terrain in the early morning and coo to each other in the ghostly dawn belong to our Argentinean neighbour.

'Well, even if they're not yours, take care. Those birds are a menace in the winter. They hang out on roofs looking for hidden geckos and small creatures and destroy the terracotta tiles with their beaks and claws. Whatever you do, don't invite them up to the house.'

'It's never crossed my mind,' replies the Scotsman giving me a surreptitious wink.

'You should give your hens a good dollop of oats, corn, dried bread and warm water every day when winter draws in,' commands Neus.

'And pasta,' adds Bernat, draining his glass.

The church clock chimes and Neus flaps her arms in the air. '*Mare de déu*! We must get to Mass.'

Llorenç insists that he give them a lift once he and the Scotsman have shifted the logs from the back of his vehicle. Minutes later we watch Llorenç driving slowly along the narrow track, carefully steering his van close to the stone wall to his right, to avoid any chance of toppling over the other side down into Rafael's orchard.

Later as I finish preparing supper, Juana and Pep drive into the courtyard.

'Good timing,' I say.

'This place gets more like Piccadilly Circus every day,' mutters the Scotsman as he pulls off his wellies at the kitchen door. 'So much for a quiet life.'

Juana, looking customarily coiffed and chic, pops her head round the front door. 'We're here!'

We exchange hugs and she hands me a bottle of red wine.

'It's a new eco-wine from Xavier's shop.'

'Excellent,' says the Scotsman. 'If Xavier's recommended it, it's got to be good.'

Xavier owns Colmado Sa Lluna, which is popularly known as the mini-Fortnum and Mason of Sóller town. Pep lumbers into the hallway clutching a small plastic bag.

'Hey, Ollie, *venga*! Look what I've brought your mad mother.'

He pulls out a comical-looking chicken made of shiny yellow plastic with a red cockscomb and enormous feet. Ollie sniggers when Pep turns a little key at its base and the chicken starts to cluck and strut about on the marble floor. After a while it falls on its side with its feet kicking, gives a squawk and stops dead.

'What a ridiculous thing!' tuts Juana.

'I found it in Inca market and thought that when Johnny disappeared for the winter you'd have another little friend to chat with on a cold frosty morning.'

I give him a prod. 'Oh very funny, Pep.'

Juana rolls her eyes. 'Well consider yourself lucky. He could have brought you one of his and Alan's disastrous bottles of home brew. We'd all have ended up in hospital.'

We both giggle while Pep gives her a warning nudge.

'You may mock, *cariño*, but one day Alan and I will be fighting you both away from the cellar.'

The plastic chicken suddenly spasms and begins clucking with what sounds like uncontrollable laughter.

Juana hoots with mirth. 'Look at that! On balance, it's not such a stupid chicken after all.'

Four

IRONING OUT THE WRINKLES

I'm standing outside the lofty entrance of the Corinthia London hotel, mobile glued to my ear. The Scotsman is rambling on about how the water is running cold and how he'll have to call up the boiler maintenance company in Palma. Distractedly, I offer a few choice murmurs of sympathy, secretly thanking the gods that I'm not there to suffer icy showers and hoping that he'll have the problem fixed before I get back.

'I'm meeting George now, so I'll have to go.'

He gives a sigh. 'OK, well look after that ankle of yours and take it easy.'

'And no overdosing on *puros* while I'm away.'

'As if!'

I thrust Judas into my handbag and with difficulty make my way up the stone steps to the main doors. Walking is not an easy option following my completion of the marathon a few days earlier. My left ankle is still swollen and I'm forced to walk stiffly with head erect, putting as much emphasis on my right leg as possible. A tall, grey-liveried doorman welcomes me with a smile into the cool white lobby. Discreetly he hovers behind me – no doubt in case I capsize – as far as the soft green carpeted steps that lead to the voluminous lobby lounge. High above an enormous crystal chandelier beams down on a casual scattering of chic mushroom-hued sofas and chairs. In the centre of the room the polished mahogany of a vast circular table beckons the light and is crammed with vases of purple blooms. Blimey, Dannie's excelled herself this time. Having had one too many tantrums at the long-suffering hotel she previously favoured, she has now settled on the capital's latest and plushest five-star as her new London home from home. I wish the staff luck, or *molt sort* as we say in Mallorca. No doubt the nervous wreck of a manager of the previous hotel has cancelled his psychiatry sessions, got out the bunting and is doing a little jig around his lobby, supping on a bottle of Krug. I notice Greedy George sitting on a large sofa to the left of the room and make my way slowly over to him across the shiny marble floor. He's already guffawing.

'Know what, guv? You remind me of that Dennis the Dachshund from the *Toytown* series. Remember how he used to walk?'

'Fortunately, that was almost before my time.'

'Yeah right, you wish! So, I take it the marathon was a joyous experience?'

With relief I sink into a soft chair and throw my legs out in front of me. 'At least it's over. Took me more than four hours, but it was worth the agony and it was rather nostalgic to be back in Cologne. I haven't been there since I was an au pair.'

'Presumably they don't have horse-drawn carriages and chimney sweeps any more?'

'Oh, you're on good form.'

'So, where are you staying while you're in London? In that dodgy female club of yours?'

'Actually, I'm staying in St John's Wood with my old university chum, Jane.'

'Not very flash, guv. You should get a room here.'

'If you paid me enough I might. Anyway, I prefer to stay with Jane. We catch up on old times.'

'Oh, that must be a thrill a minute,' he sniggers.

Quickly I divert the conversation. 'So, nice hotel.'

'Yeah, it's not bad. See that chandelier? It's got a thousand and one crystal spheres.'

'What, have you just counted them all?'

'Better than sheep. Actually your pal and mine Manuel Ramirez told me that, and he knows a thing or two about hotels. Said it cost $1.6 million and was designed by a French geezer called Chafik Gasmi and that French firm, Baccarat.'

Manuel Ramirez is my paranoid client in Panama who owns the contemporary H Hotels chain, wears bulletproof vests made by a Colombian tailor in Bogotá and owns his own private Learjet. His favourite possession is a pure gold Kalashnikov that sits on a wall above his desk in Panama City, a subtle reminder to all employees not to mess with him. He is shortly to open a new bijou hotel in St Petersburg.

'I don't think you're supposed to pronounce the "t" in Baccarat.'

'Who cares? Anyway, before Dannie arrives, I've got to tell you my news.' A pause.

'Well, go on, I can't hold my breath much longer.'

'I've found a new showroom.'

Now that is interesting. 'Where?'

'Barcelona.'

'What? But that's in Spain, I mean not far from me in Mallorca.'

'No flies on you, guv. I came across it when I was over there with Bianca. Well, technically I was with Bianca, when she wasn't being pummelled or having needles stuck into her at the hotel spa.'

'So, where is it exactly?'

'Just off the Ramblas, a warehouse with a fabulous frontage. And I met Felipe, this great Spanish geezer, in a bar who's launching a new sherry brand called "Diana".'

'A British royal family fan?'

'No, you clot. "Diana" means "bullseye" in Spanish. Bet you didn't know that.'

'Sorry, I'm not a great aficionado of darts. So, what's the sudden interest in sherry?'

'Well, Felipe's going to launch his sherry as "Bullseye" in the UK, and I suggested we collaborate.'

'Remind me of the synergy between Havana Leather and sherry?'

'Don't get all cocky with me, guv. Think about it. We're about to launch a new bull's hide leather range made exclusively in Spain – all fits nicely. We can do a joint launch in Barcelona too.'

'Still all a bit tenuous if you ask me. So, when do you plan on opening the showroom in Barcelona?'

'I reckon it will be June before we get going. The building needs a lot of work. Still, good to think we'll practically be neighbours.'

The idea of Greedy George being in such close proximity doesn't exactly fill me with joy.

I nibble on a nail. 'We'll have to think of a fun way of launching the bull's hide range.'

'What about staging our own in-store bullfight?' he chortles merrily.

'Very droll. No, I was thinking about something more artistic. Perhaps an exhibition?'

'That sounds boring. I know, how about tying it in with a local bull-running event?'

'An *encierro*? No way.'

'Why not?'

'Because it's become a hugely controversial issue with animal rights groups and it's also quite normal for one of those running ahead of the bulls to be gored to death.'

'Well, it would certainly add a little excitement to the occasion, guv.'

'Maybe not the kind we'd be looking for at a launch,' I reply.

'I wonder who first came up with the idea?'

'What, of bull running?' I ask. 'I think it harks back to about the fourteenth century when local Spaniards would heckle the bulls when they were transporting them from one place to another. It took off as a sport.'

'Trust you to know a useless fact like that,' he says with a grin.

A polite young waitress wafts over and offers us afternoon tea.

'Just a Darjeeling for me,' I reply.

'First flush?' she enquires.

'No, she's a bit past it, love,' gurgles George happily.

'Fine, thank you.' I give him a warning kick.

'I'll have a strong Royal London brew and a big slice of Bakewell tart.'

When she's gone I shake my head. 'You should go a little easy on the cake, George. I worry about your health.'

'I'm already two stone overweight, so it's hardly going to make any difference, is it? Besides, I'd rather drop down fat and happy than thin and miserable.'

Perhaps he's got a point. He suddenly jumps to attention. Dannie is gliding towards us in what looks like a beige and cream silk kimono and matching slippers – at least she'll blend in with the furniture.

'Like the Japanese look,' yells George, before slapping a kiss on her cheek.

Her brow furrows a touch and then she sinks down on to the sofa next to George before blowing me a kiss.

'Darling, you look so well. What do you think of my new London home?'

'Very nice, Dannie.'

I examine her bizarre new hairstyle, a flaming bouffant affair, rather like a hay bale on fire.

'I've got the Lady Hamilton suite. Doesn't that sound glamorous?'

George gives a sniff. 'Mind you, poor old Lady H didn't have a very glamorous end, did she? Drank herself to death.'

'A sobering thought.'

I give her an encouraging nod. 'Well put, Dannie. Anyway, how are plans for St Petersburg?'

'Wonderful, darling. The shop site is beautiful and Manuel is being such a help.' She offers me a perfect pearly toothed smile. 'Amazing that you should have two clients opening in Russia at the same time.'

'Yes, lucky old me. So, like Manuel, you're still aiming for a March launch?'

'Absolutely. But in the meantime I have something exciting to share with you both.'

In anticipation, George is already trying to mask a smirk. Dannie's elegant, manicured fingers flutter like impatient butterflies about the combination lock on a brown leather holdall. Finally there's a click and she releases the top leather flap and slowly pulls out what appears to be a small metallic desk light.

'It's a light,' says George flatly.

'Not any light,' she says confidentially. 'This is Allure Bloom, a new state-of-the-art LED anti-wrinkle device that will go exclusively on sale at Miller Magic stores next spring. It was designed by Anton Novak, an ingenious Czechoslovakian inventor friend of mine.'

I'm not sure whether to laugh like a hyena or exhibit feigned delight. Fortunately the waitress returns with a loaded tray and breaks the spell.

'And what can I get for you, madam?'

Dannie's spidery false lashes come together in prayer while she cogitates. Then she tosses her head back announcing that she'd like jasmine tea and a bowl of soya nuts, oh and also a glass of Evian water containing three green olives skewered on a cocktail stick. The waitress doesn't blanch, just nods pleasantly and pads off. Maybe she's served a lot of Dannie-types in her time and has grown immune to their peculiar requests.

'But don't these lights already exist?' I tentatively put to Dannie.

'Sure, but mine will be the latest design and combines green, red and turquoise light to achieve a faultless and smooth complexion. This is just a prototype, but I intend to launch them in St Petersburg and then go global.'

Greedy George gobbles down his Bakewell tart in a few bites. 'And have you used it yet?'

'Can't you tell?' she purrs softly although there's a hint of menace in her voice.

George grins inanely. 'Well, I always put that porcelain skin down to your impeccable Transylvanian ancestry which does a good line in immortality.'

She laughs cheerlessly. 'Yes, but even Count Dracula could have made use of one of these to add a little colour to his cheeks.'

I ask her if she's heard of Raisa Ripov. George rudely interrupts.

'Rachel's gotta be having you on, guv. No one's called Raisa Ripov. I mean, that's just too silly for words.'

'I've checked out her website and she's the real deal. A seventy-year-old Russian–Czech beautician. She's opening Radiance, a new aesthetics clinic in Mayfair. Might be worth talking with her, Dannie.'

She nods enthusiastically. 'A perfect connection. I must meet her.'

'So how much will one of these lights cost?' demands George.

'About five-hundred dollars.'

'Sadly I'll have to miss out then,' he scoffs.

Her cool emerald eyes rest on his face. 'Don't worry, dear George. I wouldn't dream of charging you. As it happens, Anton Novak needs guinea-pigs to trial the male version. He's had a little problem with skin burns among his male testers but nothing he can't iron out over the next few months I'm sure.'

George gulps hard and throws me a look of panic. For once he genuinely seems speechless.

By the time I reach Caffè Nero on Curzon Street the dark sky has opened and pearls of rain roll like tears down the front of my handbag. It is 6.30 p.m. and a crisp wind is spinning leaves into mini-vortices along the pavement, gathering darkly by drains and in shop doorways. I push open the door of the cafe and am immediately engulfed in warmth and soft amber light. Ed is sitting hunched over a copy of the *Evening Standard*, a cappuccino at his side and a plate betraying scattered crumbs. Tucked under his legs is his trusty, battered old MEK— his Medical Emergency Kit – which is full of life-saving medication and supplies should he by chance be faced by some unforeseen hazard in the course of his day. He jumps up when he sees me and quickly pulls out a chair.

'Terrible weather, isn't it, Scatters?'

'Just a bit windy.'

He gives a hearty cough. 'I think this cold air has already gone to my chest. I've been feeling a bit wheezy today.'

Ed, as a self-confirmed hypochondriac, is always on the lookout for new ailments to add to his ever-growing list.

'You look fine.'

His big hazel eyes close momentarily. 'To be honest, I'm not fine at all. The BBC is making loads of redundancies and my boss has told me I'm likely to be one of the first for the cull.'

I take off my suede jacket and hang it on the back of a chair, noting its saturated back and hoping it'll make a quick recovery. 'Why you?'

'It's all to do with the Beeb's forthcoming move to Salford.'

'If you offered to relocate, would there be a job for you there?'

'Maybe, but who in their right mind would move voluntarily to Salford?'

'Someone who would otherwise be out of work?'

He grimaces at me. 'But there's Rela to think about too. My poor girlfriend can't spend all day dodging street gangs. One of the guys in my office is actually from Salford and he told me to invest in a flak jacket if I relocated there.'

'Oh, it can't be all that bad.'

'Well, would you move there?'

'You must be joking.' I get up. 'Fancy anything?'

He dabs his nose with a bedraggled tissue. 'Maybe a small chocolate muffin.'

I return with an espresso and watch as he wolfs down his cake.

'Well, when the time comes, just take your redundancy and set up your own business.'

He regards me with terror-filled eyes. 'Doing what?'

'Computer consultancy. You're a whizz. You could start locally and expand across London.'

'But I've always worked for the BBC.'

'I know. How boring. Time for a change.'

Judas rings in my handbag. It's Ollie.

'We still haven't got any hot water and the boiler man can't come until later this week.'

Bad timing. I'll be back home by then.

'Well, tell the Scotsman to drive up to Catalina's so that you can have showers and then go to Es Turo for supper.'

He brightens up. 'Good idea. I'll tell him. Oh by the way, Inko's hurt her paw and the builders found a nest of rats up in the field. They ran like the wind.'

'Oh, how horrible. Where did they go?'

'Into the house, where do you think?' He titters when I gasp. 'Only joking!'

Ed looks at me when I finish the call. 'What's up?'

'Just rats everywhere and no hot water. A typical day in Sóller.'

He shivers in horror. 'Thinking about it, maybe Salford's not so bad.'

Dynamite PR, housed on the second floor of a modern office block off Regent Street, is a hive of activity. I reach the reception desk and a young blonde in her early twenties mouths a 'hello' to me as she juggles with several calls. Hot on my heels are two couriers, both wearing bicycle helmets and thrusting clipboards towards the receptionist while she presses the buzzer to let some unknown caller in down at street level.

'Just a moment,' she waves over in my direction.

I look at the array of national newspapers, glossies and current affairs magazines fanned out on a chunky glass coffee table and remember that buying that little lot every month used to cost me a fortune when I ran my own agency. And of course most of them never got read. Understated black and white photographs of exotic-looking destinations and tribal people line the coffee-coloured walls and a water vending machine hiccups from a corner of the room in front of an L-shaped chocolate leather sofa. From a room above I can hear the intermittent roar of an angry drill and rock music wafts in from an open window along with the sound of crashing waves, but it isn't the sea; rather London traffic ploughing through heavy rainwater.

'Cold out there,' remarks the receptionist. 'Can I help you?'

'I have an appointment with Gillian and Rachel.'

She smiles suddenly, slightly embarrassed. 'Oh, of course. Now I know who you are! I'm sorry, my name's Elisa. I'm new around here.'

We shake hands and she leads me through into a boardroom where a coffee machine gently burbles on top of a sleek black sideboard. Cups, saucers and biscuits sit patiently at its side and a shiny rectangular table flanked by eight chairs gobbles up the centre of the room. While the receptionist flits off to alert the troops, I look out of the large window and down at the sluggish traffic awash with winking red brake lights that, like a funeral cortege, winds its way slowly up Regent Street. Rachel interrupts my reverie.

'Hey stranger, how are you?' She rushes forward in her lofty heels to give me a hug, her long fair hair brushing my face. 'Gillian's on her way. Gosh, what a morning. The phones haven't stopped.'

She pours three cups of coffee which she pops onto a tray and brings to the table.

'So, does it feel strange being back in an office?'

'It's hugely liberating knowing that I'm not in charge, just passing through.'

'What about the adrenalin?'

I laugh. 'Oh, I get that in spades back in Sóller, Rachel.'

She takes a sip of coffee. 'Yes, I can never imagine you sitting still. So what's happening in Mallorca?'

'Well, La Vermada, the wine festival in Binissalem, is starting soon and a watermelon fight is coming up in Villa Franca, and then there's the Palma marathon – that's all just this month.'

'You're not going to do the Palma marathon too?'

'Are you kidding? I can hardly walk as it is!'

The door opens and Gillian breezes in, clutching a file. Her dark wavy locks fall about her face as she reaches forward to give me a peck on both cheeks 'Good to see you. Now, I don't know if

Rachel's brought you up to speed, but we could do with your help on a few accounts.'

Rachel winces. 'Only a few days a month, a bit of backup for the team.'

'It's just that we've won quite a lot of new business and it makes sense to offer you some work – if you've got time.'

'I'm rather overloaded with George and Dannie at the moment. And let's not even talk about mad Manuel in Panama, plus I have a lot of freelance writing and...'

'Come on, it would only be for a few months,' smiles Rachel. 'Just a bit of strategy stuff that you can do online.'

'And what kind of clients are we talking about?'

They look at each other and grin.

'Well, Raisa Ripov would get us off to a good start.'

'How did I guess, Rachel?'

'In fact,' says Gillian, 'We've got a meeting with Carolyn Hadden-Paton, editor of the *Weekly Wrinkle*, in an hour. She's looking for news stories.'

'The *Weekly Wrinkle*? Are you serious?'

'Deadly,' giggles Rachel. 'It's actually rather good value.'

'Well, then I've got something she's going to love.'

'Really?' says Gillian enthusiastically.

If they thought they'd got their work cut out with Raisa Ripov, wait till I tell them about Dannie's Allure Bloom anti-wrinkle light.

My mobile rings. 'Good news,' trills the Scotsman. 'The boiler man came today and fixed the hot water but he's coming back next week to give the system a complete overhaul.'

'Thank heavens. How's Inko's limp?'

'She had a thorn in it. All sorted.'

When I finish the call Gillian eyes me with concern.

'Who's Inko? Someone who ran the Cologne marathon with you?'

'No, my cat.'

'Ah.'

'So,' I say, 'I hope you're both sitting comfortably because now I'm about to tell you the secrets of Allure Bloom…'

Five

BOILERS AND BUSY BEES

An anaemic sky gives way to a thin ribbon of sunlight as cool white mist slowly rises, revealing the jagged peaks of the Tramuntanas in all their glory. Down in the valley bonfires rage like fretful volcanoes, their plumes of pungent smoke rising high into the still morning air. The Scotsman leans out of the bedroom window, a pained expression on his face.

'Pep told me that bonfires were banned until next month, so what's going on?'

'I thought they could start in October.'

'As if rules matter much around here anyway!' he snorts. 'They're just a bunch of pyromaniacs. Smell that air.'

It's long been a bone of contention that the local council turns a blind eye to the profusion of bonfires ignited early in the autumn. The crackling of kindling can be heard at dawn and roaring fires often blaze until late morning, small acrid grey clouds floating up into the clear sky like smoke signals. I jog down the stairs and find Ollie standing sleepily on the landing in his school uniform.

'Want to come and feed the chickens with me?'

'If I must.'

He follows me out of the house and down to the corral. Doughnut is circling the perimeter like a prisoner in a cell. As I unbolt the gate he attempts to squeeze past me.

'Not so fast!'

I close the gate firmly behind us and a minute later, after opening the door to the henhouse, am surrounded by flapping wings and urgent beaks. Ollie carries the seed feeder into the corral and fills it up with corn, amused at the way the birds nudge each other aside to get at the food. Salvador stands apart from the crowd, haughty and imperious, until finally heading for the water trough. He struts towards us in a ponderous and comical fashion, stretching one leg slowly forward in synchronisation with his head. I giggle.

'He's just like Professor Wallofski! I knew he reminded me of someone.'

'Who?' asks Ollie with a frown of disapproval.

'You know, Max Wall, the comedian. He had this ridiculous character in black leggings and Doc Marten boots who used to do a really silly walk.'

'Sounds hilarious,' says Ollie flatly. 'Can I get on with finishing my homework now?'

'But we're going in ten minutes.'

'That's all it'll take.'

As I watch him scramble up the steps to the back patio, I speculate with a wince on the quality of the work he'll be handing in to his teachers. As he studies all subjects at his Spanish school in either Catalan or Castilian Spanish I am finding it harder to offer any pearls. The Catalan linguistics homework he receives is, according to one of my Mallorcan teacher friends, practically university level. She is surprised that he can make head or tail of it, so it is little wonder that I struggle. Alan comes out on to the doorstep to wave us off.

'Remember the boiler man's coming again today. You must meet him.'

I love the way the Scotsman makes firm friends of every tradesman who enters the house. After exchanging polite pleasantries with our *síquier* for some years, a friendship grew and now the two greet each other with bear hugs and cheerful banter, plodding down to inspect the irrigation channels together and discussing the lack of rainwater with an endearing earnestness.

At the school gates I watch as Ollie struggles into the playground lugging his huge rucksack like Sisyphus with his rock up the hilly path. Out of nowhere a group of blazer-clad boys run over to him, patting his back as they accompany him up the slope to the classroom. He smiles and chats with them in Spanish and soon they are giggling and horsing around. The bell rings and the headmaster appears, rounding up all the latecomers and waving at the departing parents. I run back to the car and head into Sóller to pick up the *Majorca Daily Bulletin*, the local English newspaper for which I pen a column every Saturday. I park up near the station and pop my head round the door of Rafael's bakery on my way to the *estanco*, the newspaper-cum-tobacconist shop. He is wearing a white overall and munching on an *ensaimada*, the light, coiled pastry famous in Mallorca.

'Hey, you want one, neighbour?' he cries as he strides out on to his porch and deposits a sugary kiss on both of my cheeks.

I laugh. '*Graciès*, but I'm on my way to Café Paris.' I pause in front of his shop window, gazing longingly at the piles of fig rolls, almond cake, croissants, and plate of *coca de patata*, light spongy bread rolls. 'Ah, Rafael, I wish I didn't like food so much.'

He squeezes my shoulder. 'You don't want to be one of those scrawny women who live on lettuce leaves! How boring is that. You're not fat. True, you could lose a few kilos but so could I. Besides, this new outdoor gym will get you back in shape then you can eat as many of these as you like.' He sweeps a hand across the window, then rushes back into the shop. A moment later he pulls various buns and cakes from the window and returns to my side with a carrier bag. 'Here, enjoy these with Alan. Remember, life's for living not for dieting!'

I give him a hug and pick up my newspaper at the *estanco* where my brief, habitual conversation with the staff is conducted, as always, in Mallorquin dialect. The owner, a staunch flag bearer for the local lingo, makes few concessions for linguistically challenged foreign residents. As I enter Café Paris the usual suspects are already in situ. José looks up from the coffee machine and gives me a wry smile. At the back of the room I can see elderly Senyor Bisbal playing cards with 'Barney Blue Eyes', his devoted old retainer and companion who is wearing his favourite black beanie hat. They nod distractedly in my direction and mutter a *bon dia* as I take my favourite seat by the staircase. A moment later and another member of the pensioners' circle arrives. This time it's Jordí, a widower who comes in for a beer early morning and spends some hours reading through the local newspapers. He returns later in the afternoon for another pick-me-up and a chat with José. I rise to greet him and he kisses me on both cheeks with his customary warbled greeting of '*Cariñññññññññññño! Como va?*' Darling, how are you?

Once more I settle down to read the English and Spanish newspapers as José brings me over a piping-hot double espresso, mineral water and croissant. There's a shuffle and Marta, an elderly widow, pulls out a chair at the next table. She gives me a wan smile.

'How are you today?' I ask her.

She pushes out her bottom lip into a pout. 'The legs are still bad and I've got a slight cough.'

'Probably the change of temperature.'

She nods. 'At my age you have to be careful.'

I watch as she draws a linen napkin from her handbag and ties it carefully around her neck. Marta dines at Café Paris twice each day and always carries her napkin with her. The cafe has become her home from home and she is familiar enough to poke her head through the kitchen hatch to demand more butter on her pasta, or a few more olives on her plate. The front door whines open and my chum, Antonia, bustles in along with a few skittish autumnal leaves. She catches my eye and heads over to the table while José prepares her a *cortado*, a small coffee with frothy milk.

'Do you mind if I join you?'

'Of course not! How's business?'

She gives a shrug. 'The same. Everyone's being careful with their money these days, but just wait. Next month they'll all be ordering video games for Christmas and it'll be chaotic.'

'Is Albert in the shop? I was going to pass by to ask him about my temperamental mouse.'

She laughs. 'Yes, he's hiding round the back so go and wake him up.'

Albert and Antonia run Hibit, the town's computer shop, one of the main hubs of the expat community. No job is too small and Albert – tall, languid and with a well-developed sense of irony – humours all neurotic and clueless callers who drift in to the premises to ask obtuse questions about their computer problems. I head up the list. Next door Albert Junior has set up his own estate agency, Inmobiliaria Sóller Homes, so can never escape his parents.

'Hey, I saw you out running with Florentina the traffic warden, the other day.'

I laugh. 'Yes, we try to manage a run together a few times a month.'

'Rather you than me. So, want to know my news?'

'You've won the *lotería*?'

Antonia gives a hoarse grunt. *'En mis sueños.'* In my dreams. 'Actually it's better than that. I've given up smoking. For good.'

'You're not serious?'

'Sí. This morning was the very last cigarette I will ever smoke.'

One of the most familiar sights in the town is of Antonia puffing away on a cigarette while chatting with locals outside her shop. During the cold and rainy winter months she continues the tradition while huddling in the porch for shelter, before abandoning the unfinished cigarette and crushing it as if it were a tiresome insect under foot.

'A brave decision. I shall be monitoring your progress carefully.'

We get up and pay at the bar.

'I'll come back to the shop with you.'

As we pass Albert Junior's front window, she suddenly grasps my arm. 'Have you heard the news?'

'Albert Junior's given up smoking too?'

'No! His girlfriend is expecting a baby. I'm going to be a grandmother.'

And of course this is just too good an opportunity to disrupt Albert Junior's day. Enthusiastically we bang open the showroom door and with a resigned grin he welcomes us in, knowing by his mother's expression, that he's going to have to discuss the wonders of potential fatherhood for some time.

The front courtyard is awash with vehicles. There's Stefan's white grubby van, two *motos* belonging to his workers, a blue car and a dumper truck. Our Mini is holding its breath, squeezed between the latter two and, to add to the confusion, Alan is calling to me from below my office window like a slapstick Romeo.

'Can you come down and discuss the frogs!'

I stop in the middle of writing an article and plod down the stairs. Everyone is congregated in the *entrada*. A new face has appeared – that, I presume, of the boiler man.

The Scotsman waves me down. 'This is Jeroni Pinya, who's come to overhaul the boiler.'

I shake his hand. 'Is it a big job?'

He gives a cheery laugh. 'I never know until I get started, but it probably just needs a good clean.'

Stefan waits patiently and then asks me about clearing the pond.

'You want to do it this minute?'

'Soon, once we've finished off some work in the field.'

'I'll have to check that the frogs have gone. I warned Johnny about this last week.'

Stefan nods sagely. 'Ah, *si*, your talking *calàpat*.'

The Scotsman raises an eyebrow. 'She gets madder by the second. All of the frogs have gone. Not a squeak out of them for a week so it won't be a problem.'

'All the same, I'd just like to be sure,' I reply.

I potter out to the pond. Silence. Johnny is neither squatting on his favourite stone nor in his favourite hidey-hole under a craggy rock. A light breeze ripples over the water's surface but there isn't a croak or a plop. The boys really do seem to have hopped off for the winter. I return to the *entrada*.

'*Vale*, it looks as if they've left, Stefan.'

He nods and with a pert smile sets off back to the field. Jeroni now busies himself in the tiny boiler room out by the front patio, occasionally popping into the kitchen to use the taps, muttering *sucio*, or *mucho polvo*, dirt and dust, under his breath. Half an hour later, as I'm pushing a batch of muffins into the oven he returns to the *entrada* and with a look of defeat, summons us both to hear the worst. He's holding a grubby part of the boiler's anatomy and it's not looking too well.

'*Mira*. You see this? It's broken right through. That's why the boiler's not firing properly.'

The Scotsman frowns. 'Can you fix it?'

He shrugs. 'I'm sorry *senyor*, but I've just called my office and we don't have any more in stock so I must return in a few days. I'll find a temporary solution for now.'

'That would be helpful,' sighs the Scotsman.

'Where are you from on the island?' I ask Jeroni. 'Pinya is an unusual name.'

'My family is from Palma. Pinya is a Jewish name because we are *xuetas*. Do you know the word?'

I am aware of the *xuetas*, descendants of the Mallorcan Jews, many of whom were forced to convert to Catholicism during the island's murky historical past. Pronounced *chueta*, the word's etymology harks back to the Mallorquin word *xua*, meaning pork. The persecution of the Mallorcan Jewish community began in the thirteenth century at the time King James I of Catalonia and Aragon wrestled power from the Moors, accelerated during the Spanish Inquisition in the fifteenth century, and continued into the early nineteenth century. Those Mallorcan Jews who converted to Christianity were supposed to show their fervour for their new religion, and rejection of Judaism, by eating pork. It was claimed that the new converts would cook and eat pork on the streets to prove their faith. Other possible origins for the word are *chouette*, meaning screech owl, a bird of ill omen, or *jueto*, the diminutive of *jueu*, or Jew.

'I know a little about the *xuetas*,' I say somewhat diffidently. 'They had a pretty raw deal in Mallorca.'

He shrugs. 'My family all converted to Catholicism centuries ago but I still feel some sadness for how my ancestors were treated. You know they used to burn Jews at the stake here in Mallorca in what was known as the *auto-de-fe* – it means "act of faith" in Spanish. Practising Jews were supposed to give public penance for believing in Judaism and they were punished accordingly. I bet tourists know nothing about that.'

'Few, I imagine, but then again, scratch the surface of any holiday destination and you're certain to make some unpleasant historical discoveries.'

'True,' he says thoughtfully. 'You know my ancestors created three beautiful synagogues on this island and all were requisitioned by the Catholic Church. Ever been to the Church of Montesión in Palma?'

'A few times.'

'That was once a synagogue. In the seventies a new synagogue was created in Palma, a bit of a modern affair. I've never been inside.'

'Is there still a Jewish community in Mallorca?'

'Yes, there is, but Jewish people form part of the general community now. You know in the past they used to live in a ghetto known as the Call? You can still walk around the Jewish quarter of Palma.'

'Our Mallorcan friend, Pep, took us there once. He showed us the remains of a gate on the goldsmith's street which he said was used to lock the Jewish community in at night.'

He gives a grunt. 'Either to lock them in or stop the locals attacking or stealing from them. Depends on your perspective. There were gates at both ends of the street which were locked from dusk to dawn. And that was in the early twentieth century. Not that long ago.'

The Scotsman shakes his head sadly. 'Ah, such injustices, Jeroni. But then these islands have a troubled history. After the Phoenicians, the Greeks came, but they were conquered by the Carthaginians.'

'Then came the Romans,' I butt in. 'Actually, they offered some sort of respite. The island had five hundred years of reasonable stability under their rule.'

The Scotsman frowns. 'But didn't the Vandals attack the Romans?'

'Yes, and trashed most of what they had created. It was all downhill until the Moors arrived about five hundred years later.'

'We have the Moors to thank for our *bancales* and irrigation systems,' chips in Jeroni. He strides over to the rear kitchen window and points up at the *bancales* above the back wall. 'Those stone terraces have been there hundreds of years, all their handiwork.'

'True,' replies the Scotsman.

Jeroni begins packing his tool box. 'You know the *Moros* didn't have a problem with the Jewish community. Live and let live was their attitude and then 300 years later King James I of Catalonia and Aragon arrived and the Jews became pariahs.'

'And why was that, in your opinion?'

'It's complicated, but in truth they resented the Jews' fiscal success and trading ability.'

We stand in awkward silence.

'Anyway, I must be going. As soon as the spare part arrives, I'll call and pop over to replace it.'

We wave him off at the gate, watching his blue car make its way slowly along the rocky track.

'Nice guy,' muses the Scotsman as we walk back into the *entrada*, 'and a bit of a local history boffin to boot.'

There's a loud yell from the front garden. '*Que susto*! *Venga*, Alan!'

We rush out on to the porch and over to the pond where Rudi and Jaime are holding up two long, wriggling snakes. I recoil against the wall.

'If you were wondering why the fish have disappeared, here's your answer,' shouts Rudi. 'We were pulling out the last of the reeds and saw their two heads pop up.'

The sludgy, greeny-grey water serpent is known as *Natrix maura* and is extremely bad news if you happen to be a fish or a passing bubble of frogspawn. Luckily for humans it is completely harmless, although on occasion it likes to give a nasty surprise. A few months back one of the little beasts bobbed up from the stream at the bottom of our field while I was clearing weeds and gave me quite a shock. How long these unwelcome lodgers have been lurking in our pond is anybody's guess, but it explains the absence of fish.

'Shall we let them loose?' asks Rudi.

I take a step backwards. 'Yes, but not here, *gracias*. Can you take them in a bucket to the field?'

He nods. '*No problema.*'

Depositing the snakes in a bucket, he and Jaime stride off in the direction of the field while I peer into the newly cleared and emptied pond. It seems so sad and devoid of life. I can't bear to think of the silence now that Johnny and our band of frogs have gone. I love lying in bed at night with the windows flung open, listening to the throaty amphibian serenade with backing vocals from the rasping cicadas. Hopefully it will only be a temporary absence.

Stefan leans on the craggy wall that curves around the edge of the pond. 'Now we'll have to reseal it all and start again. I suggest you avoid reeds in future. The roots take over everything.'

The Scotsman gives a tut. 'We'll stick to lily pads, that way we'll be able to keep an eye out for snakes.'

'Well, if you discover one hiding in there, don't ask me to fish it out,' I retort.

'Alan would do that, don't worry,' laughs Stefan.

I notice the Scotsman give a shiver of revulsion followed by a wooden smile. It would probably be Ollie who'd save the day should a snake really decide to inveigle its way back into the pond.

'I think we've finished for the day. *A demà.*' See you tomorrow.

The Scotsman and I stand out in the courtyard as Stefan and his men noisily charge their various vehicles. A moment later and they're all gone in a large cloud of acrid smoke.

'Peace once more,' The Scotsman sighs. 'Between the broken boiler and the snakes, it's been an eventful day.'

I pull my jacket around me now that the sun has melted behind a cloud. 'Let's hope nothing else can go wrong. Although they always say problems come in threes.'

The Scotsman laughs, then suddenly sniffs the air. 'Something's burning. I hope it's not more damned bonfires.'

With an urgent squawk, I rush into the house to be greeted by the unmistakable aroma of charred muffins. The Scotsman bounds after me and offers a sympathetic hug as I pull the blackened offerings from the oven.

'But they shouldn't have burnt so quickly. I only left them for twenty minutes.'

'Oh well, that's problem three out of the way. Nothing can go wrong now.'

There's a sudden loud pop from the oven and its illuminated panel of symbols goes black. The motor cuts out. Silence.

I turn to the Scotsman. 'As you were saying?'

There's a kiss of autumn in the air and a cool wind rattles the shutters and sends leaves dancing along the stone steps that lead up to the front patio. Orlando stands like a sphinx on the wrought iron lid of our well, his bushy grey winter pelt ruffled by the breeze. Ivy has crept like a stealthy assassin over the well's smooth sides and slithered up the sturdy pillars of the porch, along the honey stone façade of the *finca*, so that it caresses the window panes of Ollie's bedroom on the first floor. I pull on my jacket and lock the front door while Ollie squats on the ground next to Inko, stroking her fur. The Scotsman is surveying the front garden while nursing an inflamed right arm.

'In the circumstances, I find it somewhat ironic that we're on our way to an apiculture fair,' he puffs.

'We can always pull out if you're in pain.'

He seems affronted. 'Absolutely not. I'm looking forward to it and besides, can you imagine what Pep would say?'

'That's the least of our problems. Even Pep would have some sympathy.'

The Scotsman winds his favourite Rupert Bear-style scarf around his neck and gently pulls down the sleeve of his shirt. 'It was such a stupid thing to do. I still wonder how those wasps built their nest on the inside of the shutter like that without either of us noticing.'

I stroll over to the car. 'But the nest was hidden in the corner.'

'How many stings did you get?' asks Ollie.

'Ten.'

'One good reason not to clean the shutters,' he replies with a grin.

'Actually, I should check all of yours,' Alan says.

Ollie shakes his head. 'No way are either of you entering my room. It's strictly out of bounds to parents.'

He slinks into the back seat of the Mini. 'So what are we doing at this bee gig?'

'I wouldn't describe it as a "gig" exactly. There are going to be a lot of the island's beekeepers buzzing about…'

He gives a groan. 'Boom, boom…'

'… and they'll hopefully be selling their products. I'd quite like to pick up some beeswax and a selection of different honeys.'

'Best time to buy honey,' Ollie replies.

I sit in the front passenger seat and turn to face him.

'Care to share your pearls?'

'I read somewhere that honey produced at this time of the year has more health benefits.'

'Such as?'

'How do I know? It's probably good for all sorts of things. That's why apitherapy is so popular.'

'Is it?'

'Are you being deliberately obtuse this morning?' he tuts.

'I've never professed to be a bee expert. Aren't the stings good for arthritis?'

The Scotsman starts the engine. 'A bit of a painful cure, isn't it?'

'The venom is administered by injection,' Ollie replies. 'Probably still hurts but if it works, I suppose it's worth the pain.'

'Where did you learn all this?' I ask.

He looks out of the window. 'In a science lesson. The coolest thing about bees is that the males do nothing all day while the females work.'

'So, not very different from the human world then?'

Alan gives me a nudge. 'Steady on.'

'Before you buy any honey, mother, it's worth remembering that it's just regurgitated nectar.'

'Thanks, a lovely thought for a Sunday.'

We take the road to Santa Maria and head inland to Inca and the gentle undulating agricultural area known as central Pla. Pep, Juana and their son, Angel, are meeting us in the *plaça* of the village of Llubi and after we've investigated the fair, we're off to lunch at one of Pep's dubious haunts.

'You know Llubi's better known for its capers?' I say as the village comes into view. In the distance the vast grizzled back of the Tramuntanas glimmers under a cold, white sun, dwarfing the low-rise clutter of stone houses huddled at its base.

'Capers, as in frivolous escapades?' suggests the Scotsman.

'Actually I'm talking about the unripened buds of *Capparis spinosa*.'

'Capers taste revolting,' Ollie mutters from the back of the car. 'And they look like tiny squashed toads.'

'Ugh! Actually the plants aren't that attractive. Rather triffid-like and prickly,' I reply.

'And I thought I was the *jardinero* around here,' grins the Scotsman as he squeezes into a narrow parking space on the edge of the village. There's a festive atmosphere and the streets are heaving with people.

The Scotsman turns to me. 'Look at the crowds. We'd never have found a space closer to the market.'

'We've got to walk?' Ollie peers out of his window. 'How far?'

'At least five hundred metres. If it's all too much I can give you a fireman's lift.'

'I'd like to see you try,' he challenges.

We follow the procession of villagers along narrow, winding streets until Llubi's old stone church tower comes into view. The *plaça* is flanked on all sides by brightly decorated stalls sporting green, candy-striped awnings and a large sign has been strung between two pillars at the entrance to the square announcing that this is *'Fira de la Miel'*, the Honey Festival. The stallholders appear to be doing a roaring trade.

'This place is a hive of activity today,' I say idiotically.

Ollie shakes his head but doesn't bother to reply.

'Now, where are Pep and Juana?' muses the Scotsman. 'Probably in a bar if I know Pep.'

'Wrong!' bellows a voice behind him. 'What kind of man do you take me for?'

Pep's wild grey locks are partially imprisoned under a black fedora, tipped jauntily at the brow.

'What's this, your Al Capone look?'

He fixes his blue eyes on me. 'Someone has to maintain standards. Ollie and I are the only stylish dressers around here. Isn't that true?'

He gives him a bear hug. 'Angel's over there buying honey cakes. Do you want to join him?'

Relieved to be free of his tiresome parents and their friends, he rushes across the *plaça* to find his companion while the rest of us exchange hugs. Juana, stylish as always, in a navy wool jacket, cream silk top and tailored trews, is already clutching a paper bag in one hand. She runs the other through her cropped, coppery locks and in doing so nearly catches a fiery gold earring hanging from her right ear.

'Nice earrings,' I mutter.

'Thanks. I got them from a jewellery fair in Bilbao. Now, what do you think of this beeswax I've just bought? Come, we've sussed out the best stalls. Over there you can try Hidromel, the honey liqueur.'

'Far too sweet,' grumbles Pep. 'But the *sobrasada* sausage and honey snacks are good. Come on Alan, we'll eat all the free samples and then find a bar.'

The idea of Mallorca's famed paprika flavoured sausage being lathered with honey doesn't appeal. I leave Pep and the Scotsman to their pursuits and set off with Juana to the honey stands.

'You know they've got producers from all over the island, even Menorca,' says Juana.

A young woman vies for our attention.

'Do you want to try some of our rosemary honey?'

I take a small spoonful. It's delicious and tastes slightly medicinal.

'My son says this is the best season to buy honey.'

She smiles. 'He's right. The honey often has a stronger flavour and more health-giving properties. It all depends on the quality of the nectar.'

'How did he know that?' asks Juana.

'Amazingly he picked up that nugget from his science class.'

'Why "amazingly"?'

'Because he's been caught twice reading a book under the desk in his science lesson. The last time he was reading about the world's most incompetent criminals. His Mallorcan teacher hadn't known whether to castigate or compliment him.'

'That's funny,' giggles Juana. 'At least he wasn't on his mobile. Look on the bright side.'

I purchase two jars of Es Raiguer flower honey which comes from the Campanet area and a kilo of Mel de Carrotja from Ses Salines. Both are produced using natural and traditional methods and are dense and golden in hue with an intense floral flavour.

'What are you going to do with all that?' Juana asks.

'We use loads of the stuff. We put it on our porridge and I use it in place of sugar in chocolate mousse and muffins.'

Juana laughs. 'I can't even make muffins, or chocolate mousse come to think of it.'

'Well, don't learn. That's how you put on weight.'

I pick up a large tin of beeswax – always good for giving a wonderful sheen to wooden furniture – and am pleasantly surprised that it only costs €3. The next stall is a profusion of soaps and beauty products all made with honey. An elderly lady in traditional peasant-wear peeps out from the pile.

'Do you want wrinkle-free skin?'

'A bit late for that,' sniggers Juana. 'Beeswax Botox might be more useful.'

The woman takes my hand and rubs a cream into it. Although it makes the skin feel smooth, the perfume is unbearably sweet. I envisage swarms of bees following me around the garden in the mistaken belief that I'm nectar on legs.

'If you stay until the afternoon, they'll award the winners of the honey competition. Menorca's tipped to win for clearest honey this year,' the woman confides.

Angel and Ollie wander over.

'Dad and Alan are in this really cool bar,' says Angel, giving me a rather awkward hug. He too is entering the bizarre world of teenage-dom where physical contact with adults is seemingly worse that being pricked with red hot pins.

'It's got a deformed animal museum,' says Ollie.

'What?'

He pats my arm and points. 'Just over there. Don't say I didn't warn you.'

'We'll meet you back at the museum.'

The boys slope off together, glimpsing the stands and studiously avoiding eye contact with any of the stallholders.

In the bar off the *plaça*, Pep waves us cordially inside. 'Just look at these stuffed animals. A deer with two heads. Imagine!'

The Scotsman is supping on a small beer and studiously ignoring the bizarre creatures with treble legs, dual tails and multiple sets of ears and eyes that lurk on shelves and in cabinets around him.

He grimaces. 'It's rather macabre, Pep.'

'Oh, I'm sorry to have offended those English sensitivities of yours, Alan...'

'Scottish, if you don't mind.'

Pep gives a guffaw. 'I shouldn't goad you. After all you are covered in wasp stings.'

Juana and I order espressos.

'Where on earth did they find all these oddities?' she quizzes.

'The world's full of weird specimens,' Pep replies.

She gives him a wan smile. '*Pues*, you should know.'

The Scotsman looks at his watch. 'So where are you taking us for lunch, Pep?'

'A nice little restaurant near Santa Maria that serves a fantastic *menu del día*, but we've plenty of time.'

Juana drains her cup and pats him on the shoulder. 'Actually, we have to leave right now because I've arranged for us to have a private visit to the apiculture museum.'

'You're kidding. Another museum?' complains Pep.

'Well, this is hardly a museum, more a warped taxidermist's fantasy,' I reply.

The Scotsman laughs. 'A bee museum sounds more edifying. Where is it?'

'It's just up the road in Moli d'en Suau, a rather beautiful restored mill.'

'*Madre de dios*! What more do we need to know about bees?' demands Pep.

Juana rests her hands on her hips. 'I thought the boys would enjoy it. They're meeting us there. *Venga*, we'll only be about an hour.'

'An hour?' Pep's eyes bulge. 'You got me here under false pretences. Just a little walk around a honey fair, you said, and then Sunday lunch.'

'There's always another agenda,' replies the Scotsman.

'Women and female bees have a lot in common,' Pep grumbles. 'They never sit still.'

'But there's another thing worth remembering, Pep.'

'What's that?' he asks me, falling into the honeytrap.

'Like bees, women can have a dangerous sting in the tail.'

He plonks his hat on his head and rises from the table. As we gather on the doorstep, he turns to us all with a grin. 'To be a bee or not to be a bee? That, *mis amics*, is the question.'

Six

OLD FLAMES

I awake to the sound of gunshots echoing in the hills. In the half-light I inspect the luminous hands of my clock and see that it is 6.00 a.m. A grey, muggy sky stares back at me from the open window. It's impossible to sleep now. All I can envisage are scores of thrushes, the much-coveted *tords*, cowering in the trees as hunters storm the mountains with shotguns. Some of the lucky ones manage to take flight and huddle like traumatised refugees among the leaves in the orchards. Every year when the *tord* hunting season begins, I feel the same familiar sense of foreboding. In the past, these small speckled migratory song birds were caught in large nets called *filats*, but thankfully widespread use is no longer permitted. In the Tramuntanas, *filats* are still tolerated and it is unlikely that they are policed to any great extent, but there is a stipulation that an individual hunter should kill no more than twenty birds in a day. Given that the season lasts for nearly four months, the odds of survival for holidaying thrushes aren't too good.

After a quick shower, I pop down to the kitchen and feed the troops, leaving the Scotsman to slumber on. Minky, Orlando, Inko and Doughnut gather at the back door, while Bat Cat sits at one of the kitchen windows tapping his paw persistently against the pane. I consider this to be the height of bad manners so serve him last. For the third day running there's no sign of Scraggy, which is rather ominous. I set to work on my winter warmer breakfast for the hens: warm porridge with mixed seeds and raisins. Sometimes I add discarded bread, rice or overripe fruit to keep them on their toes, and as a consequence am increasingly greeted like the messiah. Goneril has even taken to pecking my arm affectionately at the gate while Barney allows me to stroke her feathers. As I'm squatting on the floor of the corral discussing bird hunting with my feathered friends, I hear a van squeal across the gravel in the courtyard. Who'd be calling at such an early hour? A moment later, Llorenç yells out, *'Uep!'* and makes his way down into the field.

'Spoiling your hens as usual?'

'Of course. That way they produce wonderful eggs.'

He tuts. 'So how many are they laying a day now?'

'Five or six.'

He gives me a wink. 'Not bad. Maybe having a view of the Tramuntanas has done the trick.'

A shot rings out in the cloud-covered mountains. 'The hunters,' I say sadly.

He shrugs. 'I know you love animals but *tords* can be a menace for farmers at this time of the year. They eat all the grapes and olives.'

'I thought that was a convenient myth?'

'*Per favor*! We're not barbarians. There are thousands of *tords* and they can be very destructive.'

'There won't be thousands if they keep killing them.'

He laughs. 'You could always start a sanctuary in your garden.'

'Don't tempt me.'

'My mother makes *tordos amb col*. It's delicious – fried thrush with cabbage, pine nuts, tomatoes and *sobrasada* sausage. And you can't beat *tords* in a bowl of *arroz brut*.'

I'm a great fan of *arroz brut*, literally meaning 'dirty rice', a hearty Mallorcan soupy stew of vegetables and meat. The *tord*-free version is particularly appetising.

'So what's up?'

He beckons me. '*Venga*! I have something for you.'

We walk across the field to the orchard and up the steps to the courtyard. There's a real chill in the air and Llorenç instinctively zips up his jacket and rubs his hands together.

'Look in the van.'

I peer through the back window and see a selection of neatly sawn branches and logs of different sizes.

'My outdoor gym!'

'As you requested.'

He opens the van doors and unloads the timber onto the porch. 'So, you're going to use them as hand weights?'

'Something like that. It's all part of my cunning scheme to become as self-sufficient and fit as possible.'

He leans against his van. 'You really are a headcase. Next time I see you, I'll be expecting muscles as big as Popeye.'

The wheels scrunch over the gravel as Llorenç reverses the vehicle and heads off along the track. I look at the rather intimidating pile of logs and wonder how I'm going to shift them into the field where I've begun to create a small outdoor exercise area. At that moment, like the genie from the lamp, a yawning Scotsman appears on the porch in his dressing gown.

'Busy?' I ask sweetly.

'Not yet.'

'Good, because I've got a little task for you.'

I'm at my desk finishing a press release when the telephone rings. It's Pep.

'Listen, are you busy Saturday night?'

'I'm not sure.'

'Then you must be free. I need a small favour. Can you cook dinner?'

'For you and Juana?'

He keeps his voice low. 'And a few others. The thing is that Florence, an old French flame of mine, is visiting the island with a friend and I can't see her alone.'

'Why on earth not?'

'You know Juana. She wants to be there too. Maybe she doesn't trust Florence.'

'You, more like.'

'Huh! *Gracias*. You're a real *amiga*. I was thinking it would be nice and relaxed to meet on neutral territory and since you like cooking...'

'You really do have a cheek, Pep! But for Juana's sake I will agree to it. That way we can both keep an eye on you.'

'Listen, I haven't seen this girl since I was twenty-four. That was more than thirty years ago.'

'And a few years besides.'

'So shall we say 8.00 p.m.?'

'I suppose. So, it'll be just the four of you, and Angel of course?'

A pause. 'I think so, but you know us Mallorcans. Who knows whom we might pick up on the way?'

I replace the receiver. What was I thinking of agreeing to such a dinner? The Scotsman will no doubt consider it a risky idea. I potter downstairs to the kitchen in bare feet and am immediately upbraided.

'Where are your shoes? You want to catch the *gripe*?'

Catalina is standing in the kitchen armed with a mop. 'And now you're spoiling the clean floor. What you want? A coffee?'

'I was looking for the jolly gardener.'

'He's making a bonfire.'

I grab a pair of wellies on the back porch and make my way down into the field where the Scotsman is prodding a rather limp bonfire with a stick. As usual he's puffing on a *puro*.

He throws me a cursory glance. 'At least I've waited until November, unlike all the others who jumped the gun around here.'

'Isn't it is a bit wet for a bonfire?'

'Actually, Miss Clever Clogs, I put all of those old rushes and debris from the pond under a polythene sheet, so it's all as dry as a bone.'

I step back from the smoke and am suddenly aware of several mountains of fresh earth dotted about the orchard.

'Have we got rampant moles around here?'

He eyes me with some impatience. 'I'm planting several new fruit trees and then the broad beans and peas.'

'All good exercise. Talking of which, what do you make of our Mowgli gym?'

'As in little Mowgli from *The Jungle Book*? I thought he spent most of the time swinging on vines.'

'Yes, it's a shame we don't have any of those. Do you reckon it's taking shape?'

He looks across at the assortment of logs and branches arranged at the side of the field. 'Look, much as I think it's a grand idea, it doesn't hold much appeal for me. My days of pumping iron or lifting ant-riddled logs are long over. Quite frankly, I'd rather stick to exercising with a spade and trowel in the garden combined with a bit of gentle hillwalking and cycling.'

I shrug. 'Oh well, I can't really blame you, but I've really got to take myself in hand. Sitting at the computer for hours on end isn't good for the back.'

He gives me a playful nudge. 'Nor is scoffing muffins and drinking sugary espressos throughout the day. So, how exactly are you going to use it?'

I stroll over and pick up two of the heaviest short logs as if they were arm weights and lift them in the air. 'See?'

He nods slowly. 'What about that long, hefty one?'

'Ah, that has to be rolled along. It's quite tough work.'

In some amusement he watches as I try rolling the massive log forward. 'It's a bit slippery after last night's rain,' I add, just as my wellie boots slither on the wet grass and I am sent sprawling in the mud.

'You can say that again,' he chortles.

He saunters across with a Cheshire cat grin and attempts to haul me up but loses his balance and slides down effortlessly beside me.

'You pulled me over!' he complains.

'I didn't! You lost your balance.'

The Scotsman's trousers have somehow managed to locate the only cold puddle of muddy water in the vicinity and cursing he gets up and surveys the damage. 'I'll have to go and change now. You're a menace.'

'It could have been worse!' I giggle. 'At least you didn't break any bones.'

He gives a grunt and shaking himself down, plods off to the kitchen. A moment later I hear Catalina erupting with laughter.

The Això És Vida van draws up outside the Red Cross office in Sóller town where the usual suspects are eagerly awaiting its arrival. Teo hops out of the front seat to greet us all, sporting dreadlocks, skinny jeans and a huge smile, and throws open the van's back doors. The aroma of sweet, damp earth, basil and rosemary is overwhelming. He begins carrying wooden boxes overflowing with ecologically grown produce into the office, the rest of us following in his wake. Each of his regular customers has pre-ordered a large box of assorted fruit and vegetables, the contents of which are unknown until he arrives. This week there are ruby radishes, a bunch of carrots, potatoes, giant spring onions, leeks and spinach. Under the first layer, I find parsnips and courgettes and bunches of parsley, basil and rosemary.

Several of our group assemble their own offerings for purchase. I don't buy eggs as we have our own hens, but I scoop up a few kilos of mountain honey and organic sheep and goat's cheese. The Scotsman is buying a few packs of stoneground flour produced at Finca Es Puig d'Alanar, a local mill near Porto Cristo. Whatever he is saying to the jolly female vendor has her laughing out loud. I wonder if Alan's made one of his famous Spanish linguistic bloomers. Some people exchange goods for money, others for products. The Scotsman and I are looking forward to off-loading some of our excess vegetables in the future. We find ourselves with huge batches of seasonal vegetables such as artichokes or aubergines and spend the following weeks eating nothing else. Raiding every recipe from the tomes on my cookery bookshelf can only throw up so many varieties on a theme and there's a limit to how much pickling or bottling one can do of any one vegetable. My friend Marilo who coordinates our local Almaeco group is keen to extend the product range on offer to incorporate more varieties of fruit, and also grains and nuts. Between us all we could create a fairly self-sufficient, bucolic existence in the valley using barter rather than cash for produce.

As we stroll across Sóller's plaça, with our overladen wicker baskets, Antonia gives us a wave.

'Still not smoking, see?' She waggles her hands triumphantly in front of us as she flitters past.

'She hasn't given up, has she?' asks the Scotsman.

'You're a dying breed. The *puros* will have to go.'

'Never!' he says defiantly.

In the car park we see Neus and Bernat heading towards us, holding hands.

'Isn't that sweet? They look so happy.'

The Scotsman narrows his eyes. 'Wait till they're married. That'll wipe the smile off poor old Bernat's face.'

I give him a poke in the ribs. 'Ah Neus! How's life?'

'*Va bé*. We have some news.'

The Scotsman gives Bernat a wink. 'You've done the deed?'

He laughs. '*Si*, I've asked her to marry me. We're not getting any younger.'

'That's fantastic! What's the date?' I ask.

Neus gives a shy smile. '*Pues*, we're planning on the fifteenth of August.'

'That's months away,' says the Scotsman.

'But there's lots to organise, Alan. My son in Santa Maria has offered to hold the reception in his garden but there'll still be a lot of preparation. We hope you'll all come.'

'We wouldn't miss it for the world, Neus,' I reply.

In the car, I remember my earlier phone call with Pep.

'By the way, we're hosting a dinner on Saturday for Juana and Pep and one of his old French girlfriends will be coming along with a chum.'

'What? Is Juana happy with that?'

'I've no idea. I'll have to give her a call. Apparently this Florence hasn't seen him since he was twenty-four.'

The Scotsman frowns at the steering wheel. 'I hope Pep behaves.'

'It's your job to make sure he does.'

He drives out on to the main road. 'So how come Pep and this Florence are still in touch?'

'I've no idea.'

He mulls this over. 'Mark my words, there's something fishy going on.'

'What on earth do you mean?'

'Just an instinct. I have a feeling it's going to be a night to remember... or should I say, one we might prefer to forget.'

I walk into Ollie's bedroom and find him poring over his homework. He's holding a frayed and battered Catalan text book.

'That looks like a barrel of laughs.'

'It's about Mallorca's history. We're studying this guy called Archduke Ludwig Salvador. He was quite cool.'

'Well, he was living high up near Valldemossa. Must have been a bit chilly.'

He throws me a pitying glance. 'The worst of it is, you actually think you're amusing.'

'I know, it's a sure sign of the onset of old age. Tell me about the cool Archduke.'

He rubs his eyes wearily. 'You know all about him already.'

'I know he produced *Die Balearen*, several dense volumes covering six thousand pages worth of Mallorcan natural history which took him about twenty-two years to write. Aside from that he had a Mallorcan lover named Catalina Homar who sadly died of leprosy.'

He gives me a knowing look. 'Some say she died of a worse kind of disease.'

'Who told you that?'

He shrugs. 'I read about it somewhere.'

'Well, I think leprosy would be bad enough.'

'I suppose. The thing I like about him is that he did exactly what he wanted and he never destroyed anything on his land.

All the animals were allowed to grow old – he wouldn't even cut down the trees.'

'My kind of guy.'

'He wouldn't have killed the coatis.'

'Sorry?'

'There's a poster up at school telling people they can kill coatis if they see any.'

I laugh. 'It must be a joke. We don't have coatis in Mallorca.'

'Apparently someone brought them over from South America and started breeding them on the island and now they're all over the place. Our teacher says they're a menace for farmers but they look rather sweet to me.'

'Are they similar to aardvarks?' I ask.

'Not really. Aardvarks have longer ears and a different tail. Coatis have white-ringed tails and upturned snouts and a brown or black coat.'

'More like anteaters?'

Ollie wrinkles his nose. 'Sort of. They're carnivores, so if one got into our chicken house the hens would probably know about it.'

'So, although they look sweet they're actually quite vicious predators.'

'Apparently, but I still think it's cruel to kill them.'

'Anyway, back to the Archduke. Wasn't he supposed to have dressed like a peasant to merge in with the locals?'

He leans back in his chair and flicks his pencil against the desk. 'He did it more for fun, I think. He was an eccentric and spent a lot of time travelling around the world on his yacht, the *Nixe*.'

'All right for some. It helped that he was from the Austrian Hapsburg dynasty. They had a bit of cash.'

Orlando pads over to Ollie's chair and jumps onto his lap.

'We're visiting Son Marroig next week, one of the Archduke's estates. I'd have preferred to see S'Estaca but Michael Douglas bought it.'

'I've seen pictures. It's very Moorish.'

'It's where Catalina Homar lived. She used to look after his vineyards there. So when are Pep and Juana arriving with these dodgy French women?'

'Any time, and don't say that. They're probably charming.'

'It's Pep's old girlfriend, right?'

'So it seems. You and Angel càn make yourselves scarce after supper.'

'You bet.'

There's the sound of an engine humming.

Ollie pulls a face at me. 'Good luck.'

By the time I've reached the front door, the Scotsman has already bounded over to the car. Although lights blaze on the terraced walls and at the main gate, the courtyard is dark and I can't quite make out the number of guests standing around the car. There's the sound of swift feet on gravel, and Angel rushes up to the porch. He gives me a brief hug and heads straight for Ollie's room. I saunter over to the car wearing my best and most welcoming smile. Earlier I had telephoned Juana, who had seemed far from pleased that Pep's old flame had tracked him down after so many years. As I approach, Pep grabs my hand.

'Let me introduce you to Florence and her TV producer friend, Marie.'

Florence, a giraffe of a woman, exuding glamour and embalmed in some exotic perfume, plants a cold little kiss on both my cheeks. Her long dark hair brushes my face.

'You are our hostess?' she says in broken English. '*Enchantée*! You are so kind to invite Marie and me. What a charming house, but your little lane is so dark and narrow. Marie was so scared.'

Marie, frothy blonde hair, blue eyes and a decade younger than her friend, pops forward on precarious purple heels to kiss me. She's wearing thin red cotton pantaloons, a black halter-neck top and a red felt hat with a small black plume. '*Oui*! I said to Florence that it is like, how you say, 'ammer 'ouse of 'orror! And then we see a bat as we open the car door. I screamed!' Hoots of laughter and merriment. Juana shoots me a look of desperation.

'Well Marie, if you see Count Dracula creeping around a bush, let me know.'

Pep gives me a warning look as I sweep everyone through to the *entrada*.

'Oh, but can we see your garden and pool?' exclaims Marie. 'It is so nice with all the lights shining in the darkness. Like the walls of a medieval dungeon.'

'Yes, and last week was when Guy Fawkes tried to blow up your government, no? It's a creepy time of the year,' adds Florence.

'That was some while ago,' mutters the Scotsman. 'And he didn't succeed, so no harm done.'

I lead them from the kitchen door to the patio. 'It's a bit chilly.'

'Pas du tout!' retorts Marie, her arms already covered in goosebumps.

I notice that Pep closely shadows Florence while Juana casts a watchful eye over them. Full of bonhomie, Alan appears with a tray of cava and soon everyone's in good cheer. Florence suddenly gives a little shriek of pleasure as she approaches the pergola beyond the kitchen door, Despite the time of the year, bunches of purple grapes hang in juicy clusters from the twisted grey vine that coils like a giant snake about the wrought iron lattice frame. 'Are those real?'

The Scotsman laughs. 'I sincerely hope so.'

He jumps up and pulls down a small clump of grapes which he places in Florence's hands. With delight she pops one into her mouth.

'But it's still so sweet. Marie, you must try them!'

Her friend bends forward but squeals and throws her hands in the air when a gecko darts from a crevice in the wall. 'Oh my God! What is it?'

'It's only a little gecko,' says Juana.

'Oh, I hate lizards. I don't like anything that scuttles around,' Marie replies.

'Let's hope a rat doesn't drop on your head then,' Pep mutters.

'You have RATS? You're not serious?' says Florence.

The Scotsman tries to be reassuring. 'Not many, just a few in the field but they only really come out at night.'

Marie plucks a grape from the bunch in Florence's outstretched hand and munches thoughtfully on it. 'Delicious! Do you make juice with them?'

'Better than that,' the Scotsman replies. 'Pep and I are making our own wine.'

Florence rolls her head back and laughs. 'That's so funny. A Scotsman and a Mallorcan trying to make wine.'

'I don't see what there's to laugh about!' Pep snorts.

'I do!' says Juana with a smirk. 'You know that Pep was over here one day treading grapes and he fell right out of the barrel covered in juice?'

Florence puts a hand to her mouth in disbelief. *'Non! C'est pas vrai!'* It can't be true.

The Scotsman chuckles. 'It was such a funny sight. Poor Pep. It took us ages to mop it all up.'

'Never again in my house,' I say.

Juana giggles. 'Nor mine!'

Pep knocks back his cava and attempts to affect a casual air. 'One day, when my brew wins awards you'll all be sorry.'

This prompts another explosion of laughter from the assembled throng. I sneak a glance at my watch and decide that it's time to serve up the first course, and herd them inside. The boys reluctantly join us, sitting at the far end of the kitchen table where they talk in animated and hushed tones.

'So, Florence, how did you catch up with Pep after so long?'

She fixes her huge black eyes on me. 'You know, when my friend Marie and I hit on the idea of a weekend break on the island, I suddenly thought what fun it would be to look up Pep. And *voilà*! I found him in the telephone directory. So simple.'

'We met when I was studying at the Sorbonne,' adds Pep.

The Scotsman frowns. 'You were at the Sorbonne? I thought they only let in first-rate students.'

'Very droll, *mi amic*,' titters Pep.

'So, why did you choose Mallorca?' I ask, handing Marie the breadbasket.

She takes a slice of baguette and begins mopping up the dressing on her plate. 'Well, I am Jewish and working on a TV documentary about the history of my people during the time of the Spanish Inquisition.'

'That's quite a heavy subject,' I say.

She shrugs. 'Yes, it is terrible what happened, but the past is the past. We just have to learn from our mistakes.'

Florence waggles a fork at me. 'Where do you buy these artichoke hearts? They are divine.'

'They're from our own garden. We chargrill and bottle them in olive oil.'

'And these wonderful aubergines?' asks Marie.

I shrug. 'The same.'

'But how do you find the time to do all this? It must be so boring preparing it all,' Florence says.

'Actually, it's great to get away from the computer for a few hours.'

'Even I enjoy bottling. It's rather therapeutic,' adds the Scotsman.

'Oh, I hate cooking of any kind,' Marie announces. 'I eat out all the time.'

'And you, Florence?' Juana asks.

'I wish I had more time but in truth I buy a lot of ready-made food.'

'And there I was thinking all French women were good chefs,' says the Scotsman sadly.

'Another myth, I'm afraid,' laughs Marie.

I carry a large tray of fishcakes to the table.

'My favourite,' says Angel, bobbing up from his chair. 'Have you made those fried potatoes?'

'They're called sautée potatoes. Yes, just for you and Ollie.'

I serve the boys and then pass plates to the others. Alan raises an eyebrow surreptitiously when he sees the two French women pile up their plates.

'And are you in the film business too, Florence?' I ask.

She shakes her head and laughs. 'Oh no, I am an authoress.'

The Scotsman smiles and serves her some vegetables. 'Do you write fiction?'

She chews thoughtfully on some broccoli. 'I am a feminist, and so I write about women's issues.'

'Fascinating,' says Juana. 'Have you a book on the go at the moment?'

Marie giggles and takes a sip of wine. 'She is writing about her past lovers, so watch out Pep.'

'I hope that's a joke,' he says lamely.

Florence tosses back her mane of hair. 'No, Marie is correct. I am writing about how women can make terrible mistakes in their choice of partners, how it affects their lives and can shape their future.'

'I see,' says the Scotsman, gulping down his wine rather quickly. 'Sounds like bestseller material.'

Florence flashes a rather malevolent smile in Pep's direction. 'Sometimes I look back at the way men treated me in my twenties when I was just a vulnerable young woman.'

Pep nearly chokes on his wine. 'Vulnerable? You were as tough as old boots.'

She points a finger at him. 'I pretended to be strong but really I was just a frightened child inside.'

Pep tuts and shakes his head. 'That's not how I remember it.'

'So what is the theme of your book?' asks Juana, evidently amused to witness Pep's discomfort.

'I am tracing as many of my ex-lovers as possible to discover if and how they have changed in my eyes or whether they are still chauvinist pigs.'

'Er, can we be excused?' Ollie asks with a brief urgent smile. 'We'll come back for dessert later.'

'Of course,' I reply giving him a quick wink.

The two boys push out their chairs and head off to Ollie's bedroom.

Juana turns to Florence. 'Well I can assure you that Pep hasn't changed in the twenty-five years we've been married. He enjoys being a chauvinist.'

'Just what I would have thought,' replies Florence. 'You must be such a special woman to put up with him.'

'That's true,' says Juana with a beatific smile. 'I tell him every day.'

'So, Pep, what do you feel about my little book project?' asks Florence.

All eyes are on Pep. He gulps down the contents of his glass and then with a defiant grin replies, '*Magnifique*! I shall be the first to buy a copy.'

Juana gives a titter. 'And I'll be the second.'

The Scotsman clears away the dishes while I carry dessert bowls to the table. Juana and Florence are locked in deep conversation while Pep and Alan compare notes on the quality of the red wine. A second later, a piercing scream from Marie nearly causes me to drop the bowl of honeyed chocolate mousse I'm carrying.

'*Mon dieu*! There's a RAT on my foot! Help me!'

Without a thought Pep dives under the table and reappears with a struggling Inko in his arms. She gives an indignant meow and hurtles off in the direction of Ollie's bedroom.

Pep laughs. 'A fairly big rat, I'd say.'

Marie shakes her head. 'I'm so sorry, but it felt just like a rat was rubbing against my leg. I wouldn't have a wink of sleep living here with all these creatures.'

Pep offers her a comforting glass of wine, adding rather unconvincingly, 'It was an easy mistake to make.'

Marie raps the table with her knuckles. 'Oh Florence, did you see how gallant Pep was? Without a thought for his own safety he threw himself under the table. You know you really are mistaken. He's not such a chauvinist after all.'

It's a frosty morning and a thin layer of ice has settled on the roof and windows of the Mini. The Scotsman strides into the courtyard and exhales deeply.

'Ah, just smell that air. The thing I love about living here is having real seasons.'

I stand on the porch in my furry slippers and cotton dress.

'What on earth are you wearing?'

'Whatever I could find at close hand.'

'Don't go nutty and dress like that nervy French woman, Marie, last night. What a pair they were,' he says.

'Actually, it ended up being a fun evening.'

The Scotsman guffaws. 'Well, after all that nonsense about Florence's book, Pep rather redeemed himself in their eyes over the rat.'

Ollie comes out on to the porch yawning. 'You mean the rat that turned out to be a cat? What was that woman, Marie, on? I mean she was scared of anything that moved and that Florence was a weirdo. It was stupid of Pep to invite his old girlfriend here.'

The Scotsman places an arm around his neck. 'What did I tell you about girls? Trouble!'

Ollie shrugs. 'Angel said that after they'd dropped them off at their hotel in Sóller, his mum was laughing all the way home.'

'Can you blame Juana?' I ask. 'They were an eccentric pair but I ended up quite liking them.'

'Ah well, it takes all sorts,' sighs the Scotsman. 'And they did bring some very good French wine.'

A figure waves to us from the terrace above our front garden. It's Fernando.

'Everything OK?' says the Scotsman.

'*Bé*. But my mother's still not good.'

I walk over to the garden to hear him better. 'Are the pills not working?'

He shakes his head. 'We decided to stop the medication. For a while she seemed to be getting a little better but last night she had another ridiculous hallucination and she wouldn't listen to reason.'

'A rat in a hat?' I suggest.

He laughs. 'No, worse. She said a coati walked into the kitchen, ate the cat's dinner and sauntered out again.'

Alan tuts. 'Oh dear.'

Ollie and I exchange looks.

I glance up at him. 'Actually, Fernando. There's something I really think you ought to know...'

Seven

DOG IN THE MANGER

Beyond the open bedroom window, rain hisses like a nest of angry vipers. I watch as the Scotsman, in sopping Barbour jacket and with old tweed hat pushed firmly down over his ears, attempts to clear the drain concealed in a clump of bushes at the far end of the rear patio. Muddy grey water gurgles about his wellies and carefree plant pots skip by, some landing in the pool where they pirouette round and round at speed. The shutters rattle like chattering teeth as a wild wind blows, sending the trees into a frenzy, while torrential rain gobbles up patches of the field and orchard.

From the window overlooking the field I can see that the corral is becoming waterlogged. The silly girls are still frolicking about in the mud, their feathers clinging to their sides while Salvador shelters under a miserable, tearful lemon tree. Much as our feathered friends seem to enjoy inclement weather, I decide that they should retire to the henhouse until the rain subsides. I close the windows and shutters and head downstairs, where I pull on wellies and wrap up in a waterproof jacket and scarf before making my way across the back patio. The Scotsman gives me a wave and ambles over, holding his hat with one hand to ensure that it doesn't take off and share the same hapless fate as the plant pots.

'Guess who I found curled up in my *abajo* today? A soggy old Scraggy.'

'Well I never, I wonder where he's been all this time.'

'I gave him some food. He's very scrawny, but he'll live.'

My scarf rises up and slaps me in the face. I tuck it into my jacket. 'I'm going to coax the hens inside. It's getting too violent out here.'

He nods. 'Good idea. I'll come and help.'

We walk carefully down the wet stone steps to the field and over to the corral gate. Barney and Carmen Miranda appear at the fence, soaked to the skin and jabbering excitedly.

'Time for bed,' I shout above the gale. But of course the girls are having none of it. Despite the deluge, thunderclouds and flashes of lightning, they are shrewd enough to know that it is still only lunchtime, not their normal hour to retire for the night. Stubbornly they flit around the soggy corral, flapping their wings and darting in all directions while clucking loudly in unison. Maybe it's just my wind-rattled ears, but there seems to be a natural cadence to their song.

'Do you think they're attempting a feathered rendition of "Singing in the Rain"?' I shout in the direction of the exasperated Scotsman, who is stalking Salvador around the tree.

He looks back at me. 'What on earth do you mean?'

'You know, "I'm clucking in the rain, just clucking in the rain, what a glorious feeling, I'm happy again."'

'With any luck you'll be carted off to an asylum soon,' he mutters.

'Killjoy!'

The Scotsman now stands in a sizeable puddle, his tall frame just about level with a bunch of withered lemons hanging from a tree, the last of the season. A few grey locks that have escaped from under the rim of his hat lie flattened against his bronzed forehead. In spite of it being December, the Scotsman still remains tanned, a phenomenon that has prompted waggish Mallorcan friends to award him the sobriquet of the *moro*, the Moor. I watch as pearls of rain run down his face and drop from his chin like intrepid tombstoners to an uncertain fate below. In some frustration he makes a dive at Cordelia and curses when she deftly shrugs him off. I don't fare much better with the others. Gallingly, when we do manage to drive most of the hens into the shed, one or other will tantalisingly hang back, hopping off as soon as we approach and squawking something no doubt along the lines of 'Catch me if you can!' The whole exercise reminds me of those annoying little puzzles where you have to get all the balls in allocated holes but inevitably one fiend keeps rolling out. The Scotsman loses patience and suggests we come back later when they might have come to their senses. We secure the gate and are just about to return to the house when there's an enormous crash. We look up just in time to see part of the high *bancal* separating our land from that of Emilio our neighbour, collapse to the ground. Heavy rocks tumble down, one on top of the other and roll into the field. The Scotsman winces and blinks away the rain.

'Will the insurance cover it?' I bawl above the wind.

'Actually, I think it's Emilio's call. Whoever owns land above a boundary wall is responsible.'

We plod back to the house and take off our sopping jackets. When he removes his hat the Scotsman's silvery grey hair rises from his head like tiny wisps of smoke.

'What's happened to your hair?' I laugh.

He attempts to smooth it down. 'This damned hat always seems to create static electricity. As it happens, I need to have my hair cut, but when can I ever find the time?'

'My mother always used to say that one has to make time.'

'But then again, she would have been only too aware that living with you, that's virtually impossible. There's always another little chore lurking behind the door.'

We warm ourselves by the fire.

'Emilio's not going to be too happy.'

The Scotsman shrugs. 'Looking on the bright side, at least it's only part of the wall and thankfully neither of us was underneath it at the time.'

Indeed it might have put rather a dampener on the Christmas festivities if one of us had been flattened like a Spanish tortilla. It has rained solidly for four days now and the novelty's wearing a little thin. My sister, Cecilia, and her son, Alexander, will soon be arriving from Paris and London respectively, both hoping to enjoy the blue skies and mild weather that is characteristic at this time of the year. They may not be in luck at this rate.

'When are we picking up the Christmas tree?' I ask.

The Scotsman gives a grunt. 'That's another thing I've got to do on my endless list. The local nursery said I could collect it tomorrow.'

'You did order one that's three metres tall?'

'What do you take me for?' he says with a nervous look in his eye. 'Of course I did.'

I potter upstairs to get on with some office work, occasionally glancing out at the blackening sky. Greedy George has emailed, inviting me to Barcelona the following month to inspect the site for his new Havana showroom, and a former client and old friend, Andrea Cecile, wonders whether I might handle some freelance PR work for her new fashion brand, Number 35. The telephone rings. It's Rachel.

'Just wanted to check you're still alive.'

'Barely.'

'How's the weather?'

'Filthy, and the chickens are misbehaving.'

'I warned you about them. The bucolic dream isn't all it's cracked up to be. Well, it's lovely and sunny here in London.'

'I'm very happy for you. So how are things?'

She sighs. 'Oh, the usual pre-Christmas scramble with journalists calling in products to feature in last-minute gift guides. Mind you, I'm off on a rather jammy trip in January. I've got to visit a new hotelier client in Barbados. Tough call, eh?'

'How awful for you. I'm not remotely jealous. Is Ben going too?'

'He wishes! At least we'll have Christmas together in Yorkshire and then do the family visits. I take it you're staying put?'

'You bet. I'm a sucker for Christmas in the valley.'

'That's good, because I've got some stuff I need you to do for Raisa Ripov.'

'Oh come on, give a girl a break.'

'It's just a bit of editing and a rewrite of a brochure. You can do it standing on your head and it'll pay for more than a few chickens.'

'Well, I suppose...'

As I replace the receiver, Ollie pops his head round the door. 'You know what? I've just been on YouTube and seen that Max Wall guy playing Professor Wallofski. He's actually quite cool.'

'I told you so. Well, if you like him, I've got lots of other old comedians I can acquaint you with. One of my favourites was Dave Allen, and then of course there was Eric Morecambe and Dick Emery and what about Stanley Baxter...?'

He cuts me short. 'Perhaps that discussion can wait until you're in the old folk's home, but until then, I've got to get on with some homework.' And he slinks out of the office before I have a nanosecond to protest.

It's early evening when we hear an urgent banging at the front door.

'Whatever next?' puffs the Scotsman as he kneels on the rug, sorting through a box of Christmas tree decorations. A double necklace of fairy lights hangs around his neck and trails along the floor. Bernat stands on the porch clutching an umbrella, his face ashen and drawn. I usher him in.

'Whatever's happened?'

'I'm not sure. I promised that I'd pop by Neus's on the way home from Sóller, but she's not answering the door. Like a fool I left her spare key at my own house so I can't get in. All the lights are on, so I'm worried that something might be up.'

'Did you try the back garden?' asks Alan as he begins winding the lights carefully around his hand.

Bernat nods. 'The gate's locked though, and my legs aren't good enough to attempt climbing over it. Neither of her nearest neighbours are at home so I thought I'd come here.'

'Perhaps she's just out on an errand,' I suggest.

He shakes his head unhappily. 'But she was expecting me. She wouldn't go out.'

'Where's your car?' Alan asks.

'Outside Neus's house. The rain's so bad, I thought it safer to walk round here.'

Alan and I grab our still damp jackets and head for the Mini with Bernat in tow. Ollie is having a sleepover at Angel's, so if we're delayed for any reason, there won't be a problem. The rain is relentless, drowning the windscreen and thundering on the car's roof. Some minutes later we drive up to Neus's house which is on the end of a terrace and make a dash for the front door. Bernat peers out at us from the back passenger seat, a fearful expression on his face. I find one of Neus's white cats crying on the porch and watch as it suddenly scurries away in the rain, and leaps up and over the garden gate. Moments later it returns, brushing my legs and mewing loudly. Is it trying to tell me something? We ring the doorbell to no avail and decide that if worse comes to worst we'll have to break a window. First, we decide to take a quick look in the garden. I climb onto a shallow wall and with the Scotsman's help, lever myself up and over the high back gate, landing in an ungainly heap on other side. Immediately I hear an urgent voice and there some way off, sheltering under the broad roof of her hen hut, is Neus. She is lying on one side and appears somewhat relieved to see me.

'What happened?' I gasp.

'Oh, I stupidly tripped over while I was trying to get the hens inside, and did something to my left leg. I managed to crawl over here but I can't get up.'

I worry that Neus has broken a bone. At least she's reasonably dry under the shelter of the stone hut, although she is shivering with cold. I put my jacket around her and see whether I can lever her on to her feet but she gives a little cry of pain. The back entrance to the house is open so I rush inside and let in the Scotsman via the front door. With renewed energy, Bernat leaves the car and makes his way through the house to the back garden where he is horrified to see his beloved lying out in the rain surrounded by wet chickens. He calls for an ambulance while Alan and I keep Neus as dry and warm as can be with both our jackets and a duvet until it arrives thirty minutes later. The two paramedics are fast and efficient, lifting Neus onto a stretcher with the utmost care before transferring her to the vehicle. They tell us that she'll be checked over thoroughly by a doctor and have an overnight stay at the hospital.

She grabs my hand. 'Bernat will come with me, but would you mind feeding the cats while I'm gone and locking up the chickens?'

'*No problema*, Neus. Do you have a spare key that I can use? That way I can feed the cats tomorrow.'

'By the front door on a peg.'

We watch as the white vehicle, which has backed up to the garden gate, rumbles across the short gravel yard, its tail lights and indicators flashing red and white intermittently in the silky darkness like twinkling lights on a Christmas tree. The vehicle falters at the road before turning left in the direction of Palma and Son Espases Hospital. The Scotsman and I are drenched, our jackets lying uselessly in the mud and rain where Neus discarded them. After shooing the three cats into the house and making sure they're fed and watered, we decide to tackle the hens. We walk across the garden, relieved that the rain has been reduced to a drizzle. To our dismay we see several excitable shadows lurking in the long grass. Why the devil haven't they taken themselves to bed? In the inky blackness we fumble about in the garden, attempting to coax the reluctant birds into the old stone henhouse. They cackle and hop about enjoying our growing desperation as we try to corral them towards the building's open door.

'I can't believe we're doing this for the second time in a day,' I moan.

'This is hopeless,' hisses the Scotsman. 'I'm tempted to invite a passing genet to gobble them all up, but that wouldn't be kind to Neus.'

'It would be a whole lot easier if Neus had a corral rather than letting them run loose about the garden.'

He grunts in acknowledgement. We traipse about in the long wet grass contemplating our next move when all of a sudden the garden is bathed in dramatic white light as a full moon smiles down from the smoky heavens. The wind drops and the sky dries away its tears. Mesmerised, we gaze up at the perfect white orb until it slowly disappears behind the tips of the Tramuntanas.

The Scotsman breaks from his reverie and rubs his hands together. 'Come on, we'd better get these little horrors to bed and then we can go home.'

'I could certainly do with a hot shower and a glass of something.'

In a state of exhaustion, the Scotsman looks about him. 'Now where have they gone?'

There isn't a beak or feather in sight. We walk round to the henhouse door and to our amazement find all of Neus's ten hens huddled together on the top roosting bars with their eyes tightly closed.

'Would you look at that?' chuckles the Scotsman as he slams home the bolt of the door.

'Sweet dreams!' I coo, but they don't appear to hear me as they slumber on.

We lock up the house and yawning, head off home. Once in the kitchen, the Scotsman uncorks a bottle of red wine and gives it a sniff.

'Let's leave it to breathe while we check up on our own girls.'

Down in the field we enter the corral to find Salvador asleep on the top shelf of the hen house surrounded by his dozing harem.

The Scotsman gives a sigh of relief and quickly turns tail. 'Best not to rock the boat.'

'Indeed, let sleeping hens lie.'

'Surely lay?' he smirks as we wearily retrace our steps back up to the house. By the rosy glow of the fire we chink glasses. Never has a robust drop of red wine tasted so good.

Early on Saturday morning Ollie and I feed Neus's cats and chickens and are just locking up her house when we hear someone calling to us.

'Excuse me, are you friends of Senyora Adrillon?'

I turn to face a rather stout middle-aged woman standing at the gate, a crumpled handkerchief raised to her ruby nose. She automatically addresses me in English.

'I'm Serena Payne. I'm renting the house next door. Is the *senyora* around? I haven't seen her for a few days.'

It suddenly dawns on me that she must be the irritating new English neighbour with the multitude of allergies.

'I'm afraid she had a bad fall during the storm so is recovering in hospital. Luckily she didn't break anything.'

She sneezes heavily. 'Oh, right, it's just that her cats have been a bit of a nuisance of late and keep trying to get into the house.'

'A hazard of rural life,' I say with a stiff smile.

'Yes, but I suffer from a severe allergy to animal fur, so it's a bit of an issue.'

Ollie eyes her suspiciously. 'Maybe you should shut your doors.'

She turns to him with a look of irritation. 'But I don't want to be a prisoner in my own home. It's bad enough having to cope with all the pollen around here. I've had to get several trees removed from the garden and I'm forever clearing away seed pods from the porch.'

I wonder why it is that every new incumbent who rents the next door house to Neus always ends up being difficult. Perhaps it's jinxed.

'You have an allergy to pollen too?' I ask.

'Yes, and to certain types of vegetation and even feathers. I hate hens.'

I notice that her right eye begins twitching involuntarily. Ollie stifles a nervous giggle and turns away.

'Perhaps you'd have been better renting in the town?' I suggest.

She seems aghast. 'Oh, but I love the countryside. I wouldn't live anywhere else. I have a house outside Bath in the UK, and it's very rural there but I've had most of the trees cut down in the garden and I don't keep pets so I don't have a problem.'

'And are you working here?'

'I'm an artist. I like to have sabbaticals every few years and this time I chose Mallorca. I prefer France but it's good to have a change. Can I show you my makeshift studio?'

The woman is quite obviously unhinged but I decide to humour her for Neus's sake. After all I might be able to temper her neuroses through patient dialogue. We follow her down the path and into the house where several significant canvasses are stacked up against the white walls of the *entrada*. One shows a large Rubenesque nude lying provocatively on a bed of grass and flowers in a shady and leafy bower. Her heavy-lidded eyes are semi-closed and while one snow-white hand partially obscures her blotchy face, the other shields her modesty. Silvery hair cascades down her pink back in giant waves, coming to rest on an enormous reddish rump that resembles a lump of beef. Ollie views it wordlessly and raises his eyebrows a notch.

'I believe in celebrating the female form,' she gushes. 'I like to provoke and to inspire.'

'Yes, I can see how it would provoke discussion,' I reply. 'Your use of colour is intriguing.'

Across the room, I suddenly catch sight of a pair of crutches.

'Well, what luck! You have crutches.'

She nods. 'I always pack them in case of emergency. Why the interest?'

'Well, it's just that Neus's doctor thinks she should use a pair for a few days until the bruising and swelling subsides in her hip, but the hospital is out of stock. I was going to try to find some for her in Palma – heaven knows where. One of her sons is also making enquiries but hasn't had much luck so far. Would you mind lending them to her?'

The woman runs an agitated hand through her wiry grey hair that resembles an unravelled Brillo pad. 'But I can't let her borrow these. I might need them myself.'

'For what?'

'Well, say I had a fall in all this inclement weather? I just can't take the risk.'

'But it would only be for a few days, and it would save Neus some money.'

She hesitates then shakes her head. 'I'm really sorry, but they're not up for grabs.'

Although too stunned to answer, I'm tempted to drive a foot through her obese alter ego in the long grass. I look at my watch and explain that we must catch the early train to Palma. At the front door I turn to survey her painting again.

She studies my face expectantly. 'You like it, don't you?'

'Actually, I was just thinking that with her puffy eyes and mottled complexion the poor woman could possibly be suffering from some kind of allergy. What do you think?'

It is nearly 8.00 a.m. and we're lucky to have made the first train to Palma with a few minutes to spare. We sit on board waiting for it to depart from Sóller station.

Ollie stares across at me. 'That woman was completely loopy. Why on earth did you agree to go into her house? She could have been an axe murderess or anything.'

'Not that likely.'

'All the same, she looked mad with that scary make-up and crazy hair.'

'I suppose it takes all sorts, but I am cross that she wouldn't loan me those crutches. So much for Christmas spirit. She's being a real dog in the manger.'

Ollie peers out of the window. 'A dog's not quite right. It would give her an allergy. Ah, looks like the guard's about to blow the whistle.'

On the platform the last stragglers are running towards the wrought iron steps that lead up to the train's individual, though interlinked, carriages. Breathlessly, they make their way along the narrow aisles that are flanked on either side by simple, tawny leather banquettes. These seats have a cunning mechanism allowing passengers to face in either direction simply by pushing the back supports one way or another. Few locals use the train because the magical mystery tour through the Tramuntanas takes a good hour, whereas by road Palma can be reached in just half the time. The price is a factor too although Sóller residents, myself included, carry a card that offers a healthy discount. Despite the cost and time involved, however, nothing can beat the Sóller to Palma train experience and Ollie and I are committed fans. It seems that many visitors to the island are too, because a million of them use the privately owned train every year. It could be the nostalgia of travelling in a historic carriage with glossy wooden panels the colour of honey, or perhaps the fact that a cheery 'toot-toot', similar to that of Thomas the Tank Engine, blasts out when entering every dark, cool mountain tunnel. Whatever the weather, it is a thrilling ride into the island's capital and Ferrocarril, the local Sóller company that owns and operates the trains, ensures that they are always looking spick and span.

Ollie gives a yawn. 'Did you know that we pass through thirteen tunnels?'

'That's quite something. Just think, it will be the train's centenary soon. I wonder what kind of celebrations we'll have in Sóller?'

He laughs. 'That's a tough one. How about wine served with *sobrasada* sausage and bread? It's always the same whatever the celebration.'

He's spot on, although at least the local *ajuntaments*, the town councils, do their best to provide free entertainment and refreshments for their residents when local celebrations and fiestas take place. It could of course explain why many of them are nearly always in debt. Soon we pass over the viaduct known as Cinc-ponts, meaning five bridges. The view down to the Sóller valley is spectacular. Sunlight winks back at us from the windows of fleeting stone *fincas*, and far, far below I can see a group of wild brown and white goats ambling about the rugged landscape.

'In my history lesson, we were told that the Sóller railway was inaugurated on 15 April 1912, the same day that the *Titanic* sank.'

'Not a great omen,' I reply.

The train emerges from a tunnel and soon we find ourselves screeching to a halt at Bunyola. A few people alight and when a whistle is blown we are off again.

'Is it true the trains were made in England?'

'Loughborough,' he replies. 'And the Sóller tram was made in Staffordshire. What would they have done without us Brits?'

The train rattles through a long tunnel. When it emerges on the other side I turn to Ollie.

'Don't forget that for centuries whenever Sóllerics needed to venture into Palma they managed pretty well going up and down the precarious Coll Pass with their donkeys, so we hardly saved the day.'

We journey on through the hills, jogging by fields of naked almond trees along with olive groves and leafy orchards devoid of fruit. At one stage we pass a series of horse stables and further up the line, Son Pardo, one of two horse-racing courses known as *hipòdroms* that exist on the island, the other being in Manacor. The *trot* as it is known in Mallorquí involves horse races with two-wheeled chariots which the drivers skilfully guide around a course. It is a hugely popular local sport that goes back centuries and the famous *trotons*, the horses that take part in trot races, are famed throughout Spain. Before we know it, a jumble of buildings in shades of smudgy grey, cream, silver and terracotta jostle for space on the hazy skyline. The old boys, ruddy faced with history in their veins turn their heads from the new, brash newcomers that rise up into the sky like shiny rockets. But in reality, all are welcome in this metropolis – tall and elegant hotels rub shoulders with elderly, squat and drab apartment blocks, decrepit shops sit cheek by jowl with cool and contemporary restaurants and art galleries, and ancient cemeteries gaze wistfully over redeveloped parks. Palma in all its magnificence glimmers before us and soon the train is pulling slowly into the historic station adjacent to Plaza España. Ollie leaps out of his seat and stretches.

'Christmas shopping here I come!'

Gathering up my bag and warm jacket, I turn to Ollie. 'Just to finish our discussion about the Sóller railway, it might have been the British who supplied the trains but it was the locals who did all the spade work creating the tunnels and railway line.'

He offers me an impish grin. 'Still, there's no use in having a railway without a train, is there?'

And with that he hops down from the wrought iron staircase and saunters happily along the platform towards the exit and a tinsel-wrapped Palma.

Out on the street, we find ourselves in a man-made jungle of cars, buses, lorries and *motos* roaring along the eight-lane ring road that sweeps past Plaza España. Pedestrians swarm the pavements and cafes, and a solitary policeman wearing dark shades and blue uniform stands blowing his whistle furiously at a crossing. Ignored and practically mown down by the advancing public, he evidently decides to throw in the towel and with a shrug, purposefully heads off towards a cafe located outside the central bus station. Ollie and I are carried along in the crowds and, on the other side of the street, manage to make a quick diversion down a side street, soon arriving at Plaza Mayor and a little later, the main shopping areas of Sant Nicolas and the old town. At a novelty shop, Ollie buys a comical desk toy for his cousin, Alex, and a fake *puro* made of chocolate for the Scotsman, while in a fashion store I dither over a jumper for my sister. Is it the right size? The sales assistant, about my sister's slim build, obligingly places it over her T-shirt, convincing me that the smaller size will be best. In the old town we buy a beautiful wool pashmina for Catalina and some funky jewellery for her twin daughters. It is then that we take refuge in Cafeteria Jaume III opposite the smaller of Palma's two Cortes Ingles department stores. While I opt for a double espresso, Ollie sips at a Bitter Kas and then has the devilish idea of ordering *churros*, the deep fried sugary dough sticks that are heavenly on a cold wintry day. In an instant all thoughts of dieting and open-air gyms are thrown to the wind.

It is siesta time when we find ourselves walking through the historic Jewish quarter of Palma known as the Call Mayor. It was here that from the twelfth century until the fifteenth century at least 300 Jewish homes lay segregated from the rest of the community behind high walls. On Calle de La Calatrava stands the whitewashed Santa Fé church which was once an ancient synagogue. During Moorish times there were two further synagogues which were later requisitioned under Spanish reign, becoming the Church of Montesion and Church of San Bartolomé.

'So, why did the Spanish take the synagogues from the Jewish community?' Ollie asks.

'It's a bit of a long story, but in 1314 when King Sancho was ruler, two German Christians were converted to Judaism by the local Mallorcan Jews. Some say it was all a bit of a ruse by King Sancho and the Catholic Church to extract money from the wealthy Jewish community by accusing them of trying to make converts. As punishment, the king reclaimed the synagogues and ordered the local Jews to pay a fine of one hundred and fifty thousand florins.'

'That sounds like a lot,' he replies.

'It was. Anyway, it was all downhill from there. In 1391 locals pillaged the Jewish quarter of Palma and three hundred Jews were killed.'

'That's rank,' he says.

'Rank?'

'No worries, mother. That's teen-speak for disgusting.'

'Righto. Anyway, by 1435 all Mallorcan Jews were forced to convert to Catholicism, but most continued to practise Judaism secretly behind closed doors.'

'And did the king find out?'

'Sancho? Oh, he'd long since popped his clogs as had several successors. Far worse for the Mallorcan Jews was the reign of King Ferdinand V of Aragon and Queen Isabella of Castile in the late fifteenth century.'

'What was so awful about them?'

'Well, they created the Spanish Inquisition, a sort of witch hunt against the Jewish community. It was quite a cunning scheme because Ferdinand's old father had left him huge debts, money that he owed to Jewish money lenders, and so by removing the Jews, he removed the debt.'

Ollie looks around him. 'It doesn't seem such a bad area, but I guess it's very different now.'

'You bet. I mean if you visit Plaza Gomila today near Porta Pi Shopping Centre you'd never know that it's where they used to burn Jews at the stake.'

'So, when was it safe for Jewish people to live here?'

'Believe it or not, it was only during the Napoleonic invasion of Spain in 1808 that the Spanish Inquisition was halted, although it wasn't abolished until 1834.'

'And half our family is Catholic,' he mutters.

'I don't think any modern-day Catholics would be proud of what happened, but we are talking about a pretty pernicious time in European history.'

He rests his bag on the pavement for a moment to rub his sore fingers. 'Actually, can we talk about something more cheerful? It's not very Christmassy.'

'You're right. Let's go to C'an Joan de S'Aigo for some hot chocolate.'

He cheers up. 'I love that cafe.'

And so do I, probably because of its historic legacy. It is Palma's oldest ice cream parlour having been founded by Mr Juan de S'Aigo in 1700. In the early twentieth century the place was run by a revered Sólleric named Mateu Jaume who penned a cookery book in 1884 entitled *Llibre de gelats i quemullars – The Book of Ice Creams and Teacakes*. Aside from serving delicious ice creams, which in days of yore clever Mr S'Aigo used to produce from ice stored in his snow house known as a *casa de neu* in the Tramuntana mountains, the parlour is famous for its cakes. One of these is the *ensaimada*, the coiled pastry made from *saim*, meaning pork fat in Catalan, which is integrated into the dough. *Ensaimadas* are light and crispy and are served with a multitude of fillings such as custard, cream and angelica as well as *sobrasada* sausage. A popular drink served at the establishment is ice-cold *horchata*, traditionally made with tiger nuts – *chufas* – but also with almonds.

We stroll off through the streets towards it, loaded down with our shopping bags, stopping occasionally to admire Christmas decorations in windows. Just before we reach the cafe, a gallery catches my eye, or rather the enormous bronze bull standing defiantly in its midst.

'Isn't that amazing?'

Ollie lolls in the doorway. 'It's all right. A bit overpowering. It must be about three metres tall!'

In the windows and on the bare white walls are a variety of watercolours and abstract interpretations of bulls.

A suave, suited man approaches. '*Hola*, my name is Juan Pico. I'm the owner of this gallery. What do you think of our *toro*?'

'I think he's wonderful, but he seems so huge.'

'His creator wanted him to look like a god among bulls, illustrating the strength and power of the real-life creature. He is, how you say, larger than life.'

'Is it by a local sculptor?'

'Antonio Sanchez is from Jerez. He's a very talented young artist. The bull is called Ratón.'

'Mouse? Is the name supposed to be ironic?'

He smiles. 'Ratón is a famous bull on the mainland. He is the hero of many bull runnings at which several men have met their fate on his horns. This is a tribute to him.'

'How heavy is he?'

He laughs. 'The sculpture? About a thousand kilos. And don't ask the price.'

An insane idea crosses my mind and I ask for the man's business card which he is delighted to thrust into my palm.

In the cafe, Ollie eyes me warily. 'OK, heads up, why did you want that guy's card?'

'You remember I told you that Greedy George was going to be opening a showroom in Barcelona?'

'So?'

'Well, he's hoping to link up with a sherry brand from Jerez called Bullseye and I just thought that bull would be perfect for the launch.'

'Are you mad? It probably costs a fortune!'

'Oh, I'd only want to have it on loan in return for some free publicity.'

He takes a sip of his hot chocolate and laughs. 'And how on earth would you get it to Barcelona?'

'I've no idea, but I'm going to make it my business to find out.'

As the Scotsman drives along the country roads towards Santa Maria he continues to remonstrate with Ollie and me. 'Now listen, I definitely booked that Christmas tree. If the guy lost my order, is it my fault?'

Having pitched up to collect our 3-metre tree from the local nursery the night before, the Scotsman was told that the order had been accidentally mislaid. In some embarrassment, the owner had offered to call his supplier in the hope of locating another one, although hadn't seemed very confident. When the Scotsman imparted the news to Ollie and me on our return from Palma he was greeted with disbelief and suspicion. Had he really placed the order? Had something maybe got lost in translation? There was only one thing for it. We would have to trawl the nurseries the following day. Christmas would not be the same without a tree.

At the first two nurseries we visit, the prices are high, the trees straggly and neither delivers as far as Sóller. In some disappointment we drive on to Hortus, a nursery just beyond Santa Maria village. To our relief we see some handsome tall firs bunched up together at the back of the yard, and all are at a reasonable price, but does the nursery deliver to Sóller? A friendly assistant shakes her head sadly.

'Sorry, *senyor*, but we don't do deliveries. Maybe we could get it in your car?'

She follows our gaze to the Mini and bites her lip. 'Ah, maybe not.'

It's at this point that a mirage presents itself in the yard in the form of Michelle and her beautiful young daughter, Ellie. Michelle is a New Zealander by birth, and she and her partner Andy, an Anglo–Mallorcan, run Tramuntana Tours on Carrer Sa Lluna in Sóller and have another outlet in the port. It's a haven for hikers, cyclists and those looking for boat charters. She comes over to greet us and immediately offers to transport our tree back to Sóller in her minibus.

'I'm picking up a tree myself, so it's no trouble at all. Maybe you could pop by the shop tomorrow?'

We call Catalina who offers to collect the tree in her van the following morning before joining us for a coffee. Delightedly we head back to Sóller, stopping briefly at the local nursery to let the owner know that we've managed to get hold of a tree. He greets us with a long face.

'But you needn't have done that! I rang my supplier today and he's promised to send a three-metre tree over here in the morning.'

The Scotsman grimaces. 'If only we'd known! I thought you were going to call if you'd got one?'

'No, I said I'd call if I couldn't get hold of one. '

In the car the Scotsman shakes his head in some frustration. 'After all that, we could have got a tree from here.'

'A simple misunderstanding,' I say.

Ollie regards us impatiently from the back of the car. 'But the tree we've bought is half the price of what you were quoted for a similar one here, so what's the problem?'

'You have a point,' replies the Scotsman.

'So, we're quids in?' continues Ollie.

'It seems so,' I reply.

'Good,' he says with a satisfied smile. 'Now you haven't got an excuse for not buying a new set of tree lights and decorations.'

Alan and I don't bother to reply. We know only too well when we've been defeated.

It is Christmas Day and the house is in a state of happy chaos. Having risen at 7.30 a.m. to roast the turkey, I am surprised some minutes later to find Ollie and Alexander tripping down the stairs in night attire to begin stealthily examining the wrapped gifts under the brightly lit Christmas tree. I find it rather endearing that my nephew, at the grand old age of twenty-four, still gets a kick out of buying and receiving gifts, and always enters into the festive spirit for the sake of Ollie. My sister Cecilia and I get started on peeling vegetables and by the time the Scotsman arrives on the scene, the cats have all turned up, Horatio the hedgehog has been discovered snuffling behind the fridge and two wild peacocks have attempted to jump into the pool. And it's still not even 9.00 a.m. An hour later, the buzzer blasts at the front gate and Pep and Juana's car rolls into the courtyard. Had I, in an inebriated moment, invited them for lunch? Surely I'd have remembered? They stride into the *entrada* with bulging bags and clinking bottles.

'We're on our way to my aunt and uncle's house, but wanted to pop by with some gifts!' cries Juana.

Pep pushes past and offers bear hugs to one and all. He slips a bottle of whisky into the Scotsman's hands.

'A little something for you and Alex when the nagging felines have gone to bed.'

'We'll be up long after them,' my sister warns.

'Oh, and I have something special for you to try at lunch.'

He pulls a bottle of red wine from a plastic bag which bears a dubious homemade label with the words: 'TORO, RESERVA, BODEGA ALAN Y PEP, MALLORCA.'

'*Toro*? Why on earth have you called it Bull?' Cecilia asks, trying not to smirk.

Pep regards her with impatience. 'Because it is a full-bodied, macho wine, of course.'

'Or just a load of old bull,' says Ollie under his breath.

'Hey, *chico*, I heard that! I may take your present back,' he growls.

Juana steps over to the large French windows in our *entrada*. 'What happened about your collapsed *bancal*? I can't see it from here.'

The Scotsman points into the distance. 'It's down there in the field. Anyway, it's all sorted. Emilio was very civil about it and got one of his farm workers to fix it. It's as good as new.'

'If only all life's problems could be fixed so easily,' she sighs wistfully.

Angel has discovered our *Belen*, the traditional nativity scene we have set up on a bookshelf near the Christmas tree. He drags his mother over to inspect it. She gasps in mock horror.

'What is this? You put a plastic dog in the wooden manger? This is blasphemous!'

Ollie grins. 'Not really. It's just a sort of in-joke.'

Pep narrows his eyes. 'I know this English expression, "dog in the manger". Is it someone who's a pain in the backside?'

'More or less,' I reply.

'Payne in the backside would be more appropriate,' sniggers Ollie with meaning.

Juana takes the bottle that is still in Pep's grip and places it gingerly by the kitchen sink. She taps my sister's arm.

'You shouldn't even think about drinking this but if you have a death wish try it, although hemlock might be quicker – and pleasanter.'

'*Per favor*! It will taste like nectar,' Pep remonstrates.

Even the Scotsman can't hide a smile. 'Well, I think it really needs to rest for a while.'

'So should my husband,' says Juana pointedly. 'It might stop him talking such twaddle.'

'*Venga*! We must go,' says Pep. 'There will be eighteen of us dining together – all family. It could be a bloodbath, Alan!'

I rush to the tree and gather up the presents we have bought for them. 'Here, these are for all of you.'

Angel stands by the kitchen door eyeing up the largest. 'Is that one for me?'

'I chose it,' replies Ollie reassuringly. In other words, it will actually be something he might care to have, rather than the usual disastrous adult choices.

When they've left, we settle round the tree to open presents, only to be interrupted by a festive call from Neus. After a week of convalescence she is now able to walk slowly with the aid of just a stick. Although I had never managed to locate a shop selling crutches in Palma, another neighbour of Neus's had come to the rescue, locating a pair for sale at a clinic in Alcudia in the north and had driven all the way there and back without complaint. He could certainly teach Serena Payne a thing or two about neighbourliness. A cork pops and the Scotsman appears with a tray of glasses. Christmas has officially begun.

Later, after a sumptuous Christmas lunch, I sit by the pool in the sunshine with the telephone suctioned to my ear, listening to Greedy George regale me with his Christmas adventures or rather mishaps.

'Still got the MIL round my neck. Stands for millstone, guv.'

'I thought you liked your mother-in-law?'

'Get away. I like her money, guv. That's a different matter. She's loaded but a right old trout with the constitution and girth of a walrus.'

'Where's your Christmas spirit?'

'Somewhere on a fictional Caribbean beach with a mystery blonde. Anyway, are you doing anything nice for New Year?'

'We're off to celebrate in Fornalutx as always, trying to gobble a grape with every strike of the clock at midnight, and then a few days later the three kings roll into town and hand out presents to the kiddies in the villages.'

'I imagine Ollie's a bit old for all that malarkey now?'

'True, but he still enjoys their arrival on horseback and trying to guess which villager is playing a king. It's our annual sport.'

He wheezes with laughter. 'You certainly know how to live it up in rural Mallorca. I'm off to the Dorchester with Bianca for some swanky dinner. Unfortunately the MIL's coming too. She has to, she's paying.'

'So what do you think about my bronze bull idea?'

'I like it.'

'We need to talk it through.'

'OK, get cracking and we'll discuss it all when you pop over to Barcelona next month.'

I suddenly recall our joint meeting with Dannie Popescu-Miller back in London. 'Whatever happened about your trying out Dannie's Allure Bloom anti-wrinkle lamps?'

'Don't ask. She wanted me to do trials after Christmas but I came up with an ingenious idea. I'm getting the MIL to do it instead. If the lamp gets rid of the old walrus's wrinkles, I'll buy one myself.'

'But the trials are for men and to the best of my knowledge your MIL isn't a man.'

'You and I might know that but they won't. She's got a short back and sides, the bark of a Dobermann and wears trousers. Mum's the word.'

When he's off the line I stare out over the glittering mountains watching a majestic eagle glide by and suddenly I feel utterly at peace with the world. How wonderful it is to be no longer welded to my former frenetic PR life in London, although the odd dollop of Greedy George madness is still there to keep me on my toes.

My thoughts are interrupted by a beaming Scotsman. 'Fancy a gentle stroll by the sea?'

With the sun on my back and not a cloud in the sky, I honestly can't think of anything better I'd rather do.

We walk along Platja d'en Repic beach, throwing pebbles into gently bobbing waves and greeting other locals with the cheery Mallorquin refrain of *Molts d'anys*! which literally means 'many years', and is de rigueur during the festive season. A dog comes bounding along the beach, kicking up the soft white sand, followed by a local police officer. I recognise the animal immediately for it is Sawyer, the new one-eyed, celebrity German Shepherd that is being feted in the town. Our mayor is hoping that the energetic two-year-old will act as a deterrent for any would-be thieves or drug dealers as he prowls the streets by night, although in truth he's going to have a lean time of it. Crime and Sóller thankfully are as distinct as chalk and cheese. As the officer passes, he calls out, *'Molts d'anys!'* and gives us a wave. Sawyer, tongue lolling, doubles back to greet us and enjoys all the attention he receives. A minute later he chases Ollie to the water's edge where he shows his acrobatic skills by leaping in the air and catching a stick Alexander throws to him. As we all head towards the port in search of ice creams, I suddenly stop in my tracks. Lumbering towards us along the esplanade with a sorry look on his ruddy face is Gaspar, the newspaper delivery man. He looks relieved to see us and gives the Scotsman and Ollie a playful knock on the arm.

'Molts d'anys!' he yells and plants two smackers on my cheeks, before coyly shaking hands with Cecilia and Alexander. 'Are you heading back into town by any chance?'

'We were hoping to get an ice cream first,' I reply.

He wipes perspiration from his face. 'It's just that my *moto*'s broken down and I could do with a lift back home. I've left it with one of the cafe owners until I can get it fixed.'

'Have you time for an ice cream first?' asks the Scotsman.

'Segur! I've got all the time in the world.'

So off we set, a motley crew, towards the port's popular *heladería*, where the Scotsman treats the delighted Gaspar to possibly the biggest festive ice cream in the world. As we sit on the sand with our overflowing cones, enjoying watching the world go by, Gaspar suddenly nudges me.

'You know Neus is much better?'

I nod. 'Yes, we saw her this morning. No real harm done, thank goodness.'

'What a pair though,' he laughs.

I give him a blank look.

'I'm talking about her neighbour, you know the English artist with allergies?'

I frown. 'Serena Payne. What about her?'

'Well, I popped round to Neus's house at lunchtime to give her a poinsettia for Christmas but she was out. That was when I saw the English woman hobbling about the front garden.'

The Scotsman nearly drops his ice cream. 'What had happened to her?'

Gaspar shrugs. 'She told me she'd fallen over one of her own canvasses and had sprained her ankle.'

'A self-fulfilling incident I'd say,' mutters the Scotsman giving me a knowing look.

'Anyway,' Gaspar continues, 'I suggested that Neus might lend her some crutches now that she no longer needed them but Senyora Payne seemed to take offence and limped off without even a *Molts d'anys*!' He gives a resigned shake of the head. 'There really is no pleasing some people.'

Eight

ON A WING AND
A PRAYER

The valley is bathed in white mist and a thin veneer of frost kisses the window panes. It is tempting to stay in bed on this cool January morning, but the open road and my garden gym beckon, so I throw on my exercise gear and running shoes and set off. Out on the lane Rafael's chickens are scrabbling about in the unyielding soil in search of insects but it's poor pickings at this time of the year. Music booms from the kitchen and I decide to poke my head round the open door.

'*Com anam?*' I shout out above the din.

Rafael is gyrating to the beat in the middle of the room, a piece of toast in one hand and a mobile in the other. To my relief he isn't sporting goggles and is fully dressed.

'I'm fantastic! Yes, it's a beautiful day. You going for a run? If my leg wasn't bad I'd come with you.'

Rafael has recently had a minor operation to correct a problem with his hip which has put paid to his running for a while. In the past he has managed to clock up impressive finishing times for his marathons, three hours being his best to date.

He taps my arm. 'Hey, I thought you had an ankle problem. Is it OK now?'

'Amazingly, I've found an excellent Dutch physiotherapist in Santa Maria who has got it just about back on track.'

'Good – you can give me his details.'

By sheer good fortune I came across Jos Alkemade on a random website and was astonished to find that he'd been the physiotherapist for various top football and basketball teams in Holland. It never ceases to amaze me that there is so much talent on the island, but discovering it often requires the grim determination of a truffle hunter or one of Mallorca's indefatigable ferrets.

I watch as Rafael limps over to the kitchen table. 'When will you be up and running again?'

He shrugs cheerfully. '*Quien sabe*? The doctor thinks maybe in two weeks. In the meantime I can dance.'

I leave his kitchen disco and head off towards the port. There isn't a soul on the road although by 7.30 a.m. lorries, *motos* and buses transporting children from nearby villages to the main schools in Sóller will begin clogging up the roads. And let's not mention local mothers on the nursery run or commuters heading for the Sóller toll tunnel. I reach the turning for Platja d'en Repic beach and jog over the little bridge, where a huge surge of mountain spring water cascades down over the rocks towards the sea. In front of me is the Rocamar Hotel that sits on a strip of dishevelled wasteland like a sad old pensioner having long been abandoned to the elements and a life of solitude. Windows are smashed, tiles uprooted, furniture stolen and doors are hanging off by their hinges. Tramps regularly bed down in the dark and dank rooms during the winter making small fires to shield themselves from the bitter coastal weather. In its twilight years, the hotel has become a refuge for stray dogs, cats with their litters of kittens, and wild goats graze in its shabby grounds. An impasse between the local council and owners has meant that no one will take responsibility for putting the old boy out of his misery in his declining years, so for now the hotel remains an eyesore and an embarrassing reminder of a time when ugly, cheap structures were allowed to be built in areas of natural beauty, all in the name of mass tourism. As I slow down to watch a rat dart across the hotel's potholed drive, I hear a *'beep-beep'* and Gaspar waves from his bike, forcing it to lurch tipsily towards me. I'd rather he kept both hands firmly gripping the handles.

'Want a lift?'

This is our customary jokey little routine.

'Not today, *graciès*.'

'When can we go running again together?'

'You only have to ask,' I reply.

'I'll call you.'

He teeters off with a huge grin on his chops and an elongated *'beeeep'*. Running along the esplanade I see ahead of me the huge grey carcass of Atalaya, newly acquired by the international hotel group Jumeirah, which intends to turn it into a deluxe five-star haunt for those with ample wallets. Many jobs will be created for locals when it opens. It sits high on a hill directly overlooking the sea, and I can only imagine how heavenly the views will be when it's finished. Perhaps if I win the *loteria* I'll get to sample its charms one day. I study my watch and head back along the esplanade. The sea is choppy and pale and disconsolate gulls skim the surface forlornly, but there are few fish to be had. Perhaps they're all slumbering on the seabed, swaddled in a blanket of soft white sand and too bone idle to face the new day. I jog back along the main road that leads to Sóller town and at the first roundabout, peel left onto the American Road and towards home. Nearing the turning to my *camino*, I suddenly remember that I am meeting my friend Cristina at 10.30 a.m. and before then have some urgent emails to deal with. As a spit of rain pricks my skin and the sky rumbles I luckily find myself right outside the courtyard gate. I am tempted to run dutifully down the slope into the field to do a quick workout with the wooden logs but the lure of a shower and a strong coffee wins. There's always tomorrow. As they say, *poc a poc.*

The rain has subsided by the time I park up outside El Convento de los Sagrados Corazones, the former Convent of the Sacred Hearts, which now comprises a Baroque church and state primary school. The grand old sandstone building was constructed in the eighteenth century and is an imposing sight as one approaches Sóller from the direction of Palma. Cristina zooms up on her powerful motorbike, clad in black leather outerwear. She pulls off her huge white helmet and we exchange kisses.

'I'm sorry I'm a little late. The traffic from Palma was unbelievable.'

'Don't worry. How was work?'

She grins. 'Frantic as ever.'

Christina juggles her consultancy work at a busy medical clinic in Palma with life in Sóller with her husband Ignacio, a naval architect, and eight-year-old daughter Lola. We originally met at an art exhibition in Sóller to launch the work of Ignacio's younger brother, and have been firm friends ever since. Cristina is a direct descendant of the swashbuckling Capità Joan Angelats, famed for his heroics in vanquishing marauding Tunisian and Moorish pirates when they made a surprise attack on Sóller Port on 11 May 1561. The bravery of the locals, in particular the *valentes dones* – the valiant women folk – in such tempestuous times is legendary, as is the quick thinking of Guillem de Rocafull, governor of Ibiza, who sent warning to Capità Angelats of an imminent attack after the Moors stopped off in Ibiza for water supplies en route to Mallorca. With the aid of commanders from nearby Bunyola, Santa Maria and Alaró, Capità Angelats and the townsfolk defeated their aggressors and lived to see another day. Cristina, her husband Ignacio and young daughter, Lola still live in the beautiful historic home – more a museum – once owned by Joan Angelats, and I always feel a frisson of excitement and privilege when tiptoeing around the vast edifice with its ancient family portraits and vestiges of heavy, dark and solid furniture from a past epoch.

Today we are meeting the legendary Padre Bartomeu Barceló i Roig, a man who loves bees possibly more than anything else in the world. This retired teacher and priest from the small inland town of Porreres has for many years made Sóller his home and now resides in comfortable quarters within the *convento*. Cristina and Ignacio are happy to allow Padre Barceló to use a slice of their mountainous terrain to cultivate honey, his great passion.

Cristina presses the bell at the rear gate and a moment later, a rich, velvety voice hits the intercom, '*Si, quién es?*'

Cristina explains that she's arrived with the Englishwoman who wants to know all about him and his excellent honey. He chuckles, and in a matter of minutes the gate swings open and an athletic-looking man with a thick crop of white bushy hair and laughing eyes set behind heavy, crimson-rimmed spectacles welcomes us in. We find ourselves in a quadrangle overlooking a neat and well-tended garden. The sprightly *padre* strides through an elegant cloistered gallery and along a high-ceilinged airy corridor that leads to his own simple rooms. He turns to me and shakes my hand warmly, keen to know my name and country of birth. When he learns that I'm a mongrel of Celtic, mainly Irish origin, he claps his hands together in delight, telling me that in the 1960s he spent two summers hitchhiking around Ireland while studying in a seminary and had a whale of a time. I wonder what the Irish must have made of a hitchhiking Mallorcan priest. He was surely the toast of the town.

'You know how old I am?' he asks.

'Well, maybe seventy?'

He gives Cristina a nudge and laughs. 'Did you hear that? She's a flatterer. No, I'm eighty-seven and you know what? Twice a day I climb up the mountain to tend my bees, and that is why I'm in such good health. And of course I eat lots of honey.'

I stare at him in amazement. If this is what beekeeping can do for you, I might take it up myself. But what would the Scotsman say? I fear adding bees to the ever-growing menagerie might just finally send him over the edge. We sit in his cosy study and talk bees.

'You know I simply couldn't live without bees,' he tells me. 'When I was young I used to be a *blavet* at Lluc Monastery. We *blavets* studied there and acted as choir boys.'

'Doesn't *blava* mean blue in Mallorquin?' I ask.

'*Si*, we were known as the blue collars. You know, it's one of the world's oldest boy choirs similar to those in Vienna and Regensburg in Germany.'

I nod. 'I know about the *blavets* because my neighbour Rafael's musical son also went there from the age of nine until fourteen.'

'*Idò*, then you've got the picture. Well, in 1939, right at the end of the Spanish Civil War, the monks decided to put six old beehives in order. There was a lot of deprivation at the time and food was scarce.'

Cristina chips in. 'Didn't the monks take on a famous beekeeper to help?'

'Indeed. His name was Mestre Pere Penya and he came from Fornalutx. He had a terrible temper and a wooden leg.'

I try not to catch Cristina's eye as we both smother grins.

'Having said that, the man had a huge heart. He inspected the beehives and got some of the students to assist him but they hated being stung. I was only fourteen but for some reason I became entranced by his work, and in a nutshell he chose me to be his apprentice. I learnt all about beekeeping thanks to him and when he left, I was put in charge.'

'But weren't you frightened of being stung?'

'Bees only sting to defend themselves, and it's God's will that they pay with their lives.'

'Yes, it's a bit of a double-edged sword.'

He beams across at me. 'Ever since that time I have tended my own hives. Cristina and her husband Ignacio kindly let me keep my fifty beehives in one of their olive groves.'

'Yes, but you give us fantastic honey in return,' she replies.

Cristina has often given me pots of Padre Barcelo's delectable mountain honey. Once you taste it, it's hard not to metamorphose into Pooh Bear and consume the lot all in one go.

'The thing about bees,' he continues, 'is that they do so much for humanity. If they didn't pollinate the flowers on the planet we wouldn't survive.'

Padre Barcelo suddenly breaks into impressive English. 'In 1951 when I was director of studies here, an Englishman with an enormous moustache came to the convent one day from the village of Deia. He asked me if I'd allow him to visit the bell tower every Tuesday to be stung by the bees up there. He suffered from rheumatism. Imagine!'

'So, what did you say?'

He rolls back his head and laughs. 'I agreed, of course. He came every week like clockwork.'

'But can't stings cause anaphylactic shock?' I ask.

'Only one person in every twenty thousand is likely to have a really severe allergic reaction. Anyway, he was all right. He used to thank me profusely after every visit.'

I wonder who the masochist with the moustache was. Maybe he wore a hair shirt too, just for good measure. I shall have to ask my chums in Deia if they can identify him.

'Would you let me visit your hives one day?'

'Of course, it would be my pleasure. Now, another thing I should mention is that bees aren't venomous. Those stung who happen to have very severe allergies simply die of asphyxiation because their throat swells up.'

I'm not sure if that's such a comfort but the good *padre* explains that if one acts quickly and uses a knife to create an opening in the throat, a life can be saved. I'm beginning to get cold feet about the visit to his hives. I'm not sure if I fancy my throat being slit open in the unlucky event of an allergic reaction.

'So, when did you learn to speak English?' I ask.

'Oh, a long time ago when I studied in Oxford and Ireland. I taught English here and in Madrid although I've forgotten a lot over time.'

Cristina and I exchange glances, deciding that we've taken up enough of Padre Barceló's time.

'Now, before you leave, let me give you my book.'

He disappears into another room and returns with a slim volume sporting the title, *El Mundo de las Abejas – The World of Bees*.

'It's for you. A little gift.'

I offer him a hug of gratitude. We get up to leave.

'We'll arrange a date for a visit,' says Cristina.

'Indeed,' he replies thoughtfully. 'But the poor bees have had a very hard time of it this summer without rain.' He taps my arm. 'Did you know that if I were to put a queen bee in a purse and secrete it on your person, every bee from the hive would follow? In fact they'd start creating honey on you. Isn't that extraordinary?'

It sure is, and I hope he doesn't get any ideas about experimenting with the concept. When I visit his hives I'll be giving a thorough search to my pockets before I leave.

We walk through the silent, dark cloisters back to the gate where another visitor, an elderly man, awaits him. The rain has started again.

'One more thing,' he says animatedly. 'I know a man in Asturias who lives on milk and honey alone and he is in perfect health. He has all the minerals and nutrients he needs, which is why bees are God's little miracle.'

He smiles and waves goodbye. I give Cristina a hug, and pushing the book into my bag make for the car as heavy drops descend. I look up at the darkening sky. Someone up there was obviously listening to the bee-loving *padre*. I imagine the inhabitants of his fifty beehives buzzing about happily in the rain, grateful that their owner is a man with a seemingly direct line to their creator.

We're on our way to the *plaça* in Sóller when Judas rings. With some difficulty I extract the phone from my pocket while keeping the wicker carrier balanced on my lap. I hear Rachel's chirpy voice.

'Good time to call?'

'Well, it's not perfect timing, Rachel. We're off to the Beneides de Sant Antoni.'

'What's that?'

'The annual blessing of animals in Sóller town square – it happens every year on 17 January. Quite frankly Horatio and the hens are none too happy.'

'What? You're bringing your hens? And who's Horatio when he's at home?'

'Our hedgehog. Do you remember nothing I tell you?'

She hoots with laughter. 'Oh, this is the best, I can't wait to tell Sarah and the rest of the girls in the office. You've finally flipped.'

'I've done nothing of the sort. I just felt it would be good to have the new hens blessed. After all, I did the same for the cats a few years ago.'

'Yeah, right. I remember; you lost them up a side street.'

'Well, the hens will remain in their wicker carrier and I shall just ask the *padre* of Sant Bartomeu church to anoint them through the open lid.'

'What on earth do Ollie and Alan think about it all?' she giggles.

'Ollie has little to say on the subject and Alan is demanding a huge whisky when we return home.'

'Look, I won't keep you; I just wanted you to know that Rasia Ripov loved that proposal and all the brochure changes you did for her. She's dying to meet you.'

'Great stuff. Maybe on a future trip.'

'She's even offering you free Botox at her Mayfair salon. Just think, an end to wrinkles.'

'It might be worth mentioning to her that just four kilograms of botulinum is capable of killing off the entire human race. I think I'll pass and keep the frown lines.'

'You are a joy. So when are you back in London?'

'Oh, heaven knows. I'm rather preoccupied with helping Alan dig up the soil ready for planting this month and we're about to start picking the new crop of oranges. In the middle of everything I've got to flit over to see Greedy George in Barcelona.'

'You get more like Worzel Gummidge every day.'

'I know, it's sad. Talking of which, we could do with a scarecrow. The pigeons are dive-bombing the corral for grain every day, and let's not mention their attacks on the new broad bean shoots. It must be the cold.'

She stifles a guffaw. 'Well, I've got to go back to the real world now. I'll catch up soon when you're less frenetic.'

The real world? London? Huh! She's got it all wrong. The real world is here ploughing the land, planting seeds, growing vegetables and producing our own eggs. I mean, tell me, what is real about frenetic London life? Commuting, pollution, endless stress, buying pre-packed foods from supermarkets and...

'What's going through that mind of yours?' asks the Scotsman warily. 'I don't like it when you're quiet.'

'No, nor do I,' chimes in Ollie from the back of the car.

'I was just thinking…'

'Burrrk… burrrk,' rasp the hens.

'Stop it, Barney. You too Carmen Miranda. Pipe down. Now what was I saying?'

'Nothing remotely interesting,' replies my son with ennui.

I ignore him. 'Actually I was thinking about the wonders of a bucolic existence, the harmony with nature and… ugh!'

'Now what?' says Ollie.

I look down in my lap and see that Barney and the other girls have deposited a sizeable amount of prize guano into the wicker cage which has somehow seeped straight through on to my jeans.

'Fancy a bit of fertiliser?'

'Yeuch! Gross!' whines Ollie, peering over my shoulder.

The Scotsman glances at my trousers. 'You can't go to the blessing like that!'

'Why ever not? I'll reek so badly that they'll send me right to the top of the queue.'

We find a parking space close to the town hall and, in a delicate joint operation, manage to remove Horatio in his straw-filled box from the backseat and the squawking girls from the front. A few stragglers have already arrived and are talking animatedly with the priest while four donkeys wait patiently for their brush with the Almighty. The priest offers us a smile and seeing the state of my jeans, offers to deal with our pets first. He leans down into the box and blesses the recumbent spiky form hiding amid the straw, and then with extraordinary skill and patience manages to anoint the heads of each of the girls. They suddenly stop their gabbling and raise their eyes towards him rather flirtatiously. He makes the sign of the cross and after a brief chat, we turn to see Jacinto, our donkey whisperer. As usual he is wearing one of his hobgoblin outfits – a brown jerkin with green moleskin trousers, ankle boots and a little Tyrolean cap. He has arrived with six donkeys and to my delight I see that Minny and Della, our own mother and daughter, are among them. I carefully lower the wicker carrier to the ground and rush over to fondle the donkeys' ears. Ollie strolls over, keeping his cool demeanour though unable to hide his delight at seeing our donkeys.

Jacinto gives Ollie a hug. 'I knew you'd be here, so I thought I'd bring Minny and Della along. They're champing at the bit to return home, so when you're up and running, let me know.'

The Scotsman sighs. 'I think Stefan will start building the new shelter next month. The rain's made the job impossible of late. Hopefully it'll be finished by the spring.'

The old man pats his arm. 'They can stay with me as long as you like. Just call me when it's ready.'

We set off home as more people arrive in the *plaça*. Some carry guinea pigs, chinchillas and rabbits, others dogs and ferrets on leads and several farmers arrive with sheep and goats. It would be fun to catch up with some of our acquaintances but the hens are getting restless. I wave at the *senyora* from La Lareña, my favourite bakery. Just seeing her makes me hungry for one of her cappuccino croissants.

'Well, the first thing I'm going to do when I get home,' I declare, 'is to make myself a cup of tea.'

'Ooh no!' retorts Ollie, winding down the window of the car and gasping in fresh air. 'The first thing you'll do is change those foul-smelling trousers.'

'Hear, hear!' says the Scotsman.

'Burrrk,' say the girls and deposit another huge dollop of the Scotsman's favourite fertiliser right in the middle of my lap.

The taxi driver pulls out to pass the car in front of us which has inexplicably drawn to a halt in the middle of Las Ramblas. I haven't been back to Barcelona for some time but it seems that traffic and frayed tempers continue to be a hallmark of the city. My driver pumps the horn and, prodding the side of his head with a plump finger, fixes the man with a fierce glare as we screech by.

'*Madre mia! Que tonto!* You see that idiot? *Mira!* He's consulting a map!'

I peer out of the cab's rear window and see a rather gormless-looking man with a map spread out on the steering wheel. He has stopped dead in the middle of traffic and seems oblivious to the hooting and tooting going on around him.

'A lost tourist, I'd hazard.'

He gives a grunt. 'Lost brain more like. And where's the Guardia Urbana mob when you need them? Happy to pull us cabbies off the road for a missing fog light, but fools like that can cause traffic jams and the boys in blue are nowhere to be seen.'

He revs the engine and, muttering darkly, suddenly takes a sharp right and careers at speed down a lean side road. He darts from street to street avoiding delivery vans, speeding *motos*, stray dogs and cats and dilatory pedestrians who step out into the road with shopping bags, but without a by-your-leave. Soon I haven't a clue where I am. Hopefully still in Barcelona.

'We're now in Bari Gotic and this is Carrer de la Portaferissa. You need the next turning.'

We have arrived in a rather chic street with tall elegant buildings. Shoppers are milling about and there's a feeling of prosperity in the air.

'So *reina*, what does this place look like? Number ten you say?'

So it's not just in Mallorca that people use the pally '*reina*', queen, when talking to women.

I shrug helplessly. 'He said it was a warehouse of some kind. Apparently it doesn't have a number outside because it's in a bad state of repair.'

'Huh. No number. My day keeps getting better.'

He drops his speed and on identifying number eight, a stylish men's shirt retailer, hugs the wheel, and narrows his eyes in search of number nine.

'See that? The next shop is thirteen. Where the hell have the other numbers gone?'

'Looks like the next buildings are all being redeveloped. It's bound to be one of them. Why not let me out here?' I suggest.

He pulls over and rubs his forehead. 'I wonder why I do this job. Barcelona gets more impossible every day. New buildings and one ways. It's not what it used to be and now every cretin's got a car. You drive?'

'*Si*, but I live in rural Mallorca. It's a bit different on the roads.'

'Well don't move. The city is an *infierno*.'

'Still, it's not always idyllic in the countryside. You know what they say, *pueblo pequeño, infierno grande*.'

He turns to me and laughs loudly. 'I like it. An English woman who knows one of our little idioms. "Little village, big hell." Who told you that?'

'One of my Mallorcan friends. She said I was lucky to live outside a village away from the gossips.'

He shrugs. 'It won't make much difference. They'll talk about you anyway, except they'll just make everything up.'

He gives a manic laugh and at that juncture I decide it's time to alight. He takes my note and gives me a wink and a smile when I tell him to keep the change.

'*Benvingut a Barcelona i molt sort!*' he cries and drives off. Welcome and good luck. Luck I will certainly need. Crossing the street, I walk along to where number ten should logically have been. An old terraced building stares glumly back at me, its facade smothered in scaffolding. Could this be it? I yawn and look at my watch. It's 9.30 a.m. and, having caught an early flight from Palma, I've already been up about four hours. I walk a few blocks on and find myself on the corner of an intersecting street. There's an icy wind blowing in from the sea and a spit of rain in the air. Oh, come on George. Where the hell are you? I'm just fumbling in my bag for Judas when I hear a 'Cooooeeeeee!' I look up and down the street but can only see a few fast-walking commuters and some workmen in overalls hunched over their crunchy *bocadillas* and coffees on a bench. This is the normal time for *a merienda*, a little mid-morning snack.

'Up here, you dozy cow!'

I look up and see Greedy George waving from the third floor window of an ancient and dowdy building on the intersecting street. He points to the street below him and beckons me over. With some irritation I leave the street I'm standing on and walk along the pavement towards the boarded-up building. Some moments later a maroon door caked with dust and grime creaks open and George's corpulent form appears before me.

'Wotcha, guv. What were you doing on that street?'

'That is Carrer Pol, the street you told me to go to.'

'Did I? Well it's not the right one.'

'I might never have got here.'

'Course you would. If you'd have just given me a bell, I'd have known exactly where you were. As it was, you're lucky I just happened to be looking out of the window.'

'But what were you doing on the third floor? Haven't you bought the ground floor area for the showroom?'

'Hold your horses!' He grabs my arm and pushes me towards the entrance. 'I've got three whole floors. All pretty groovy. I can keep stock on the top floor, and display products on the bottom two. I've got a swanky wrought iron and cherry wood staircase being designed that'll take clients to the upper level.'

'Isn't it better to get the showroom finished before you start ordering up designer staircases?'

'Don't be boring. The guy who's making it is a friend of Philippe Starck.'

'I'm getting goosebumps with excitement.'

'Cut it out, guv. Come on, let's do a grand tour and then go and get a fry up, Barcelona-style.'

I walk through the gloomy open space on the ground floor. Although the windows are boarded up and the bare floorboards moan at the touch of a shoe, the place has potential. The ceilings are lofty and some of the original art nouveau features are still intact. An immense marble fireplace and an ornate mahogany dresser dominate the room.

'How amazing. It's very Belle Époque.'

'Don't go all French on me again. Listen, guv, it's cheap and classy and that's all I care about. A lick of paint and some pretentious fittings and Bob's your aunt.'

We walk up a rather precarious wooden staircase without railings to the next floor. The area is huge and empty.

'Used to be a fabric company up here apparently. Lots of girls on sewing machines.'

'What were they making?'

'Frilly knickers for all I know. Come on, let's go up one more flight.'

On the top level, the ceiling is made up of old wooden beams and the floors are tiled.

'Why did they have tiled floors up here when they're all made of wood below?'

'I haven't got my crystal ball with me today, guv. How do I know?'

'You must find out. The history of the building is part of your new story.'

'Oh, don't go all cosmic on me. I haven't got time to research all that tosh.'

'Well, if you're too lazy, give me the contact details for your property agent and I'll find out.'

He huffs and puffs but agrees. 'Anything to keep you from nagging. Who knows, it could have been a brothel at one time.'

'How on earth would you deduce that?'

'Pure fantasy, guv. It's all that talk about sewing frilly knickers that did it.'

I bestow my most withering look in his direction and together we turn tail and head off down the dimly lit stairs and back out into the street. He spends an age locking the enormous wooden door.

'You've got to take the door back to its original grandeur,' I say.

'Yeah, my mate Felipe who owns Bullseye sherry is sorting that out. He's chummy with an ace carpenter.'

'Am I going to meet this Felipe?'

'Felipe Cañas? Yeah, we're having lunch with him.'

'Excellent. We need to discuss logistics for the launch and how his sherry will feature on the night.'

'He'll do whatever you tell him, guv. So let me get this all straight. You're going to get Antonio Sanchez, this Spanish geezer who's created Ratón, to loan the brass bull to us for the Barcelona launch where we'll exhibit it along with my new range of bull's hide products?'

'Well, I was thinking of taking it further. You know, having a general bull art theme in the showroom with the bronze bull being the *pièce de résistance*.'

'And what about Bullseye?'

'Obviously we'll serve the sherry at the event and it fits in perfectly with the bronze bull theme because the artist also comes from Jerez.'

'Clever, guv. And how much d'you reckon all this will cost?'

'Not sure. I'll have to talk to the gallery owner in Palma.'

George gives a loud yawn and, leading me by the arm, enters a narrow and shadowy passageway that gives on to a lively square with a church and numerous cafes.

He claps his pulpy hands together. 'This is the heart of the Gothic area. You up for breakfast?'

George can't function without shovelling vast quantities of food into his belly throughout the day. He reminds me of an old steam train constantly being fed with coal every time it needs more oomph. We step into a welcoming cafe and take a table in the warm interior. I notice that my hands are frozen.

'By the way,' he yells, 'Felipe owns a strip joint in El Ravel area. It used to be the red light district but it's gentrified now. More's the pity.'

I look at him in horror.

He gurgles with laughter. 'Keep your hair on, guv, we're not meeting him there today. Sadly it's closed at lunchtime.'

He opens the menu and slaps it shut after a few seconds of browsing.

'I'm up for a tortilla with bacon, fried potatoes and mushrooms. What about you?'

'Scrambled eggs for me and a double espresso.'

A diminutive waiter with a droopy moustache appears and gives George an affectionate pat on the shoulder.

'Your usual, Jorge?'

'Yeah, and lots of toast and butter on the side, Manuel.'

The waiter smiles across at me and takes my order.

When he's gone, George starts giggling. 'I love the way he calls me Jorge and the way he says it, *whore-hey*.'

'It's not *whore-hey*, more *ho* as in hot and then *hey*.'

He sniffs. 'Stop being pedantic, guv. Fancy him being called Manuel. He's a dead ringer for the geezer in *Fawlty Towers*, don't you think? Remember how he used to say *"que?"* all the time? *Que? QUE?*'

'Keep your voice down,' I hiss.

He shakes with mirth. 'All we need now is for Basil himself to turn up.'

The waiter returns with our drinks. 'What's making you laugh so much, Jorge?'

I kick George beneath the table. 'Oh, it's just a silly joke,' I mumble in Spanish.

'*Que?*' he replies.

Greedy George dissolves into hysterical giggles while I shrug helplessly at the bemused Manuel. If this is the shape of things to come, it's going to be a long, long day.

It's 6.30 p.m. and Felipe Cañas is pulling into a parking space at Barcelona Airport. He, George and I have been together since lunchtime and have thankfully agreed all plans for the launch quite amicably. I have tried not to think about Felipe as a dodgy geezer with a dubious nightclub in a sleazy corner of the city, and tried repeating the mantra that he is a successful businessman with a fantastic, synergistic new product which will greatly enhance the launch of Havana's new Barcelona showroom.

'So,' he says, turning off the ignition. 'As soon as you know more about the bronze bull's creator, let me know. If this Antonio Sanchez lives in Jerez, my hometown, and the bull is returned there from Palma, I can visit him and negotiate the transport of it by boat to Barcelona. We still have many months to plan.'

I nod. 'That's very good of you. The Palma gallery owner did mention that Ratón would be returned to Jerez next month after the exhibition at his showroom was over. I just hope transporting it won't be a palaver.'

'A what?' he says.

'It means a bit of a nightmare. A nuisance.'

'No,' he says with a grin. 'I have friends everywhere. I know a man with a boat that I think would be perfect.'

'It's not better going by road from Jerez?'

He shakes his head. 'This captain owes me a favour. Why pay to send it by road? Leave the detail to me.'

Felipe Cañas seems worryingly self-assured.

I pull open the passenger door. 'Well, thank you for the lift. It's been great meeting you.'

'You too. Maybe I'll pop over to Mallorca some time.'

'Great,' I say.

He offers me a polite air kiss on both cheeks before I step out on to the pavement.

'So *hasta luego*!' I say unconvincingly and before I can stop myself, 'by the way, I hear from George that you have a nightclub?'

He breaks into laughter. 'Ah, the old rogue told you this? It is a strip club, not a real nightclub. You want to visit some time?'

I rear back. 'Oh heavens, no!'

He smiles. 'That's good, because the girls are getting a bit old and ugly. I need to ditch them and hire some young, sexy birds. Then you should come with George. It'll be a great night out.'

He blows me a kiss and drives off. I stare after the car in some shock. I was definitely right about flashy Felipe Cañas. He's horribly self-assured and worst of all, a completely sexist pig.

Nine

COPS AND ROBBERS

A wedge of sunlight appears between two rocky outcrops high up in the Tramuntanas. I watch from my outdoor gym of boulders and logs, willing it to spread and lighten up the dull, grey sky. Despite having plodded off for my early morning run, the air still feels chilly on my bare arms and legs. Three of the cats have come down to the field to spectate. They watch with expressions of irony – or is that just my imagination? – as I lift heavy logs into the air. Minky and Doughnut discover my skipping rope and begin lethargically knocking it about under a lemon tree. Meanwhile, Orlando stands perfectly still, his head bobbing up every time a log is raised high, although he can't disguise a large yawn when I attempt a few feeble plank exercises. The Scotsman must have set off to school with Ollie while I was out running and will expect me ready for action in the garden on his return. I've promised to help plant the beetroot, peas and potatoes. The first crop of broad beans, planted back in the autumn, are nearly ready and the artichokes' thick stems are shooting up from the soil. Broad beans, known as *habas* in Spanish or *faves*, in Mallorquin, are best picked when young and tender. I normally prepare them with a little olive oil and lemon juice, smashed garlic, sea salt and black pepper, and sprinkled with chopped parsley. If we have a bumper crop, we steam cook them and store them in jars of olive oil for a rainy day.

As I'm groaning on completion of my twentieth press up, I hear a child calling. I pull myself up and see Clara, one of Fernando's young granddaughters, peering at me from the lower gate.

'What are you doing?' she asks in a rather disapproving tone.

'Good question. Actually, I'm exercising.'

'It looks like fun. You've got a skipping rope like mine.'

'Have I? That's good to know.'

'Can I come in?'

I open the stiff gate and watch as she skips over to one of the tree stumps, wiping it clear of mud before sitting down. Her honey-brown hair is pulled back into a pony tail with a red ribbon and she flutters the sort of lustrous black eyelashes that Dannie Popescu-Miller would kill for. She swings her spindly legs back and forth against the bark. With envy I notice she's wearing warm woolly tights and a thick red quilted jacket.

'Show me some of your exercises with the skipping rope.'

I laugh. 'I'm not very good.'

Grabbing it from the branch of a tree, I do about ten jumps on the spot and stop.

'Can't you do any more? Here, let me show you.'

She takes the handles and begins frenetically sweeping the rope in the air, never missing a beat as her tiny, seemingly winged feet lift high above the ground. After a while she drops the rope. To my dismay I notice that she isn't remotely out of breath. Inspecting one of my spongy exercise balls, she bounces up and down on the largest and then points to my wobble board which for some inexplicable reason I call my Ouija board.

'Can I have a go?'

'OK, but be careful, it's not called wobbly for nothing.'

She steps onto its surface and giggles when she can't keep her balance.

'This is really fun.'

After several attempts, gripping my arm, she manages to stay aloft. I look at my watch.

'Haven't you got school today? Ollie left ages ago.'

She shrugs. 'I suppose so. Granddad's taking us today because we stayed with him last night. He's out feeding the hens and sheep.'

'Well, you'd better go back or he'll start worrying.'

Reluctantly she heads for the gate. I accompany her to the communal track whereupon Fernando's anxious face appears from the orchard above.

'That's where you are, you little monkey. I hope she hasn't been a nuisance.'

'Not at all.'

He looks at me in my running top and shorts and shakes his head. 'Aren't you cold?'

I rub my hands together and realise that I am indeed freezing.

'Can I come back and play some time?' Clara whines.

'OK, but only when I'm here. I don't want you hurting yourself.'

She grins and runs off up the track just as I see the black Mini slowly coming into view. The Scotsman stops to speak to her while I jog back to the house. With any luck I'll just have time for a shower and a cup of tea before he gives me my marching orders.

'The hens loved their porridge today,' I announce to the Scotsman as we push in the last of the seedling potatoes. He stands up to stretch out his back.

'I think you're spoiling them, and I notice that my muesli's gone down. Have you been giving them that too?'

'Only a spoon or two as a treat.'

He mumbles some incantation and tuts loudly. 'Well, no more. That stuff costs me a fortune.'

'But you have to admit that the hens are laying fantastically well.'

'They should be laying bars of gold for the cost of keeping them.' He points towards the orchard. 'Have you seen the blossom on that almond tree?'

I follow his gaze to the clusters of delicate pink petals that have all but obscured the branches of a fine old almond tree. This is one of my favourite times of the year because when the exquisite almond blossom arrives, it's certain that spring won't be far off.

He turns to me. 'By the way, do you fancy popping over to an almond fair in Son Servera this Sunday?'

'Sounds good. Presumably they'll be offering some tastings?'

He gives me a push. 'Always thinking of your stomach. Anyway, looks like we're done here. Shall we brave Eroski?'

Neither of us likes trekking to the local supermarket too often and we try where possible to supplement our own home-grown produce with supplies from the town's individual shops. I still feel we are privileged to have the choice of at least six bakeries, three butchers, two excellent grocery stores, and a vegetable and fish market. There used to be a wonderful old grotto housing a *bodega* at the far end of Carrer Sa Lluna, the main shopping street in the town, but it sadly closed, only to be replaced by yet another women's fashion emporium. Mobile phone shops and estate agents have popped up faster than bamboo shoots all over the town and one really has to wonder how any of them makes a living. Fortunately the die-hard Sóllerics continue to run their quirky and unique little stores across the town, but that will only continue if locals support them.

'We need some more gas canisters as well,' sighs the Scotsman. 'I'll have to go down to the port tomorrow and wait for the gas van.'

As the valley does not have access to mains gas, as homes do in Palma, we are reliant on butane gas to feed our cooking stove. The exceptionally big and bulky orange canisters usually last us at least four months and then need replacing. The tricky part – for a woman, at least – is manoeuvring the empty canisters. Ours are stored at the back of the house behind the outer kitchen wall and they are a devil to budge without developing a small hernia. Our ritual is to take the canisters down to the car park in the port of Sóller where the gas van hangs out a few mornings each week, ready to receive hobbling clients. Without the Scotsman's intervention, I'm not sure how competent I'd be completing this task alone. Perhaps I should consider sticking an empty canister in my outdoor gym. If I worked out with one every day I'd probably be able to give even Popeye a run for his money.

The supermarket is crowded, which is unusual for a Tuesday lunchtime. We split up, stalking food products up and down the different aisles in the hope that we'll be finished faster. I bump into Rafael at the shelves filled with washing powders and cleaning agents.

'So boring! What you buying?' he asks.

'Nothing very exciting, I'm afraid.'

He suddenly brightens up and punches my shoulder.

'You know I go backpacking to India, Nepal and Sri Lanka?'

'You lucky thing. When?'

'In a few weeks. I not back until end of April. You wanna come?'

'Just give me the ticket.'

He breaks into loud, honking laughter and sets off along the aisle. 'Hey, when I go, you look after my house, neighbour. I don't want no burglars!'

As I head towards the checkout counters, I notice a small commotion taking place at one of the tills. The Scotsman is gesticulating wildly in the middle of the group. Now what's he been up to? I'm tempted to slink up an aisle until the brouhaha has died down, but decide that would be cowardly. I breathe deeply and enter the fray. Two of the friendly cashiers who know me well are tutting sympathetically.

'Your poor husband has just been robbed, *senyora*!'

'What?'

The Scotsman is looking very downcast. 'I was just taking some Dijon mustard off a shelf when a large man wearing a black suit, hat and shades knocked into me with a heavy holdall. He had a little chap with him wearing a tight white suit...'

'Sounds like one of the Blues Brothers and a diminutive John Travolta lookalike. You're not just making this up?'

The Scotsman flaps his arms in the air. 'Can you try to be serious? These men took my wallet.'

'One of them would have distracted the poor *senyor* while the other picked his pocket. They are very cunning, these foreigners.'

'Were they English?' I ask.

One of the cashiers looks horrified. 'Of course they wouldn't be English. There are all sorts of foreign gangs operating across the island. We rarely get them up here though.'

The manager bustles over in great excitement. 'A vigilant shopper just noticed two men acting suspiciously in the store car park and rang the police. One was small in a white suit and the other was tall with shades, a hat and...'

'See,' says the Scotsman jubilantly. 'I am vindicated.'

I can only imagine that these jokers are the Chuckle Brothers on a secret filming mission for BBC television. What thieves in their right minds would draw such unnecessary attention to themselves?

The manager receives a call on his mobile. He shoots the Scotsman a hopeful look as he gabbles into the telephone and smiles. 'You would never believe it! Apparently the police picked up the trail, chased them up a side street where the robbers promptly crashed the car.'

The assembled throng claps and whoops. Justice, it seems, has been served.

'This is better than *Starsky and Hutch*,' I say. 'Mind you, I hope they weren't injured.'

'*Que va!*' shouts a nearby shopper. 'If they were stupid enough to mess with the police, they got what they deserved.'

'They're shaken but not injured,' says the manager. 'They're being taken to Sóller police station this minute.'

Shoppers appear thrilled by the thieves' arrest and the manager is evidently delighted to have been able to report such good tidings.

'What about my wallet?' asks the Scotsman.

'You will need to visit the police station, *senyor*. That officer just told me that there's a good chance they'll get back your wallet unless the thieves disposed of it immediately.'

We rush to the car and head for the town's police station but the Scotsman suddenly gives an anguished squawk and drives off in the opposite direction.

'Have you completely lost your marbles?' I ask.

'Gas!' he shouts.

'What?' I look up and discover that a gas canister lorry is two cars ahead. The Scotsman is like a dog with a bone, gripping the wheel and following the van wherever it goes.

'He's got to pull over some time soon,' he mutters.

The van lumbers up a narrow, cobbled lane, turns sharply into a broad street and finally follows a road leading to the town's cemetery. When the van slows down and pulls over by a grocery store seemingly to make a delivery, the Scotsman leaps out of the car and taps on the driver's window. The man has barely had time to turn off the ignition. He jumps in his seat.

'*Que susto*! You gave me a fright. What's up?'

'Do you have any spare canisters?'

'Sure, you can have as many as you like.'

We exchange the two empties stowed in the boot for two new ones extracted by the driver from the back of the van. The Scotsman returns to the car with a smile on his face. 'Car chases are actually rather good fun. Now, for the police station. I can't wait to get my mitts on Little Travolta.'

I'm sitting at my desk trying to make head or tail of a long email from Dannie when the telephone rings.

'Hello?'

Silence.

I'm about to hang up when I hear a long sigh. A heavy breather, in Mallorca? Surely not.

'It is Manuel.'

That's all I need. Mad, paranoid Manuel Ramirez, my hotel client from Panama.

'Is there anything wrong?' I ask.

'Listen. I have a hitch with the new St Petersburg hotel. My personal security team has been informed by the Russian secret police that I may be targeted by the mafia over there.'

'How so?'

'Extortion, blackmail, anything. As I have told you many times, enemies surround us. Don't trust anyone – not even your dog or cat. Every creature has its price.'

I look across at the grey ball of fur dozing at the opposite desk and whisper, *'Et tu, brute?'*

'What did you say?'

'Nothing, Manuel. I was just asking Orlando to bring me a cup of tea.'

'Who is Orlando?'

'My cat.'

He sounds amazed. 'I have heard of cats fetching fish for the ancient Egyptians but this is something else. You must have a very special animal.'

'I like to think so. What do the Russian police want you to do?'

'Keep a low profile and if anyone suspicious makes contact, to inform them immediately.'

'Maybe they try their luck with all new business owners arriving in the country. I imagine there's quite a protection racket going on.'

'My problem is connected with a deal that went sour in Russia many years ago. I made one or two dangerous foes so I must watch my back.'

No doubt Manuel will be glad of his wardrobe of bulletproof jackets, courtesy of his tailor in Bogotà.

'It is tiresome, but I must delay the launch of the hotel from April to June. I need time to sort out this problem. All the press information will have to be altered.'

'That's easily done, but how are you going to resolve things?'

A manic laugh echoes down the line. 'Sometimes it is necessary to find the source of the problem and eliminate it completely. You know the best way to kill a verruca?'

Now he's worrying me. 'Marigold oil?'

'By gouging it out. It may cause pain for some but it's swiftly gone. Forever.'

I'm about to tell him how I'd rather hold with my marigold theory but the line goes dead.

Perhaps the gold Kalashnikov on his office wall may soon see active service.

Catalina is bustling about in the *entrada* with a pail of soapy water and a mop.

'You coming up to Fornalutx for the Carnival next week?'

'Gosh, I'd completely forgotten about it. But we don't have any silly outfits.'

Catalina shrugs. 'You got a nice purple Sri Lankan outfit in your cupboard. You can wear that with a black wig.'

I laugh. 'I don't possess a black wig and I'd have to try to darken my skin. No one's fluorescent white in Sri Lanka.'

'Just go to the Carnival shop in Palma. It's cheap and you can get everything. Alan can go as a gardener. Is easy.'

'A gardener? That's not very exciting.'

'*Si*, but it's simple. He can just bring a rake and some gardening gloves.'

She taps my arm. 'Hey listen, you never told me the end of the story about the robber in Eroski.'

'Didn't I? Well they caught Little Travolta and the Solo Blues Brother but they'd apparently flung the Scotsman's wallet out of a window. However, the police did get back most of the contents. Needless to say the money had conveniently disappeared.'

'Hmm... at least they were caught. *Venga*, I'll just finish cleaning the floor and you can try a piece of my homemade *gatò d'ametlla* over a coffee.'

Catalina's almond cake is nothing short of heaven on a plate. 'Well, believe it or not, we're off to the Fira de la Flor de L'Ametler on Sunday. I love almonds so I hope they'll have lots of different products on sale.'

She rests her hand on the handle of the mop. 'If they have salted, toasted almonds, bring me back a pot. You always seem to be hopping off to food fairs these days. What's going on?'

'I suppose I just want to learn more about local producers. I'd rather buy fresh fare direct from farmers than use supermarkets.'

She rubs her forehead and frowns. 'The trouble is that people are busy and think it's too time-consuming to visit farms.'

'But it's not difficult to plug into a local network of cooperatives. Most will even deliver to the door. I think I'm going to make it one of my missions to get the word out about local produce. The only way I can do that is by visiting farms and fairs for myself and making the contacts.'

'A new crusade,' she smirks. 'As if you haven't got enough to do already.'

'Yes, but it's important, so I'll just have to make the time.'

She resumes her cleaning just as the Scotsman opens the kitchen door.

Catalina growls. 'Take those muddy boots off!'

He steps back outside, yanks at his gardening boots and returns a moment later in his woolly socks. He gives her a radiant smile. 'Have you seen the mimosa, Catalina?'

She walks over to one of the kitchen windows. '*Si*, I noticed that it's flowering. Those yellow blooms are beautiful and the Judas tree is fantastic – it has a lot of blossom.'

'It's a wonderful time of the year for gardening, but there's so much to do. I've still got to pot all the herbs.'

'*Poc a poc*. My father is the same, always in the garden but complaining that he never has time to do everything.'

He nods enthusiastically. Catalina's father, Paco, is a gardener of the old school for whom the Scotsman has the utmost respect. He will always consult him should a lemon tree be in a forlorn state or if a particular vegetable is not taking to the soil. Invariably Paco has the solution.

'My mother wants you to come up for lunch one day with the family. You haven't been over for a while.'

'Tell Marta we'd love to come for lunch, and also to see your grandmother.'

Lunch at Paco and Marta's is always a delicious and simple feast. All the food on the table is brought straight from the land and everyone mucks in. Her grandmother, now in her nineties, peels vegetables while Marta and Catalina dart around the kitchen, things sizzle and hiss from the stove and the most delectable aromas waft throughout the house. The entire family, Catalina's three brothers, her aunts and uncles and all the grandchildren join in and conversation is lively to say the least. Marta's home-prepared figs in anise are scrumptious, as are all the other bottled specialties that grace the feast.

Miquela potters downstairs and empties a wastepaper basket. Wordlessly she takes over the job of washing the marble floor of the *entrada* and then empties the frothing soapy water on the front steps. 'All done.'

Catalina smacks her hands together. 'Well, in that case it's coffee time and you can all sample my almond cake.

'What about the diet?' I ask.

'What with Carnival coming up? Impossible! I thought it might wait until *Cuaresma.*'

'Lent? Ash Wednesday's still a few weeks away.'

'I know,' she beams. 'So until then, I'm going to eat, eat, eat.'

It's a gloriously sunny day as we trundle along the country roads in the direction of the small inland town of Son Servera in the east. As far as the eye can see a quilt of white and pink petals spreads across the landscape as delicate blossom rains down from the abundance of almond trees that come alive at this time of the year. On the outskirts of the town, I am momentarily transported to the world of Cecily Mary Barker's *Flower Fairies* as petals pirouette and perform *petits sauts* all about us, dropping like mini-parachutes on to the tarmac road. Soon we see signs for the Fira de la Flor de L'Ametler, the festival of the almond flower, and turn up a narrow track that will hopefully lead us to Ses Cases de Ca S'Hereu, an *agrotourisme* or rural guesthouse where the event is taking place.

'Look!' says Ollie, from the back of the car. 'See the black fence coming up? There's another sign.'

The Scotsman dutifully turns left and we follow an elegant drive that leads to a señorial stone house flanked by *algarrobas* – carobs, almonds, lemons and orange trees. A smiling steward beckons us to a parking space and we step out on to a well-maintained lawn bordered by huge pots of herbs, creepers and seasonal shrubs. The Scotsman is in his element.

'Ah! Look at that beautiful *Schinus molle*!'

'What?' grumbles Ollie.

'The Peruvian pepper tree. Just look at that, it's still got its red berries.'

I turn to see a handsome specimen with feathery dark green leaves to the side of the house. 'Is that the tree that produces pink peppercorns?'

The Scotsman nods.

'Any chance of your planting one? I like using them in cooking.'

Ollie yawns deeply. 'Can we end *Gardeners' Question Time* and go and see this almond fair? You're both so boring when you talk about plants.'

We follow a group of people heading over to stands in an adjacent strip of land. As we draw closer I notice that there are various old pieces of machinery on show.

'Is that harvesting equipment?' I ask.

The Scotsman nods sagely. 'Yes, looks like it. Ah, I can see an almond liqueur stand. That should be interesting.'

Ollie and I potter over to various stalls selling crafts on an almond theme. I buy almond soaps and some heavenly smelling candles. At a cake stand we buy a delicious-looking almond cake and home-made almond milk bread. I see a sign for *orxata amb ametlles* and head towards it. A cheery, avuncular man offers to pour us a glass each.

'Has milk been added?' I ask.

'*Non*, it's just almonds, ice, cinnamon and sugar, the traditional way.'

'Just how I like it.'

The *horchata*, as it is known in Castilian Spanish, tastes delicious and Ollie and I drain our glasses quickly. He refills them.

'Have you ever had *orxata amb xufles*?' he quizzes. 'Now that's a special drink. In fact the original drink used *xufles*, not almonds.'

I nod. *Horchata* made with *xufles*, meaning tiger nuts or earth almonds, is quite a different-tasting drink; perhaps richer, creamier and more, well, nutty. The etymological root for *orxata* appears to originate from the Catalan word for barley, but today it simply refers to the white, ice-cold drink made from the crushed essence of either the more authentic tiger nuts or almonds. The tiger nut is the root tuber of the chufa sedge plant and was cultivated with gusto by the ancient Egyptians and revered for its health-giving properties. During the first century AD the Moors brought the edible tuba from the Middle East to the Valencia region of eastern Spain where they cultivated it successfully for hundreds of years. Somehow it never took off in the Baleares or in other regions of the peninsula.

The man serving at the counter gives me a knowing wink. 'Any idea how *orxata* got its name?'

I laugh. 'No, but I have a feeling you're going to enlighten me.'

'*Pues*,' he says, 'back in the first century James I came to a small Catalan village and was given a drink by a little girl. He drained the cup and asked her, "What is that?" to which she replied, *"Es llet de chufa!"* – It's milk of the tiger nut. And he said, *"Aixo no es llet, aixo es or, xata!"* That isn't milk, that is *or*, meaning gold, *xata* meaning my sweetie. Get it? "It's gold, sweetie."'

He throws his head back and laughs.

'*Molt bé*,' I reply. 'I hadn't heard that one before.'

The man leans forward on the counter. 'Do you know that there are five million almond trees on this island? Aside from the algarroba and olives it's one of Mallorca's leading crops.'

'I read somewhere that in the nineteenth century when the pest phylloxera destroyed all the grapevines, Mallorcans took to planting almond trees instead.'

'That's exactly what happened. Trouble is that it's hard to make a living by them these days. Most of us smallholders just produce enough for our families and friends. And then last year many almond trees were destroyed by the termite *xiófago*. It attacks the tree bark.'

'I remember reading about it,' I reply.

The man nods. 'And this year the *picudo rojo*, the red palm weevil, has arrived from the mainland and is attacking the palm trees. Let's hope it doesn't like almonds!'

I give him a reassuring smile. 'According to the local press, the insect only attacks palms, so your trees should be safe.'

'All the same, the island's almond trees are under threat. There's so much competition now from the likes of America that local farmers are pulling up all their trees and replanting them with olives, which are much more profitable. Makes more commercial sense.'

'The end to the beautiful almond blossom on Mallorca?' I say.

'Let's hope not.'

As we head off in search of the Scotsman, Ollie turns to me. 'Things can't be that bad for the farmers here.'

'Don't you believe it. Some are hanging on by their fingernails.'

Ollie and I find the Scotsman still lingering at the almond liqueur stand in deep conversation with a woman dressed in traditional peasant gear.

'Still here?' asks Ollie impatiently.

'I've had a good look round, but this charming lady invited me to try a snifter. That almond liqueur with honey is something else.'

He picks up a large paper carrier bag, bottles tinkling within, and bids farewell to his new friend.

'Looks like you cleaned out most of her supplies,' says Ollie.

'Well, I bought a few bottles for Pep too – purely for research purposes.'

'What kind of research?'

'Oh, didn't I tell you?' he says nonchalantly. 'Pep and I are considering making our own almond liqueur.'

'Well, not in my kitchen,' I reply.

'Pep's got so many almond trees it makes sense to brew it over at his house.'

'Great,' I say with some relief although I dread to think how poor Juana would cope with the likely chaos engulfing her kitchen. I'm tempted to forewarn her but then with any luck Pep and the Scotsman will never get round to it. After all, they still haven't even started on the *limoncello* yet. Or have they?

It's a cool blustery day and I am in ill humour. Returning from my habitual early morning run, this time down to the port, I discovered that some intruder had been in the field, and more specifically tampered with my outdoor gym. Logs had been pushed around, my skipping rope had vanished, but worst of all was the absence of my wobbly board. Who would bother to do such a thing? It wasn't so much the expense of the item but more the inconvenience of having to order another from the UK. As I buy my cheese and *jamon Serrano* in Colmado de Sa Lluna in Sóller town, I tell Javier, the owner, about my woes. He shrugs philosophically.

'What can I say? Nothing is sacred these days. People often take things that they see lying about. They don't even consider it stealing. Few of us still have manners.'

He nods rather pointedly at a tourist who barges into the shop and begins taking photos of the interiors without even acknowledging us.

'Can I help you?' asks Javier in English.

The woman with the camera shakes her head and carries on taking photos. I can't decide what nationality she is, perhaps German or Scandinavian. When she's had her fill, she walks out without purchasing anything or thanking Javier.

'See what I mean?'

I laugh.

'And another thing. When the summer comes, it's fatal to leave your front doors open, especially in a village likes Fornalutx. Some tourists come straight off the street and walk into the house as if they're entering a free museum.'

Javier is absolutely right. A good German friend once told me that she was sitting in her townhouse eating lunch when she heard movement from the tiny front courtyard and found two tourists rifling through a box of books she had left there to give to a friend. She was forced to chase them away.

'*Idò,*' said Javier. 'It seems to me that it's the work of some opportunist. There's been a spate of petty thefts in the town of late. It's the way of the world.'

Maybe, but I still like to think that crime is a rarity in my beloved Sóller. I sigh and leave the shop, consoling myself with a strong espresso and a croissant at Café Paris. Tolo, our friendly deputy manager of the Banca March is having a *merienda* and advises me to hurry back home because torrential rain is expected. On the way to the car I bang into Antonia. She tuts when I tell her about the theft.

'Robbers everywhere! You got to watch your back all the time. What have I told you? Don't be so trusting. Be careful.'

Duly chastised, I drive home and take my purchases into the kitchen. I decide that the only thing to lift my mood will be to cook, so I bake two dozen poppyseed teacakes and bottle some lemons with salt and herbs, Moroccan style. Feeling much better about life, I make my way up the stairs to the office with a pot of Darjeeling tea and two cakes which I polish off while replying to emails. The phone rings. It is Ed.

'I've just heard that I'm going to be made redundant. After twenty-five years they've finally cut me loose.'

'Oh come on, it's not all that bad. There are so many other things you can do and you will get a redundancy package.'

'It's hardly a fortune,' he says gloomily. 'And they're only giving us another six months' employment.'

'Look, when I'm back in London, we'll have a brain-storming session about all the things you can do.'

'Such as? I may not want to be a computer consultant as you suggested.'

'Well, perhaps you can manufacture MEK bags for hypochondriacs just like you. There's a mad English woman locally with lots of allergies, whom I'm sure would jump at the idea of a MEK.'

'Now you're being silly.'

'Never fear, something will come up.'

There's a loud banging at the door. The Scotsman is at a nursery in Santa Maria so I quickly finish the call and run downstairs. Fernando is standing on the doorstep sheltering from a sudden deluge of rain and looking contrite and horribly angst-ridden.

'Fernando, whatever is wrong?'

'I have a terrible confession to make. Clara was here for supper last night. This morning her mother called me to say that she had admitted to taking a skipping rope and an exercise gadget from your field. She had left them in my garden.'

I laugh. 'So, she was the robber?'

He gives a long sigh. 'You know what children are like. She said that she meant to bring them back to your house last night but completely forgot. At least she owned up to her mother and I found them exactly where she said she had left them.'

He bends down and carries the wobbly board into the *entrada* and deposits the wet skipping rope on the piano stool.

'The trouble is, she thinks you have an exciting playground down there.'

'I realised that when she popped over to see me. Perhaps the best solution is for her to come and play whenever she likes, but on the understanding that she leaves everything just as she's found it.'

'That's very good of you. She's such a scallywag.'

'Fancy a cup of coffee?' I ask.

He nods enthusiastically. 'I wouldn't mind. It's so chilly today. Just look at that rain!'

'But it's great for the vegetables.'

'True, but we don't want more flooding.'

We walk into the warm kitchen and I brew some coffee. 'I'm so relieved that it was your Clara, because it backs my theory.'

'Which is?'

'That it is always best to try to see the good in people. I was so disappointed to think that someone here in Sóller, of all places, would do such a mean thing. It just seemed unthinkable.'

Fernando laughs. '*Si*, but you shouldn't be too trusting. There are plenty of chancers around.'

I bring the cups over to the table. 'Oh, I'm sick of being told that. You're all too cynical.'

The front door flies open and a huffing and puffing Scotsman breezes in. He bangs it shut and sets down a bramble plant and two saplings.

'It's filthy out there! What a time I've had.'

'I like the plants,' says Fernando, getting up to shake his hand. 'Come and get warm.'

I make another coffee and bring it to the table. The Scotsman waggles his umbrella at us.

'You won't believe what happened to me. I popped into the Schlecker store in the port to buy some cat food and left my big green umbrella in the bucket by the door but when I went to fetch it, it had been nicked. The poor girl at the till was mortified.'

'But isn't that it?' asks a puzzled Fernando, staring at the umbrella in his hand.

'Indeed it is. I ran out of the shop and caught the scoundrel waiting for his wife to reverse out of a parking space. I told him to give it back immediately.'

'What did he say?' says Fernando in evident amusement.

'He tried to make excuses but he had no choice but to return it. Just a chancer!'

'Was he Mallorcan?' I ask with disappointment.

'Very much so. He got in the car pretty damn quickly and sped off.'

Fernando roars with laughter and taps me sympathetically on the shoulder. 'Now can you tell me again about your theory?'

Ten

FROM RUSSIA WITH LOVE

At first, the sound is almost indistinguishable from the raucous din of the cicadas, but instinct tells me that they've arrived. I sit bolt upright in bed and focus on my alarm clock. It is 7.00 a.m. and the sun has already beaten me out of bed. The Scotsman is still submerged in dreams, no doubt of a horticultural nature, so I throw back the covers on my side, trying not to disturb him and scuttle downstairs. In my long white cotton T-shirt, I walk out on to the porch and pull on some gardening boots. The sound is getting louder. Can it really be them?

A swift dashes past, momentarily distracting me and then to my chagrin I nearly step on a corpulent dead rat. It stares blindly back at me, a sharp incisor sticking up defiantly from its gaping mouth. A swarm of ants have already commandeered its body, and are industriously forming queues at its ears. I watch as they make their sure-footed and vertiginous ascent up the pale pink legs, across the torso to the back of the head. They move in methodical, neat and orderly lines like skilled mountaineers. An urgent croak from the patio reminds me why I have dashed to the front garden with such alacrity. I reach the pond and peer into the greeny-white depths. A few robotic, coppery carp are listlessly swimming up and down like bored regulars in a municipal pool, while small frenetic goldfish dart about the rocks. After the massacre of our old fish at the fangs of two rogue water snakes, Ollie and I were forced to go on a shopping spree for some new bedfellows for our frogs. We decided that there was little to beat a hardy carp or a skittish goldfish. All our enormous reeds have now been replaced with rather elegant and understated lily pads which the Scotsman tells me should always be referred to as *Nymphaea*. I ask you. As I examine the burgeoning pond life, I hear a distinct '*plop*' and just catch sight of a tiny, bendy green leg as it disappears beneath the surface. A moment later a pair of bulging eyes appears below a rock.

'Ha! I can see you. No use hiding. So, you're all back at last?'

No response.

I dare to poke around Johnny's favourite hideout, but he's not there. In the gloomy crevices of the rocks overhanging the pond, there isn't the slightest movement. Water trickles from the thick stone ledge above, over the skin of soft green moss that covers the rocky wall and into the pool where it bubbles and splutters by a gathering of upturned stones.

'Now you see me, now you don't.'

I look up sharply and there he is, sitting high up on the slimy ledge of the wall.

'Johnny! How on earth did you get up there?'

'Ever heard that toads can jump? Jeez, they don't teach you much in school.'

'I'm glad you're back. What do you think of the new-look pond?'

He chews thoughtfully for a few moments and then unzips his tongue and catches a tiny insect. He gulps hard. 'Mmm. De-li-ci-ous!'

'Ugh. That was horrible to watch.'

'Way of the world, missus. First things first. Those new fish of yours are complete boneheads. Just swim like zombies up and down every day. What did you do, shop at Deadbeat Carp R Us?'

'Oh come on, give them a chance.'

'And another thing, me and the boys feel a little naked without the reeds. These lily pads are OK, but we got no protection from that busybody heron poking his nose around here every day, and what about those damned cats?'

'We can buy a few more pond plants and put in some larger rocks.'

'Well, make it snappy. Uh-oh, gotta go. There's your postman.'

In ungainly fashion he dives into the water with an immense splash, displacing several lily pads and upsetting one of the exercising carp. Now the poor fish will never know what length he was on. Jorge approaches with a large parcel and several letters.

'Let me guess. You've been having a long conversation with your imaginary toad, Johnny.'

'*Perdóname.* There's nothing imaginary about Johnny, trust me.'

'Sure,' he sniggers. 'Anyway, looks like somebody loves you.'

'Oh?'

'A big parcel from Russia.'

I get up and pull it from his clasp. 'But I don't know anyone there.'

'Maybe it's from an unknown admirer, then?'

'Huh. I don't think so.'

'Looks like you've got some bills too.'

'Now, why did you have to spoil everything?'

He laughs and saunters off towards the front gate. 'By the way, I think the outfit's got a certain style, but those boots aren't going to catch on anytime soon.'

He grins and marches off with an *'Adeu!'*

The Scotsman is in the kitchen making some coffee. He steals a glance at me as I wander over to the table, and frowns.

'You never let Jorge see you in that get up, did you? It's hardly decent and as for those clodhoppers on your feet...'

'But they're all the rage!'

He tuts and stands by the kitchen door, peering through the glass. 'Thank heavens spring has nearly sprung. I saw a wonderful martin and a white egret just now and best of all, the jasmine's about to flower.'

I put on the kettle and yawn. 'It's my favourite. I love the smell. By the way, isn't Stefan supposed to be starting on the donkey hut this week?'

He nods. 'He rang yesterday. Now that the rain's cleared up, his guys can get cracking. They'll be up tomorrow. He reckons it'll take a week to get sorted.'

'It'll be nice to have the girls back.'

He looks at the parcel in my hands. 'What's that?'

'It's from Russia.'

'Who do you know in Russia? Maybe it's from mad Dannie Popescu-Miller or possibly Manuel Ramirez. They're both over there a fair bit now.'

I sit down at the table and begin tearing off the brown paper. 'That would be disappointing. I mean if it's from Dannie, it's bound to be something boring to do with Miller Magic and if it's something from paranoid Manuel, it could be dangerous.'

'What do you mean?'

'Well, it would probably contain a self-destruct message along the lines of, "I will tell you only once and... BOOM!"'

I break through the wrapping and open the elaborately decorated inner cardboard box. White foam chips fly out like wild snow as I thrust in my hand and grapple with the strange wooden object within. I pull it out onto my lap.

'That's a *matryoshka*. It means little matron in Russian,' says the Scotsman.

'I didn't realise you were a Russian scholar,' I reply with a raised eyebrow.

'I've always been fascinated by Russian dolls.'

'Any other dark secret you'd like to share with me?' I twist the brightly coloured torso of the bulbous wooden female figure and smile when a smaller one stares solemnly back at me. There are fifteen layers altogether. At the final twist a tiny piece of paper falls out. I unwind it and read the minimalist message of, 'Enjoy. Luv yu, Dannie.'

The Scotsman looks on, evidently mystified by it all. 'There's something else.'

A small folded envelope is enclosed in the same box. Inside are several antique Russian coins with another cryptic note which reads, 'For Ollie'.

I regard the Scotsman. 'Has she gone mad?'

'So Dannie's sent some coins and a set of fifteen Russian dolls for no apparent reason?'

'Looks like it.'

'Those dolls are rather well made. I bet they cost a small fortune.'

'Surely not?'

He examines one closely. 'Very fine workmanship. These aren't the usual tat produced by large factories. Perhaps she just felt like sending you a thank-you gift for all your hard work?'

I shrug. 'Maybe. But somehow, knowing Dannie, there has to be another agenda.'

The agenda presents itself some hours later. I am at my desk, basking in the warmth from the open window and enjoying the angelic choir of frogs when the telephone rings.

'Darrrrrrling! How are you?'

'Dannie, how nice to hear from you. I just sent you an email thanking you for the beautiful *matryoshka* and the coins you sent Ollie.'

'I know,' she gushes. 'I just this minute received it. It was only a small gesture to show my appreciation for all you are doing for Miller Magic. Everything is in place for the launch this week thanks to you. Oh, and Aliona Muchinskaya at Red Square PR has been such a help. It's thanks to you that I found her.'

Aye aye, something's up. Why is she being so ultra-sweet?

'I'm delighted to hear that everything's going so swimmingly well, Dannie.'

A pause.

'Actually, I was calling you about another small matter.'

'Yes?'

'A dear old Russian school friend and her husband are flying out to Mallorca next week and I told them all about you.'

'Aha?'

'Anyway, their names are Boris and Valentina Arsov and they are simply dying to meet you, and I did say you'd be only too delighted to show them around Sóller and maybe even invite them to stay for a night or two.'

I take a sharp intake of breath. 'STAY?'

'Oh, you'll love them, darling. They're charming and so undemanding. They'll be staying at that nice little hotel in the village of Deia near Robert Graves's museum. What's it called, La Residencia?'

'It's the first hotel we ever stayed in when we came to the Sóller Valley. It's part of the reason why we fell in love with this area.'

She gives a small impatient sigh. 'How charming, darling. Well Valentina and Boris will be taking the best suite, naturally. Apparently it even has its own private pool.'

'So, they won't need to stay with me?'

'Well, I think they might like to experience a typical rural peasant home.'

'Peasant?'

'What I really mean is, quaint and traditional, which George tells me yours is. Valentina is very erudite and loves local history. She is part Hungarian and speaks six languages, so don't underestimate her. Oh, and be careful with Boris. He's a former KGB agent, or maybe he still is. Anyway be discreet. Thank you, angel heart. Luv ya!'

I stand by my desk not entirely sure what to do next. Then I remember. I stride to the top of the landing and shout.

'Alan!'

He plods over to the bottom of the staircase. 'What now?'

'Houston, we have a problem.'

'What do you mean?'

'Think *perestroika*, *glasnost*, *uskoreniye*, cold war and KGB. The Russians are coming!'

He sighs deeply. 'I've no idea what you're twittering on about. Until further notice I shall be planting my celeriac and carrots in the garden. When you've come to your senses, you'll know where to find me.'

Ollie and I enter the corral with fresh water and a bowl of lukewarm porridge and seeds, carefully trying to avoid stepping on our excitable hens. Cordelia manages to fly as high as my arm and gives me a sharp peck when she can't reach the bowl I'm balancing in both hands.

'That was very bold and rude. What's got into you, Cordelia?'

She gives a cluck and waltzes off to the lemon tree in a sulk. Barney now tries her luck and lands on my head.

'Oh, classic!' My son yells in great merriment. 'I wish I'd brought my mobile. I could have taken a great image for Facebook.'

I kneel down and shake Barney off my head and in so doing, slop some of the bowl's contents onto the soil. I give her a good scolding.

Ollie shakes his head. 'You do realise that they don't understand a word you're saying?'

'Of course they do. They just pretend that they don't.'

He watches as Salvador pecks at the girls' coxcombs when they impede his route to the food bowl.

'Poor Salvador, he never gets a look in with that lot. They're so greedy.'

We lock the gate and head off across the orchard to where the Scotsman is standing meditatively with a pitchfork in one hand and a large *puro* in the other.

'Have you seen my *Echiums*? They're going to be whoppers this year.'

Ollie pokes at one of the deep blue flower heads. 'Is this an *Echium*? More like a triffid.'

'I know, they're going to be huge.'

'Look, if you guys are going to go all gardening gaga, I'm off to do some homework.'

He plods off towards the house.

'Wait, there's a package for you from Russia,' I say.

He stops in his tracks. 'For me?'

'Come on, I'll show you.'

Back at the house, Ollie examines the three coins carefully. He has a large collection that he's been gathering since he was a small boy, but these days he chooses quality over volume and rarely discusses the hobby with his friends. He says that it's considered naff to collect coins or stamps these days, but I imagine that if he ever came across a Guyanese one cent 'Black on Magenta', estimated worth about three million dollars, he might want to shout about it.

Ollie looks up at me. 'They're really beautiful. This one's a Soviet silver rouble from 1921. That was after the Russian Revolution, mother.'

'I know that.'

'Yes, but it's different from the Russian rouble. This one was produced under the communists so it has the communist insignia on it, the red star on one side and hammer and sickle on the other.'

'Ah, now I see. What are the other ones?'

'One is a Nicholas I copper kopek from 1842 and the other's a Nicholas II good-quality poltina – that's fifty kopeks – dated 1913. Nicholas and his family were bumped off a few years later.'

'It was in 1918, wasn't it? I've never forgiven Lenin for having the Romanovs murdered.'

Ollie titters. 'Yeah right, I'm sure he'd have cared what you thought about it.'

'Imagine having not only Nicholas, but also his wife and all those poor children slaughtered in cold blood. The man must have been a monster.'

'Oh well, it's all in the past. No point losing sleep over it, mother. Now if you don't mind, I've got things to do.'

I rise from a chair at his desk and head for the door.

'Oh, by the way, we may have a Russian couple dropping by next week.'

He narrows his eyes. 'Any particular reason why?'

'They're friends of Dannie's. Those coins were a sweetener.'

The penny – literally – drops. 'No such thing as a free coin, eh?'

'*Exacto.*'

He shrugs philosophically. 'Well, I'll check with one of my Internet coin dealers, but I reckon these three coins are worth a few hundred dollars, so as far as I'm concerned Dannie can invite whoever she likes to stay.'

The Tramuntanas are twinkling under a hazy sun and the orchard is a blaze of colour as fat lemons and oranges hang lazily from bowed branches; the ones nearer the base practically brush the soft grass with their leaves. Kneeling on the back patio by the pool, the Scotsman has dismantled his wormery and is talking to the various Josés, Jorges and Juans within. He never seems to have contemplated awarding them female names despite their hermaphrodite state. No doubt he'd claim that they had fewer female reproductive cells, so should surely be more macho. He has taken the slop bucket in which we throw all digestible, safe waste from the kitchen and begun to disgorge its contents into the top compartment of the wormery. I study his progress with some concern.

'Hey, don't forget the hens. They'd like some of those veg peelings too.'

He sits back on his heels. 'My worms have a greater need. They're looking a bit peaky.'

'Peaky? How in heaven's name have you deduced that?'

He gives a frustrated tut. 'I can just tell by their body language. They need a little fortification.'

'A tot of rum?'

'Don't be silly.'

I rub my hands together. 'When you've finished with your diminutive chums, is there any chance that you'll get started on cleaning the pool?'

He takes a puff of his *puro* and smiles. 'Any other jobs you'd like me to contemplate in the course of my day?'

'Plenty.'

'Well you'll have to wait. Stefan's men are working on the donkey hut, so I'll need to supervise and I have some pressing work to do in the garden.' He points vaguely in the direction of the field. 'I've got all those shrubs and saplings to transplant. You've no idea!'

I leave him to his ramblings and set off upstairs to the office. Both sets of French doors in the *entrada* are thrown open so that as I walk by, Johnny and the frogs' lively jamming session fills the air. Lulled into a false sense of security I arrive at my desk and begin checking my emails. I receive a surprise one from Rafael which includes images of him grinning to camera surrounded by groups of friendly natives in what looks like deep jungle terrain. He tells me that he's having a ball in India and is soon off to Bardia forest in western Nepal to track wild elephants. I wonder what the locals must make of him. Ed has also sent me an email saying that he's been sent an official redundancy letter from the BBC. At least he's seriously considering setting up a computer technical support website now which, given his techie skills and the fact that he's welded to his computer day and night, isn't such a bad idea. My eye is suddenly distracted by a light flashing on the telephone. It seems that I've missed a phone call from someone unknown. Intrigued I dial the number back and give a start when a booming voice fills the earpiece.

'It is Valentina here. You are friend of Dannie. I am so excited that Boris and I spend time with you. We are now at La Residencia hotel but perhaps we can come over tomorrow?'

'Ah, Valentina, how marvellous to hear from you! I'm afraid tomorrow might be a little too soon. Maybe Wednesday. What might you like to do?'

She breathes heavily into the receiver. 'You show us town please, and we come stay maybe one night in your authentic peasant dwelling.'

'It's not a peasant dwelling really, more a traditional farmhouse. They're called *fincas* here.'

'OK, whatever you want. We have chauffeur so give address and we come Wednesday morning, 10.30. Goodbye.'

I sit at the computer trying to decide my next move. It would be a good idea to speak with Sven Gevers, La Residencia's director. Perhaps he can at least let me know how many nights they'll be staying and an idea of their general demeanour. I search my emails and see that I have an early deadline on a magazine article, which isn't helpful when I also need to finish an urgent PR proposal for the All Man Clinic by the end of the day.

Catalina pops her head round the office door. 'I just come by with some seedlings from my father for Alan. Everything OK?'

'No. I've got to entertain a Russian couple all day Wednesday. They're friends of Dannie's and I've no idea what they're like.'

'Come and have paella at my house in the evening.'

'Are you serious?'

'Why not? They can experience a real Mallorcan supper.'

'You're an angel.'

'Wait until you've tasted the paella before you say that!'

She darts off leaving me feeling slightly better about my visitors – but how on earth will I fill their day?

A sleek black car rumbles into the courtyard and a moment later an impeccably dressed elderly man exits from one of the back seats while a liveried chauffeur politely holds open his door. The man looks about him, takes in the amber stone frontage of the house, the wooden shutters, old ivy-choked well, and then glances up at the front garden to the left. He fixes his gaze on the silvery-grey olive tree in the centre of the lawn, before studying the pond and *bancales* high above the stone wall. He removes his dark shades and seeing me standing on the front porch, strides over and takes my hands in both of his.

'I am Boris Arsov.'

He gives me a little bow and then beckons to his chauffeur. The young man comes over, and after being issued with an incomprehensible instruction, rushes back to the car, apparently to retrieve Valentina. A vision of blue and white Chanel couture wafts from the back of the car. She sports enormous shades and long golden tresses that reach her tiny waist. The legs are long and luxurious, and enclosed in sheer tights the colour of alabaster. Miraculously, in towering and spindly heels she makes her way over the spiky gravel like a graceful gazelle, bobbing up on to the top step with hand extended and a winning smile on her oval face.

'Darrrrrling! What can I say? We are honoured to arrive at your little home. Thank you from bottom of our hearts. Dannie said you are true friend.'

She pulls off her shades to reveal a pair of startlingly emerald eyes. I give a little gasp.

She giggles and gives me a flamboyant air kiss on both cheeks.

'You like? They are not real. Contact lenses, you know. I wear different colour most days. Sometimes lilac or brown.'

Her husband gives a tiny yawn and a rather stiff smile. 'Our chauffeur can bring in the bags?'

I shudder to think what they might have brought in the way of luggage. To my relief they will only be staying one night, and when I telephoned Sven Gevers at La Residencia he assured me that they were discreet with impeccable manners. As I welcome them into the *entrada*, and straight through to the patio by the pool, the chauffeur begins hauling various pieces of Louis Vuitton luggage from the boot. Without the slightest expression he follows my instruction to take them all down to the basement suite where he loads them onto two of the old wooden chests. He isn't remotely out of breath.

'Are you Mallorcan?' I ask.

He shakes his head and replies in word-perfect English. 'My father was Russian and my mother is from Venezuela. I speak six languages and I live in Palma.'

'Wow, that's impressive.'

A shadow of a smile crosses his handsome visage. 'Well, you know, there are good clients to be had if you can communicate effectively. I am never without work and clients hire me in advance through international agencies.'

'Gosh, you are organised.'

'Yes, I need to eat like everyone else.'

'By the way, they are just staying for one night, aren't they?'

He glances around the room with a look of mild disappointment. 'One night here will be more than enough. They are in the top suite at the hotel with a private pool and big terrace, so this will not suit them for long.'

There's nothing like honesty to bring one down to size. All the same I'm relieved to hear it will indeed be a super-short stay. He ascends the stairs with a very straight back, leaving me to wonder whether he's man or robot. Outside on the patio, my Russian guests appear to be basking in the sun and are stretched out on loungers.

'So Mr Arsov, how is the hotel?' I ask.

'Very good, thank you and please, call me Boris. We have nice room with pool and they serve us very good Catalan caviar from the Garona River in the Pyrenees. You try Nacarii?'

'I don't think so.'

'No problem. We bring you some. At home we eat Beluga but this local sturgeon is very impressive.'

'That's very kind of you. Now can I get you some coffees?'

He shrugs. 'Maybe an espresso.'

Valentina asks for Darjeeling tea with lemon.

'Do you have a little biscuit too?' she asks.

'I've made some lemon and poppyseed muffins this morning. Would they do?'

She looks confused. 'You made them?'

I laugh. 'I'm afraid the cook's on holiday and the butler too, come to think of it.'

'You poor thing!' she cries.

'You have a gardener?' asks Boris.

'Oh yes, the old Scotsman, but he's very stubborn and never takes instruction.'

Valentina shakes her head sadly. 'That's too bad. Sometimes you need to discipline staff.'

I dive into the kitchen, re-emerging some minutes later with their drinks and a plate of freshly-baked muffins. Valentina seizes one and bites it with a startling ferocity.

Boris sips his coffee slowly. 'By the way, where is your husband?'

'Oh, he'll be here soon. He's just dropping off our son, Ollie, at school and popping by the nursery.'

'Ah, nursery? You have another young child?'

'Actually our only son, Ollie, is thirteen,' I explain. 'I'm talking about a plant nursery.'

He laughs. 'That's funny. '

Valentina leans forward for another muffin. How can she fit them into that tiny body?

'You make these with fresh lemons?'

'From the garden and stoneground organic flour from a local mill.'

She rolls her eyes. 'But I am amazed you cook these. Did your mother teach you?'

'Well, my family all love cooking but I do rely on some good cookery books too.'

'Valentina doesn't know how to cook. We have many staff.'

Lucky old Valentina. I take the empty plate from her hand and place it on a table.

'So, where would you like to go today?'

She regards me with a well-sculpted face devoid of lines or wrinkles. I wonder how much is down to good genes rather than the expert scalpel of a plastic surgeon.

'We are in your hands. We do as you ask,' she smiles graciously.

'Great. Well I shall take you on a grand tour of Sóller. We'll go to Café Paris, and Sant Bartomeu church, the *ajuntament* – that's the town hall – and take in some art.'

Boris seems interested. 'What kind of art?'

'Well, there's Can Prunera on Carrer Sa Lluna, an art nouveau museum displaying the works of well-known local artists, and there's the permanent Miró exhibition at Sóller station.'

He nods. 'I have several Mirós and Picassos as well as ceramics. You like Henry Moore? I have a few at one of my properties in Switzerland.'

'Gosh, lucky you. We could visit the Sóller Natural Science Museum too. It has a wonderful example of Myotragus, the ancient mouse goat that lived here three thousand years ago.'

Valentina shakes her head enthusiastically. 'I know all about this creature. It was unique to Mallorca and Menorca. I would like to see this museum.'

The woman has immediately gone up in my estimation. Quite obviously she's not just a pretty face. I offer them more drinks but they're keen to hit the road. As I'm getting ready to lock up the house, the Scotsman rolls up in the Mini and hauls a crate full of plants from the back seat. I grab his arm.

'They arrived early so I think we should set off soon.'

He enters the *entrada*. 'Where are they?'

'Out on the back patio.'

He strides through the kitchen in his old beige chords and wearing his tweed cap and habitual Rupert Bear tartan scarf.

'Ah! You must be Mr and Mrs Arsov?'

Boris and Valentina eye him warily but seem taken with the shrubs in his hands. The Scotsman dumps them on the patio.

'As you can see, I'm just the gardener.'

They smile awkwardly.

'You have made a very nice garden here. Well done,' says Valentina courteously, flashing two rows of gaudily white teeth.

Boris catches me smirking in the doorway.

'Wait! This is British humour, I think. You are husband, not gardener?'

The Scotsman smiles genially. 'Actually, I'm both. Do call me Alan, but as the gardener I'm very grateful to your elegant wife for her compliment.'

After pleasantries we head for the car. The chauffeur stands to attention.

'Please,' says Boris. 'You come in our car. There is plenty of room.'

I feel rather awkward swanning around my adopted hometown in a limo, but then it will make Catalina howl with laughter when I catch up with her later, and what a joy it will be to see Antonia's expression when I pop by Hibit to tell her the story. Somehow, despite my initial reservations, I think with Boris and racy Valentina in the car, we may be in for a fun ride.

In a wide, cobbled passageway lined with terracotta plant pots overflowing with brightly coloured spring flowers, we arrive at the house of Catalina and Ramon. Having arranged to meet on Wednesday evening, Catalina had to alter plans at the last minute because her favourite Sóller pink prawns, *las gambas rojas*, which she liked to use in her paellas were not landed by the fishermen in the port that day. Although forced to take Boris and Valentina out to supper that night, we could at least reassure them that we'd be enjoying homemade paella with Catalina and her husband Ramon the following night. Their twin daughters have decided to spend the evening with their cousins and Ollie is having a sleepover with his school friend, Juan. Ramon welcomes us into the house and instinctively raises an eyebrow when he catches sight of Valentina. She is no longer wearing her Chanel twinset, having changed into a chic turquoise silk blouse and black palazzo trousers, back at the house. She has her hair pulled back into a chignon, and dons a pair of patent leather skyscrapers on her feet. I notice that her eyes now match her blouse.

'I love your top,' says Catalina, pushing past Ramon to welcome them into the house.

Valentina who has bought up half of Sóller town, is in high spirits.

'Oh, I'm so glad you like it. I adore shopping. When we were staying at the George V in Paris I bought this blouse at the Yves St Laurent show. They were so fabulous that I had to buy three in different shades.'

'Good idea,' says Catalina, giving me a surreptitious wink. 'Please come and have some cava.'

Kisses are exchanged and seats taken. To my amazement, the reed-like Valentina digs into the salted almonds that sit in a large pottery bowl on the table, and knocks back her glass of cava in two glugs. Boris is still busy by the front door, dipping into various bags he has brought with him. Finally he approaches the hostess.

'Where is your kitchen, Catalina?' he asks.

She leads him up the stairs and a few minutes later they descend with plates of Nacarii caviar on tiny wafer biscuits. A bottle of Stolichnaya Elit vodka has apparently been placed in the freezer for later. Ramon seems rather taken by his guests and is keen to know about sport in Russia. Boris pulls a face.

'Football is our number one game, but our teams aren't so hot. I mean Barcelona is fantastic.'

'My team,' beams Ramon.

'Ah, well you are wise. My team is Moscow Dynamo but it is nothing to Barça. All the same, I support Chelsea in London. An old friend owns the club.'

'No surprises there,' I say quietly to Alan.

He gives me a nudge and reaches across for one of the caviar-coated biscuits.

'Have you ever played?' asks the Scotsman as he takes a mouthful.

'Of course in my youth, but I don't do much sport now, just a little gym and skiing.'

'And are you retired?' asks Ramon.

Boris grins. 'Not quite. I do a little business with close Russian friends. One day we were poor and now we are rich. Isn't that funny?'

The Scotsman laughs. 'Well, you must all be doing something right.'

Boris turns to him. 'No, not always, in truth. Maybe we have done terrible wrongs in the past but we try to make things better as we get older. I have learnt to live with my own sins. Wisdom comes with age.'

'It can't be that bad,' laughs Ramon. 'As long as you haven't murdered anyone!'

Boris fixes him with a cool gaze. 'Death comes to us all in one way or another. A bullet is sometimes the kindest way.'

I take a gulp of cava and try not to focus on what Boris's role might have been with the KGB.

'So how did you and Valentina meet?' I say as brightly as possible.

'When I was a young soldier, barely eighteen, I was sent to Hungary to quell the anti-communist uprising in 1956. The Hungarians were challenging the rule of Moscow and there was a lot of bloodshed. While there, my Russian commander met and fell in love with a Hungarian woman named Gizela and brought her back to the homeland.'

'They were my parents,' interrupts Valentina. 'My father treated Boris like a son when they returned to Russia and remained close friends long after they served in Hungary.'

'So, how did you end up marrying?' asks Alan.

She laughs. 'He was the only man I knew apart from my father and we got married when I turned twenty. I had our two sons before I was twenty-five.'

'What a romantic story,' says Catalina.

'Yes,' smiles Valentina. 'Little did I know that I would be marrying such a powerful man. He had to travel so much for his work but he always came back to me.'

'Were you in sales?' asks Ramon pleasantly.

Boris is evidently amused by the question. 'I was more of what you might call... a troubleshooter. Yes, that's good.' He shakes his head in what appears to be silent mirth. He doesn't share the joke.

Valentina soldiers on. 'My husband had an important role within our government.'

Boris suddenly looks up, a furious expression on his face. 'You have said enough.'

There's a rather ponderous silence, thankfully broken by Catalina who gives a deep sigh of pleasure as she tastes the caviar. 'This is *molt bo*! I could eat a plate of this.'

Boris is quickly back to his old self. 'Ah, but the pleasure comes in having small amounts so that you're left longing for more.'

The Scotsman nods. 'It's wonderfully delicate and so clean on the palate.'

Ramon gives an amused shrug as he wolfs down three helpings. 'Tastes fine to me. So this sturgeon is from the Pyrenees?'

'The fish journey all the way from Siberia to the Garona River in the mountainous Aran Valley,' Boris replies. 'Nacarii has a sustainable farming programme.'

'And is this caviar expensive to buy?' he asks matter-of-factly.

Boris smiles. 'It's about two hundred euros for one hundred grams.'

Ramon's jaw drops. '*Que*?! Stop eating, everyone. We should be out selling this on the street – by the egg.'

I notice that Valentina doesn't try any caviar. She catches my eye. 'I love this stuff, darling, but I eat it all the time. I'm saving myself for Catalina's paella.'

On cue, Catalina, who has returned to the cosy kitchen, reappears and announces that dinner is served.

'And now, Boris, you will try the best paella in the world,' she announces.

Boris rubs his hands together. 'I can't wait. And afterwards, you will sample best vodka in the world.'

And indeed Catalina's seafood paella proves an unmitigated success, although I continue to be amazed by Valentina's voracious appetite. At one stage she whisks a langoustine off Boris's plate and sucks at it noisily. Ramon stifles a smile with his napkin. Moments later she pulls a crab's leg from the communal paella dish and cracks it noisily with her teeth and begins licking her fingers. Beneath the table the Scotsman nudges me with his foot and it is all I can do not to start giggling. I wonder if she behaves like this at the George V in Paris.

At the end of dinner Boris rises to his feet. 'How privileged we are to have made such good Mallorcan and English friends in just a day.'

Valentina fiddles with her eye. When she looks up, I see a tear wending its way down her cheek.

'Yes,' she says with a gulp. 'We are truly blessed to meet such good, kind people.'

Catalina and I exchange glances as we raise our glasses, now filled to the brim with Boris's special Stolichnaya Elit vodka.

Alan chinks glasses with Valentina. 'Good health!'

'Salut!' Catalina and I chime together.

'Cheers!' says Ramon.

We look expectantly at Boris who raises his shoulders and laughs. 'Well, I suppose we would say *Za vashe zdorovye*!'

Alan slaps him on the back, 'And so say all of us.'

At the end of the evening, we exchange hugs with Catalina and Ramon and make our way with Boris and Valentina back to the village car park where their chauffeur is patiently waiting. Just as we are about to say our goodbyes, Boris opens a large holdall.

'We have a few gifts for you.'

He produces jars of caviar, premium vodka, Cuban cigars for the Scotsman, and a beautiful inlaid Russian gold antique cross for me. Finally he holds up a black hoodie with the Russian initials КГБ written in red across the front.

'This is for Ollie. It means KGB. You think it's funny?'

'Brilliant!' I say merrily. 'After all, where would we be without the secret police?'

'Where indeed? It was a sad day for Russia when it was dissolved in 1991.'

'All good things come to an end,' I say inanely as Alan looks on uncomfortably.

He shoots a glance at the Scotsman, 'But maybe your son would have preferred real KGB gun?'

'No, I think this is perfect. We're not great gun lovers in our household,' he replies.

Boris gives a nonchalant shrug. 'Pity. Guns save lives... and of course, remove problems.'

After exchanging kisses with Valentina and handshakes with Boris we watch as the blood-red tail lights of their sleek limousine disappear into the smoky darkness.

'What on earth did you make of all that?' I say.

'Very curious altogether. He certainly seemed to have an unnatural fixation for guns.'

'I'm beginning to think old Boris was some kind of top spy for the KGB. Do you think he was a trained assassin?'

The Scotsman offers me a lean smile and fakes a Russian accent. 'You might think that, but I couldn't possibly comment.'

Eleven

KIDDING AROUND

A fine mist of spring rain greets me as I stride across the orchard in search of the Scotsman. A few minutes earlier, having returned to the house after my customary morning run and workout, I discovered that the kettle had vanished from the kitchen. How was I to make my first cuppa of the day? Having interrogated the five cats to no avail, it struck me that the Scotsman must surely be the guilty party. At the bottom of the orchard I inspect the trail of evidence that suggests he must be lurking nearby: an abandoned spade, pitchfork, trug, trowel and a messy pile of old canes which he's resurrected from his *abajo* for growing the French beans. Where is he hiding?

A moment later Judas rings from the back pocket of my running shorts.

'Hello?'

It's the Scotsman.

'Why ever are you calling me on the mobile and more to the point, where are you?... The *torrente*?... A goat?!'

I snap the phone shut and head off in the direction of the stream at the far end of the field. The Scotsman appears to be in a pickle and has summoned my help, but of course the only real reason I'm heading over there is to ascertain the whereabouts of the kettle, and perhaps to enjoy a little spectator sport. Minny and Della, our donkeys, are now back at the far end of the field and enjoying their new stone shelter with its roof of terracotta tiles. A sturdy fence has been erected between them and the rest of the land, affording them a little peace from chickens, cockerels and cats. They both look up at me as I approach the long grasses and labyrinth of squat palm trees that dominates the strip of land in front of the stream. Neither seems particularly bothered by the very strange sight before them. The Scotsman is standing in the stream's shallow water in his wellies and manhandling a rather hefty old billy goat which is maaaaa-ing very indignantly. To the untrained eye one might assume the pair were enjoying a rather vigorous dance together, perhaps a jive, as the creature rears up onto its back legs and thrashes against the Scotsman's chest as he tries to pull it towards the verdant little bank on the other side.

'Having fun?' I yell.

'You took your time! Can you give me a hand? The stupid creature must have slipped in.'

'Do you know where the kettle is?'

'Kettle? For God's sake, can you help me with the goat? It weighs a ton.'

With some impatience I make my way to the stream and take a tentative step into the shallow and freezing cold water.

'This is going to ruin my trainers,' I moan.

'Too bad! Can you grab it on the other side so that we can haul it up onto the bank?'

I get a grip on the animal's hairy back and stomach and together we heave it over to the side of the stream, finally helping it to get a footing on the grass. It gives a long and plaintive cry, shakes off the water and haughtily saunters off into an adjacent orchard.

'Well I like that! Not so much as a thank you very much,' the Scotsman complains.

I clamber back onto the dry grass. 'He did seem in a bit of a hurry. Maybe he's got to attend to some important goat business. Now, back to pressing matters. Where is my kettle?'

'*Our* kettle is outside my *abajo*.'

'Whatever is it doing there?'

'I was using boiling water to kill weeds growing in the walls. It's a very good organic way of shifting the blighters. Mind you, perennials tend to re-sprout so they need an extra dose.'

'I need it for my tea.'

He exhales deeply and trudges off through the palm trees with me following along behind.

'Here's the kettle,' he says impatiently as we reach his lair. 'Perhaps you'd be good enough to make me a cuppa too.'

'A cup or two?'

'Now you're being deliberately silly.' He looks at his watch. 'Remember, we're off to see Llorenç at noon, so we'd better leave at 11.00 a.m.'

'Two hours only, and I've got to finish a press release for Dannie and put the lemon honey marmalade into jars. It just needs to cook a little longer.'

'I'll give you a hand. When you're ready, give me a shout.'

In the kitchen I take off my wet trainers and socks and make tea. The Scotsman takes his mug gratefully and potters off into the front garden while I line up the cooked and softened lemons that I boiled the previous night, discarding the pips and cutting them into thin shreds. Carefully, I tip them into the leftover strained cooking water that I have divided between two big cooking pans and add six kilos of sugar, two of honey and a handful of chopped stem ginger. It's good to make use of four kilos of lemons from the orchard all in one go. While the mixture bubbles I stir vigorously, pouring in a generous tot of whisky until it's time to test the temperature. In the past I used old-fashioned methods to see if the marmalade was ready to bottle, such as the crinkle test, achieved by placing a small dollop of marmalade on a saucer to cool in the fridge. If the marmalade crinkled when pinched, it meant that the setting point had been reached. Now I just use a preserving thermometer for the task. When the temperature reaches 104.5°C I turn off the heat and leave the marmalade to cool while I set to work on washing the jam jars and drying them off in the oven.

By the time I've located the Scotsman in the garden shed, and waited until he's kicked off his boots, we're ready for filling. We work hard for half an hour pouring the marmalade into jars, sealing and labelling them, until finally rewarding ourselves with another cup of tea. In total we've made twenty pots of marmalade which will last for two years or more. Scanning my watch, I rush upstairs to work on the release, finish it off with a flourish thirty minutes later, shower and change just as the Scotsman begins impatiently calling me from the *entrada*. So much for a *mañana* existence in the Sóller Valley.

As we drive towards Lloseta in the central *pla*, the arable farming area abundant with crops and fruit trees, the drizzling rain gives way to a pale blue sky and a cautious sun that skims the horizon. Can Morey Farm, owned by Llorenç, is reached from the main road to the town of Inca, past a small brook and up a solitary stone track. As we park the car beyond the metal gate, a dog barks ominously from the wide courtyard but it is secured on a long chain and wags its tail as we draw near. The door of a nearby barn swings open and Llorenç walks jauntily along the cement path to greet us. Bearded with his grey hair swept back, he sports a bright red T-shirt, jeans and open-toed shoes, seemingly unperturbed by the recent drizzle.

'Welcome to Can Morey. I hope by the time you leave, you'll be an expert on Mallorcan goat's and sheep cheese.'

'We'll do our best,' I laugh.

He leads us across the broad, cemented courtyard to a field where sheep roam lazily about the furrowed earth, chewing on clumps of hay. Barely acknowledging us as we cut a path through their midst, they appear content and well-fed, their long brown ears twitching occasionally when troubled by a passing fly. Beyond is dense forest.

'These are traditional *ovejas rojas Mallorquinas*,' Lllorenç explains. 'They are an unusual breed characterised by russet-coloured heads and legs. You'll notice that they have long ears and a pronounced Mediterranean nose.'

The Scotsman and I inspect them more closely.

'Do they originate from Mallorca?' I ask.

He beckons us to follow him to a series of open-air pens where goats and sheep are feeding from large troughs of hay.

'There are two main breeds of Mallorcan sheep; the white mountain variety which you find in the Tramuntanas, and the red sheep which has its roots in Africa and southern Europe. It's perfectly adapted to the island's climate and rocky terrain and produces excellent milk for cheese making. I've got two hundred of them.'

'Well, it's a lovely peaceful spot for them to graze,' I say.

'Not so peaceful. At night many have been savaged and killed by local dogs. It's a serious problem but it's almost impossible to identify the culprits. In a rural area like this everyone keeps dogs and many roam around untethered.'

He opens one of the metal gates to the pens and invites us in. We tramp through the thick golden hay scattered on the cement floor and are approached by several of the flock. They're not remotely timorous and enjoy having their woolly heads and pelts stroked. I notice that the sheep have broad, short white tails and although some have rust-coloured coats, most are creamy beige.

'Unfortunately the Mallorcan sheep is in danger of extinction. There is only a small population on the island – maybe one thousand at most. It's not a good situation.'

'But why is that?' Alan asks.

He puffs out his cheeks. 'To be honest, there aren't many people producing natural organic sheep cheese on the island any more. It's too expensive for a smallholder to try to compete with dairy giants that can churn out pasteurised cheeses at a much lower cost.'

'Doesn't the government offer any concessions?'

He offers a wry smile. 'I wish! The problem is that small traditional businesses like mine with forty goats and two hundred sheep have to bear the same costs as a large concern with, say, two thousand animals. There are so many protocols now in place with regard to sanitation and health and safety. You can get swamped by all the bureaucracy.'

'Is it any easier producing goat's cheese?' I ask.

He shrugs. 'It's the same really. Producing organic live cheese of any kind using natural plant rennet, as I do, is very rare now. The whole process is a labour of love that you can't compare with the fast mechanised processes of a commercial company.'

He takes us to a sheltered area of the pen where a group of ten brown kids are maaa-ing plaintively. They allow us to stroke their furry noses and long ears.

'I could take one home,' I say.

Llorenç laughs. 'They're nice creatures and very tame.'

The Scotsman frowns. 'I'm sure they are, but we don't need to add more animals to our menagerie for a while.'

'How far back have goats and sheep been used for cheesemaking in the Baleares?' I ask.

'Oh, a long time, hundreds of years. They even recently found a cheese rind that dated back to 1500 BC and there are historical documents from the fourteenth century that mention sheep cheese from Mallorca.'

'That's not so surprising when you think that migratory paths for sheep and goats were established at least eight hundred years ago in Spain,' muses the Scotsman. 'Urbanisation's had a big impact on them.'

'That's why Spanish shepherds defiantly march with their sheep through Madrid city centre every year to make a point,' I add.

'*Pues*, it's certainly a challenging time to be a sheep farmer of any kind,' Llorenç replies.

'Were your family involved in the business?' I ask him.

He looks over at me and laughs. 'Not at all. They made shoes in Inca. I've just always had a passion for local traditional farming. When I finished university I worked for the Ministry of Agriculture and have collaborated on two books on the subject of Mallorcan cheese production and also the *matances*.'

The *matances*, the slaughter of fattened pigs, is an annual tradition celebrated by many local Mallorcan families. Two hundred years ago whole communities would use nearly every part of the pig to make cured sausage together, particularly the famed *sobrasada*, prepared with paprika, spices and sometimes honey to last them the whole year. In more recent times the *matances* has been continued less out of necessity and more as a cultural ritual to be enjoyed among family and friends, but new health and safety regulations imposed by Brussels have put a dampener on the event. Pigs can no longer be killed on the premises unless a vet and a ministry official are present, so families either take their pigs to the abattoir or risk being caught doing the deed at their homes illegally.

'So,' says Llorenç, clapping his hands together, 'let me show you where I do my milking.'

We bound after him to a simple stone building, partially open to the elements, in which perfunctory cement stalls have been created to separate the goats and sheep for milking. Although the animals used to be milked manually, Llorenç now uses a rudimentary milking machine with a pump whose coloured plastic suction tubes spew out from its centre like the tentacles of an octopus.

'This machine allows me to deal with a few of them at a time, but it still takes me nearly two hours to milk them all and I do that twice a day, starting at six in the morning. It's tough work and you can't have a day off, not even for a *fiesta*, and that's from October until June. After that it's too hot for milking. That's when we gather hay and make up the stores for the winter.'

He whisks us off to a hygienic kitchen-cum-laboratory in adjacent premises where he makes the cheeses. He shows us the dried flowers of *Cynara cardunculus*, a vegetable rennet that he uses to help coagulate the raw milk into curds and whey.

'We put the milk into this large stainless steel and sterile container and heat it to about thirty-two degrees, add the rennet and leave it for about thirty minutes until it curdles. Then we cut the curd with vertical lyres to drain the whey.'

We study the slim metal slicers that he wafts in front of us.

'Then the curd is placed into square moulds in cotton muslin for at least eight hours. Even the cloth has to be bought from a special supplier. If it was treated with soap or some chemical it would contaminate the cheese.'

'Has that ever happened to you?' I ask.

'Believe it or not, it did. We got hold of some cotton cloths from another source once and the batch of cheese had a slightly perfumed taste. We've never made the same mistake again.'

The Scotsman takes a seat on a wooden stool. 'So, why is the cheese cut into squares?'

'It's an old tradition in Mallorca. It's called *una fogassa*, a shape used to make traditional bread or cheese.'

I potter over to examine the muslin moulds. 'What happens next?'

Llorenç demonstrates a pressing machine. 'This presses the moulds for at least eight hours, after which the cheeses are salted then cured for two months in a cool and airy storage room. Once cured, we rub the rinds with olive oil.'

'Gosh, it's some process,' I say.

'*Si*, you have to be passionate about Mallorcan cheese to do this.'

He takes us to the dry storage room and shows us two similarly shaped cheeses.

'This one is Ruat, produced from my goats and the other which has a creamy colour, is branded Can Morey, and is from my sheep.'

'And how would you describe the taste of each?' I ask.

'The sheep cheese has a very particular flavour on account of its fatty milk and the use of natural vegetable rennet. Try it.'

He cuts us a piece of sheep cheese. It has a creamy texture and salty, slightly acidic taste. I find myself having another chunk. The goat's cheese is dry and smooth with a slight ammonia aftertaste. I can't decide which I like better. The Scotsman is making appreciative noises. 'Well, I think we might stock up on a few more cheeses while we're here. What are the smaller ones up on the shelves?'

Llorenç pulls two down and lets us examine them. The charcoal-grey cheese is apparently flavoured with *algarroba*, carob beans, while the other, which is reddish in hue, is infused with red pepper. We decide to buy one of each and leave his store with a bag of aromatic wares.

When we've said our farewells we walk back towards the car, patting the farm dog on the way. It's only when I reach the passenger door that I notice a corpulent ewe patiently standing there chewing thoughtfully on a mouthful of hay.

'Want a ride into town, old thing?' asks the Scotsman.

'You could come and live in our menagerie,' I add encouragingly. 'I think you'd get on famously with the donkeys, cats, hens, snakes, rats, hedgehog and of course the singing frogs and Johnny. What do you say?'

The rusty-hued sheep offers me an apprehensive stare and then with a loud '*baaa*' trots off as fast as she can in the direction of the field.

On the way back home we collect Ollie from Llaut, his Spanish school, off the road to Valldemossa. He approaches the car slowly, rucksack slung lazily over one shoulder, blazer over the other, with his light-brown hair falling into his eyes.

'I think we should get you a haircut soon.'

He collapses on the back seat of the Mini. 'Chill, mother. It's fine.'

The Scotsman fires the engine. 'Ollie, we've had such an interesting day visiting a sheep and goat's cheese farm.'

'Mm, that sounds thrilling,' he mutters. 'Shame I missed out.'

'Actually, you would have enjoyed it,' I reply.

'Do you know about the fainting goat phenomenon?' he asks.

'You're kidding?' says Alan inanely.

Ollie groans. 'Don't try to be funny, it doesn't suit you. Anyway, these goats have a genetic disorder that makes them collapse when they get overexcited. They just fall down for several seconds.'

'That's extraordinary,' I reply. 'Don't they get hurt?'

'How do I know? They probably just hit the grass, hardly a big deal.'

We travel in silence for a while. Suddenly Ollie gives a deep sigh. 'I've been thinking...'

'But you're a teenager, that's against the rules,' chortles the Scotsman.

'Gosh, you two always think you're so funny,' Ollie mutters. 'Anyway, I've been wondering about moving.'

'Moving?' I ask.

'I really like my school, and I've got great Spanish mates, but I keep wondering what it would be like to study at an English school.'

'Gosh, that would be quite a change,' I reply.

'My *Chicken Licken* book sort of triggered the idea,' he continues.

'What on earth has *Chicken Licken* got to do with it? He never went to boarding school, did he?'

'Don't you start with the silly comments. It's just that it was one of my first books when I was little. When I rediscovered it in my bookcase it made me realise how things have changed.'

'In what way?' asks Alan.

'Well, just that I'm a lot older now. I can't imagine the days when I read *Chicken Licken* every day.'

'I do. It was one of your favourite books along with *Where the Wild Things Are* and *The Elephant and the Bad Baby*.'

'Yes all right mother, you don't have to dredge up the entire list. I was only five. Anyway it got me wondering about the future and possible options.'

'Carry on,' says the Scotsman calmly. 'Are you talking about boarding school?'

'I kind of like the idea. I want to play rugby and learn in English rather than having to switch between Catalan and Castilian Spanish for every lesson. It's getting tougher and I miss English literature and even English humour.'

I'm not quite sure how to respond. The thought of sending my son away to boarding school in England fills me with anxiety. I also can't bear the idea of not having him at home with us every day. But am I considering his best interests? Clearly not.

'Wouldn't you get homesick though? And what about all the animals, they'd miss you.'

Ollie catches my eye and grins. 'What the heck? That's such a ridiculous and sentimental thing to say. Of course the animals wouldn't miss me. You would, mother.'

'I know. I'd hate you being away.'

He taps my head from the back seat. 'Well, you'd just have to put on a brave face. Besides you'd see me in the holidays.'

'If you went to boarding school, you'd have to study on Saturdays.'

'You probably get used to it. Anyway, they have these things called exeats when you get weekends off.'

'And what about the freezing winters in England? You love the sun.'

'I'd hardly be studying in a tepee in the snow, mother. Besides, when you're stuck in classes all day, you don't have time to notice the weather.'

I'm rather unnerved by his maturity but also his sangfroid. The simple truth is that he will soon be fourteen and is becoming more independent and sure-footed about what he wants from life. Perhaps he's right, and boarding school would herald opportunities that he'd never have on the island. His current school only offers English as a foreign language and as quite an accomplished linguist, the lack of other lingos would probably become frustrating for him in time.

'Well, whatever is best for you, works for us,' says the Scotsman thoughtfully. 'Let's have a good chat about it when we get home and start looking at options for next year.'

'You really are being serious? This isn't one of your little jokes?' I ask.

'Yeah, I'm just kidding,' he says, then turns to me with a smile, 'Of course I'm being serious. I've thought about it for some time.'

'It's not cheap. I'll be cleaning doorsteps until I'm ninety,' I mumble.

'Better than being in an old people's home, and besides it'll keep you fit,' he quips.

The Scotsman laughs. 'Yes, the fees will give us a new sense of urgency and purpose, that's for sure.'

Fifteen minutes later, we arrive back on the track and just as we enter the courtyard, Wolfgang strides over from the house next door. He shakes Alan's hand and gives me a peck on both cheeks.

'So, your German neighbours are back to terrorise you. Be warned.'

I squeeze his arm. 'Well, our frogs are back from their holidays so they might be terrorising you.'

He pulls a face of mock horror. We have a long-standing joke with him about the din the frogs make just a stone's throw from his and Helge's bedroom window.

'So, we do dinner soon?' he asks as he heads back to his house.

'Come to us. Maybe Friday?'

He smiles. 'Sounds good. I'll confirm with Helge.'

The cats are perched on each of the squat, sandstone pillars that flank the front wall of the lawn, in readiness for their supper. We enter the kitchen and I set about feeding them while Ollie disappears to his bedroom to do his homework and the Scotsman begins making a fire before putting the hens to bed.

'What time is Cristina arriving?' The Scotsman asks.

'Any minute, so you mustn't disturb us.'

'Have I ever?' he asks innocently.

For the last month, my friend Cristina and I have been meeting twice a week at one another's houses to speak English and Spanish – much to the amusement of her husband Ignacio and the Scotsman, who think it's just a good excuse for a gossip. We both want to keep improving our language skills so, in the spirit of self-sufficiency, decide to help one another without the cost of expensive lessons. It's an *intercambio*, a language exchange. When Cristina comes to my house she must only speak English and vice versa when I visit hers. We swap copies of English and Spanish gossipy magazines, books and films which sometimes act as conversation pieces for the following week. The best part about it is having fun with a really good chum a few nights a week when otherwise we'd probably concern ourselves with household chores. It's such an ingenious arrangement that I wonder that we never thought of it before.

There's a distant rumble like thunder followed by a roar as Cristina's macho motorbike zooms into the courtyard, upsetting the gravel as it grinds to a sudden halt. Standing next to her gleaming white beast in customary black biker gear, leather boots and heavy white helmet, she looks as if she's stepped right out of the pages of an edgy *Vogue* fashion shoot. When she pulls off the helmet, a mass of honey-blonde hair tumbles onto her neck. The pretty face is petite and her blue eyes full of mischief.

'*Hola* biker girl,' I say as we exchange kisses.

She gives a groan. '*Que día*! Oh, we're speaking English. I nearly forgot.'

In the kitchen we settle down at the table with glasses of fresh orange juice and begin discussing our respective days and plans for the rest of the week. Cristina has an excellent command of English but occasionally finds certain grammatical rules rather tricky and wants to improve her vocabulary. Don't we all! I get frustrated when I can't think of the exact word I want to use in Spanish, often having to adopt a more mundane alternative in its place. Part of our lesson is spent discussing idiosyncrasies of the two languages and we love to share very colloquial expressions and phrases. The Scotsman saunters in giving Cristina a hug.

'Can I join in?'

'No, girls only,' I reply.

He picks up a copy of *Hola!* and drops it back on the table. 'How can you read all this rubbish – and as for this one, *Grazia*, it's pathetic! Nothing but fashion and celebrity tittle-tattle.'

Cristina shoos him away. 'We like gossip and it's easy to read, so leave us alone.'

He stops by the kitchen door. 'One quick question, Cristina, do you know of a local seamstress?'

She ponders the question for a few seconds.

'I know lots of locals who seem stressed. I don't quite understand.'

I laugh. 'Now that's a perfect reason why we're having these get-togethers. Alan's talking about a *costurera*, a seamstress, but you interpreted it as "seem stressed".'

She rolls her eyes. 'Goodness, I must write that word down. It reminds me of our conversation last week.'

At Cristina's house we'd had a rather odd and confused moment when our conversation in Spanish involved her daughter Lola and the words *hola*, the magazine title which also means hello, *ola*, wave, and *olla*, meaning saucepan.

'So, why do you need a seamstress?' asks Cristina.

The Scotsman falters at the open door. 'I need some trousers taken in. I've been watching my weight and have lost a few inches around the waist.'

'Lucky you,' she replies with a grin. 'Are you doing it for Lent?'

'No, I just thought I needed to shed a few pounds.'

'I can see the difference. I'll give you the number of a friend before I leave.'

'Fantastic. Right, now I'm off to see the chickens,' he says.

'Good,' I reply. 'Stay out there for a while.'

He suddenly steps back in. 'Guess who's here? Horatio. I haven't seen the old chap for a while.'

Cristina and I peer out of the back door where Horatio our resident hedgehog is snuffling about the plant pots on the patio. He winces in the light and with a twitch of the nose edges his way past us into the kitchen and takes up his position behind the fridge, his favourite retreat.

'Isn't he sweet?' says Cristina.

'He's adorable, but he's always trying to snaffle the cats' food, so he's becoming quite fat.'

The Scotsman grins. 'Our resident kite's flying over the house. Do you want to see it?'

I give him a push. 'Stop distracting us. Go and commune with the chickens.'

He saunters off with a chuckle.

We resume our seats at the kitchen table.

'So, Cristina, where were we?'

It's only later when we've cleared away the supper dishes that I notice the answerphone is flashing. It's a message from Jaume Jaume, an almond grower and sheep breeder, whose organic lamb we have been buying through our local Almaeco group. He's inviting us to visit his farm near Petra, a trip I've been longing to make for some time.

'How exciting is that?' I squeal.

'What is?' mumbles Alan.

'Jaume Jaume has invited us to visit him next week.'

He is kneeling on the rug sorting through some heavy logs to put on the fire. 'Another sheep outing. We'll be baaa-king mad by the time we're done.'

I giggle and look up to find Ollie standing in front of me. He shakes his head as he regards us both.

'You two really are so sad. The thought of boarding school seems more attractive by the second.'

Alan and I share complicit smiles as he grabs a bottle of Bitter Kas from the fridge and with a stern, headmasterly glance at us both, potters back up to his room.

As we hurtle along winding and country lanes in the central Pla area known for its fertile and arable land, we finally arrive at a Roman road that seems to stretch like a never-ending piece of grey elastic to the edge of the horizon.

'This is the road that takes us straight to Jaume's farm,' I say. 'We just take a sharp right at the end of it and *voila*!'

'That's if it does actually have an ending,' comments the Scotsman wryly.

Fifteen minutes pass and we both exchange anxious glances.

'We're already quite late, should I call him?' I ask.

No sooner have I spoken than we see a crossroads ahead and moments later we pull up at Jaume's gate. It's easy to find on the empty lane because, to our relief, Jaume himself is standing helpfully at the stone entrance in anticipation of our arrival.

He offers us a roguish smile. 'So, you found us! Did you get lost?'

We apologise for our tardiness but he laughs and claps Alan on the back.

'I've got all day. *Venga!* Come on! Let's take a walk around the grounds and we can have a chat.'

The sun is strong for early spring and the sky cloudless and vibrant blue. Lambs gambol about the fields under their mother's watchful eye while others graze lazily on clumps of long grass. Jaume Jaume strolls along pointing out trees and plants on the way.

'We've got eight hundred acres of land and our nearest neighbour is more than two kilometres away.'

'So you don't pop round for a coffee too often?' I jest.

He smiles. 'Actually, we do get together a fair bit. It makes for a nice walk or horse ride but you're right, it's a fairly solitary existence. You have to like it.'

'Did you find that hard when you were growing up here?' Alan asks.

He shakes his head. 'When I was a child, the place was full of people – family and extended family, farm labourers and local farmers. This place was thriving. As children we used to walk or take the donkey over to our neighbours who had children of our own ages. We didn't mind.'

I stop to stroke a baby lamb that has run out on to the stony path. Its mother appears, baaaing loudly, and gives me a wary look.

Jaume laughs. 'You'd better watch out!'

I rise to my feet and scuttle out of the ewe's way. 'So, how long has your family owned this place?'

He turns to face me. '*Pues*, at least two hundred years. My parents still live on the farm but it's not the same any more. Times change.'

We reach an orchard of almonds. 'See all these? I sell through a local cooperative, but it doesn't make any money any more. Even sheep farming is hardly viable now. I could never afford to employ people so I do it all myself.'

I find it hard to imagine how Jaume manages to take care of such a vast area of terrain on his own but he seems to take it in his stride.

'It's a wonderful place to live and I enjoy my life, but upsetting things happen. This weekend for example, people came to my farm at night and shot twenty of my baby lambs. The Guardia Civil came the same day, but what can they do?'

'Who would do something so barbaric?' I ask angrily. 'Did they take the lambs away to eat?'

He gives a sigh. 'No, it seems they just did it for sport. They shot the lambs with rifles and rode off. I think it's people who live around here.'

'Do you think you know them?' asks Alan.

Jaume shakes his head. 'I hope not. Perhaps it's just bored teenagers from Manacor, the local town, who think it's macho to go on a night hunt in the countryside.'

'Damned cowardly to shoot at defenceless animals, if you ask me,' I reply.

'*Es la vida*,' he shrugs.

The sun burns on our backs and we head off towards an enormous field of plants.

'What are you growing here?' I ask.

'*Habas*, beans.'

'One of my favourites!'

He shakes his head and laughs. 'Not this variety. They're not for human consumption.' 'Are they for the sheep?' suggests Alan.

'Spot on. They love them. And see over there?' He points to a strange group of what look like igloos made of slabs of stone.

'Many years ago pigs were quarantined in these huts to stop the spread of infections and diseases. There was a fairly substantial village of stone huts here at one time – each one housed a family of pigs.'

I find it rather novel to think of pigs having their own mini villages. It gets me thinking of *The Three Little Pigs* and I imagine any wolf would have a hard time trying to blow down one of these well-constructed buildings. I'm about to share my thoughts with Jaume but wonder how I'd explain in Spanish a children's story from the nineteenth century about anthropomorphic animals building homes of straw, sticks and bricks. He might think I'd lost the plot.

'How many sheep do you have?' the Scotsman asks.

'I've got a flock of about two hundred white Mallorcan sheep now and two token machos. They have all the fun!' He gives a hearty laugh. 'This is the lambing season, so it's a wonderful time to visit. Look at them all.'

In truth I haven't seen such a mass congregation of sheep in one place, all of them jostling for space and baaing at the top of their voices. I close my eyes and am immediately transported to the House of Commons with the speaker shouting, 'Order! Order!' to an unruly crew of MPs who bleat loudly and gesticulate wildly with cries of, 'Baa humbug!' and 'Shame on ewe!'

The Scotsman pats my arm. 'A penny for them?'

I blink. 'Oh, I was just thinking about British politicians.'

He looks up at the sun and grins. 'Hmm, maybe we need to get you in the shade. You know what they say about mad dogs and Englishmen?'

Jaume stares at us. '*Bien*? You're not too hot? We'll be at the farmhouse in a minute.'

'Do you have *ovejas rojas* too?' I ask.

'The red sheep? No. They were only introduced when the island was suffering from a drought a century or more ago and our own sheep were dying. I always think the white variety is best for livestock farming.'

We reach the house and hear his dog barking from its outdoor stone kennel. It's so grand it resembles a small home. We sit in the original kitchen of Jaume's large and sprawling country house which for two centuries has quietly witnessed the comings and goings of the Jaume family.

'Fancy some homemade *sobrasada*?'

'Wonderful,' smiles the Scotsman.

Jaume places three glasses and white china plates on the table, and begins slicing a loaf of crusty white bread. He pulls down a large *sobrasada* sausage that dangles from a hook above the table, and cuts it into chunks.

'Help yourselves. I'll just get a bottle of something.'

As we spread the paprika sausage onto the bread, he fills our glasses with a robust red wine and sits down on a chair between us. 'You know if this house could speak, it would tell you some tales. It's been a silent guest at all the family's christenings, marriages and deaths for two centuries in good and bad times.'

'It's an extraordinary thought,' I reply.

The *sobrasada* is delicious and when we've had our fill, Jaume takes us on a tour of the house. We visit the enormous wine cellar, and a maze of unused rooms and studies that bristle with authenticity and untold stories. Framed sepia photographs of Jaume's family and neighbours in traditional Mallorcan country wear hark back to an epoch when agriculture was critical to the island's economy. Now – sadly – it doesn't seem to hold such importance. I stand in front of the picture frames.

'From what other farmers and smallholders have told me, when tourism took off here in the 1950s many farms that had been productive bit the bullet. Is that true?'

He gives a little shrug. 'Some survived for a while, others suffered a slow death. Many farmers could no longer afford to employ labourers who began to take jobs in the tourism sector where understandably they could make more money. Farming took a blow and when the EU began imposing restrictions, health and safety regulations and bureaucracy, most Mallorcan farmers waved the white flag. There was only so much they could take.'

'But aren't there government or EU subsidies?' asks the Scotsman.

Jaume nods. 'There were some for the development of agrotourism and viticulture, but not really any more. Tourism has taken over from agriculture.'

'It's nearly eighty-five per cent of the economy now, isn't it?'

He turns to me. 'Something like that. I just carry on with my work and thankfully have some very loyal customers who want natural organic lamb which keeps the farm going.'

'Is it costly to buy sheep?' I ask.

Jaume rolls his head back and laughs. 'Not at all. Unfortunately they now fetch the same price they did twenty years ago and don't even ask about wool. When I had my entire flock sheared recently, I was only offered one hundred euros for the lot!'

We leave the house and amble past some nearby fields of *algarroba* trees, carobs, which Jaume tells us are only worth cultivating for animal feed.

'No one will give you much for the carob pods any more,' he remarks.

He leads us to the family's historic chapel situated next door to the house. The walls are covered in paintings, most by amateur local painters which give it a quaint and intimate air. There's a large portrait of Friar Juniper Serra by the door. Jaume seems pleased that I know who he is.

'My wife and I were married here. This place used to be the very heart of the local farming community, and Sunday Mass was held here every week.'

'Did you have good attendance?' I ask.

He throws up his hands. 'It used to be packed! In fact, our local priest who's now in his nineties, still returns to give family services here and he often officiates at neighbourly gatherings and fiestas such as our annual traditional *matança*, the pig slaying.'

'That must be some event,' I say.

He breaks into giggles. 'It's a riot and everyone mucks in.'

In the sunshine we walk back through abundant fruit orchards towards the car, stopping on the way to explore the remains of an ancient talayot situated on his land.

'You know there are many Bronze Age talayots on Mallorca and Menorca that date back to the late second millennium BC. They were thought to have been watchtowers.'

'How amazing that you have a piece of Mallorca's history in your own backyard,' I reply.

He laughs. 'Maybe I should turn it into a tourist attraction!'

After hugs goodbye we find ourselves heading back along the broad Roman road. Despite the evident hardships I contemplate whether the warm and hospitable Jaume Jaume would ever, like so many Mallorcan farmers of the past, abandon farming altogether. As if voicing my thoughts, the Scotsman gives the wheel a hearty thump and turns to me.

'What a blissful day, and wasn't it a magical idyll? I know times are tough for anyone working in agriculture here but if I were Jaume Jaume, I wouldn't change my life for all the world.'

Twelve

FRIARS, FASHION AND FADS

I t's Saturday morning and normally I would be up in the village of Deia attending a Pilates class with a group of highly entertaining local women led by the effervescent Marilyn, but today I have been persuaded by Ollie to go into Sóller town for a coffee and croissant. In truth he didn't have to twist my arm too hard, because if there's anything to raise the spirits and create an intense feeling of happiness, it's a visit to Sóller on the busiest day of the week. And of course it's almost impossible to go into town *just* for a coffee. The marketholders will lure me to their stalls with a friendly smile and wave, Tolo from the bank will stop for a chinwag, the lady from the jewellery shop will want to give me a progress report on the state of her varicose veins and aching back, and the welcoming *senyora* in La Lareña will engage me in conversation about the weather and the vagaries of the Mallorquin dialect. Let us not forget neighbours and friends. For every two metres covered on foot, one is sure to meet some acquaintance or other, happy to gossip, and pass the time of day without the need to clock-watch.

As Ollie and I sit in Café Paris enjoying our breakfast, Senyor Bisbal and the seniors who like to commandeer the table at the far end enter the bar. Stopping by our table they ceremoniously take it in turn to shake my hand, pinch Ollie's cheek and exchange pleasantries. My neighbour Pedro joins them within a few minutes, offering me a hearty greeting on the way over to their table. Moments later Antonia arrives. She is in a rush and has quickly popped by to pick up her customary *cortado* coffee.

'My gosh, you won't believe it!' she yelps in my direction. 'I've had a cigarette today, but only one. I'll be back on the straight and narrow tomorrow. I promise!'

'A likely story, Antonia.'

She utters a hoarse laugh and runs a hand through her short fair hair. 'The trouble is I get busy, and it's so nice to have a relaxing fag break outside the shop.'

I watch as she gulps down the contents of her cup and rushes from the cafe to return to Hibit, where no doubt Albert will be sitting like a spider in his web at the back of the shop, gold-rimmed glasses perched on the bridge of his nose as he peers into the recesses of a sick computer. I always think he should wear a white coat and stethoscope around his neck, because he really is the valley's computer doctor. With great care and concentration he spends his days opening up the backs of tired, confused, virus-ridden or elderly machines, inspecting the circuit boards, fans and tiny coloured wires that run like veins throughout with an expert and sympathetic eye. He rarely loses his patience, and when he's restored an ailing computer to peak form and issued it with a clean bill of health, his satisfaction is palpable. My computer adores him and would probably refuse point-blank to go for its medical check-ups anywhere else.

Ollie looks up. 'Oh, now here's Gaspar. Why don't we invite everyone to sit at our table?'

Gaspar ambles over and stoops to kiss me on the cheek. He pats Ollie on the head with a pulpy hand. 'Everything good at school, *chico*? Working hard?'

Ollie dutifully nods, flashing me a look of intense impatience when I begin to converse with Gaspar about the opening of the new Jumeirah hotel in the port.

'It's going to be very swish,' Gaspar tells me. 'Mark my words, they'll have millionaires staying there. I passed it the other day when I was on my newspaper round and there were hundreds of men working on the site. What does that tell you?'

'That they want to finish the building soon?' I hazard.

He touches his nose and gives a wink. When he wanders off, Ollie prods my arm.

'What the heck was that all about?'

I burst out laughing. 'I've no idea. Sometimes people just like to create an aura of mystery about things for no apparent reason.'

He sighs and pushes the empty plate away from him. The tell-tale crumbs of chocolate cake cling to the surface.

'I do wish people wouldn't keep pinching my cheek and patting me on the head as if I'm some baby or pet dog. It's really annoying.'

'They mean to be kind. It's just they forget that you're not a child any more.'

'And what is it with adults? They always ask you about utterly boring and mundane things such as school or exam grades. Who in their right mind wants to talk about school on a Saturday morning? Or at any time, for that matter?'

'It's because adults often don't have a clue what to say to teenagers. School is safe territory. What could they ask you?'

'I dunno, maybe about whether I'd seen any alien aircraft recently or...'

'But you haven't, have you?'

He throws me an exasperated glare. 'Only the one you come from. Actually UFOs or OVNIs as the Spanish call them, have been spotted in Sóller.'

'Never!'

He cocks an eyebrow. 'Oh, yeah? A Sólleric named Josep Climent claimed to have seen an alien aircraft on a dark rainy night in 1979. It circled the Ofre peak several times.'

'Did anyone believe him?'

'There was a TV programme all about it, and he even had a photograph to prove it but the police took it away and it was never seen again.'

'Spooky stuff.'

He taps my hand. 'In all likelihood it was the people from your own planet. Maybe they've been trying for decades to find the ideal location where they could beam you down onto the earth without you causing too much havoc.'

I squeeze his arm. 'You're sooo funny.'

'I know, mother. Come on, let's get the bill and go for walkies.'

In the busy street, we make for the olives stand where the friendly *senyora* encourages us both to try a new red chilli-flavoured variety. It makes my eyes water but Ollie knocks several back without a problem. The stallholder knows my penchant for *boquerones* too, so offers me a mouthful of the delicious little anchovies in olive oil. We buy a selection of green and black olives and potter through Plaza de Sa Constitució to Colmado Sa Lluna where Teresa and Javier are fending off a scrum of excitable elderly French tourists. Impatiently the oldies scoop random items off the shelves, waving them wildly in the air as if at a bring-and-buy sale in an attempt to attract Javier's attention. Politely he tries to keep the vociferous Gallic mob happy as he serves them one at a time, while Teresa quells others in the group with a tray of salami slices and tiny chunks of manchego.

'I think we'll come back later,' I say to Teresa.

She raises her eyes and grins. 'Yes, give us fifteen minutes.'

In Can Matarino, the butcher's shop, I order some breasts of *pollastre*, chicken, and a *rollada*, a heavenly pork roll filled with chopped egg, onion, carrot and sausage meat that is made on the premises. Catalina, always serene and sublime, beams at me as she brings a gleaming knife down on the head of a hapless chicken. At least the poor creature is no longer alive to witness its decapitation. I notice that they have home-made vegetable *croquetas* on sale, usually made with *acelgas*, Swiss chard, which grows in abundance in our hedgerows. I order twenty and, with our wares, we walk up Carrer de Sa Lluna to Art i Mans to collect the framed photo of my crossing the finishing line at the Cologne marathon. This little emporium that does framing and sells artists' materials and stationery is for Ollie an Aladdin's cave. Angela wraps up the framed picture carefully.

'I love walking in the hills, but running isn't for me. The event must have been so exciting though.'

I nod. 'Yes, it's the atmosphere and the spectators that keep you going really.'

Ollie stocks up on some pencils and buys himself new ink cartridges. He's recently taken to writing in fountain pen which, being rather anachronistic, appeals to me. I always sign personal letters in brown or violet ink because it seems so much more civilised somehow.

Out in the street, I glance at my watch.

'OK, we need to pop by Calabruix to get your new Catalan science book and then go back to Colmado for some cold meats.'

Ollie groans. 'That's so boring, and there'll be a huge queue in Colmado.'

'No, it'll be fine now. Come on.'

In Calabruix bookshop Margalida, the wry owner, greets us in Mallorquí. My attempts at conversation in the dialect always bring a smile to her face and she enjoys correcting me. All the same, I know she'd rather I try than not. Luckily she has Ollie's textbook in stock, and as we browse around the store I notice that a title by my friend Ignacio Ricalde is in pride of place on a bookshelf. In spite of being a busy marine architect in Palma during the week, he somehow managed to pen this dense tome concerning the Spanish Civil War in Mallorca in his free time. It is entitled *Los submarinos italianos de Mallorca y el bloqueo clandestine a la Republica*, and offers a fascinating insight in to how the tranquil port of Sóller was once a submarine base for the Italian navy during the war. My friend Cristina despairs when I begin to quiz her erudite husband on naval history, particularly international maritime subjects and the ancient traditions of the island. We can talk for hours, and his passion for the subject is manna for a Mallorca history aficionado like me. Of late while Cristina and I have been exchanging gossip magazines, I've been passing on copies of *Private Eye* to Ignacio. He finds English satire hugely entertaining.

'This is a great read,' I say to Margalida, pointing at his book. 'It's incredible to think that seventy-odd years ago, the port was full of young Italian sailors and warships.'

She smiles wanly. 'I know. It wasn't a great time in our history. I'm glad that it's long gone.'

Just as we're on the point of leaving, Jackie Waldren, an American academic who has lived in Deia for many years, enters the shop. She runs the Deia archaeological museum which she and her late husband, Bill, created.

'Just the woman I'm after,' she drawls. 'Listen, we're about to celebrate the museum's fiftieth anniversary. We'll have all sorts of talks and exhibitions and a display about Myotragus. Any chance of your writing about it in the *Majorca Daily Bulletin*?'

'Of course. Did you say Myotragus?'

She nods as Ollie pulls me towards the door. 'Please don't get her started on that damned mouse goat. It's an obsession.'

Jackie gives me a wink. 'OK, we'll talk about it next week in Deia when we're both not skiving from our Pilates lesson.'

Out in the sunshine, Ollie and I stop briefly by Colmado Sa Lluna, now empty of tourists, and make our purchases. As we leave the shop, Victoria Duvall, a well-known Hollywood film director in her day, stops for a chat. As she waves goodbye and sets off up Carrer de Sa Lluna, Ollie draws to a halt. He seems suddenly overcome with exhaustion and ennui.

'Can we go home now? I really need to chill out for a while in my room.'

'You poor old thing. How about an ice cream on the way back to the car?'

He narrows his eyes. 'This isn't a devious way of getting me to visit yet another shop, is it?'

I regard him with feigned shock. 'How can you think such a thing?'

We head along Calle Romaguera towards Fet a Sóller, the town's ice cream factory, and I make a quick diversion into Sa Botiga de sa Plaça to buy some celery and spinach. Catí laughs when she sees Ollie's face.

'Having a hard morning?'

'You could say that,' he mumbles.

She leans over the counter and hands him a packet of chewing gum. 'That'll calm your nerves.'

He thanks her and smiles before popping the packet into his pocket.

At the factory Ollie orders a large helping of chocolate and cookies ice cream and, somewhat surprisingly, we make it back to the car park without further distraction or intervention, to my son's huge relief.

It's late afternoon and I'm in the kitchen surrounded by lemons. Aside from making fresh lemonade and juice for freezing most weeks, I have taken to bottling, or rather preserving, batches of the fruit with salt and water to make Moroccan-style lemons. Years ago I remember buying a small jar of the fruit preserved in this way from a deli in London at an eye-watering cost. Now I just make my own for nothing. They're so easy to prepare and last for at least a year, once sealed. Absorbed, I bend over the work surface cutting a lemon lengthways, as if making quarters, although the trick is to cut it only partially through before rubbing sea salt into the hollow. Ollie enters the room and takes a seat at the table, slapping a heavy book down in front of him.

'I've got this project to do all about some guy called Fray Juniper Serra.'

I blink and look up. 'Juniper Serra? The Franciscan friar who was credited with founding California? What a coincidence.'

'Is it?' he asks with some impatience.

I waggle my knife in the air. 'Recently, when I went into Palma for the fiftieth anniversary party of the *Majorcan Daily Bulletin*, I met the president of the Friends of Juniper Serra Association. His name's Tumi Bestard.'

'Fascinating, mother, and how does that help me with my project?'

'Well, he was telling me that it's the three-hundredth anniversary of Juniper Serra's birth coming up and they're already gearing up for the big day.'

He twiddles a pen between his fingers. 'That might be worth mentioning in my project, I suppose.'

'I'd say so. I find it all rather interesting.'

'Why's that?' he asks.

'Well, in the eighteenth century people would have been totally reliant on boats to travel to far-flung places in the world. Friar Junipero, as he was known, would have had to endure long and uncomfortable sea voyages to reach Mexico, his first port of call.'

'It must have seemed like quite an adventure though,' he replies.

'On one level, but just think of the culture shock. He wouldn't have been able to communicate with the indigenous people and the conditions would have been tough, to put it mildly. What have you learnt about him so far?'

'That he was bitten by an insect in Mexico that infected his leg for the rest of his life.'

'The extraordinary thing is that despite a horribly ulcerated leg, he walked twenty-four thousand miles in California alone, setting up nine missions that still exist today.'

'I think our teacher's planning on taking us all to visit the museum in Petra in the next week or so.'

'Ah good, we'll be able to compare notes. When have you got to hand in the project?'

He rubs his eyes. 'Not for a while.'

Rising slowly from the table he stretches and comes over to watch me packing the partially cut lemons into sterilised jars. Afterwards I fill each one with lemon juice, peppercorns and herbs.

'They look revolting.'

'Actually, in a month or so they'll be delicious.'

He laughs. 'Well, don't try feeding them to me.'

'You've eaten them loads of times, you just don't know it. I chop them up when they're softened and use them in rice and couscous dishes all the time.'

He looks surprised. 'So you don't eat them whole?'

'Good heavens, no. They'd be horribly bitter. Fancy helping me label them?'

In some disgust he looks at my hand-made efforts. 'Why don't you do these on the computer?'

'I'm not technical enough to do that.'

'I'll have a go tomorrow. What do you want written on them?'

'Just what's contained in the jar and the date.'

'No problem, but I'll have to do this batch by hand for now.'

At the end of an hour we stand back to admire our handiwork.

'Maybe you should open a stall in the market,' he suggests wryly.

'I might have to if you want to go to boarding school.'

He pats my arm and offers an indulgent smile. 'That's what parenting's all about, isn't it? Making sacrifices for your darling children?'

The Scotsman bangs open the kitchen door, a bulging trug under one arm. 'Just look at these artichokes and beans! If you're not too busy, we could have a go at bottling some.'

'Don't try your luck,' warns Ollie, giving him a reproachful look.

His father thumps the trug down on the table and is suddenly aware of the jars of bright yellow lemons glowing on the work surface.

'Ah, I see you've already been busy. Just look at all those!'

'A labour of love, but worth it,' I say.

Ollie pulls open the fridge door and helps himself to a Bitter Kas. 'Fancy anything, you two?'

Alan looks at his watch. 'Good God, it's a Saturday night and we haven't even had a drink yet. How about a glass of *vino tinto*?'

He opens a bottle of red wine and sniffs the cork appreciatively.

Sometime later in the evening, after a supper of home-made fishcakes followed by sorbet and fresh cherries, we sit by the fire discussing Easter which is almost upon us.

'Two whole weeks of holiday,' says Ollie.

'Perfect timing,' replies the Scotsman with a wink. 'You can help us with bottling and freezing the new season of artichokes and broad beans.'

He gives his father a playful smile. 'No can do, old thing. I'll be tied up every day.'

'Really? Doing what?' he asks.

'Sleeping – or playing tennis – of course.'

And with a yawn, he hops off upstairs to his room.

I sit in the office, sorting out some paperwork. Tomorrow morning I'm off to London for a few days, meeting with Dannie at her hotel and – for my sins – Raisa Ripov at her new Mayfair salon. I've promised Ollie an enormous Easter egg by way of compensation for my temporary absence during his holidays, and said that I'll be back for the festive parades and for a spot of egg-rolling in the field. Every Easter we hold a series of silly competitions. First, we decorate boiled eggs and then have a 'smashing' time rolling them down our steep cement slope to the field. The overall winner of the various heats is the one whose egg reaches the bottom of the slope the most times without disintegrating on impact.

The windows are flung open and a warm sun rests its gaze on my bare arms. I bask in the warmth as I tap away at the keys. Moments later the telephone rings. It is Greedy George's rather pedantic-sounding Spanish property agent.

'You left me a message last week enquiring about the history of the building Mr George Myers has just acquired in Barcelona city?'

'I did indeed. Thanks for getting back to me. George said that it was a clothing factory at some time.'

He gives a throaty cough. '*Si senyora*, during the fifties and sixties, but after that time it was a warehouse for building materials. Of course two hundred years ago it was an elegant house. How times change.'

There's a pause.

'But do you know who owned the property at that time?' I enquire.

'Of course. A famous bullfighter lived there in the nineteenth century and...'

'A bullfighter?'

'He was called Enrique Martinez, quite a hero in his day.'

'Do you have any information you could email me?'

'*Pues*, I do have a background sheet on the property that I could forward you, but it'll have to wait until tomorrow. I'm run off my feet.'

When he's off the line I call George.

'Bullfighter? I love it, guv. Couldn't be better.'

'Exactly, so it's a perfect way to link the building with the new bull's hide leather range, Ratón the bronze bull and Bullseye.'

'Maybe we could invite a famous bullfighter along?'

'Rather controversial, and you'd probably be charged an enormous appearance fee, but maybe we could invite a descendant of Enrique Martinez?'

He breathes heavily into the phone. 'See what you can do, guv, and call me when you've seen Dannie in London.'

'Why?'

'Well, she's been a bit frosty towards me after I chickened out of trialling her new Allure Bloom LED lamps for men. Turned down the MIL, as well. She sussed out the old trout wasn't a man at all. I didn't want to be a guinea pig for her inventor, Anton whatever-his-name-is and end up with burns all over me mug.'

'She'll get over it. As it happens, Dannie's already got them on sale at her new Russian showroom and they're selling like hot cakes.'

'Really? Hot cake's the word, all right! So no Russian's been burnt to a crisp using one yet?'

'Not that she's mentioned.'

'All the same, I think I'll wait till they've had a proper airing before trying one out.'

A kerfuffle below my window forces me to cut short the call. I peer down at the patio and see that a heron has flown down to the pond and is standing on one of the rocks, his beak snapping at the water. Orlando eyes him warily from the lawn while the frogs have disappeared from view. In fear that it'll attack the new fish, I grab a pen and hurl it into the pond. The bird rises up into the air, indignantly flapping its wings and flies off, reminding me that we need to buy some new pond plants to afford our fish and amphibians some cover from such predators. I'm about to start a new email when the Scotsman bangs open the door.

'It's hopeless. Half my worms are dead and the rest are lethargic.'

I try to imagine how a worm can be lethargic when it's already recumbent and hardly leads a frenetic lifestyle. All the same, I feel a pang of sorrow for the Scotsman because I know he has tended them carefully.

'Could it be something in the soil? Some man-made fertiliser?'

'I don't use anything harmful on our land, you know that. I wonder if it's the cold.'

'Hardly in April.'

'Perhaps it's because I mixed different worm species.'

'Look, why don't you call the company I bought the wormery from in the UK, and ask for some advice.'

The wormery was an inspired birthday gift that I had shipped over from England together with a thousand live worms some years earlier. Much as the Scotsman appreciated the gesture eventually, he wasn't too happy when, impetuously plunging his hand into the box on its arrival by special delivery, he extracted a handful of pink, wriggling worms.

'Have you got the phone number?'

I look through my contacts file on the computer and write down the company's details.

'Call them now and see what they say.'

He takes the piece of paper from me. 'Maybe the worms are just hungry and I'm simply not feeding them enough.'

Deep in thought he wanders out of the office.

All this talk of hungry worms has me thinking about the batch of cranberry muffins I made earlier. I slip downstairs and make myself a pot of Darjeeling tea and, carefully balancing it on a small tray together with a mug and two of the cakes, return to my desk. A simple, decadent moment like this is yet another reminder to me of just how lucky I am to work for myself and on my own terms. Best of all is that no one need ever know just how greedy I really am in my cosy eyrie at the top of the house.

It's a bright and crisp morning in London when I find myself back at Dannie Popescu-Miller's rather swish hotel. Rachel's instructed me to take the elevator to the Lady Hamilton suite on the seventh floor, where we'll be meeting with Dannie and Raisa Ripov, proprietor of the new Radiance spa in Mayfair. If this is karmic justice, I must have done something rather dubious in a former life to deserve such a meeting of mad minds. One of the doormen helpfully pushes the button when he shows me to the lift. I notice that the doors' silvery metallic surface is decorated with falling leaves cast in bronze. He catches my eye.

'You know the designer hand-picked leaves from the streets around the hotel and replicated them on the doors of the lift.'

'Any reason why?'

He looks at me in some astonishment as if the answer is blindingly obvious. 'Well, to give the hotel personality – a sense of place.'

I nod. 'Ah. Of course.'

On the seventh floor I head down the hushed white corridor in search of the Hamilton Suite and feel a wave of nostalgia sweeping over me when the bell rings out with a loud and reassuring 'DING-DONG'. It's literally a dead ringer of the one used in the sixties' TV commercial when a smiling Avon lady presses the doorbell. Rachel opens the door and welcomes me inside the cool and contemporary hallway. With a cock of the head, she directs my gaze to a cream marble staircase that winds up to another level.

'Dannie's getting dressed upstairs. She's apparently only just woken up, and Raisa's due to arrive any time. I've ordered coffee.'

I give a yawn. 'Good thinking. This is a nice pad.'

'Sure is. Wait till you see the view from the terrace above.'

We wander through to an airy lounge full of beige and cream furniture. A large kidney-shaped desk beckons from across the room.

'Looks more like a piano,' I mutter.

'Yeah, right. I hate to think how much this place costs a night. Probably more than my salary for a month.'

There's another 'DING-DONG' and soon a waitress is serving us with coffee and delicious croissants. A few minutes later, Raisa Ripov arrives with aplomb. The candyfloss-coloured hair is heavily lacquered into fierce little peaks that rise up all over her scalp, giving her the appearance of an exotic reptile. The facial skin is as smooth as a pebble, the cat-like eyes drawn upwards towards the temples as if by an invisible thread and the lips taut and swollen like two overblown beach balls. She throws off a fur coat – animal unknown, but the pelt is sleek and black – and teeters on tall, spindly heels through to the lounge. Rachel rushes forward to give her a peck on both cheeks while I extend a wary hand. She shakes it vigorously.

'Darling! How lovely to meet you. Rachel and Dannie have told me so much about you.'

'Oh really? And so you've already met Dannie?' I ask.

Rachel gives a rictus smile. 'Yes, Raisa showed Dannie around her new Radiance spa only yesterday and has agreed to sell her Allure Bloom lights there. Isn't that wonderful?'

I nod obediently just as Dannie sweeps into the room in an emerald kimono, a turban of green silk piled up on her head. At least, thank the stars, she's already assembled her various layers of make-up so we don't have to endure too ghastly a spectacle before 10.00 a.m. Dannie embraces me in Hollywood style with much air-kissing and hand-holding.

'What do you think of my new home from home? You know I have often felt a great affinity with Lady Hamilton. She and I were born on the same day – 26 April.'

'But fortunately not the same year,' I trill.

'No, thank heavens,' she laughs. 'And from the upstairs terrace I can even see Nelson perched on his column staring lovingly through the window, perhaps in search of his lost love.'

Rachel has an involuntary choking fit and with tissue to the face, trots out of the room. The coward!

'You know Lady Hamilton didn't enjoy a great fate. She ended up penniless in a French poorhouse, if I recall correctly.'

Dannie gives a long sigh. 'Yes, a tragic end for one so beautiful. And so how is life in glorious Mallorca?'

'Still glorious. The Scotsman and Ollie are both fine and the chickens, cats and donkeys are all in fine fettle.'

Raisa gasps. 'Chickens? But what use are they?'

'Well, they give us eggs for one thing.'

She attempts a frown but the brow is as tight as leather on a drum. 'Don't tell me you eat the yoke? Think of all that cholesterol, darling!'

· 'That's all a bit of a myth, Raisa. It's not the cholesterol in eggs that's harmful, but rather the way they're often eaten with saturated fats such as oil and butter.'

'All the same, I have a phobia about flapping feathers. I often dream that wild birds are attacking me while I sleep, their sharp beaks pecking at my eyes.'

Rachel has only just stepped back into the room but now has yet another coughing fit and hurries out into the corridor.

'Is she all right, dear?' asks Dannie with some concern.

'Just one of those spring colds,' I reply. 'Now, before I forget, I've brought you and Raisa a few goodies from my garden.'

They sit up expectantly as I carry over two bags containing oranges and jars of salted lemons and dried tomatoes in olive oil.

'My oh my!' exclaims Raisa. 'Did you buy these or make them?'

'All home-made.'

'How divine! And do you eat them or use them as a facial product?' enquires Dannie with sincerity.

'I had intended them for the stomach, but if you want to try them as a beauty aid, that's your prerogative.'

They return earnest glances and smile graciously.

'So Dannie, I've just heard the great news that Raisa will be selling your anti-wrinkle lights soon?'

Dannie clasps her hands together. 'Yes, it's so exciting! We must work on a joint promotional plan. Perhaps you and Rachel can do that together?'

'Of course, and I'd like to visit the spa.'

'We can go straight from here,' suggests Raisa. 'If you're in town long enough you can try a few procedures.' She leans forward to study my face. 'I see you don't use Botox. Such a shame. You have a vertical line developing between the brows and you could use some filler treatment for lip deterioration. You wouldn't know it, but I have Botox and fillers everywhere, darling.'

I smile. 'Gosh, that's remarkable. I'd never have guessed, but you know I think I'll stick with the imperfections.'

She looks disappointed. 'But why, when you can do something about it?'

'I have a mental block about botulinum. It's the idea that the needle might slip and I'll end up like Frankenstein.'

Dannie manages to raise a stiff eyebrow. 'You'll change your mind one day soon, but until then I'll give you one of my lamps to try.'

'Actually, I think George is quite keen to have one.'

She puffs out her bottom lip. 'He wasn't very cooperative with my trialling of the lamp, so he will have to wait. He's a very naughty boy. You know he even tried to pass off his poor old mother-in-law as a man?'

'Really?'

With a wobbly lip, Rachel re-emerges and pours more coffee for everyone. Her eyes are still watery following her attack of uncontrolled laughter. She mouths, 'Sorry' as she passes me a croissant and bites her lip hard when Raisa begins chanting quietly over her coffee.

'Just my morning energy prayer,' Raisa breezes when she's finished. She takes a gulp of black coffee and adds a generous dollop of some liquid from a small silver hip flask secreted in her handbag. Rachel and I pretend not to notice.

Dannie touches my arm confidentially.

'I have a little favour to ask before you leave. Would you know anyone who can rustle me up a little outfit for a cocktail reception at the American Embassy tonight? I'm already bored with the dresses I brought over.'

I suddenly remember my old friend Andrea Cecile. Could she cope with Dannie, I wonder?

'There is someone I know. A very good dress designer with some fabulous creations.'

She stands up and stretches. 'Excellent. Send her here with a selection of items at 12.00 p.m. I have a lunch meeting at 2.00 p.m.'

'I'll have to check if she's available, Dannie.'

She flashes me a warning grimace. 'It would be in her interest. Besides, she may need to alter something.'

Twenty minutes later Raisa, Rachel and I make for the front door, but Dannie insists we visit the vast bedroom suite upstairs and take a stroll on the roof terrace, so that we can wave at Nelson on his column and admire her private jacuzzi. Afterwards, as we file out into the corridor, she grabs my hand, her sharp crimson nails brushing my wrist. 'Remember to tell your designer friend that I need her here at midday. And perhaps it's wise to warn her now that I don't like to be disappointed. Ever.'

I'm about to reply when Judas rings. 'Hello?'

It's the Scotsman. 'Terrific news! I've sorted the worms out.'

'Great. Look, can I call you back later?'

He burbles on. 'The nice chap from the wormery website told me I'd made the soil too acidic by throwing in citrus peel. Imagine!'

All eyes are fixed on me.

'Ah, righty-oh!'

'He's sending me a thousand *Eisena fetildas* to get it going again.'

'What?!'

'Tiger worms.'

'Oh no, we're not having more worms sent by post. Remember what happened last time.'

Dannie squirms against the door and pulls a face.

The Scotsman laughs. 'This time I'll be ready for the package, don't you worry. It'll be here the day you're back.'

'Just my luck. Well, must fly.' I pop the mobile back in my handbag.

'Did you say WORMS?' yells Raisa in her heavy Russian accent.

'Yes, my husband has a wormery.'

'Please don't tell me you eat them!' gasps Dannie.

'Of course not. We use them to make good fertiliser.'

Dannie pats my arm in conciliatory fashion, rather like a priest might to a penitent parishioner who has just confessed to some guilty secret.

'You know at times, darling, I think we're like tectonic plates. Our worlds rarely collide.'

And with a scrunch of the nose and a saccharine smile, she turns tail and leaves us to find our own way to the lift.

Back in Rachel's office, with mobile welded to the ear, I am in pleading mode. Andrea Cecile is in her fashion emporium on Fulham Road and apparently has a day groaning with meetings and fittings.

'You're asking for one heck of a favour,' she tuts. 'If I help you out, I'll have to cancel an important appointment at midday.'

'It'll be worth it. You'll love her.'

'Liar. I can tell by your voice that this is going to be challenging.'

'Exactly, and you know how you've always loved a challenge.'

She gives a breezy laugh. 'You owe me big time. Can you email me an image of her together with her vital statistics?'

'Well, she's part vampire, so I'm not sure she'd show up on any photographs.'

'Stop being an idiot. Vampire or not, I need to get an idea of her figure.'

'She's hourglass with the body mass of a grasshopper.'

'That's for me to decide,' she retorts.

I promise to send her everything she needs and after a call with Dannie's saintly and ever-efficient anorexic secretary at Trump Tower in New York, the image and measurements are soon winging their way to Andrea. Rachel gives me a long look.

'I hope this Andrea's a very good friend. If not, you'd better get the next plane home.'

It's 8.15 p.m. and Rachel and I have just finished putting the finishing touches to a joint PR proposal for Raisa and Dannie. Earlier we spent a few hours over at the All Man virility clinic in Harley Street conducting interviews with its specialists and learning about the wonders of Viagra. We're now the only ones left in Dynamite's offices and I groan when from the window I see sheets of heavy rain battering the snarled-up traffic in Regent Street.

Rachel gives a big yawn. 'Shall we go and get a bite to eat?'

'Only if I can share your umbrella.'

She laughs. 'I can even lend you one. Fancy an Italian?'

'All depends on his looks and how well he cooks.'

She taps me on the head with a file and gets up just as my mobile rings. It's Andrea Cecile.

'Well, thanks for one of the weirdest days of my life. That woman has only just let me out of her clutches.'

'You haven't been with Dannie all this time?'

'Practically. She loved everything I brought over to the hotel and then cancelled her next meeting so that she could visit my shop. She's just about cleaned me out of stock.'

'So you owe *me*?'

'Not so fast. I spent the entire afternoon getting her outfit ready for tonight and now she wants me back at 6.00 a.m. with the rest of the stuff being altered before she catches her flight back to New York.'

'Isn't that what BFs do?'

'Eh?'

'Best friends.'

'I think I'll keep her as a client, if that's OK with you.'

'Well, hang in there. Her company, Miller Magic, is worth a cool forty million dollars.'

Andrea laughs. 'OK, I'll bear that in mind.'

When she's gone I wearily gather up my files and follow Rachel to the lift.

'What a day.'

She passes me a black telescopic umbrella and giggles. 'Just like old times, eh?'

'It sure is.'

'Come on, I bet you miss the office, just a bit?'

I step into the lift's cool, marble interior and watch as she pushes the button for the ground floor. As we make our descent, the lift suddenly draws to a halt.

Rachel curses. 'Oh no! I think it's gone again. It's got stuck twice in the last week.'

'You're kidding me?'

'Don't worry, I'll call Harry the caretaker and he'll get hold of the lift engineer. His office is only round the corner.'

As she reaches for the emergency telephone I give her a smug grin.

'So Rachel, what was it exactly you thought I might be missing about office life?'

Thirteen

BATS AND BULLS

The Scotsman is hovering over his wormery and poking at the soil as hundreds of lean, pink little bodies squirm about his fingers. On the lid of the sturdy green wooden box with its chunky legs are the words HOTEL DES CUCS, the worm hotel, and indeed it is just like a five-star paradise for the over-indulged little devils.

'The other thing I learnt from that nice wormery chap was that crushed egg shells are an excellent way of creating a more alkaline sort of soil.'

'Fascinating,' I say, stifling a yawn.

'He sells his own lime-based mix online, but I thought with all our hens, it'd be a waste not to use the shells and do our own thing.'

'Absolutely.'

'I worry about acid soil.'

'Yep. Acid rain's one thing, but soil? It's the stuff of nightmares.'

The Scotsman nods genially and then narrows his eyes. 'You're not taking this seriously, are you?'

'Actually, no. I'm a little wormed out.'

Ollie emerges from the kitchen with a bottle of Bitter Kas. 'Wow, it's hot.'

I look up at the baby-blue sky. 'I know, you wouldn't think it was May. More like July.'

He strolls over to the wormery and eyes his father quizzically. 'What are you doing?'

'Feeding my worms some treats.' Alan pops another handful of spinach and broccoli scraps into the seething soil.

'Sweet!' exclaims Ollie as he watches a long worm coil affectionately around the Scotsman's finger.

'There's nothing sweet about it,' I say, recoiling. Hard as I try, I'm not a natural at worm-bonding.

'I don't mean *sweet*, mother. I mean awesome,' he replies.

'Teen-speak,' says the Scotsman cheerily. 'Tsk, even I knew that!'

I stomp off to the sunlit kitchen for some sane conversation with Minky and Orlando, who are both stretched out voluptuously on the warm, terracotta-tiled floor.

'Did either of you know that "sweet" means "awesome"?'

Minky blinks at me uncomprehendingly while Orlando offers me a cursory glance before resuming his nap.

'Thought not,' I say triumphantly and slipping off my espadrilles, walk through the *entrada* to the front patio. The stone is rough and warm underfoot, a sensation I relish as soon as the better weather arrives. In fact, I'll find any excuse to kick off my shoes and it's rare to see me in any kind of footwear around the house come spring. Johnny is puffing out his chest and sitting plumb in the middle of the pond on a large rock. He studies me for a moment.

'You seem a bit aimless. The good life getting you down?'

'Quite to the contrary. I've just finished freezing the last crop of broad beans and have planted all the tomato seeds.'

'Oh aren't you Miss Goody Two-Shoes? And how are the worms?'

'Wriggly.'

He gives a cackle. 'Huh! For all the rhetoric, you're still a bit of a townie, scared of a few worms. Give me a break!'

'So, how do you like the new lily pads I bought you?'

'They're OK, but we need more plants. As for the carp, they're still miserable buggers.'

'Maybe I could interest you in a few piranhas?'

'Oh, I'm laughing so hard, I nearly split a side. Look all I want is a few lively, communicative fish. Is that too much to ask?'

I'm about to remonstrate when there's a tooting at the front gate. No more chatting with my inner toad. I potter over to the porch and see Pep's grinning face behind the wheel of his battered old white van. He parks sloppily and takes his time exiting the vehicle.

'Lost a leg?'

He slaps my arm. 'When you get to my age, you'll learn that it pays to pace yourself.'

'Fifty years hence, I'll let you know.'

'Aren't you sweet?' he growls.

'Ollie tells me that "sweet" means "awesome", so you chose wisely. Are you after the Scotsman?'

He shrugs and follows me into the *entrada*. 'Not really. Juana's gone shopping in Palma, so I was wondering who I could pester for a few hours in her absence. I thought of you.'

'I'm touched. Fancy a coffee?'

'A beer would be nicer.'

I take a can from the fridge and pass it to him, knowing that he prefers to drink it without a glass. He sets it down on the kitchen table and helps himself to a chair.

'You know it's the Moors and Christians battle on Monday?'

'I do indeed. We'll be down at the port for the kick-off and later in the *plaça*. Are you and Juana going?'

He swallows a long draught of beer. 'I don't know. I think I'm getting a bit old for all that hysteria and noise with guns blasting every few seconds. There are other fiestas that are easier on the ear.'

'What is wrong with you? Ah, wait a minute! I've got it. This is all about your birthday.'

He sniffs and examines his hands. 'Sixty is a major milestone. One foot in the grave.'

'Oh for goodness' sake, don't be pathetic! Aside from smoking those stinky mini-*puros* which make you cough and splutter like a decrepit moped, you're in peak condition... for an oldie!'

He breaks into a wide grin. 'So, what are you cooking for my birthday dinner next week?'

'Baked beans on toast. You wanted something very British.'

'Oh, no you don't. You promised me a feast!'

'It'll be a surprise.'

The Scotsman walks in and looks delighted to see his partner in crime.

'Ah, if it's not the birthday boy himself! Only six days to go.'

'The beginning of the end, *mi amic*.'

'Nonsense,' he replies. 'I've already crossed the border and I'm in fine fettle.'

'Yes, but you Scots have unique genes.'

'That's true, we are a special breed. Talking of which, are you coming with us to the Angus beef farm tomorrow?'

Pep offers him a blank stare. 'Scottish beef, here on Mallorca?'

Alan throws up his hands. 'Do you ever listen? I told you and Juana all about it last week.'

He looks bemused. 'My memory's going, old chap. Be kind. No doubt my little piranha of a wife will have it in the diary.'

'It's called Angus Son Mayol. The beef melts in the mouth,' I chip in.

'Naturally it's organic?'

'Of course – the cattle are fed on clover. And Manuel, the farm manager, uses the traditional rotation method so that while they're grazing on one piece of meadow, the previous area has time to recover.'

He gives me a rascally smile. 'You know I'm very sceptical about all this organic and ecological mumbo-jumbo.'

The Scotsman laughs. 'Well, it can be confusing.'

'Confusing? It's a veritable minefield, *mi amic*! There are so many worthy types on the island – mostly foreigners – chattering on and on about sustainability, ecology, biodiversity, biofuels and organic farming and most haven't a clue about any of it. Just buzz words. They all buy from Al Campo like the rest of us.'

'I think that's a trifle unfair,' I reply.

'Oh yes, and what about these seminars on permaculture being run here in Sóller? I thought they were for hairdressers until Juana put me straight.'

'You do have a point, Pep. I prefer the term natural farming, by which I mean animals are fed natural food, and farmers use traditional methods to grow crops without chemical fertilisers and synthetic herbicides.'

He nods. '*Exacto*. That is how our forefathers operated. They didn't need to dream up fancy names for everything. All this eco and organic labelling is just an excuse to charge more. You look in the supermarkets.'

'If that's the case, why don't you buy natural products directly from Mallorcan farmers and smallholders across the island like we do? They actually charge less than the supermarkets.'

The Scotsman taps Pep on the shoulder. 'If you want to help Mallorcan farmers, buy direct.'

'Who said I want to help anyone?' he taunts.

I give him a nudge. 'Fair enough, but for taste and price alone, it's a better deal and so despite yourself, you'd be keeping local farmers going.'

'OK, so we'll come to this Angus cattle farm with you tomorrow but remember, it's only because I'm partial to anything Scottish. I'm not into all this organic rubbish and I don't think the beef will taste any better.'

Alan smothers a smile with his hand. 'I'm pleased you'll come, even under duress. We may convert you yet.'

He finishes his beer and rises to his feet. 'I doubt it. I'm a Mallorcan through and through. No one pulls the wool over my eyes. So, tell me, how is the wormery?'

The Scotsman beams. 'Fantastic! The new worms are settling in well, and you wouldn't believe how much they're eating.'

'So our Mallorcan worms weren't good enough for you. You had to buy their English cousins?'

The Scotsman rears back in mock indignation. 'What? But I'm a Scotsman through and through, and no one pulls the wool over my eyes. They're the finest Scottish worms on the planet.'

Pep breaks into laughter and gives Alan a good-natured hug. 'Touché, *mi amic*. We Scots and Mallorcans have a lot in common and I have a feeling that when your Scottish worms get together with their new Mallorcan friends, anything could happen. We could have a new super-breed of worm on our hands.'

'That's an awesome thought,' I say.

'Sweet,' replies the Scotsman.

It's Sunday morning and a thin grey ribbon of cloud dogs the blue sky hinting at rain to come. Juana and Pep are standing in the courtyard staring up at the Tramuntana mountains beyond.

'If it rains, I'll be happy!' exclaims Juana. 'We can go hunting for *cargols*.'

Both Juana and Pep are great fans of snail stew and spend rainy evenings in May searching the hedgerows for the slimy little creatures which they pop into plastic carrier bags and bring home to soak in brine before cooking.

'Poor little snails, may they escape your clutches!' I reply.

Juana scrunches my arm. 'As a gardener, Alan will appreciate our efforts. They're a menace in the garden.'

'True,' replies the Scotsman robustly. 'An absolute pain!'

'So how do we get to this Angus Son Mayol?' asks Pep, rather flatly.

'It's near the university and the Parc Bit technical park where Ollie's school is. When we get there we have to drive up a narrow country track to the farm. Best to follow our car.'

Juana is just giving me details of the forthcoming snail fair in Sant Jordi when Alan beeps the horn impatiently and taps his watch face. Pep gives a grunt and directs Juana to the front passenger seat.

'Stop jawing, woman, and get in. The sooner we're there, the sooner we can leave.'

Ollie gives Pep a smirk and slides into the back seat of our car. I notice Pep returns the smile in conspiratorial fashion. Angel waves at Ollie from Pep's car where he is lying across the back passenger seat reading a comic. At least the boys can hang out together once we get there.

'Why the heck we have to go to this farm beats me,' mutters Ollie.

'You'll enjoy it,' Alan says brightly.

'Yeah, right,' grunts the teen from the back of the car. 'Thank heavens Angel's going as well.'

As we're setting off along the track, my mobile rings. It's Neus.

'*Hola, reina*! Are you at home? I just tried the main line but it kept ringing.'

'Sorry Neus, but we're on our way to a beef farm near Valldemossa.'

She gives a sigh. 'Ah, *no problema*, but would you have time to pop by when you're back? I have a little problem with the neighbour.'

I groan. 'Not Serena Payne again?'

'*Si*, she is at my house because of the bats.'

'Bats?' I yell.

'She ran round to my house just now and said that she has loads of bats flapping about her attic.'

'Bats in the attic? Whatever next!'

'She's hysterical because of her allergies, but I can't ring the council for advice because it's Sunday.'

'Tell her it's not your problem.'

Neus rebukes me. 'That's not a very Christian attitude on a Sunday. She isn't the best neighbour, but I can't leave her in such distress.'

'Well, she's not been so thoughtful to you.'

'*Es la vida, reina.* She's a sad woman. I think I'll have to take her with me to church. She won't return to her house and I can't climb up to her attic to sort it out.'

The Scotsman frowns. 'Not that bloody woman causing problems again?'

I hold a finger to my lip. 'We'll be back in a few hours, Neus. Don't do anything until we get there.'

'*Vale i graciès.* Bernat is coming for lunch so we can invite her to dine with us.'

When I put Judas back in my bag, Ollie laughs.

'Don't tell me, that mad woman has killer bats and she's allergic to them?'

'Something like that. I've said we'll go round when we get back.'

'No way!' replies Ollie. 'She's a nutter. It's probably just a ploy to lure us into the attic where she'll chop us up into pieces.'

I turn to the Scotsman. 'You see what violent computer games do to the teenage mind?'

'Actually, I side with Ollie. The woman's not normal.'

'Whatever the weather, we can't leave Neus at her mercy, so we'll have to pop round.'

'Great. Bats and bulls. A typical Sunday in the lives of my deranged parents,' says Ollie.

'Beats homework,' I reply.

He groans. 'Talking of which I've got to finish the Juniper Serra project today.'

'Well, later we could drop you off at the house to carry on with it before driving round to see Neus.'

Ollie appears to carefully weigh up his options. 'On second thoughts, I think I'll come with you to Neus's. I'd be better than you lot at climbing up into the attic and I quite like bats.'

'Excellent,' I smile. 'Do you remember that song about bats by Carly Simon?'

The Scotsman shrugs at the wheel. 'Can't say I do. How does it go?'

I break into raucous song.

'Ah yes!' He says, beginning to hum the tune. 'It's all about bats, or rather "de bat" flying in your face.'

Ollie holds his head in his hands. 'You two are so sad.'

And because we're so sad, we sing at the top of our voices about 'de bat' all the way to Angus Son Mayol, offering Ollie only the slightest reprieve when we find ourselves lost in the middle of the estate and draw to an abrupt halt.

'I don't think we should have followed the track to the right,' I say.

'Well, there wasn't a sign. It seemed the most logical way,' the Scotsman sighs.

'This place is weird,' Ollie pipes up from the back of the car.

'What on earth do you mean?' I ask, scanning my map.

'Look outside.'

The Scotsman and I peer out of the windows and suddenly become aware of strange immobile figures lurking under trees, in the fields and by outhouses. There are petrified grey horses too.

'How very bizarre!' I exclaim. 'They look like soldiers.'

'Exactly. They're replicas of Emperor Qin Shihuang's Terracotta warriors,' Ollie replies. 'He had eight thousand buried with him.'

'Why?'

He tuts at me. 'To defend him in the afterlife, of course.'

'What on earth are they doing here?' I ask.

'Search me,' he grunts.

'They look a bit eerie, don't they?' The Scotsman remarks. He fires the engine. 'I think we're going to have to turn round and retrace our steps. This rough road is just leading us into farmland.'

We reverse up a drive. Not a soul is about.

'Let's find our way back to the entrance of the farm and this time take the turning to the left,' he says.

As we make our way along the winding track, we spot more grey stone horses and sober-faced warriors lurking behind hedgerows and standing guard at trees.

'It would freak me out coming here at night,' Ollie mutters from the back seat. 'I bet they cost a fortune too.'

We arrive back at the entrance and take the turning to the left, and in some relief find ourselves in the forecourt of the farm. Manuel, the farm's manager, strides over to the car to greet us. It was some months ago that I met Manuel, a Spaniard with excellent English and German, at a mutual friend's house and learnt all about the Angus cattle he was rearing at Son Mayol farm for the Swiss owner. He invited the Scotsman and me to visit and it's only now that I've found the time to take him up on the offer.

'Got lost?' he asks with a smile.

'Yes, we ended up inside the estate. We saw some interesting sculptures everywhere.'

He nods. 'They belong to my boss.'

'It must have been some feat getting them here. I find them a bit creepy.'

Manuel laughs. 'If you find them unnerving now, come back at night-time.'

Pep, Juana and Angel have already arrived and amble over to us. We exchange greetings after which Manuel directs us to an open-topped Jeep.

'We have eighty hectares of land, so it's better if I show you around by car. Pep, can you take your vehicle too? We won't all fit in mine and that Mini won't cope with the wild terrain.'

Pep cackles loudly. 'You're right about that! Only the English would buy a Mini for our sort of roads.'

'Leave Oscar alone. He's served us very well so far.'

'She even has a name for the damned car! That's how mad the British are. OK, Alan, you want to come with me and we'll let the others go in the Jeep?'

We set off in convoy along a steep muddy track flanked on either side by verdant pastures brimming with clover and wild flowers. The distinctive silhouettes of the Angus herd can be seen sheltering beneath leafy trees and resting in the shade of old stone walls. The heat is oppressive and soon we are all throwing off our jumpers. Warm, fragrant air wafts in through the windows. There's a distinct smell of wild rosemary and lavender.

'The cattle like the shady forest,' remarks Manuel. 'We move them around the land every few weeks to make sure that they always have plenty of grass.'

'What else do they eat?' asks Angel from the back of the Jeep.

'We give them special cereals that are produced here in Mallorca without the use of pesticides or fertilisers, and the young calves feed on their mother's milk until they're about ten months old.'

'Has it been hard for the cattle to adapt to a Mediterranean climate?'

Manuel smiles. 'No, not really. We make sure that they are relaxed and happy in a natural environment with plenty of clover and grass and places where they can find shade. They're incredibly healthy.'

'How many cattle do you have?' Ollie pipes up.

'Now we're up to a hundred and sixty-four. Anything different you notice about them, *chicos*?'

He stops the car and allows us to stroll around one of the nearby pastures. Pep and Alan park up behind us, both puffing on *puros*.

'The animals have got very dark skin,' Angel proffers.

I look across at the sturdy cattle's sleek, chocolate brown hides that glint in the sun. They have beautiful doe eyes and seem very laid back and at ease in their environment.

'And no horns,' mumbles Ollie.

'*Exacto*!' They're quite unique. You know that from about the middle of the eighteenth century the Aberdeen Angus cattle that roamed about the Scottish Highlands became famous for their succulent meat. Now it's exported all over the world and many countries have their own herds.'

'Are you the only Angus beef breeder on the island?' Alan asks.

Manuel nods. 'More to the point, we treat them with the utmost care and use nothing harmful on the soil. The meat is fantastic. Nothing can compare.'

Pep gives a sceptical sniff. 'But Manuel, can you really tell the difference between Angus beef and an ordinary breed here?'

'Of course. If you try it, you'll notice the difference.'

We return to our vehicles and visit different parts of the farm. The boys run through a field of flowers, enjoying the freedom and the hot sun on their backs. Back at the main farm building where the meat is prepared and packaged for sale, we are treated to coffee and *ensaimadas* on the terrace.

'You know there's a whole Chinese Terracotta Army on the estate,' I whisper to Pep.

'What are you talking about?' he giggles.

'Seriously, there are stone horses and warriors all over the estate.'

He smirks as he lights up a *puro*. 'Maybe the owner is preparing for an imminent attack.'

'Do you want to see them?'

He laughs. 'I'm not entirely sure you're being serious. I think this is one of your bizarre English japes.'

Manuel strides in from the office with some promotional leaflets for us to hand out to friends. He is keen to increase his customer base and is even starting up a home-delivery service.

'This is the life,' sighs the Scotsman, facing the sun, with his eyes closed.

Juana drains her cup of coffee. 'It's so blissfully tranquil here. What a wonderful job you have, Manuel.'

He laughs. 'I love my job, but I am busy all day long. There's little time to down tools.'

He takes us into the cool storage rooms with their glinting, clean stainless steel surfaces and explains about the way the meat is processed.

'As you can see, we have a simple system here. The meat is matured for three weeks and then is vacuum packed for freshness without the use of preservatives or additives.'

Juana is keen to buy some meat and manages to extract €50 from Pep's wallet. His eyes bulge.

'What on earth do you need all that for?'

Juana ignores him. 'Manuel, can I buy some steaks and meatballs. Oh and you have mince too!'

With bags in tow, we head back to the cars.

Pep pulls a face. 'We've got lunch round at Juana's parents' house now so we'd better say goodbye here.'

We exchange hugs and kisses.

'Don't forget your birthday supper,' I call after Pep.

'As if we'd forget!' he replies.

Manuel waves us goodbye as we make our way slowly along the muddy lanes.

'Now for the bats!' exclaims the Scotsman. 'This is certainly turning out to be an intriguing day.'

At the gate I have a sensation that someone is observing us, and turning quickly I see a grey stone head peering out from behind a grizzled rock. Sightlessly its eyes bore into the car, its cold features in marked contrast with the lush and vibrant green grass all about it.

'Intriguing indeed,' I say with a shiver. 'And we never did find out why there is a Terracotta Army on the estate.'

The Scotsman turns into the lane. 'Perhaps that little conundrum is best left for another day.'

'Too right it is,' Ollie replies and bunking down in his seat, soon falls into a deep and peaceful slumber.

We pull up in front of Neus's house and knock at the front door. Bernat appears and with a wry smile welcomes us into the *entrada*.

'Are you good with bats?' he asks.

'Only one way to find out,' replies the Scotsman.

Neus and Serena Payne are sitting out on the back patio drinking orange juice. They look relieved to see us, though why I'm not sure. None of us has experience of dealing with bat infestations, although we're used to entertaining the winged beasts in the garden at night. A few disorientated young chaps even enter the house, circling low and in some panic until we turn off the lights, open all the doors and allow them to escape.

Neus gets up to greet us. 'Do you want some juice or wine... or maybe some food?'

I laugh. 'No, Neus, we're fine.'

Serena Payne extends a hand in my direction. 'So nice to see you again. I'm very grateful for your help. Can you believe my nightmare?'

Ollie stifles a giggle.

'Are you sure they are bats, not rats, in the attic?' asks the Scotsman.

The woman gives a little cry. 'Oh, heavens! Don't tell me I've got rats too! No, I definitely saw winged things shooting out of the attic window late last night and I can hear all sorts of noises up there, like scraping wings.'

'Could be ghosts?' suggests Ollie helpfully. 'Or vampire bats.'

She runs a hand over her forehead which is beaded with sweat. 'Can you take a look?'

We follow her round to her front door and enter the quiet house. She tiptoes behind us and indicates the staircase.

'Keep going.'

On the landing everything seems in order but as we all stand huddling under the attic's wooden door, a soft scuffling sound can be heard.

'Sounds like rats to me,' I say.

Serena Payne clutches at the banister of the stairs in apparent horror. 'Would you mind going up there for me?'

The Scotsman is directed to a stepladder and soon has it erected and is making his way gingerly up the steps.

'Don't let any of them out, will you?' Serena Payne cries in a tremulous voice.

Once unbolted, the attic door creaks open and the Scotsman, with torch in hand, levers himself up on the ledge.

'Can I come up?' asks Ollie.

'Just a minute,' replies Alan. 'Let's see what we're dealing with first.'

He disappears into the gloom while we stand below, listening to his heavy tread overhead. Finally he re-emerges.

'Fascinating! You've got a little colony roosting up here.'

'Oh no!' she cries.

The Scotsman descends the ladder. 'It's very dark, so I can't make out which variety they might be. There's a tiny hole between some roof tiles and that's how they've probably got in.'

Serena Payne fixes him with panicked eyes. 'Can we get the council to flush them out?'

Ollie shakes his head. 'You can't do that. Some species are endangered or very rare. In the UK you normally have to let them stay.'

'No way!' she yells and sets off down the stairs. 'I've been jinxed with this property. It's been one thing after the other. First of all my allergy problems, then I sprained my ankle, and now this. This house has definitely got bad karma and since it's obvious that I'll be allergic to bats, they'll all have to be flushed out.'

Ollie and I go up the ladder one by one and are amazed to see the shadowy outline of the little creatures hanging in the darkness under the tiles. Making sure that I don't shine the torch directly at them I bend forward to examine their wings. They have the appearance of old tobacco leaves and are folded closely about them.

'There are quite a few up here,' Ollie whispers. 'She wasn't exaggerating.'

'I think an expert will need to come and identify the species. It could be quite exciting. Imagine if they were barbatelle bats or even the grey long-eared variety,' I reply.

'Imagine!' replies Ollie with feigned excitement. He backs up and begins descending the ladder. Alan has already gone downstairs and is trying to comfort Serena Payne. When we explain our findings to Neus and Bernat, they promise to call the council the next day.

'How nice it would be if we'd discovered a rare species,' says Neus.

Serena Payne, sneezing heavily, runs a shaky hand through her wild hair.

'I need some fresh air. This bat thing is doing my head in. To be honest, I'm not sure I can take much more of this.'

She disappears up the path.

Ollie laughs. 'Oh well, that's one way to get rid of her, Neus. Did you put those bats up there?'

'Of course not! What a thing to say, *chico*!'

We head for the door as Bernat appears, rosy cheeked from the kitchen where he's been dozing in an armchair.

'How are the wedding plans going?' I ask.

'Everything's under control,' he replies. 'Less than four months to go.'

'Oh, don't remind me!' clucks Neus. 'So much still to organise.'

'Stop fussing, woman. It'll all be fine.'

We bid them goodbye and are amused to see them chattering and laughing together on the porch. No doubt they're still discussing Serena and the bats.

As we head up the track, Rafael runs towards the Mini in a pair of skimpy shorts and a tight T-shirt, flapping his hands wildly in the air. Alan leans out of the car window.

'I'm back *mi amics*! What a trip I had. I go India, Nepal, Sri Lanka, everywhere! You wanna see the photos?'

The Scotsman nods encouragingly. 'Of course, maybe later tonight?'

'Sure, I come round later. You like my tan?'

I lean out of the car window. 'Better than that horrible brown oil you were using.'

He slaps the roof of the car. 'I don't use that no more. It didn't work too good.'

'I'm pleased to hear it.'

He gives a manic laugh and jogs off to his kitchen.

Back at the house I rustle up a late lunch of cold chicken and salad, and later potter upstairs to the office. The Scotsman is out in the garden digging up artichokes and Ollie is poring over his Juniper Serra project which he must complete before the day's end. Although I have few work deadlines pending, I'm keen to make sure that plans for Greedy George's Barcelona showroom launch are under control. Thanks to the assistance of his rather exacting Barcelona property agent, I was able to track down the contact details for a great-grandson of Enrique Martinez, the famous bullfighter who once occupied the building. The great-grandson, Josep Martinez, though not a bullfighter like his famous ancestor, told me that he would be delighted to attend the launch of Havana Leather, especially as he lived only a few streets away.

Meanwhile, George's new best friend, Felipe Cañas, the dubious owner of Bullseye sherry and a dodgy strip joint to boot, has organised for Ratón, the bronze bull, to be taken by road from Jerez to Cadiz from where it will be taken by sea to Barcelona and transported by lorry up to the Barcelona showroom. Apparently Felipe's chum, Mateo, the trawler's captain, will do the trip cost free because he has to make various deliveries to different ports along the way. Antonio Sanchez, the sculptor from Jerez who created Ratón, has insisted that he accompany his beloved bull on the boat, and the voyage has been insured for some crazy amount. So far so good, but I am fretting about the detail and, more to the point, what will happen if there's a problem at sea. Although I requested that Ratón be delivered at least a week before the launch, Antonio Sanchez refused, explaining that it was being displayed at a local exhibition in Jerez until a few days beforehand. I just hope that there won't be some maelstrom or other unforeseeable delay during the journey.

As I'm contemplating bronze bull mishaps, Ollie drifts into the office.

'I've just about finished this project. D'you want to see it?'

'Of course. By the way, how was your trip to the Juniper Serra museum in Petra? You never told me very much.'

He shrugs. 'It was OK. Lots of statues, models of the Franciscan missions he set up in California, that sort of thing. I liked the house where he was born. It's tiny and it's got a cool pigsty in the garden.'

'Intriguing. Well Tumi Bestard, the museum's president, is giving me a guided tour next month.'

'Bully for you. We went to San Joan too. It's where this guy Lluis Jaume Vallespir lived. He was another Franciscan friar who went out to Mexico after Juniper Serra but he came to a grisly end.'

'Poor chap. What happened to him?'

'The indigenous Indians torched a whole load of buildings and a church he set up and then they fired hundreds of arrows at him and beat him to a pulp with rocks.'

'Charming.'

He grins. 'At least they weren't cannibals.'

'Perhaps a cooking pot wouldn't have been so bad in the circumstances.'

'You think being eaten alive would have been better? Then you're mad. Anyway, at least the poor guy died a martyr.'

I read through his project, all written in Catalan, and am satisfied that it'll keep his form teacher reasonably happy. He takes the file from me and heads for the door.

'Did you understand all of it?' he asks.

'Most. Some words foxed me.'

'Such as?'

'Er, what does *innat* mean?'

'*Innat*, guv?' he says with a Cockney twang. '*Innat*'s a native, innit?' He gives me a wink and wafts out of the room.

The rain is gushing from the sky and thunder rolls overhead as we cower under umbrellas and head for the polling station. Today the local and regional elections are being held, and for the first time we are able to vote. Although we have had resident status for some years, the previous time we attempted to vote our voting forms were mysteriously lost so we never got the chance. At the front door of the local nursery school, which has been given temporary status as a polling station, a sombre Guardia Civil officer inspects everyone entering and leaving the premises. He gives a cursory glance at our voting forms and seems surprised to see foreigners entering the fray. Inside the cramped building, people are forming different queues and it becomes apparent that we have joined the wrong one. We are eligible to vote in the local elections but not the regional ones, and so have to fill in the right forms and stand in the right queue, but it all seems muddled and no one knows where we should stand or what forms we should complete. Eventually Florentina, the local traffic warden and my regular running companion, comes to the rescue.

'Hey you two, this is the wrong queue! *Venga!* You need pink forms!'

We follow her to a quiet desk where a woman takes our details and NIE registration numbers and hands us voting cards.

'You got a pencil?' Florentina yells. 'You want help filling it in?'

'*Gracias*, but it looks fairly straightforward.'

'None of them are worth the vote!' shouts an old lady. 'You'd be better tearing it up.'

The Scotsman smiles genially. 'Well, let's give one of them a go.'

We return our voting cards and head for the front door with Florentina. The rain has stopped and a bright sun has popped out from behind a grey cloud. Grabbing my hand, she rushes over to the Guardia Civil officer and introduces me to him.

He dares to smile. 'Do you run? I think I've seen you in the port.'

'That's her!' says Tina. 'And this is her husband. One of the best gardeners around. They grow their own veg and keep chickens.'

The officer nods approvingly while two local women come over to chat.

'I heard that you give your hens Scottish porridge and you get ten eggs a day,' one says.

'Well, we only have six hens so that would be a miracle,' replies the Scotsman laughing. 'But it's true. Scottish porridge is magical for hens.'

'Really?' says the other lady in hushed tones. 'Fancy that!'

We feel a spit of rain and, saying our goodbyes, hurry back to the house. Pep is coming for his birthday supper, and I have a lot to prepare.

It's 1.30 a.m. and Pep, Juana and Angel are finally about to take their leave. We sit outside on the patio, listening to the sounds of the dark night. The Scops owl is making its eerie, single-note cry and a lone dog barks from a distant orchard. Pep points to a smudge in the sky.

'Look, bats! There are loads of them.'

'Let's hope they don't set up home in our attic too,' I laugh.

'What happened about that woman?' asks Juana.

'Serena Payne? The bats are going to stay. The owner of the property that she rents took advice from the council and is allowing the bats to roost. Apparently it could do them harm if they were moved. Of course, that means that Serena Payne is moving out.'

'Neus must be thrilled,' laughs Pep.

'Actually, she feels rather sorry for her. Serena Payne is apparently looking for a studio space in Palma now.'

'It'll suit her better,' chuckles the Scotsman. 'Although she'll probably develop a whole raft of new allergies in the town.'

Juana examines the last vestiges of red wine in her glass. 'I have to admit that this wine isn't too bad. Well, after the third glass!'

Pep thumps his hand down on the table. 'Ha! Finally you have to admit that Alan and I are maestros. Our wine is sensational.'

The Scotsman beams while Juana and I exchange pitying glances.

'Well, sensational isn't quite the word,' I say, 'It's certainly robust and quite fruity but it's got a slightly acrid aftertaste.'

'What, have you suddenly morphed into Jancis Robinson?' sniffs the Scotsman.

'Who's she?' asks Pep.

'A famous British wine critic,' I reply.

'A woman? God help us!'

I give Pep a warning nudge with my elbow.

Juana drains her glass and fumbles in her handbag, producing a pen and scrap of paper. 'It'll do, I suppose but there's room for improvement. Now before I forget, can you give me the recipe for those carrots you cooked tonight, and what about the steak sauce?'

She rests a pair of reading glasses on the bridge of her nose, pen poised.

'You just fry a little olive oil and butter in a pan, add some mustard seeds, let them bubble a bit, add your diagonally sliced carrots, some mild curry powder, fresh chopped coriander and parsley…'

'Wait! You're talking too fast.'

'Then add some cumin seeds and a little black pepper and salt…'

She looks up. 'It's all a bit complicated.'

'Not at all. I'll show you next time. As for the sauce, it's just crème fraîche, Dijon mustard, lemon juice and green peppercorns.'

'And what about the mashed potato?'

'Ah yes, I added celeriac and a little garlic.'

'That was good. Take down the recipe, Juana,' instructs Pep.

'Oh, you'll have to give me a demo some time. I'm too tired to write it all down,' she sighs.

'We should do an exchange, Juana. I'd love to learn how to make your scrumptious *fideus*.'

'It's so simple, just noodles, meat, you know...'

'You might think it's simple, but I probably won't.'

Juana laughs. 'OK, we'll start a cookery exchange club. Good idea.' She stretches. '*Venga*! We must go home.'

We all rise to our feet and walk slowly into the *entrada*. The boys are both very sleepy.

'Thank you for a wonderful birthday dinner and for my present.' He holds a packet of Cuban cigars – a gift from the Scotsman – close to his heart. They put on their jackets and, yawning, head for the car. Pep turns to me as he opens the car door.

'Much as it pains me, I must admit that the steak you served tonight was the best I've ever eaten. You were right about Angus Son Mayol. The knife just glides through the meat as if it were cutting warm butter. It's the most superb beef, even if it is organic!'

He offers me a wide grin and jumps into the car. 'Oh, and the vegetables were good too. Perhaps when you next see Almaeco, you'll sign us up for regular supplies?'

We watch as the car's red tail lights disappear into the chocolatey night. Ollie has already crept upstairs to bed while the Scotsman and I stand on the porch admiring the myriad of tiny white stars burning in an infinite dusky sky.

'Did I hear right? Is Pep really going to start buying eco-veg?' says the Scotsman.

'So it seems, but in truth I think he was always a convert. He just likes to have something to beef about.'

'Ooh, terrible pun.'

'Or perhaps something to get his teeth into, given how bullish he can be?'

The Scotsman shakes his head. 'Even worse. Time for bed.'

I turn off the porch light and together we close the wooden shutters and head wearily upstairs just as something dark whirs over our heads and swoops down into the *entrada*. We exchange glances and plod back downstairs, knowing that yet another bat saga is just about to begin.

Fourteen

HOT POTATOES

A fiery sun melts like liquid gold on the tips of the Tramuntanas. It's still only 7.30 a.m., so it has no intention of taking full stage up high in the sky for at least another hour. Barefooted and wearing one of the Scotsman's old shirts, with hair dishevelled after a blissful night's sleep, I stand on the back patio with a mug of tea waiting for the valley to waken. The cats are circling me like a shiver of sharks, waiting for the moment when I'll potter back to the kitchen to fill their bowls. Doughnut suddenly swings a right hook at Minky. Orlando, perhaps out of filial love, flattens his brother's assailant in one bound. Stepping over the wriggling, hissing mass of grey and brown fur, I inspect the pool. For some months the Scotsman and I have been discussing the merits of switching from chlorine to a saline system. Aside from producing water that's softer on the skin and less stinging to the eyes than man-made chlorine compounds, we would avoid handling toxic chemicals and it would also prove a lot cheaper to maintain in the long run. The problem is the initial outlay is very steep, so this summer we will have to keep with the status quo until we might possibly win the *lotería*.

Once again a mass of frogspawn is floating at the end of the pool and tiny frogs are leaping about in the early sunshine. Why they have to journey here from the front pond is beyond my comprehension. Surely natural pond water in a tranquil setting has to beat chlorinated water? I grab a bucket and fill it with water from the hose, then carefully use the pool net to transfer the jellied mass into the bucket. It falls inside with a plop. Carefully I target the tiny frogs and catch two in a matter of minutes. Just one to go. I lean in and just as my hands close around it, I lose my balance. Splash! The cool water has me issuing some loud expletives. I swim over to the side and haul myself out. What a buffoon. The cats survey the scene like gormless spectators.

'Can one of you lend me a paw?'

No response.

I glower at them. 'Cheers, but remember that if ever one of you lot falls in, you're on your own!'

Dripping wet, I grab the bucket and look up when I hear guffawing from the upstairs window. The Scotsman pokes his head out.

'Having an early dip?'

'Ho ho ho.'

I walk round to the pond and drop my wards into the water. Let's hope they stay put this time. As I turn round, I see that Doughnut has discovered something fun on the front lawn and is attempting to play with it. I walk up the stone steps to take a closer look and see that it's moving. By Jove, it's a big tortoise! I shoo Doughnut away and examine the creature. It has beautiful, distinctive black, yellow and brown markings and robust sinewy little legs with pronounced claws. He looks up at me contemplatively – it has to be a male by his macho stance, I think – and blinks. Then without the slightest hesitation he begins chomping on some grass and leaves at my feet. There are three indigenous tortoises on Mallorca to the best of my knowledge:

the *Testudo hermanni*, which tends to hang out in the eastern part of the island in the Parc Natural de Llevant; the less common *Testudo graeca* that can be found mostly in the Parc Natural de Sa Dragonera; and the *Emys orbicularis*, the freshwater terrapin that is often seen in the *torrentes* of S'Albufera nature park. On a much larger scale is the *Caretta caretta*, the Mediterranean sea turtle, which is located in protected reserves around Mallorca. The tortoises are all protected species and I am concerned that this intrepid little fellow has found his way onto our land. Three of the cats, Minky, Orlando and Bat Cat, have now wandered nonchalantly over to witness the spectacle while Doughnut, duly chastised, keeps a wary distance. They look at the tortoise and then at me with a look of confusion on their faces. It evidently doesn't offer as much appeal as a mouse or bird.

I decide to move my new friend to a safer place, take him down into the field and install him among some leafy greens on the vegetable patch, which seems to suit him well. I put down a saucer of water and set off back to the house. The Scotsman greets me on the porch.

'What are you doing in that wet shirt and no shoes? You'll go down with a cold. Now don't forget we're setting off in less than an hour.'

'I've found a tortoise. Go and see him in the veg patch.'

'Really?'

In some excitement the Scotsman strides off in the direction of the orchard.

After a very quick shower and change of clothes I knock back a double espresso and mug up on tortoise species online before getting on with some work in the office. Manuel Ramirez has emailed to say that the opening of his new boutique hotel in St Petersburg is being postponed until October because dark forces are still at play. In truth, I'm rather relieved. Greedy George's Barcelona launch with Ratón the bull is now happening in early July, and I could do without two client events happening in different countries around the same time. Meanwhile, Greedy George appears to be happy with developments for his showroom launch and has even approved the Barcelona caterer's selection of canapés without a murmur. She is planning – not surprisingly – a bull theme, and the menu will include beef brochettes, mini-beefburgers and other red meat novelties on sticks. I am just finishing the corrections to a press release for Rachel about the All Man Clinic when the Scotsman calls from the patio below my open window.

'It's midday. Are you ready?'

I look at my watch and turning off the computer, scurry downstairs and join the Scotsman in the car. Today we are off to visit the potato fair in the agricultural town of Sa Pobla and afterwards will drive to Petra, birthplace of Friar Juniper Serra. Aside from visiting the good friar's childhood home, we will pop by the museum to meet Tumi Bestard. Ollie is spending the day and having a sleepover with Angel, so we shan't be experiencing any teen wisecracks from the back of the car. The Scotsman pulls out of the courtyard.

'What a handsome chap that tortoise is. But if he's endangered, perhaps we should inform some official body?'

I nod. 'Let's ask Catalina what she makes of it. I've just compared him with others online and I think he's a *Testudo graeca*. They have symmetrical markings on the head and a more oblong shape, thigh spurs and large scales on the front legs.'

He laughs. 'Did you make a note of his inside leg measurements too?'

As we reach the end of the lane, we nearly collide with Catalina's car.

'*Uep!*' she shouts from the window. 'You off to Sa Pobla?'

Miquela waves from the front passenger seat as I dash from the car to speak to them.

'We've found a wild tortoise in the garden. Do we need to inform anyone?'

She frowns. 'Hmm. I don't think so, but it's best to leave it to roam freely. It'll probably go when it suits.'

'I think it's a Greek tortoise, so I'm going to christen him Homer.'

She laughs. 'Don't get too fond of it. He won't hang around for long. OK, now we go to the house to clear up your chaos!'

She toots and speeds up the track like a rally driver on acid, leaving a trail of dust hanging in the air. The sun has now shifted from behind the mountains and is sitting squat in our line of vision. The Scotsman winces with the light and pulls down his visor.

'It's going to be a scorcher today. I'll have to do a double dose of watering tonight.'

We decide to take the country route, first following the road inland to Santa Maria and then to Inca.

I've long had a fascination for the town of Sa Pobla. In truth, there's not a lot to it. Like other small towns in the central Pla, it crouches low beneath dusty-brown undulating hills that form a narrow ridge to the north, behind which are the more spectacular Tramuntanas. If you blinked you might miss it, but that would do the town a disservice, because despite its lack of visual splendours, a few jewels lie hidden in its lean, labyrinthine streets, not least a contemporary art and toy museum and the Museum of Sant Antoni and the Devil. Sa Pobla sits on the edge of S'Albufera's nature park and two Englishmen, a certain Mr J. L. Bateman and a Mr Green, are credited with having initiated the draining works of part of S'Albufera in the late nineteenth century, which enabled locals to break up land to create a hundred wells. These they used to turn dry terrain into arable land, and potatoes became one of the chosen vegetables. As we approach the town, a reddish-brown smudge on the horizon dotted with a few stone and whitewashed buildings, the Scotsman turns to me.

'This town was given Royal status in the fourteenth century by King James II. Bet you didn't know that?'

'True. But did you know that a fellow Scot by the name of Archibald Findlay from Auchtermuchty had a big influence on the town?'

He tuts. 'Presumably he brought a variety of potato here.'

'Damn! How did you know that?'

'I didn't, but any decent gardener would recognise his name. He was a prolific potato breeder from the late nineteenth century to the early twentieth, and was responsible for keeping the nation from starving during the two world wars with both his British Queen and Majestic potatoes.'

'Quite a hero.'

The Scotsman warms to his theme. 'Indeed. He even created blight-resistant potatoes, but rather shamefully no one gave him any recognition. It's only recently that he's received a commemorative plaque from his hometown of Markinch.'

I'm beginning to wish I'd never started on the subject.

'Well, it was he who introduced Royal Kidney potatoes to Sa Pobla. Of course there's a lot of controversy about it all now.'

The Scotsman shakes his head. 'That poor chap was dogged by controversy. When he created the Eldorado strain, another breeder claimed it was just a genetic variation of another potato called Evergreen and it just about ruined him. So what's this new controversy?'

'It's just that many think Sa Pobla began wrecking its soil when it started its potato obsession. There's an unnaturally high level of nitrates in the subterranean waters of the S'Albufera nature reserve that is probably caused by over-use of fertiliser for agricultural purposes.'

The Scotsman ponders this. 'Are potatoes the main crop grown here, then?'

'Put it this way, the town went from producing twenty-five tons of potatoes a year in the early days to a thousand tons by 1925. Back in the tenth century the Moors had successfully grown rice and so locals had the bright idea of reintroducing its cultivation at the beginning of the twentieth century to counter the monoculture of potatoes. They've done it again in recent years as part of a crop rotation system.'

'Why, how many potatoes do they produce a year now?'

'About fifteen thousand tons, I think. They're mostly exported, many to the UK.'

'That sort of level of production would naturally put a strain on the land if not carefully monitored, particularly on the wetlands of S'Albufera.'

'Well, there are many that worry about the enhanced use of fertilisers to keep up production. It's a bit of a hot potato, if you'll excuse the pun.'

The Scotsman pulls a face. 'Actually, I won't!'

As we drive into the centre of the small town, it becomes apparent that locals are in festive mood and are preparing for their big *Fira nocturna de la patata*, the evening festival of the potato. Most of the activities will take place over two evenings, but the bars and restaurants are serving up potato specialities during the day too, and according to posters there are potato-cooking demonstrations in the main square. We park the car and make our way to Plaça Mayor where a number of bars and restaurants are offering the chance to sample different potato dishes for just a few euros. It's lunchtime and the owners are doing a roaring trade. We settle on one of the busiest bars where the aromas wafting from the basement kitchen are too delectable to ignore. We're lured to a small table on the pavement, and within a short while a friendly waitress offers us a selection of mouth-watering potato-based treats. We choose salt cod casserole, seafood and potato platter, baked squid and potato, *patatas bravas*, *tortilla español*, and potato ice cream with figs and honey. A large bowl of *aioli* is placed on the table together with a pannier of crusty brown bread, home-cured green olives and a jug of earthy red wine. With the sun on our backs, we dip our bread into the garlicky mayonnaise and await our potato treats. The savoury dishes arrive in small terracotta bowls and we share them between us. The Scotsman raves over the squid served with *jamon Serrano* and baked sliced potatoes and garlic. I prefer the salt cod with sautéed potatoes which is served with roasted peppers and green beans in an exquisite tomato salsa. By the time we reach the potato dessert, we are struggling to consume even the smallest morsel.

'The ice cream's delicious, if a bit starchy,' muses the Scotsman. 'But the local honey's a nice touch, and the figs are heavenly.'

He looks at the bill and smiles. 'All that for thirty euros. You can't complain.'

We step inside the dark interior of the bar and make our way to the kitchen where we compliment the chef on a fine selection of dishes. He explains that different potatoes were used for each one. We apparently enjoyed a combination of Royal Kidney, Lady Cristal, Majestic and Charlotte, but if we'd been asked to distinguish between them all, it might have put us on the spot.

In the square a woman invites us over to observe her cooking demonstration. She is preparing *patatas bravas* with tomato, paprika and chilli, a dish which Catalina has taught me to prepare and which is delicious served as *tapas*. The pan sizzles as she flips potato pieces in hot olive oil, while at the same time preparing the sauce in another pot. She stirs paprika and chopped red pepper into the beef broth, and adds tomato sauce with a little wine vinegar.

'I don't normally add vinegar. Maybe I should?'

The Scotsman looks mystified. 'Well don't ask me. I have the culinary skills of Orlando.'

'Can he cook? I didn't think he was bright enough.'

I take out my notebook and remind myself to revisit the recipe when I get home. A young man at my side suddenly taps my arm. 'You a journalist?'

'Of a kind.'

'So, you're writing about the potato fiesta?'

I laugh. 'Not necessarily.'

He shrugs. 'My family has grown potatoes here for many years.'

'Are you involved in the fiesta?'

He balks at that. 'No, I am studying agriculture at the university but I don't want to grow potatoes. Production has become too aggressive.'

'But it's always been the town's main industry,' I reply. 'What's so different now?'

'There are harmful nitrates from the fertilisers that are contaminating the waters. We need to find a better way to grow our crops on the island.'

'I imagine, as it's the main source of profit for the town, it'll be hard to find converts.'

He nods. 'Maybe for now, but with competition from other countries in the EU and high costs of production, it's a case of diminishing returns.'

'So, what do you want to do in the future?'

He laughs. 'Forget my parents' business, run an organic farm with some friends and sell locally.'

I wish him luck. He walks off into the crowd, one of a new generation of Mallorcans daring to question traditional forms of farming.

I turn to the Scotsman. 'We need more like him.'

'Indeed, but he and his generation will have an uphill struggle. The organic world's still not understood here.'

'As they say, *poc a poc*.'

We stroll by displays of old farming equipment used for harvesting potatoes and pass a stall selling seed potatoes, at which the Scotsman can't resist buying a tray of the Royal Kidney. We usually plant the Pentland variety, but decide it would be interesting to try a new breed. Before heading off for Petra, we pay a brief visit to Can Planes, a beautifully restored nineteenth-century mansion that serves as a cultural centre. The building includes a big white space on the ground floor displaying works by well-established Mallorcan artists and foreign residents from the 1970s to the 1990s. Upstairs is a historical toy museum with over 3,000 exhibits: veteran cars, carousels, board games, dolls houses, and trains. It takes the Scotsman all his might to drag me away from the place.

Once on the road, which is devoid of cars, we drive to the country town of Muro and then on to Santa Margalida and finally Petra.

I peer out of the window at the rolling countryside. 'Don't you think it's incredible how many attractions this island has to offer? I mean, that toy museum could hold its head up in any major city.'

The Scotsman considers this. 'It's true. Given its size, Mallorca has a huge variety of galleries and museums. I mean, think of the Sóller Valley alone. We've got the natural history museum of the Baleares, the naval museum in the port and the Robert Graves Foundation up the road in Deia…'

'… and don't forget the Can Prunera art gallery and the Miró exhibition at the station.'

'And best of all, the Botanical and Alfabia gardens,' he replies.

'A gardener's dream,' I say with a smile.

The Scotsman scans his watch. 'We should be bang on time to meet Catalina Font. Remind me why we're here?'

'Because we were invited. Besides, it's good to learn about some of the more notable figures in Mallorca's past.'

The quiet and unassuming town of Petra is still in *mañana* mode when we arrive. A few stragglers are drinking coffees in the little *plaça* outside a cafe which overlooks an imposing statue of Juniper Serra, erected in 1913 to commemorate the bicentenary of his birth. Soon the town will be celebrating another hundred years since the friar set foot on the planet, and the pressure is on to make it a date to remember. In fact, without good old Juniper Serra, Petra wouldn't be much of a town to write home about. It's a charming little enclave of the Pla, a stop-off point for a stroll and a coffee, but the main draw is the famed founding father of California: the friar who put Mallorca on the map.

We make our way up the cobbled side street to the museum, passing a series of large colourful tiled panels depicting the different missions in California founded by Serra, and wait for Catalina Font, secretary of the Juniper Serra Foundation, to arrive. Since she leads a busy life teaching in Palma and her work with the museum is totally voluntary, she has warned us that she might be running late. Standing in the quiet narrow street outside the museum's tall green gate, we peer through the bars at the traditional patio formed from tiny grey pebbles beyond. The honey-coloured building with its wide arched portals nestles among an abundance of green foliage and trees. A large palm dominates the forecourt together with a curious blue pole, at the top of which is a large old-fashioned bell. Several locals pitch up, concerned to see us standing forlornly outside the closed building, and kindly offer to take us first to Catalina's home and then to that of Isabel Riera Galmés, the custodian of the museum. We explain that we are happy to wait. By the time Catalina arrives we have been made several kind offers from hospitable Petra folk, ranging from a cup of coffee to a quick tour around the town.

A cheerful woman with a mane of glossy brown hair and a mischievous smile, Catalina plans our trip with precision. First, she takes us to the broad-shouldered old Church of Sant Bernat, a stone's throw away, whose windows the young Franciscan friar apparently cleaned in his youth. We meet the resident priest who gives us a whirlwind tour of the historic building with its meticulously refurbished altars and frescos. By now Isabel, the museum's custodian, and Tumi Bestard, the former American Consul who these days devotes his free time to the museum's future, have arrived. With enthusiasm, he shows us the simple terracotta-hued terraced home in which Juniper Serra lived as a child. The ceilings are low and the rooms tiny. Upstairs is the four-poster bed in which the friar slept, and below, the indoor stable where the horses were kept – a poor man's alternative to central heating. Similarly to Ollie, I'm rather taken with the stone pigsty in the narrow garden built like a mini-igloo and resembling those I saw at my sheep-breeder friend Jaume Jaume's farm.

'How did Serra become a friar?' I ask.

'His family sent him to the local Franciscan school in Palma at the age of fifteen, and it soon became apparent that the boy was gifted academically. He was ordained into the Franciscan order while young and became a professor of theology by twenty-four,' Tumi replies.

'That's some achievement,' says the Scotsman.

'It was, when you think of his humble background,' says Catalina.

She whisks us off to the museum along the same street to admire wooden models of the nine missions set up by the friar when he arrived in Alta California.

'I presume he learnt the local lingo?' I ask Isabel.

'Of course.' She leads me to a model showing Juniper working in the fields with a group of swarthy men. 'How else do you think he taught the locals to build, grow crops and raise livestock? He became an integral part of their lives.'

One wonders if the indigenous people took kindly to being shown new skills when they'd lived quite peaceably for many years doing things their own way. On a scientific expedition some years before, I had pondered the same question when visiting a remote Amerindian tribe converted in the 1950s to Christianity. Undoubtedly the tribe had picked up new skills and wholeheartedly embraced Christianity, but they soon forgot their own traditional medicinal cures and instead of bartering with their neighbours began exchanging money for goods. In a short space of time the tribe became dependent on external sources for supplies and lost their self-sufficiency.

We wander round the exhibits of the museum where there are copies of Juniper's letters, historic artefacts from California at the time and many paintings of the friar at different periods in his life. Having read up on the Spanish conquest in the eighteenth century of Mexico, Baja and Alta California, it is easy to see why there has also been criticism of the brutal methods employed in the colonisation of the Native American Indians. All the same, viewing history from a contemporary standpoint is never comfortable and can lead to misconceptions.

'There will always be detractors, I suppose,' says the Scotsman. 'But Junipero Serra undoubtedly brought a lot of new skills to the Indians and his legacy lives on in the California missions, which are visited by thousands of people every year. They do a lot for charity, I believe.'

'True,' I reply. 'Many Mallorcans view him as one of their most successful exports.'

Tumi, joined by his wife Olga, claps his hands together and with a wry grin declares that it's time for refreshments. He takes my arm and leads me out on to the patio. The sky is darkening and it's only then that I realise how long we've spent roaming the two floors of the museum.

Catalina smiles. 'So, time for a celebratory drink and a snack in Juniper's honour,' she says.

'But we should head off home,' says the Scotsman. 'We've taken up enough of your time.'

Our new friends won't hear of it, and together in a posse we set off along the street to enjoy the wonderful hospitality of Catalina at her own home. In her cosy living room, whose walls are adorned with the works of her artist brother and many well-known contemporary Mallorcan artists, we sit drinking beers and feasting on home-made *sobrasada* and manchego cheese served with fresh brown bread.

It is late by the time we set off from Petra.

'What an entertaining day,' I yawn. 'We must do this more often.'

'What exactly? Visit the home of famed friars? Eat too much good food and wine?'

'No, get out and about more and see the hidden parts of the island.'

He gives a sigh. 'Hmm, good thinking. So are you still hungry?'

'You've got to be kidding.'

'I was thinking that we could pop by Es Turo for a light dish. It's the start of the orange festival in Sóller so they might be serving up some scrumptious orange-based dishes.'

'Well, I suppose...'

And despite a day of culinary extravaganzas, we arrive an hour later up in Fornalutx village just in time for last orders. A perfect end to a perfect day.

Fifteen

THE BULL FROM THE SEA

A hot sun beams down at me as I toil away in my al fresco gym. I'm following a book written by a personal trainer that suggests daily exercise routines in a natural environment. The idea is that one starts with gentle jogs, press-ups, lunges, skipping and log-lifting before gradually progressing to more challenging exercise. I'm still at wimp level. All the same, I'm really enjoying exercising in the fresh air away from the hot and sweaty atmosphere of an indoor gym. There's no one to guffaw at my mismatched and tatty old gym wear and no one to criticise my lack of technique. And, of course, the best thing about it is that it doesn't cost me a penny. I've managed a run to the port and am now attempting to do a little log lifting. Sweat runs down my face as I stop to catch my breath. Why am I doing this? Ah, I remember, so that I can justify the chocolate croissant warming nicely in the oven. After a few feeble efforts with the heavy log I abandon it for the skipping rope. Halfway through some brisk jumps I hear the bottom gate swing open.

'You're much better at skipping now.'

I look up to see Clara smiling at me. She has her little sister Maya in tow who is watching me with what looks like a mixture of pity and embarrassment. Why on earth is an unfit woman trying to skip? she seems to be asking herself.

'Can we play?' asks Clara.

'What about school?'

She shrugs. 'Granddad's not ready yet. We've got a few minutes.'

Maya in shorts and a T-shirt begins bouncing on one of the balls, while Clara unceremoniously whips the rope from my hand and begins skipping.

'You know in England most school children have to wear uniform.'

Clara pulls a face. 'How stupid. In Palma I've seen a few kids from private schools wearing uniforms, but it's much nicer to wear what you want.'

'It's not so stupid. It means everyone looks the same.'

'What do you mean?'

'Well, there are many children who can't afford expensive clothes while others can. It's fairer that pupils don't judge each other on what they wear.'

She laughs. 'No one has expensive clothes at my school. Mind you, Guillermo's rich because everything he wears is Quicksilver or Billabong, and he's even got his own BlackBerry.'

'That's my point.'

She stops skipping and jumps on the Ouija board and gives it a spin. 'It's hard to keep your balance on this. Let's both try and stand on it.'

'That'll break it, given my weight.'

'Even you're not that fat!'

'Thanks a lot.'

Against my better judgement I step onto the wobbly circular board and by grabbing hold of each other's arms we manage to keep upright. Clara giggles and paddles her feet so that we both lose balance and have to jump off. A voice calls from the gate.

'I don't know who's the bigger child!'

I turn to see Fernando grinning through the bars.

'Clara's a very bad influence on me.'

He laughs. '*Seguro*! *Venga*! Time for school.'

The girls scuttle out of the orchard and up the path to the track. They wave. 'See you tomorrow!'

'Maybe. Have fun.'

Just as I enter the house I hear the telephone ringing from the kitchen.

'*Hola?*'

It's Marina, the daughter-in-law of my old friend, the poet, Michel Ripoll. 'I have to tell you that Michel passed away peacefully in his sleep last night. Ignacio is making the necessary arrangements. He wanted you to know.'

I feel an instant blow to the stomach. I saw Michel and his family only a few weeks ago and, although in his nineties and reliant on the use of a stick, he had seemed in fine fettle.

'Had he been feeling ill?' I ask, trying to sound normal. My eyes are pricked with tears.

'Not at all. He took a book to bed as usual and in the morning I went to give him his cup of coffee but he didn't wake.' She hesitates. 'It sounds odd, but he really seemed to be wearing a smile. A sort of knowing smile.'

I feel a rogue tear escape down my cheek and for a moment it's impossible to swallow.

'What was he reading?'

'A poetry book. The page was open at *Vientos del pueblo llevan* by Miguel Hernández.'

I laugh through my tears. 'He gave me that poem to read last year and got very cross when I misinterpreted one of the verses.'

'But poems are subjective,' she says sweetly.

'To a degree, but of course he was right. It was my Spanish that tripped me up.'

An embarrassed pause.

'He didn't want to be buried so we'll be scattering his ashes from the *faro*, the lighthouse in the port. He loved to walk there. Maybe you'll come with us?'

'I leave for London tonight and won't be back from Barcelona until this Friday.'

'Don't worry. We'll wait until you return and we can celebrate his life together.'

After she's gone I take a chair from the kitchen and drag it through to the bookshelves in the *entrada*. On the third shelf I find my prize, the little brown leather-backed book of Michel's own poems that he gave me. I take it with me upstairs where I can weep in private.

The Scotsman bursts into the house with a large potted sapling. He must have popped round to one of the local nurseries while I was out running.

'You're going to be so happy.'

'Really?' I say.

He sets the pot down. 'You don't sound so chirpy. Didn't you have a good run?'

'Marina called when I got back. Michel's died.'

He strides over to me and gives me a hug. 'I'm so sorry. He was such a lovely old chap. Was it sudden?'

'He died in his sleep.'

He puts on the kettle. 'I'll make you a tea. We have to remember that he was well into his nineties. He had a good innings.'

'I suppose.'

'He never got over losing his beloved Sofia during the Spanish Civil War.'

'No. In truth,' I add, 'I don't think he would have chosen to hang on this long without her. She was the light of his life.'

'Let's hope he'll be with her now.'

'Apparently he was reading Hernandez before he died. He was a Spanish poet, a Republican, imprisoned by Franco after the Spanish Civil War.'

'Did he survive?'

'No, he was sentenced to death but given life imprisonment instead. He never made it out of jail. He died in 1942 of tuberculosis leaving a wife and young son.'

'What a waste.'

'Indeed. Listen, forget the tea. I need a walk so I'll pop into town and get a few groceries.'

I scoop up my handbag by the door.

'Before you go, let me show you the tree. It's a lime.'

I laugh. 'You finally got me one?'

'It wasn't for want of trying. Tramuntana nurseries rang me when you were out to say they had a beauty. Where shall we plant it?'

'Perhaps in the front garden.'

'Perfect.'

I walk off along the fragrant track – now heavy with the smell of lavender and rosemary – and stop to say hello to my neighbours, Pedro and Silvia, who are enjoying a coffee on their front patio. As I reach the road I hear, mingled with the sound of hissing cicadas, a 'beep-beep', mechanical spluttering and a smell of acrid smoke. Gaspar draws to a halt on his decrepit *moto* and gives me a radiant smile. Beads of sweat cling to his upper lip.

'Want a lift into town?'

'Don't worry. It's a nice day for a walk.'

He seems crestfallen. 'You won't have a lift with me? What have I done?'

Reluctantly I get on the back of the bike. So much for the contemplative walk. Gaspar sings and chatters as we bump along in the glaring sunshine, his rusty *moto* ricocheting off stones and potholes in the narrow lanes as we head towards the town. By the time we reach Sóller's main *plaça* I'm covered in dust, but my spirits have lifted because it's simply impossible to feel glum with Gaspar around.

In Café Paris I join Antonia at one of the tables. Her fair hair has been cut short and she is wearing a floral summer dress.

'Still abstaining?'

'I'm trying. Just one cigarette today.'

'But it's only 9.30 a.m. and you've already had one.'

José comes over with a double espresso, water and a croissant and places them in front of me with a wink.

'*Si*, but think about it. I could have had two cigarettes by now, but I've just had the one.'

'Hmm. That's a sort of twisted logic, Antonia.'

She breaks into a grin. 'Albert Junior's baby is due next month. You know it's going to be a boy?'

'Wonderful, and what'll they call him?'

She falters. 'Tyler. In memory of our dear son.'

Antonia and Albert's younger son died in a traffic accident when only nineteen.

'I can't think of a more fitting tribute.'

She smiles. 'That way he'll always live on.'

She knocks back the last of her coffee and, tapping my arm, says she must return to the shop. I leave a few minutes later just as Tolo from the Banca March enters.

'Shall we all meet for dinner soon?'

'We'd love to. Can I call you when I'm back from my travels later this week?'

He nods. 'Of course. *Bon viatge*!'

I head off to C'an Materino in Calle Sa Lluna to buy a chicken and opening the door, bump into Viktoria and Krisztian who run the Village Café in Deia. I often pop by this bijoux Hungarian eatery for a coffee and slice of one of their delicious cakes –

usually straight after a Pilates class, which of course undoes all the good work. Catalina pulls a fat chicken from the display case and sharpens her knife.

'Want its head?'

I wrinkle my nose and she laughs. A familiar ritual. Pathetically my guilt at eating chicken is assuaged if the bird's head is removed. I don't want to look at its eyes and imagine it whispering, *'Et tu brute?'* These days I feel a tinge of hypocrisy, fawning over my pet chickens at home while happily roasting one of their chums for Sunday lunch. I leave the shop and pop by Colmado Sa Lluna for some *jamon Serrano* and buy some light bulbs at the electricians. At the *correus*, the post office, I wait patiently in the queue for fifteen minutes to buy some stamps and am rewarded with smiles from the counter staff, who ask about the hens and the Scotsman's vegetable growing. After a brief chat with Cati at Sa Botiga where I buy some blueberries, I scan my watch. Time for home. With perfect timing the creaking, old wooden *tramvia* is just trundling through the *plaça* so I wait outside Botiga de sa Plaça just as it makes a stop.

Back at the house I find the Scotsman digging up lettuces and radishes. Under the sun the colours seem so vibrant. He is surrounded by flourishing beetroot, potatoes, cucumbers, French beans, peppers and tomatoes. It breaks my heart to leave such a bounty even for just a few days.

'I shall miss all this.'

He leans on his fork. 'It'll still be here when you get back. Anyway, the food in Barcelona is always damned good. By the way, have you seen how the figs are growing?'

I look over at the tree that produces sticky green figs and see that its branches are already weighed down with fruit. The tree that produces purple figs is over by Emilio's wall. I love both varieties.

'When I get back we can prepare all those peppers you picked and stick them in jars. It's going to be a bumper crop this summer. I'll make you some bottles of fresh lemon juice before I go though.'

He smiles. 'Don't worry about me. Just get yourself organised. Remember you've got a plane to catch.'

Six hours later I arrive in London. Nothing has changed. Traffic roars, there's the on-off urgent cry of police and ambulance sirens, and hordes of people are marching this way and that like programmed ants. I leave my case at the club in Mayfair and take a taxi to the Havana showroom in St James's. The windows display the new bull's hide range of products with a mischievous retro twist. Full-size, black and white cardboard cut-outs of well-known Hollywood names from the 1940s and 1950s stand smiling by each range. Each has a speech bubble with catchphrases such as 'No bull?', 'Bullseye!', 'Feeling bullish?', 'Foxy Oxy', 'Why not take the bull by the horns?' and 'Let's not lock horns.'

Richard, Havana's longstanding showroom manager, greets me like a long-lost friend.

'Darling! How are you?' He air kisses me and distractedly runs a duster over my jacket as if I'm one of the store's grubbier products. 'How d'you like the new window display? Not too cheesy?'

'It's fun and rather eccentric. I love the turquoise handbag mirrors.'

'Gorgeous, aren't they? And you'll see that they have a dinky strap and popper to keep them shut. They're available in five colours.'

He snatches one from a glass shelf and sniffs the white leather. 'All the guests at the Barcelona launch will get one of these, won't they? I sent them all by courier to George two days ago.'

'We're giving them a choice between a mirror or business cardholder.'

'So why haven't I seen these cardholders yet?'

I give him a wink. 'They've been specially designed by George in Barcelona. They're not for sale here yet.'

He gives a huffy shrug. 'Typical of George not to think about the showroom in London. It's all about Barcelona now. And what's happening with this bronze bull?'

'Hopefully everything's under control. It's due to arrive by boat late morning on Thursday and then a pick-up truck will take it to the Havana showroom. The art exhibition, which is all on a bull theme, is going up in the showroom tomorrow. It's going to look amazing.'

'And what about Dannie's Allure Bloom lights?'

'Hmm, those are going to be on display, though I think they'll be a bit out of place.'

He slaps my arm. 'Don't you believe it. They've been flying out of the showroom here. Women will try anything that might erase wrinkles. Actually a lot of us men would too!'

He floats off to answer the telephone. 'Hellooooo! Havana Leather, how can I help you?'

I look at my watch. I've got lunch with Raisa Ripov and Rachel, then a meeting with Dannie and Andrea Cecile. It seems that Dannie is keen to promote the Number 35 brand to friends and clients of hers in the States. I hope it won't all end in tears. I value Andrea too much as a friend. Later I'm meeting Ed for a quick supper before getting an early night and catching a flight to Barcelona in the morning.

'You'll never believe who that just was on the phone!'

I throw out my hands. 'Well, who?'

He does a stage whisper though with no one else in the shop but the two of us, I'm not sure why.

'The royal household. They want some of the new bull's hide range.'

'Who's it for exactly?'

'She didn't say. Maybe it's for the Duchess of Cambridge. Imagine!'

'Now Richard, I need to check that you couriered off all the press and guest info packs last week.'

He rolls his eyes. 'They don't call you Miss Double-Check for nothing. George confirmed he received everything yesterday. It's all awaiting you. Who'll be helping you with the guests and press on the night?'

'The new Spanish showroom staff. I haven't met them yet.'

'God help you. The manager's as mad as a hatter. Her name's Celestina and she told me she's a clairvoyant.'

I give a guffaw. 'A likely story.'

He pouts. 'Don't laugh, it's no joke. She's apparently got the eye. I met her when she came here for training.'

'If things get boring we could use her as a star turn on the night.'

Richard stands on the doorstep as I hail a cab. 'Oh, look at that!'

He picks up a shiny coin from the pavement and hands it to me. 'Here, love, this is your good luck penny. Trust me, you're going to need it.'

It's 10.00 p.m. Ed and I are sitting in Tempo restaurant in Curzon Street, owned by Henry Togna, a close friend, and Ollie's godfather. As usual the Italian fare has been scrumptious.

'You don't think I could order another slice of lemon tart?' asks Ed.

I'm still eating my amaretto semifreddo and am amazed to see that he's demolished his dessert so quickly.

'If it makes you happy.'

'It's only a few hundred calories. Not that much in the scheme of things. How's yours?'

'Excellent. I suppose you want some?'

'Just a soupçon.'

He pulls the plate towards him and with his spoon, takes a generous portion. 'Mmm…'

I order coffee. 'So when are we going to talk about the elephant in the room?'

He fiddles with the handle of his MEK at his side. 'Oh, who wants to talk about work?'

'I do. You need a plan otherwise you'll spend all your redundancy and end up on skid row.'

'That's what Rela says. Actually, I've decided to apply for a part-time computer consultancy job I've seen. It's just up my street.'

'Well, do it. And what about the website?'

'I just need time.'

'Working for yourself isn't as scary as it sounds.'

'It's just that I've always worked for the BBC. I don't know anything else.'

'Exactly – so see it as escaping from a prison.'

'Not quite how I view it, to be honest. Rather more that I've been dumped at sea.'

'Nonsense. It's just a question of confidence. In fact I've a feeling Greedy George could do with computer help.'

'But he sounds terrifying.'

'Funnily enough, I think you and he would get on. You're both deranged.'

'Thanks.'

The coffee arrives. Ed piles sugar into his cappuccino and passes a critical eye over my double espresso.

'Doesn't drinking that make you hyper?'

'Just how I'll need to be to survive the next few days.'

He gives a startled cough. 'But you don't envisage any problems with the delivery of this bronze bull, do you?'

'No, but the unexpected can sometimes happen. I mean, it weighs over a thousand pounds. Say the trawler can't handle such a load?'

'Well, how big is the boat?'

'I think George said it was a sixty-foot trawler. It's probably a wreck if I know Felipe and his Spanish chum who's organising things.'

He laughs. 'Oh come on, I'm sure it will go swimmingly well.'

I wonder if Ed's choice of maxim is deliberate or purely subliminal.

The phrase 'rats deserting a sinking ship' crosses my mind, or rather, *Ratón deserting a sinking ship*. God forbid! I shake my head. No more of these crazy thoughts.

We split the bill and get up to go. At the door, he pats my arm.

'Cheer up old thing. It'll all be plain sailing. Just mark my words.'

Greedy George is pacing up and down the marina of Port Maso on the outskirts of Barcelona. It's gone 2.30 p.m. and there has still been no word as to the whereabouts of Ratón. All we know is that two and a half days ago the bronze bull was safely transported from Jerez to the port of Cadiz by road and then transferred onto the trawler. The old vessel set sail successfully, in good sailing conditions and was due to arrive late morning here at Port Maso. Despite my having left umpteen messages for the sculptor, Antonio Sanchez, his mobile presumably has no signal out at sea and there's been no communication from the crew. Felipe Cañas, he of Bullseye and strip club fame, seems relaxed as he walks in a sharp suit at George's side, a huge *puro* jammed in his mouth. I walk on the other.

'The point is, guv, it would be a disaster if that bleedin' bull didn't turn up here. I mean, we've got the press all fizzed up and the Spanish dignitaries are coming, and what about the geezers from the British and Spanish Embassies?'

'I'm sure it'll be here before long. Sea voyages vary according to conditions on the way.'

What twaddle am I spouting? I don't know the first thing about sea crossings.

I turn to Felipe Cañas. 'Tell me, if as I understand it, the crossing is only six hundred and twenty-five nautical miles, why is it taking your chum Mateo more than two days to get here?'

Felipe Cañas gives a spirited yawn. 'You obviously know nothing about trawlers. If my friend had a super-yacht or, say, a ferry, he could travel at twenty-six knots and get here in about eighteen hours.'

'So what speed does his trawler go at?'

'Maybe eleven knots?'

'For goodness' sake! It would have been better going by road or possibly on foot.'

Felipe Cañas glowers. 'But my friend is doing this as a favour. He is making a few little deliveries at ports en route and then bringing Ratón here. On the road any mishap could happen, such as theft.'

George gives a hollow laugh. 'I'd like to see someone try to steal Ratón from the back of a lorry. He's a thousand pounds of solid metal. They'd end up with a hernia.'

Felipe offers us a slippery smile. 'Look, I bet they're just taking their time and enjoying a few beers on deck. My old *amigo*, Mateo, is a very relaxed captain and knows these waters like the back of his hand.'

'Have you tried contacting him?' I ask curtly.

'I don't want to bother him unless it's an emergency.'

'Well, bearing in mind we kick off the event at 8.00 p.m., we won't have a lot of time to play with unless he pitches up soon,' George replies.

'At least everything else is under control,' I say as breezily as possible. 'The exhibition in the showroom looks stunning, the staff are all brilliantly prepared and the caterer's hugely organised.'

I try to forget the words of Celestina, the new Barcelona showroom manager, who told me the previous night that she'd had a premonition that the boat had sunk.

'Don't give me all that PR baloney, guv. We're screwed if that bull does a runner.'

'I'm not sure how a brass bull would manage such a feat, but it would certainly make a good headline.'

'Oh be quiet, guv. I'm in no mood for your inanities.'

Felipe Cañas suddenly grips his chest dramatically. Oh heavens, he's not having a heart attack, is he? Surely there's a time and a place for everything? A second later, to my and apparently George's relief, he plucks a vibrating mobile from the chest pocket of his jacket.

'*Si, si. Que? Que? Mateo! No es posible!*' Felipe's head is lowered and now he's gripping his forehead with his free hand as though it might by the force of gravity drag him to the ground. '*Madre mia! Joder! Puta madre!*'

Greedy George stands transfixed, listening uncomprehendingly to the stream of invective pouring forth. With a furious snap of his mobile, Felipe Cañas stamps the ground, muttering under his breath, '*Que gilipollas es este tío!*'

'What's he saying, guv?' asks George.

'He's saying that some guy, presumably his chum, Mateo, is a…'

'Wanker?' suggests George.

'Something like that.'

'OK, guys.' The slippery smile is back. 'That was Mateo. Apparently the motor of his old trawler failed last night in a terrible storm and has dropped anchor near Platja de La Ribera, a beach off the coast near Sitges, a nice resort, not far from the Port de Vilanova y La Getrú.'

'We don't need a ruddy tourist travelogue, you twit. Where exactly is that?'

'An hour from here by car,' he replies.

'That's not so bad,' says George in some relief.

Felipe sighs. 'Ah, but we have a slight problem. The boat needs to transfer the bull to the beach but has no means.'

'So what's the solution?' I ask.

'*Pues*, Mateo has sent for a boat with a *grua*, you know a crane, from Vilanova port to take Ratón from the trawler and transfer him onto a raft.'

'A raft?' yells George.

'Yes, the same boat must tow a raft behind it so that the bull can be transferred from the sea to the beach where a tractor...'

'A tractor?' I squeak.

Felipe wipes a drop of perspiration from his lip. 'Yes, at the water's edge the raft must be attached to a tractor which will drive it across the beach to a track where a lorry...'

'A lorry?' I giggle nervously.

'... will be waiting to transport it to the Barcelona showroom.'

'Are we planning on doing this within the next year?' barks George.

'*Tranquilo*, George!' soothes Felipe. 'Everything will be fine. If we're lucky we can have the bull at the showroom in a couple of hours.'

'And how are we going to get it from the lorry into the showroom?' I demand. 'Don't forget, it's three metres long and two metres high. It's enormous.'

'Mateo said that it has been affixed to a wooden base with wheels for easy transport.'

'Thank God for that!' I reply.

George stabs a finger at Felipe's ribcage. 'But why the hell can't we just get a boat to tow the trawler with Ratón to the nearby Port de Vilanova where it can be transferred directly to a lorry?'

'Yes, why the need for a raft and tractor?' I ask.

Felipe exhales a plume of smoke. 'Because too many boats have been washed up into the port during the night's storm. It is chaos there apparently!'

George hangs his head. 'What do they say about best laid plans, guv?'

I pat his back. 'As there's nothing we can do here, I suggest we return to the showroom and have a soothing cup of tea and await news.'

'A soothing bottle of cava more like,' growls George as he stomps off to the car.

Felipe catches my arm. 'Listen *mi amiga*. It's going to be – how you say – touch and go that we get this bloody bull to the showroom tonight. My friend, Mateo, is pulling every rope...'

'... string...'

'... that too, and he says that even though he went to school with the harbourmaster of Vilanova, it will be tricky.'

I close my eyes briefly. The sun is pounding and the glare from the sea is giving me a headache. 'Now listen, Felipe. We could have easily taken the bull over land, but you insisted on organising the voyage by sea through your *amigo*. It is therefore your responsibility to sort this mess out. Maybe you should send your strip club girls down to Vilanova. They might prove a motivator for the harbourmaster and his chums.' I wipe a bead of sweat from my forehead. 'Call me.'

Felipe seems lost in thought, then he smiles. 'Bring on the dancing girls. What a clever idea. Why didn't I think of it myself?'

It is 4.30 p.m. and George is charging around the showroom like a raging bull.

'If that little shmuck lets me down, that'll be the end of him. What the hell's going on?'

The caterer gives me a panicked glance as she polishes glasses and her maître d' shakes his head sorrowfully.

'Listen, George,' I say. 'The last call I had from Felipe was to tell me that the rescue boat from the port was on its way. Shall I go down there myself?'

He runs a bulky hand over his mouth. 'Actually, I'd feel less edgy if you did. At least I'd have someone sane on the ground.'

'That has to be the nicest compliment you've ever paid me.'

'And the last,' he sniffs. 'Go on, get that chauffeur geezer to run you over there. It'll take about an hour, I reckon.'

I try calling Felipe again on his mobile but all I can hear is static. I give it another go. This time he picks up.

'*Hola*! *Si*, Felipe here! Ah, *mi amiga*, come and join us.'

'Felipe, is that you? It's a bad line…'

I can hear giggling and what sounds like girly laughter in the background.

'Felipe, are you on La Ribera beach?'

More explosions of laughter. I feel a trickle of panic. Has the man gone AWOL? The line goes dead.

George frowns at me as I throw the mobile into my handbag. 'Is he pissed?'

I give a groan. 'God alone knows. I could hear girls laughing.'

'He's not gone back to his strip club, has he?'

'I hope not. Look, I'm going to La Ribera now. It's the only way I'll find out what on earth's going on.'

George grabs my sleeve. 'When you find Felipe, poke him in the eye for me.'

As I'm about to leave the showroom, Celestina grabs my hand and hisses in my ear. 'Be careful. I have a bad feeling. I see high waves, destruction and people thrashing about and screaming.'

'Great. I'll bear that in mind.'

The 'chauffeur geezer', otherwise known as Raul, has been hired for the evening to collect random VIP guests and to be at George's bidding. He smiles laconically as I get in to the black limo.

'I hear from the staff that you have a small *problema*.'

'He's actually quite a big and bulky *problema* with two horns, Raul. Now please drive like a maniac.'

He nods. 'Strap yourself in.'

As we speed off down the road I see to my horror a huge traffic jam ahead of us but Raul isn't perturbed. With one deft move and the screeching of tyres, he turns down a dim side street, and after a few sneaky manoeuvres is on the motorway heading along the coast towards Sitges. At times I close my eyes, as Raul races along, overtaking lorries and coaches and weaving between lanes like a maniac with much hooting and tooting and arm waving. I just wish he'd keep both hands on the wheel. With any luck we may just make it there in one piece.

Forty minutes later we arrive with a screech of tyres on the track leading to La Ribera beach. Stepping out of the air-conditioned car we both look at the scene on the sand before us and in some disbelief regard each other. Standing tall on an inflatable raft attached to the back of a tractor is the magnificent form of Ratón surrounded by half-naked, gyrating girls. Nestling in the bright rays of the sun, he looks golden and somehow celestial. A veritable god. Music booms and an assortment of holidaymakers, fishermen – and oh heavens, photographers – are clapping and dancing while the girls scream and whoop.

'Well, Celestina was right about the screaming and thrashing about,' I mumble.

In the far distance I can see an old blue and white trawler bobbing about on the waves.

'Know much about boats?' I ask Raul.

'A bit. That looks like an old tug to me.'

'It's a 1938 German North Sea trawler according to Felipe.'

'As I thought, a bit of an old wreck. You're lucky the bull didn't end up in the deep, storm or no storm.'

I call Felipe on my mobile. 'I am here at La Ribera. What in heaven's name is going on?'

A drunken splutter. 'Oh great, you come for the party. Ratón is, how you say in English, "the bee's knees"! I bring down my girls and everyone helped to put Ratón on the raft. Now we will transport him to the lorry.'

I pull off my shoes and march across the burning sand in bare feet towards the crowd. Standing by his beloved bull, seemingly exhausted and in the depths of despair, is the sculptor, Antonio Sanchez. One arm is thrown around the bull's neck while the other rests on his own forehead. When he sees me, he brightens up.

'Thank God. Are you here to save me from this madness? I've been travelling for days on that stinking boat, and then we had a night of sheer terror in the storm and now...'

I grab hold of Felipe's arm as he chats with the driver of the tractor, a bottle of beer in his grip. He smiles cheerily.

'Glad you came down. The press heard about it and we've been besieged by photographers. Tomorrow Ratón will be a hero!'

I'm fast losing patience. 'Get this tractor moving NOW and remove those girls from the raft!'

He jumps back. 'OK, *tranquilo*!'

Moments later the giggly girls are skipping on to the hot sand and the tractor begins its slow and lumpy ascent up to the track. It seems to take forever as crowds of people lean forward to touch Ratón's sides and photographers hop about, snapping enthusiastically. On the track Raul is giving instructions to the driver of the lorry.

'Come on! Let's hit the road,' he yells. 'There's not a minute to lose.'

Thirty minutes later, with the help of a portable crane, Ratón is secured onto the lorry. Antonio Sanchez refuses to join me in the limo, preferring to remain at his bull's side, and so we set off in convoy to Barcelona. Felipe Cañas jumps into his car and brings up the rear. As we drive off, holidaymakers wave and shout out, 'Ratón! Ratón!', presumably none the wiser as to why a bronze bull was washed up on to their beach in the first place.

It's 7.50 p.m. and Ratón is at last in place in the centre of the showroom. There's tumultuous applause when he is given a final polish by Antonio Sanchez. Photographers scuffle to take pictures of George, Antonio and Felipe, raising glasses happily as they pose beside the bull. Elegantly attired guests arrive in droves, and soon both floors of the showroom are awash with excited and affluent locals and press sipping on cava and Bullseye sherry, admiring the exhibition and products alike – even Dannie's dreaded Allure Bloom lights. The tills ring as the new colourful bull's hide leather range is quickly snapped up by the merry revellers and George, for the first time today, looks relaxed and happy. He sidles up to me and places a glass of fizz in my hand.

'Go on, be a devil. You only live once. When we get rid of this lot, we'll go and have a quiet dinner somewhere. I owe you.'

'Great, but now we need to do the speeches. Say five minutes' time? The embassy personnel are waiting for the sign.'

He nods. 'Yeah, and before the guy from the embassy speaks we've got to get the old geezer, you know Enrique Martinez, the bullfighter, up to the mike...'

I push him his notes. 'Quickly look through these again. Enrique Martinez is the great-grandson of the original Martinez who used to live here. Remember. He isn't a bullfighter like his famous ancestor.'

'Of course not, guv. He looks about a hundred. A bull would have him for dinner.'

We both have a fit of giggles and only manage to compose ourselves when gathering the troops. The Spanish tourism chief suddenly taps my arm.

'What a great event this is. So effortless. Just a few nice pictures, a bronze bull centrepiece, great canapés, sherry and cava. It's how launches should be done. No hysteria, no fuss. These days in Barcelona people overcomplicate things. I take my hat off to you British. Simplicity is always best.'

I stare at him for a second. This is irony at its best? But no. There's not a hint of guile, humour or subterfuge, and why should there be? After all, only a few of us have been party to the madness of the last eight hours.

George breathes into the mike. '… and so my good friends – *mis amigos*, rather…' There's a light titter from the guests. 'Without further ado, I'd like to introduce…'

I listen to the applause and smile. If only Rachel were here. How she would laugh. I take a sip of cava and savour it, dreaming of the moment tomorrow when I'll arrive back in my beloved, tranquil Mallorca. I'm wondering how the Scotsman is faring and the cats and the hens and… someone nudges me. It's Felipe.

'You see, I told you it would all go smoothly. My Bullseye sherry's going down a treat and tonight after the reception I am treating you, George and Antonio to supper at one of the town's best restaurants…'

'Oh no, that's really not necessary. In fact…'

He raises a hand to silence me. 'It is the least I can do for such good promotion. And later we will go to my club. In your honour I have organised a very special show…'

I catch George's eye across the room. He puts two fingers to the side of his head in a deadly salute and grins.

Felipe is wittering on, slurring his words and swaying slightly like a boat on choppy waters. '… and so to conclude, your idea for the dancing girls on the beach was a master stroke. The harbourmaster and the fishermen fell over themselves to help us and that in fact gave me my idea for a new strip dance routine for the girls in my club. I'm going to call it "A Bull from the Sea". And you know what?'

'Surprise me,' I say with a tight smile.

He gives me a bear hug and kisses my cheek exuberantly. 'I'm going to hire you to promote it.'

Sixteen

A WALK ON THE
WILD SIDE

Beneath my window the frogs are quacking with such gusto that it's quite impossible to hear the hum of my computer, let alone hear myself think. Hot and sticky with the unremitting sunlight seeping under the wooden slats of the shutters, I get up and position myself in front of the gently whirring fan at the far end of the room. The air that caresses me is warm but at least simulates a breeze. I close my eyes and try to imagine I'm on a boat out at sea, the wind in my hair, but it's no good. I'm too fidgety to carry on working. With some satisfaction I have managed, in a lengthy phone call this morning, to convince Felipe Cañas that I am not the person to promote his strip club. Instead, rather naughtily, I suggested an overbearing and pushy British PR woman I once met in Barcelona. She'll certainly give Felipe a run for his money.

Now that the excitement of the Havana launch is over and the full heat of the summer is upon us, I'm feeling rather sluggish and, dare I say it, *mañana*-ish. Perhaps what I really need is a long glass of home-made lemonade with ice and a sprig of fresh mint. I patter downstairs and am just helping myself to a brimming glassful from a jug in the fridge when the Scotsman barges into the kitchen. He's clutching a grubby trug full of lettuces, plums, beans and cucumbers which he thumps down on the kitchen table.

'Heavens, I'm parched. That looks like just what the doctor ordered.'

I take a gulp. 'It's heavenly.'

I pour him a glass and watch as he drains it in seconds.

'Poor old Salvador's got a bad leg. He got caught between the wooden perches in the henhouse this morning and tripped when he was coming down the ladder.'

'Why such an ungainly bird keeps trying to climb up to the top shelf of the henhouse beats me. He never used to attempt it,' I reply.

'He wants to be with his harem I suppose. It must be lonely sleeping on ground level when all the girls are having a hen party up above.'

This is the second time that Salvador has hurt himself climbing up to the top level of the henhouse, and I think his precarious ascents have more to do with comfort and warmth than anything else.

'If we bought him a cat basket with a cushion, he might be tempted to stay down below. He's probably a bit cold on ground level, despite all the hay.'

The Scotsman ponders this nugget. 'Well, I'm off to Hens in a minute, so I'll ask for their advice.'

I love the fact that our local supplier of agricultural appliances and sundries in the valley is called Hens, an acronym for something or other. One day we'll have to tell the owner what it means in English. He'll doubtless enjoy the irony.

'The frogs have been a bit raucous this morning.'

The Scotsman nods. 'That damned heron was back, that's probably why. I shooed it away, but it's a menace. By the way,

Homer's still with us. I found him chomping away in the vegetable patch.'

'I suppose if he's happy we should just leave him. It's rather nice to have a resident tortoise.'

'As long as the cats give him space. They seem to be keeping a wary distance. Now, before I forget, what time are you off tonight?'

'Cristina and Ignacio have suggested we meet at 10.00 p.m. by the old washstands in Biniaraix.'

'Are you sure you're up for this walk? It'll take at least eight hours I'd imagine.'

Ollie slopes into the kitchen. 'You're barking! Walking all night in the Tramuntanas and for what? It'll be pitch-black and so boring you'll probably voluntarily jump off a cliff.'

'Thanks for that vote of confidence. As it happens Ignacio has chosen tonight because there's a full moon.'

'Well, then you should be really worried. There'll be werewolves and vampires creeping around the undergrowth.'

'Sure neither of you want to come along?'

'In your dreams,' mutters Ollie as he takes a Bitter Kas from the fridge.

'I'd love to come, but I can't leave Ollie.'

'That's a feeble excuse! I could have had a sleepover at Angel or Juan's house. You're just not up to it.' He gives the Scotsman a playful punch and potters back to his room.

'Actually, I'm not sure if my walking boots are up to it. They're a bit over the hill.'

'Thinking about it, I haven't used my lightweight ones for a while either.'

'Oh, they'll be fine. You'll have a whale of a time.'

He saunters off to the front door which is flung wide open to let in the warm air. 'I'm just off to Hens before Catalina gets here and starts giving me jobs to do.'

In bare feet I walk through the *entrada* to the pond. Johnny fixes his beady eyes on me.

'Ever seen *The Texas Chainsaw Massacre*?'

I wince. 'Not my kind of film, Johnny.'

'Yeah, well there could have been an amphibian version played out today with that murderous heron. He nearly did for us all, and what do you care?'

'That's not fair! We've put in more pond plants and rocks to give you protection. Perhaps the only answer is to hang CDs from the pond's ledge.'

'Are you completely nuts?'

'Apparently, the glare from the sun bouncing off the CDs is a great visual deterrent for birds.'

He chortles merrily. 'That's the stupidest idea I ever heard.'

'Well then, I'll just have to prove you wrong.'

I hear the telephone ringing from the kitchen and dash through the *entrada* in time to pluck it from its perch.

'Ed here. How go things?'

'Fine,' I pant. 'It's about ninety degrees today, so I'm a bit hot and bothered.'

'Oh, how dreadful! Do you have smelling salts?'

'Fortunately not.'

'Well, take it easy today and don't overdo it.'

'Easier said than done. I'm off on an all-night walk to a local monastery later, but hopefully by then it'll be a little cooler.'

'Are you completely nuts?'

'That's the second time I've been asked that in a matter of minutes.'

'Proving that Alan and I are in accord about your mental state.'

'Except that my toad Johnny asked the question, not the Scotsman.'

'Well, then you are completely bonkers. Talking toad indeed! Anyway, my good news is that I've been offered part-time work at a recruitment agency, resolving its computer problems.'

'Fantastic. So you see, there is life after the BBC.'

'Let's hope. It's only a three-month contract to start with, but if I cut the mustard there might be full-time work at the end of it. The irony is, I'll be earning more per week than at the BBC for doing two days' fewer work.'

'That'll teach them a lesson.'

When he's gone, sounding more upbeat than for as long as I can remember, the telephone rings again. At this rate I'll never get any work done today. This time it's Alison, an old friend who works in marketing at the Jumeirah's Carlton Tower Hotel in London.

'I'm coming over to Sóller next week to see how the new hotel's shaping up in the port. Fancy meeting up?'

'Of course. Can you come for dinner?'

'I wish! It's just a flying visit, but I'd love to introduce you to the new team.'

That visit will be of interest to the local press. I must remember to mention it to my editor on the *Majorca Daily Bulletin*.

Just as I replace the receiver, Alan wafts into the *entrada* clutching a cat basket while dragging a bale of straw with his free hand.

'I've bought Salvador a new bed at Hens. It might stop him trying his luck up with the girls, and I picked up a wonderful bale of fresh hay there too. Isn't it a beauty?'

Strands of golden straw break free and settle on the marble floor in carefree abandonment. The Scotsman stops in his tracks. 'Ah, maybe not such a good idea to bring it into the house.'

I nod. 'I'm sure Catalina would heartily agree.'

There's a crunching of gravel and a car door thuds. A moment later Catalina appears like Boudicca in the doorway, a modern-day warrior with broom in one hand and a stern expression planted firmly on her visage. With some dismay she regards the floor and the bale of hay in the Scotsman's grasp.

'What is this mess? You get that hay bale out of here immediately!'

And with a threatening waggle of the brush, she has the Scotsman hurrying into the sunshine, a small maelstrom of straw following in his wake.

There isn't a soul about as we take the narrow and winding back road up to Biniaraix village. From the car window I study the grey, marbled sky, seeking out the moon, but there's only dim cloud and the vast spectre of the Tramuntanas looming in the distance. Ollie sits hunched in the back seat in shorts and T-shirt, humming some unidentifiable rock anthem to himself while the Scotsman grips the wheel, occasionally emitting a soft yawn. At the old washstand I catch sight of Cristina and Ignacio consulting a map. They give us a wave and amble over. Ignacio is sporting sensible hiking boots, shorts and fleece, and carries a bulging rucksack. Both are wearing head torches. Curiously Cristina is braving a skirt.

'Ah, it's so hot,' she sighs as I remark on her bold choice of dress. 'I've got a fleece if I get cold.'

Ignacio examines my sturdy cross-trainers.

'Are these OK? I've got my heavy leather ones in the boot.'

He shakes his head. 'They look fine. There isn't much mud at this time of the year.'

We say our farewells to the Scotsman and Ollie who casts me a malevolent little smile and a wink. 'Don't do anything I wouldn't do,' he chirrups.

Before he gets back in the car he pulls at my sleeve. 'Watch out for the vampires.'

Way back last summer I had asked Ignacio and Cristina, both serious hikers, what it was like to attempt the famous night-time walk from Palma to Lluc monastery in the rugged north-west of the island. They told me that the popular annual event, though fun, could be monotonous given that much of the route was taken by road. Far more challenging, Ignacio had said with a glint in his eye, was to do the entire trek over the mountains in the dead of night, without noise or fanfare.

So it was a few weeks ago that I reminded them both of our conversation and we resolved to take the original and ancient pilgrims' mountain path all the way to Lluc.

We set off in high spirits, chatting and striding up the cobbled stepped path of the Barranc de Biniaraix with relative ease. We're all used to regular mountain walking and know this section of the route well. It is after about forty minutes on the rough, cobbled track that I look down to discover that the right sole of my hardy – and costly – cross-trainers is coming loose. Five minutes later it has peeled off completely. I stop and face the others.

'Er, slight problem.'

I lift my foot for them to see.

Cristina tuts knowingly. 'How long have you had those boots? More than three years?'

'About five.'

'That's bad news then. There's a new bacterium about that's been affecting rubber-soled walking shoes – it started happening a few years ago and is brought on by extreme heat.'

'I've lost walking shoes because of it,' says Ignacio. 'Let's have a look at your sole.'

By the light of his head torch he examines the base of my foot.

'Here, I've got some masking tape I can wind round it. If it gets too uncomfortable we can turn back.'

Cristina agrees. '*Si, si*, we can do this another day. *No problema*!'

There's no way I'm turning back. 'I'll be fine. Come on, let's keep going.'

Handyman Ignacio's prowess with a roll of sticky tape is impressive. He envelopes my shoe with the shiny brown stuff and soon we are off. There is now the gentlest of breezes and from behind the peak of the Ofre emerges a shiny full moon. I let out the sound of a would-be werewolf and we all laugh. A moment later, Cristina grabs my arm when some dark, animal form scurries at speed across the rocks below the path.

'*Que susto!*' she shouts, laughing with the shock. 'What do you think it was? A rat?'

'A goat maybe,' I reply.

'Or perhaps a small vampire?' Ignacio jokes.

Two hours later, somewhere on the Coll de l'Ofre, the sole on my other trainer disappears. This time the tape proffered by Ignacio won't stick on to the damp base, so I carry on regardless. It's like walking in a pair of thin slippers, ensuring I can feel every rock underfoot, with the accompanying discomfort.

By the light of the moon and a clutch of dazzling white stars we walk past the vast treacly-black Cuber Reservoir, and onwards to Tossals where Ignacio suggests we refill our water bottles which are all but empty. He strides off into the shadowy trees to find the exact location of the spring and leaves us in the dense wood, where small unidentifiable creatures scamper about in the dark and sturdy goats clatter their bells, causing us both to shriek in the stillness.

'I hope he comes back soon,' whispers Cristina.

'Imagine if he abandoned us. Do you think we'd get to Lluc on our own?' I ask.

Cristina explodes with giggles. 'You and me? They'd be searching for us for days.'

We're still chortling when Ignacio returns with good news.

'You two are always laughing. Now what? Come on, I've found the spring.'

We fill our bottles and set off up the curving, craggy hill of the Coll de Massanella. The sweet aromatic air and warmth suddenly changes as we climb higher, and soon we are pulling on fleeces shivering with the chill. At the peak, over 1,000 metres high, the view is spectacular, with the golden lights of Palma twinkling in the far distance. We take a brief break and pull a selection of edible goodies from our rucksacks. Cristina has made a delicious Spanish tortilla, a potato omelette, wedged between hunks of fresh baguette. I bring out goat's cheese, *jamon Serrano*, fat, ripe tomatoes and a selection of salted nuts. We sit on the dark rocks, the moon having slipped behind the hills, and, with our head torches as a guide, swap food parcels.

'I wish Ignacio hadn't been so boring and let us bring a bottle of wine,' declares Cristina.

'Yes, that was mean of you!' I say.

'Listen, the idea of leading you two through the dark hills with a few glasses of wine inside you doesn't bear thinking about.'

'We'd be fine, singing songs and dancing.'

'*Exacto!*' he laughs.

For dessert we feast on Cristina's home-made honey and blackberry cake. I find that I'm still ravenous and devour two enormous slices. A light rain begins to fall and Ignacio expresses concern about my shoes.

'Do you think they're going to be all right? We'll be tackling some very steep paths full of sharp rocks. Your feet will be weeping in the morning.'

'Well, they'll just have to get over it. We're halfway there aren't we?'

Cristina examines her watch. 'It's 3.00 a.m. We've done five hours already.'

We plough on, amazed at our lack of fatigue at this quiet hour of the morning. The mountains are magnificent to see even in silhouette form, as is the pearlised sky, streaked with dark blues, greens and greys like the heart of an oyster shell. A reluctant moon tiptoes behind us as we follow a steep and winding track up towards Coll de sa Batalla. The rocks needle and gnaw at my feet but, when we begin our descent on the other side of the hill, it is the lack of grip on the sole that proves the greatest threat as I slither and stumble across the slippery dark rocks at some speed. We stop for some water on a shallow spot of terrain, a fierce wind pricking our ears, and survey the circle of ghostly black peaks that spring up like jagged teeth around us. It is a strange, alien landscape; unfamiliar territory that in my sleep-deprived mind has me wondering whether we have landed on another planet. It is 4.00 a.m. and quite suddenly as we clamber up on to the ridge in the silky darkness, a sea of luminous alien eyes surrounds us. We stop to gawp and in that moment they are on the move, accompanied by much baa-ing and clumsy clattering of rocks, their ghostly bells clanging and echoing throughout the still mountains.

It is at Cases de Sa Neu, not far from where we startle the sheep, that a rosy dawn illuminates the sky and every mountain peak. We stand in wonderment, unable to steal our gaze away from the glorious tableau before us. A choir of ghostly birds begins a pure, unworldly chant that echoes about us, and then comes a distant bellow of a bull. It is nearly 5.30 a.m. when, in anticipation of reaching our goal, we make the twisty and lengthy descent, white mist curling about us, to the monastery of Lluc. In the distance we can see the elegant sweep of the building's reddish roof, the tall church tower and the skeleton outline of various outbuildings. It resembles a medieval fortress, self-contained and gloriously sheltered from the outside world. The last hour plodding the rocky path seems interminable as we wend our way ever downwards towards our goal. The paths are now less rocky and covered in sandy soil. On either side of us are vast virgin forests of bushy Holm Oaks and pine trees which remind me of the magical terrain described in the *Narnia* children's adventure books. It is on the final stretch that I dare to look down at my mummified feet, but the brown tape has all but peeled off and is trailing in sticky pieces from the mangled soles. I chuckle to myself as I limp onwards, a hobbling, ill-shod and weary pilgrim in a strange land. Cristina is rubbing her eyes and yawning loudly and using Ignacio as a support for her weary limbs.

I stride ahead, ecstatic to be nearing the end of our magical journey. Cristina suddenly gives a snort of laughter as she prods at the ground with a makeshift walking stick.

'Do you ever get tired? What's wrong with you?'

'It's true,' says Ignacio. 'Even on the upper slopes you didn't draw breath.'

'I suppose marathon running does build up stamina, although I rarely stop to think of the benefits. It just feels like a real slog most of the time.'

'Well, give me some of your energy!' Cristina laughs.

In the silent car park of the monastery we regard our watches with some incredulity. It is 7.45 a.m., and nearly ten hours have passed since we set off on our night-time adventure. With an unspoken euphoria at having reached our goal, we stand and admire the beautiful and imposing monastery church built from pinky-cream limestone. Parts of the monastery were built as far back as 1250, but the church was a later addition in the early eighteenth century. The huge wooden doors are closed, but having visited before I know what lies within. Thousands of tourists are usually buzzing about the place, most coming to pay homage to La Moreneta, 'the beloved dark one' – the black Madonna statue made from aged and darkened limestone. At this hour of the morning, there isn't a soul about and the silence is palpable. It's a rare privilege to see this splendid monastery free of bristling humanity. Cristina and Ignacio's car is a welcome sight after so much walking. Our competent guide yawns as he fumbles for the key in his voluminous rucksack. He had driven over here the previous afternoon, with Cristina following behind on her motorbike. Once parked, they had both returned to Sóller on her powerful *moto*. A deep weariness sweeps over us and Cristina slumbers on the journey back to the valley while Ignacio keeps awake aided by the breeze gushing through the window and my attempts at lively chatter. At the house, Ollie and the Scotsman sleep on. I creep upstairs, undress, examine my battered and bruised feet and with relief snuggle up under the duvet. Pain stabs at both soles, but I don't care. We did it. Physical suffering has never felt so good. With a smile I evaporate into a land of dreams.

In the afternoon, after a refreshing sleep and shower, I visit what promises to be one of the jewels in the crown of Sóller port but, with the swirling dust kicked up by grinding dumper trucks, and the sheer volume of bustling humanity in florescent jackets and hard hats, it's hard to visualise. Alison smiles.

'I know it's a real building site at the moment, but just wait until it's finished.'

During my site visit, Fernando Gibaja, the newly appointed director of the hotel and his associate, Sandra Farrero, show me detailed plans of what the final building will look like. I contemplate the bizarre prospect of having a luxury spa and gym on my very doorstep. Ah what a decadent thought! But of course – as I sternly remind myself – I have my very own jungle gym in the back garden and how could anything, ahem, possibly top that?

'When is the hotel going to be finished?' I bellow above the din.

'Hopefully spring, but better to get it absolutely right,' replies Fernando with a grin. 'Luxury comes at a price.'

Luxury is something that I've learnt to do without since moving to Sóller. Occasionally I think back to the days when I used to buy sharp suits, hurtle about the streets of London in black taxis and think nothing of dining at chic West End restaurants or stopping by a five-star hotel for a business breakfast or drink with a friend.

Working all hours gave me some sort of justification for the expense, but do I miss it? Now my hens provide my breakfast, lunches are mostly hearty soups made from our own home-grown vegetables and nights out usually involve homely fare and a bottle of *vino tinto* up at Es Turo or any other favourite dining den. I'd be a fibber if I claimed not to mourn the passing of certain indulgences and treats that before I'd taken for granted, but the pangs are a rarity and I'd not swap my rural idyll for all the world.

'So, shall we leave Fernando and Sandra to it and go for a drink?' yells Alison. 'I can't take this noise much more.'

We set off down the winding road to the harbour and promenade and sit under the shady canopy of the Albatross cafe and drink iced coffees.

Couples walking along the promenade stop to take photographs of one another in front of gleaming yachts, and large groups of day-trippers pour from boats, herded along the streets by benevolent Mallorcan guides holding brightly coloured umbrellas. The tourists wander about the harbour like evacuees in a new territory, clutching their hotels' packed lunches in cardboard boxes and eyeing the fishermen with genuine wonder. Soon they settle in the various waterfront bars to order drinks while nibbling on sandwiches and fruit from their packs. Next they'll hop on to the Sóller tram to the town and while away some hours buying gifts and knick-knacks, visiting the Can Prunera art museum and the Sant Bartomeu church before being rounded up and shunted back on to a boat bound for the popular resort whence they came. High above a craggy rock across the bay, Far des Cap Gros, the lighthouse of Sa Muleta, sparkles under the sun, and coming into view across the waves is an old veteran of the high seas, a traditional brigantine liveried in dark blue and white. Alison turns from the sea and pushes the shades back on to her forehead.

'I hadn't realised how beautiful it was here. Now I really understand why you're so in love with this place.'

Seconds later someone tugs at my shoulder. It's Antonia and Albert, with what I presume is baby Tyler in a pram. I introduce Alison to them.

'If you need computer help you know where to find us.'

'I'll let the new director know,' Alison replies with a wink.

'So what do you think of baby Tyler?' asks Albert, the proud grandfather.

'I think he's beautiful,' I say as both Alison and I coo over him in the pram. He slumbers on peacefully, his tiny face shaded by a parasol.

'Of course, now that he's born, you've got no more excuses.'

Antonia gawps at me. 'Excuses about what?'

'Smoking,' I reply.

She slaps my arm. 'As if I'm still smoking! I gave it up months ago.'

'Yeah, right,' hoots Albert sneaking a half-opened packet from her handbag. 'So how did that end up in there?'

Antonia throws her head back and laughs. 'OK, I'll start again tomorrow. Just you wait and see. I'll surprise you yet.'

And at that moment baby Tyler opens his big eyes and awards her the largest grin. Even he seems to know that I'll be waiting for that surprise for some time yet.

Seventeen

LITTLE DEVILS

Music is blasting from the kitchen as I arrive back from the field clasping an empty scraps bucket. Catalina is stationed at the ironing board when I stride in and gives my shoes a disapproving look.

'I'm going to wash the floor, so you can leave those outside.'

Dutifully I abandon the old trainers by the door and fill up the kettle. Catalina edges over to the CD player and turns the volume down. 'I love the Gypsy Kings on a sunny day like this. The music's so happy. OK, so what you been making? What are all these bottles doing on MY table?'

'Well, the ones on the left are jars of home-made chilli and pepper jelly and on the right, pesto. I made them first thing this morning. You can take some to try if you like.'

She nods. '*Si*, I will. Are they easy to make?'

'Simple. For the jelly, I just take a few handfuls of red chillies and bell peppers from the garden, deseed them and blend them with raspberry vinegar, salt, sugar, fresh lime juice and pectin.'

'What's that?'

'A gelling agent. The pesto is simple too. Just a blend of pine nuts, basil and coriander leaves, parmesan, garlic, olive oil and lemon juice. It's so much cheaper and tastier than the stuff sold in supermarkets.'

'I agree, but it's all a question of time. I spend my life running.' She props the iron on its perch and peers at the sink. 'You seen all those ants?'

'I know, the little devils have just arrived in force. One of the perils of the hot weather.'

'Use that spray I told you about. All around the brickwork.'

The Scotsman suddenly appears with Orlando bundled in his arms. 'I just used that spray this morning, Catalina! It should kill off the little horrors. Now we have another problem. I found Orlando in the field next to a huge dead rat. He's limping badly.'

I take the cat from him and gently try to examine his leg. He lets out a low warning growl and is evidently in great discomfort.

'It looks like a bite, but it's hard to see through all that grey fur. He didn't come for his breakfast this morning so I thought something was wrong.'

Catalina strokes his head affectionately. *'Pobre bicho.'* Poor little bug.

I pull the cat carrier from the outside bathroom and after laying an old towel down gently coax Orlando inside. 'I'll quickly pop over to the vet with him.'

As I stand on the patio I look over at the two strings of shiny CDs that I rigged up on either side of the pond to deter the heron and birdlife from plaguing the frogs and Johnny. To my dismay I see that several birds, including an inquisitive blackbird, are boldly perched on the strings and singing tauntingly in my direction.

'The little devils! Now how can that be?' In some confusion I set off in the car to the vet, wondering why my experiment hasn't worked.

A kind God is looking down on me as I turn into the market's tiny car park. A space has just become available outside the vet's surgery, so within minutes I am inside the waiting room with a whimpering and wounded cat sitting miserably in his wicker carrier on my lap. Tomeu escorts a man with a black *ca de Bestiar*, a traditional Mallorcan shepherd dog, from the premises and welcomes me into his surgery. Maria Angeles, his second in command and also a qualified vet, gives me a smile.

'So, what can we do for you today?'

I show them Orlando's wounded leg. Tomeu gently shaves away a little fur and disinfects the area.

'It's a very nasty bite. Look how deep it is.'

'Could have been a rat judging by the puncture mark,' Maria Angeles adds.

I tell them about the dead rat in the field.

'In that case, he's a very brave cat,' smiles Tomeu. 'And he came out the victor.'

Forlornly and with a degree of indignation, Orlando has his temperature taken at his rear end and nobly suffers an anti-inflammatory injection and antibiotic jab. The course of antibiotics I'm handed fills me with dread. Trying to get any of our cats to swallow pills is a veritable nightmare. Wedging a pill in the jaw, clamping the mouth shut while gently stroking the throat is all for naught when the little rotters break free and spit the offending item onto the floor. Minky in particular has learnt from the maxim 'beware Greeks bearing gifts' and is never fooled by my occasional buttery offerings, studiously licking away the butter while leaving the dreaded pill intact. And then I've tried cutting up and sprinkling antibiotics in the cats' dinner bowl, but as soon as they sniff an alien substance, the food goes untouched. Most galling of all is watching a vet administering pills to cats. Effortlessly they plop the item in the back of the mouth, and the next instant it's down the hatch. How do they do it?

Back at the house, Orlando rushes from the cat basket and hides in the downstairs cupboard, licking his war wounds. Nothing is going to induce him to leave his safe haven for some time. Catalina grabs her car keys and heads for the front door.

'You coming to the *Nit de Foc* tomorrow night?'

'Of course. We're meeting Juana and Pep there. Ollie's been buying up stores of bangers, so I'll bring ear plugs.'

The *Nit de Foc*, the night of fire, is a pyromaniac's dream ticket, and the biggest celebration held in August in Sóller. Dancing devils and demons with pronged forks dash about the main *plaça* prodding locals brave enough to gather en masse in front of the town hall. Most people dampen socks and shoes and wear long sleeves to avoid the sparks from bangers thrown continuously at the ground by children and the mischievous devils. A combination of thumping music, laughter, banging and popping is the name of the game and the noise can be excruciating for those with feeble ears. Savvy locals often fill their lugs with cotton wool before attending, a habit I've also developed. For all that, the event is spectacular and enormous fun with impressive fireworks, and a lively if rather manic atmosphere. For Ollie, it's a liberating time when he can let off bangers and crackers to his heart's content and instil mild terror in his parents.

'I've got to meet some visitors coming from the airport that evening, so I hope they're on time,' says Catalina.

Catalina holds the keys for a number of rental properties whose owners hire her to offer a meet-and-greet service to holidaymakers.

'Do you have to take them to their rental property?' I ask.

'Yes, they'll need the keys and for me to show them how the heating and air-conditioning works and where to put out the rubbish. The usual thing. Fingers crossed I'll be free before it all kicks off.'

She pads across to her car and throws her straw pannier onto the back seat. 'See you, sweetie!'

The Scotsman slaps my arm. 'Are you ready?'

'For what?'

In some frustration he shakes his head. 'Do you never remember anything? We promised to pop by Es Puig d'Alanar this afternoon.'

Of course. This ecological farm managed by some young Spaniards in the south-east of the island has long been on my agenda for a visit. We have been regularly buying their produce through Almaeco, particularly stoneground flour and wholegrain bread, and we'd both like to see how they operate.

'That's perfect timing, because I've run out of flour. But what about Ollie?'

'He's being picked up by Juan's father and the boys will do their homework back at Juan's house. We agreed all this last week.'

And indeed we probably did. The problem these days is that I am frequently indisposed by flights of the imagination that occur just when the Scotsman begins to impart some salient or critically important – and dare I say it, dull – morsel of information. Apparently I nod and appear to be attentive in a glassy-eyed sort of way, but the reality is very different. I am in fact far away in a land all of my own invention, happily absorbed in a make-believe world that bears little resemblance to reality. I hunt out my handbag, pop on some loafers and head for the car. The Scotsman casts me a suspicious glance.

'Are you sure you have everything you need? Did you switch off your computer?'

'I never got round to actually turning it on. So much for clearing my desk today.'

He sighs and plops a map on my lap.

'Are you sure you don't want me to drive?'

He frowns. 'No thank you, I'd rather travel at a speed where the landscape doesn't just resemble a blur.'

We set off for Manacor, a good hour's journey from home. Taking the country roads through Es Pla proves a good move and soon we are at the town of Montuiri.

'Barely an hour,' says the Scotsman triumphantly.

'We're not there yet.'

We push on, and after a troublesome moment when we lose our bearings near Porto Colom, finally find the right road to the farm. We follow the directions given by Gemma, our point of contact, and after taking a sharp left down a muddy track, turn left again, passing the quaint old school building of Puig d'Alanar, now sadly abandoned. Presumably it had outgrown its use when larger, more modern schools began opening in the main towns. We continue downhill until we reach a large metal gate. I hop out and open it while the Scotsman drives through. Another gate lies up ahead so I follow the same procedure. Gemma has warned us that there will be stray animals about and as I attempt to return to the car a group of inquisitive sheep rush up and begin sniffing at my hands. To our left is thick forest and to the right rocky pasture land. Soon a series of old stone outhouses come into view, lush and verdant meadows and neatly cultivated fields. We park the car and are greeted by Gemma – pronounced *Hemma* in Spanish – and her husband Marc who explains that we've arrived on a busy day. Aside from their current activity of harvesting, threshing and winnowing their crops, they are in the midst of baking a batch of wholewheat bread. The farm is a hive of activity.

'So, you already buy our flour and bread?' Gemma asks.

'We certainly do. We're great fans.'

'What can we do for you today?'

The Scotsman smiles. 'We'd like to buy some flour, but it would be great to know more about the farm.'

'And how you got started,' I butt in.

She laughs. 'Well, it all began about four years ago when Miguel Sureda, who owns this terrain, decided to reintroduce traditional farming techniques using natural methods such as animal power and renewable energy, and offered us the opportunity to tend the land and create a traditional stone oven.'

'Quite a big step,' I say. 'What methods did he use before?'

She shrugs. 'Like so many traditional farms on the island, it had ceased to produce for profit, so much of the land had fallen fallow. Miguel set about contacting consumer cooperatives with whom he could collaborate, and soon we came along and formed Puig D'Alanar. We care passionately about natural methods of farming. For instance, we use a horse and cart for harvesting. It's a very simple process. As the two wheels turn, a blade cuts the wheat which is then raked up, ready for threshing.'

'Is that done by hand too?'

'Absolutely. We use two horses that drag round conical rollers that take the stems from the wheat and separate it from the grain.'

'Do you winnow grains?' asks Alan.

Marc nods. 'Yes, one method is to use a reconditioned winnowing machine that's operated by an old pedal bike. As someone pedals, it powers the machine which in turn separates the chaff from the grain.'

Alan raises an eyebrow. 'Great way to get fit.'

'Yes, for whoever picks the short straw that day!' he replies.

'So, how many cereals do you grow here?' I ask.

Gemma replies. 'We produce xeixa and kamut wheat, black oats and Mallorcan barley.'

'What a selection!' exclaims the Scotsman, who is lost in wonderment at the productivity around him. 'And is that your chicken house over there?'

Marc nods. 'I made it from an old wagon cart. Basically it's movable so that the hens always have fresh grass. The corral fence is temporary, so we just move it every day.'

'Ingenious idea,' I say.

Gemma strides off towards a building fashioned from dense wooden beams in which a white, rounded stone oven, shaped rather like an igloo, has been fired and is roaring merrily.

'This building is beautifully crafted,' I say.

Marc raises an eyebrow. 'It was a ruin when we came. My previous work was as a carpenter on boats, so I built it all myself including renovating the oven.'

'A labour of love,' I reply.

'It certainly was.'

Gemma turns to us. 'You know most of the bread people buy has no nutritional value at all. Our bread retains the bran and the germ so that all the proteins, vitamins and fibre remain.'

'And it tastes better,' says the Scotsman.

'We think so. It's quite labour intensive, but the aroma and taste make it worth the effort and our customers love it.'

In the muggy building Gemma pours freshly milled wholewheat flour into paper bags for us and with our booty we emerge into bright sunlight.

Gemma points into the far distance. 'Over there is where we mill our flour. The current task is renovating a stone mill.'

'So, where do you sell your bread and flour apart from to our eco group in Sóller?' I ask.

'Mostly through small cooperatives, and markets or directly here. We're expanding all the time.'

'And do you grow your own vegetables?' asks the Scotsman.

'We've created a garden in which we grow herbs in the centre to attract the fauna and in concentric circles around them vegetables, using bio-intensive techniques. We use varieties from the island and have our own seed bank. In fact, we're working with local farmers to preserve and protect our own generic stock.'

The Scotsman looks on admiringly. 'Presumably you plant them that way according to the season and their individual cycle.'

She nods and then points over at a huge pile of hay and compost. 'You might find this interesting. We can have a supply of hot water from that lot that will last us two months.'

'How?'

Marc points at the centre of the pile. 'We bury the hose beneath the compost and as it breaks down, releasing microorganisms and gases, heat is generated. It can reach eighty degrees.'

'I could do with a compost stack like that at home,' mutters the Scotsman. 'It would save a fortune in heating bills.'

Gemma smiles. '*Exacto*! Of course, we use solar panels too.'

'So what next?' I say, pushing the damp hair from my forehead.

She laughs. 'A glass of home-made lemonade, I'd say.'

Two hours later we set off on the main Manacor road. After our welcome refreshment, we went for a hearty walk through the woods before stopping off later for a cool beer.

'Isn't it heartening to meet a new generation of young Spaniards reintroducing natural farming techniques?' says the Scotsman as we head towards Palma.

'Well, self-sustainability is what it's all about these days. About ninety per cent of food produce is brought into Mallorca, which is crazy. Locals should be supporting these farming cooperatives but it's hard to get the message across.'

He nods. 'Take Pep. He was completely blinkered until we forced him to visit Angus Son Mayol. There's this misconception that buying organic or eco-produce is going to cost you an arm and a leg.'

I tut. 'Trouble is, in supermarkets it is expensive. We'll just have to spread the word.'

It's after nine when we pick up Ollie from his friend Juan's house and make our way home to Sóller. Yawning heavily, he attempts to sound enthusiastic as I give him a blow-by-blow account of our trip to Es Puig D'Alanar.

'Whatever makes you happy, mother,' he sighs. 'I'm glad you had a fun day. School was a little more challenging.'

'Oh poor you.' I change the subject. 'Remember it's the *Nit de Foc* tomorrow night and the day after Juan's coming for a sleepover.'

He brightens up. 'Yay. Can't wait.'

Despite the late hour, the sky is still flushed with light and a dozing moon finally asserts itself and begins a slow ascent above the Tramuntanas as the car crunches across the gravel of the courtyard. In the house, Ollie hunts out Orlando and is alarmed to see him limping badly. When he hears about the rat bite, he folds him up in his arms and takes him off to his room, no doubt for a night of luxury slumbering on his duvet. I slip upstairs and scan my emails, noting that Rachel is chasing me for a press release and that Dannie is now thinking of collaborating with my friend Andrea Cecile on a fashion line. Whatever next! I turn off the computer. It can all wait until tomorrow. In the morning I must call Neus to find out how she is getting on with final plans for the wedding. Along with one of her daughter-in-laws, I've offered to help with hair and make-up on the big day. She may live to regret it. In the bedroom I stare out at the moon and listen to the throaty cry of the frogs. The air is balmy and a soft hazy aura surrounds the mountains. I drink in the sweet perfume of rosemary and warm earth and listen to the cicadas whispering under a darkening sky. Down in the field I can hear the Scotsman chatting to the chickens as he tucks them up for the night and then comes the familiar sound of the garden hose as he begins his night-time watering routine. I close my eyes and, reflecting on a glorious and lazy day, drift off into blissful sleep.

It's late afternoon and Ollie and his friend, Juan, are playing in the field. Occasionally I can hear the distant dull pop of a banger being ignited and know that the two boys are up to some mischief. The Scotsman is in the kitchen, nursing a glass of lemonade in his hand, his eyes idly wandering over the page of the local *Veu de Sóller* newspaper.

'There's an advance notice about Neus's wedding in here. Isn't that nice?'

I peer over his shoulder. 'Well deserved, but she's in quite a state about it all. It took me a while to calm her down yesterday.'

'Bernat's quite oblivious to all the fuss.'

'That's because he's a man.'

He stands up and extends his head towards the open kitchen door. 'Are those boys letting off bangers? I thought Ollie had exhausted his supply at the *Nit de Foc* last night?'

'Unfortunately, Angel gave him reinforcements before we left. I won't be surprised if Ollie is introducing Juan to the local sport of igniting bangers in lemons and watching them explode, the usual wheeze.'

'Well, they'd better be careful. The grass is so dry at this time of the year. We don't want a fire on our hands. By the way, what's that huge box doing by the door?'

I smile. 'Ah, I wondered when you'd notice that. It was delivered while you were in the field. It's a crate of Bullseye sherry, a small gift from Greedy George, for all my help with the Barcelona showroom launch.'

'Pretty good of him. And where's the bronze bull now?'

'I've no idea. I think it was going back to Jerez with the sculptor, but by road not boat this time.'

'Thank heavens for that.'

There's the sound of urgent feet and a worried-looking Juan and Ollie race into the kitchen just as the telephone rings. The Scotsman offers me a perplexed look and answers the call. *'Si, soy Alan. Ah, Marga! Que tal? Que?!'* He shakes his head.

I turn to Ollie. 'What's going on?'

'We've had a little accident,' replies Juan sheepishly. 'We were exploding lemons and a banger flipped into one of the palm trees and it sort of caught light. We didn't realise.'

'It's only smoking a little, but we thought we'd better run up and get some water,' says Ollie awkwardly.

'What?!' I leap from my chair just as the Scotsman thumps down the telephone.

'That was Marga who lives down by the stream,' he growls. 'Apparently, she just saw smoke coming from the heart of one of the small palm trees and drenched it with a bucket of water, but she thinks it needs more. What were you both thinking of?'

The boys apologise but the Scotsman's in strident mode. 'Right, all hands on deck. We'll form a relay with buckets. Come on, poor Marga and her husband haven't got time for this nonsense.'

We grab a pile of buckets and run down into the field, filling each one with water from the hose and carrying them over to the smoking tree. The boys run as fast as they can with the heavy buckets, keen to put an end to the fiasco. Five minutes later the drama is over and the tree looks none the worse for its violation.

'Now you see how dangerous bangers can be? You've got to use common sense, especially when the land is so dry. Just because a banger's spent, doesn't mean it can't catch light.'

They exchange embarrassed glances and apologise to Marga and her husband, Manuel, who find it hard to hide their amusement.

'I remember doing that sort of thing at their age,' remarks Manuel somewhat nostalgically. 'It was always good fun, but the lemons were best. We once threw a banger under the priest's robe. I got a hiding for that. Mind you, some boys at my school did really horrible things. They even blew up frogs.'

'What? That's too awful. I love my frogs,' I say.

The boys attempt a penitent stance.

'We'd never blow up frogs,' says Ollie.

'I don't for a minute think you would, but don't forget that trees are living things too,' says Marga kindly.

She strolls off to her kitchen and comes back with some home-made biscuits. 'Go on, you little devils. Perhaps you'd be better swimming or kicking a ball for now.'

They thank her and when given a nod from the Scotsman, rush off towards the house.

'The tree will be all right. Luckily it had only just started to smoke,' says the Scotsman as we return with the buckets to the house.

'Yes, I think they've learnt their lesson,' I chuckle.

Ollie rushes out of the kitchen door to greet us.

'Now what's up?' I say as my nostrils detect the unmistakable smell of acrid smoke and burnt flour.

He pats my arm sympathetically while trying not to grin. 'Bad luck old thing, I think you might have left your muffins in the oven.'

Eighteen

WEDDING BELLES

The gentlest of breezes is caressing the clumps of dry, blond grasses down by the stream. Both Minny and Della amble about the palm trees, occasionally taking long draughts of water from the big metal tank by their shelter and flicking the buzzing flies from their tails and long brown ears. The stream is completely parched. No change there then. The grey earth at its base is fractured with deep and dark hollow veins that run in wiggly lines across its surface. Flies swarm over the carcass of a heron that has long seen better days. Its leg is wedged under a rock. I can only imagine that it must have been caught unawares in a sudden deluge of rain and drowned, poor thing. I get up and make my way over to the girls. Della has been making strange honking noises the last few days and now has a streaming nose. Do donkeys get summer colds? I often fret about their welfare, taking to the telephone to consult with poor Jacinto if either seems below par. He tells me I'm worse than a mother with my fussing. The donkeys' pelts feel warm and luxurious to the touch, the fur soft and dense. Both appear to be in peak condition and have healthy appetites. It's only when I set off for the gate that little

Della sneezes loudly and regards me with rheumy eyes. That's it. I must call Jacinto even though the Scotsman and I are running late.

Today we are off to the small inland town of Porreres to visit Barbara Mesquida, joint owner with her brother Jaume of Jaume Mesquida wines. Aside from being one of Mallorca's most cherished wineries, having been founded in 1945 by the siblings' great-grandfather, Mesquida is the first to create biodynamic wines on the island. Knowing of my interest in naturally grown local fare, Barbara has invited the Scotsman and me to sample some of the new wines and to visit the vineyards. Afterwards we'll be popping by Xampinyones de Son Fullana to pick up some of its excellent mushroom compost before collecting Ollie from school.

I race into the kitchen and call Jacinto just as the Scotsman appears before me, pointing sternly at his watch face with an agitated finger. Jacinto listens patiently as I discuss Della's symptoms. This time he sounds concerned and agrees to pop by to examine her while I'm out. I replace the receiver and relay the news to the Scotsman.

'She's got a very hoarse cough.'

'A horse cough? That is worrying for a donkey.'

'This isn't a time for silly jokes.'

'That's normally your prerogative.' He scrunches my shoulder. 'Oh come on, don't start worrying. It's probably nothing. Jacinto will know what to do. Now, let's get going or we'll never get there on time.'

We jump in the Mini and with the Scotsman at the wheel as usual, we pull out of the courtyard. As we drive onto the track Helge rushes over to the car.

'Wolfgang and I are here for three weeks. Let's get together soon.'

She waves and disappears down the steps into her garden. The Scotsman smiles.

'Good to have them back. It's sad when they go away.'

As we pass Rafael's house there's the sound of wild music. The Scotsman shakes his head. 'It's a wonder he's still got any hearing left.'

At the mouth of the track, Pedro emerges from his orchard. I lean out of the passenger window as he saunters over. He greets us cordially and announces that he has some important news. His daughter Catí has just got engaged and will be marrying the following summer.

'What brilliant tidings, Pedro. Do send our best to Catí.'

Beaming, he wanders back to his orchard to get on with some pruning. We turn onto the road.

'Anyone else you'd care to chat with en route?' says the Scotsman.

I elbow him in the ribs. 'As my Irish granny used to say, manners maketh man.'

We decide to take the country route, first following the road to Santa Maria and then to Inca where we follow directions for Sineu, Montuiri and Porreres. Unlike the Sóller Valley, the landscape here is smooth, a seemingly never-ending carpet of soft verdant grasses and arable farming land only broken by the occasional orchard of olives or almonds, flanked by gentle undulating hills in the background. The little town of Porreres today appears to be dominated by elderly matrons in vans and battered cars who drive along the narrow streets with cheerful abandonment, riding the kerbs and kicking up dust as their tyres squeal around the tight bends. Alan narrowly misses scraping a wall as he attempts to avoid one of the old dears careering towards us in her grey jalopy. We park on a quiet side street and head for the shady *plaça* where earlier we spotted some cheery-looking cafes.

'I need something for my nerves after that drive. That last old girl must have been pushing ninety,' he says.

'At least, but you've got to hand it to them. They're still on the roads even if they can barely reach the wheel or remember which pedals to hit.'

'At what cost to the rest of us?' he retorts.

We sit at a table outside the main bar, Sa Plaça, and enjoy freshly baked croissants and strong coffee. A shaft of sunlight hits our table and we both briefly bask in the warmth before paying the bill and setting off across the neat paved *plaça*. In the far corner is a rather unusual metal sculpture shaped like a boat which is supported by a tall, flowering palm tree while on the other side, raised above the ground, a series of square, stone structures showpiece grey pebbles and water. Each bears the name of a local spring, the most unusual, displaying pretty pebbles of different hues, being Sa Fontassa, and is sealed with glass.

'Rather novel,' I say.

The Scotsman squats on his haunches to examine them more closely. 'Rather nice that they're promoting the natural springs on the island. No artifice, and such a simple idea.'

'You know that Padre Barceló, the honey priest, grew up here and look how fit he is. Maybe there's something in the natural spring water that keeps the local elderly so sprightly.'

'Let's hope they bottle it soon then,' replies the Scotsman. 'So, first we visit the winery and then the vineyards?'

I nod. 'That's the idea. Then we can find a spot for lunch.'

We stroll along to the chunky limestone church dominated by a vast circular window and, at the side, an imposing clock tower whose inky black spire resembles a tall witch's hat. The car is parked nearby and after a five-minute drive we arrive at Jaume Mesquida. Although housed in a traditional and modest building in a quiet part of town, the winery is a masterpiece of contemporary architecture. Barbara is there to greet us at the reception with little Barbara attached to her hip like a baby monkey.

'It's so lovely to see you! Come in and have a peek around. I hope you don't mind if Barbara junior joins us?'

The little girl smiles up at us and when we take seats at the tasting table, is keen to explore the contents of my handbag, particularly my keys and purse. Barbara is eager to tell us about her new wines.

'As you know, my brother Jaume and I took over the business from our father in 2004 and made a conscious decision to make really exceptional wines.'

'But weren't they already?' asks Alan wryly.

'What I mean is wine that was produced from really healthy soil. We didn't want to use fertilisers and pesticides any more and decided to take on a consultant in biodynamics.'

'A pretty radical step,' I say.

She laughs. 'You have no idea! We stopped the use of tractors which impacted the soil – and anyway they made far too much noise – and instead began to nurture the land. We now use mules and carts and handpick the grapes. It involves more work but the results are fantastic.'

'Do you use biodynamic agricultural methods for all your vines?' I ask.

'When we saw how fertile the soil became, we decided to convert all twenty-two hectares. It's been a revelation and now we are about to launch the Mesquida Mora first biodynamic wines.'

Alan extracts a pen from little Barbara's clutch. 'Are other Mallorcan vineyards following your lead?'

'There are some who produce eco-wines but none using biodynamic methods. You know, for me it's about preserving the land for future generations. You don't feed your children junk food, so why spoil the land they'll inherit with harmful pesticides?'

She gets up and prizes my keys and perfume bottle from her daughter's hand.

'Come and try the new wines from the barrel.'

We follow her into the quiet winery where she offers us a taste of the four different wines. There's Acrollam – it's Mallorca spelt backwards – a fresh and fruity-tasting white and rosé, and Sotil and Trispol, both reds. The former is delicious and light, while the latter has more body.

Barbara explains the story behind the names. 'Sòtil means ceiling and trispol, tiled floor, in Mallorquin. In other words sky and earth – the two ingredients needed to make and harvest superb wine.'

'Well, they're jolly good,' purrs the Scotsman. 'I particularly like Trispol. What wonderful old barrels you have here.'

'They're French oak casks and take up to about three hundred litres of wine. We have to replace them every four years.'

'So, what's the timescale on your wine production?' I ask.

'Well, we prune in January and when the grapes ripen in August we harvest until the end of October. The extraction, fermentation and bottling process goes on until June.'

'So, you're busy all year?'

She laughs. 'There's always work to be done! Now you must visit the vines.'

After a fifteen-minute drive through Es Pla with its golden fields, wild terrain and orchards brimming with fruit trees, we find ourselves at Son Obra, where healthy and bushy vines like an orderly forest of miniature trees run in rows towards the horizon. The ripe grapes are already being hand-picked by locals and hurled into an old wooden cart drawn by a mule, its dark, glossy coat shining under the sun's rays. It passes slowly up and down the rows with the aid of a smiling veteran in an old pair of faded dungarees and a straw hat. An imposing almond tree and an old stone outhouse are the only obstacles to the sun's rays as we walk among the vines, breathing in the aroma of fresh moist soil and sap.

'What do you think?' smiles Barbara.

The Scotsman scoops up a handful of red soil and sniffs it carefully like a connoisseur breathing in a fine wine's bouquet. 'Interesting. It's ferrous. Good for growing and you can see how magnificent this soil is. I could do with some of this at home.'

'We have eight vineyards and the soil varies. At Son Pòrquer there's a lot of clay but the vines still grow well. It's all about how you tend the soil. We're now using biodynamic compost which we produce from the stems of the vines, and we prune according to the lunar calendar.'

'Many of our farmers in the Sóller Valley do the same.' I reply.

The Scotsman shields his eyes from the sun's glare. 'How do you treat any potential diseases affecting the vines?'

'With medicinal plant infusions,' she replies. 'We try to find natural solutions where we can.'

'Impressive,' nods the Scotsman.

She heads towards her car. '*Venga*, I'll show you another of our vineyards before you go.'

An hour later we find ourselves on the main road from Porreres to Llumajor with the sound of clinking bottles coming from the back of the car. Aside from buying a few boxes for our own consumption, we have purchased a gift crate for Neus and Bernat who will be getting married in two days' time.

'There! I think this is Cami de Son Fullana,' I say.

The Scotsman indicates left and we hurtle down a muddy and bumpy lane. Normally we buy our mushroom compost from a local distributor, but as we were in the vicinity of the farm, we thought it would be fun to pop by. In a large clearing to our left is an enormous mountain of mushroom compost and around it the telltale dried tyre tracks of hefty lorries.

'This is where the compost is loaded up and taken off to different sellers across the island,' remarks the Scotsman. 'Now, I wonder how far down this track we have to go.'

We carry on along the unmade road a few kilometres until we finally reach another clearing. Here we find a series of old derelict barns to the right, and to the far left up a muddy slope a Portakabin with the word *oficina* scrawled on the door. A wide track runs to the side of it down to a large gaping hole, possibly the mouth of an enormous cave.

'What goes on down there?'

The Scotsman stands at the entrance to the track. 'Maybe that's where they grow the mushrooms. Who knows?'

At the office a young woman instructs us to walk over to the white *naves*, warehouses where Joan, one of the farms owners, is expecting us. After a brisk walk, we arrive at a series of large white buildings and enter through one of the metal doors. A stocky man with a cheery bespectacled face comes to greet us, introducing himself as Joan. Young men and women in blue overalls, gloves and caps pass us, pushing metal trolleys laden with cartons of ghostly white button mushrooms into various bunkers. With a blue-gloved hand, Joan beckons us to look through the window of a large workroom in which mushrooms are being packed in cartons and labelled by a group of women. They nudge one another and wave and giggle when they see us. Joan slaps his hands together.

'We're right in the middle of organising a supermarket delivery, but I can give you a very quick tour of the place if you're interested?'

'That would be fantastic,' I reply. 'So, is this where all the mushrooms are grown?'

He swings open a door and we find ourselves in a vast, cool and dimly lit store room in which large metal stacking shelves are laden with row upon row of lengthy compost bags brimming with perfectly white mushrooms.

'We have many store rooms like this. This is where we grow the button mushrooms. They take about thirty days to grow from spores and we keep the temperature at about fifteen degrees.'

The Scotsman points to the bags. 'And what kind of compost do you use?'

'It's our own natural mix made from hen and horse manure among other things. We use a different kind for the *setas*.'

'Ah, so you grow wild mushrooms too. Where are they?'

Joan smiles at me. 'Did you see the entrance to the old quarry when you came in? That's where we grow the *setas*. I'll take you there in a minute.'

'Presumably you sell to the supermarkets on the island?'

'Many, and even to some outlets in Ibiza and Menorca, but transport's an issue. It's critical that we pick and pack the mushrooms and deliver them to the stores all on the same day to keep them fresh.'

'And what about those packets of pre-sliced mushrooms I see in supermarkets?'

He frowns. 'We wouldn't supply them. Once cut and exposed to the air, they oxidize so you'd need preservatives to maintain the colour. Our mushrooms are one hundred per cent natural and we intend to keep them that way.'

He strides out into the cemented entrance hall and answers queries from various employees before bustling us out into the sunshine. 'We'll take my van from here.'

We jump into his old, dusty vehicle and soon we're rattling down the muddy and winding slope deep into the cavernous quarry. Dim light is emitted from a string of electric bulbs that, like giant fairy lights, run along the uneven surface of the roofs of the caves. As the car twists and turns through narrow passages I fast lose track of where we're heading in the labyrinthine tunnels. I sure hope Joan doesn't abandon us down here. It would be some years before we might resurface, like two giant disorientated mushrooms gasping for air.

Joan turns to us. 'In the last century they quarried for *mares* stone down here. Now it's a great place to grow *setas* because of the ambient temperature.'

With a jerk of the wheel, he turns right through a narrow and rocky arch and parks. He leads us over the rocky path to a natural cave alive with fully and partially developed *setas*. They pour out from compost sacks, growing in beautiful conical formations that resemble gigantic, oyster-grey pine cones with the young *setas* growing from the heart.

'They're quite miraculous!' I gasp.

He shrugs. 'They are special, that's why they cost more to buy. We carefully have to pick off the heads as they reach full size.'

'Do they take longer to grow than ordinary mushrooms?' I ask.

'About the same length of time.'

We jump back into the car and head back the way we came. I look out from the backseat of the car, wondering how Joan knows which tunnel to take but presumably after so many years working here, he could do it blindfolded.

'Is your whole family involved in the business?' The Scotsman asks.

He stifles a big yawn. 'A fair few. My cousin Rosa and her brother. The company was originally formed some forty years ago by an Englishman called Sampson.'

'I take it you start your day early?'

He laughs. 'You could say that. We begin at 6.00 a.m., but on delivery days such as tomorrow I'll be starting at 3.30 a.m. and I don't leave until every order's complete.'

We drive out into the clearing and with some relief I look up at the blue sky. He walks us back to our car and while Alan places the compost in the back of the car, shakes my hand.

'Mushroom growing is a full-on job, as you can see.'

'Yes, I don't think I'll be taking it up anytime soon, but it's fascinating to look round. How on earth do you manage to muster any energy at such an early time of day?'

He throws out his hands and grins.

In the car I turn to the Scotsman. 'What a slog. Up at 3.30 a.m. every week! What do you think his secret is?'

He offers me a smile. 'Perhaps he'd rather keep us in the dark, rather like his mushrooms.'

I tut and reach for the map. 'Ho ho. Now then, where do you suppose we might find a little place that could conjure us up a scrumptious mushroom omelette?'

We arrive home to find Della gone from the field. Jacinto has left a note in the porch explaining that he has taken her to his land. He suggests that she might have a virus and thinks it best to keep her in isolation and to summon the vet in the morning.

'Do you think she's got influenza?' I ask.

'Look, she's in the best of hands so let's wait and see,' Ollie replies.

The Scotsman tries to put on a brave face but I can see he too is worried. She's a young donkey and we've been warned that respiratory diseases can be serious. After rustling up supper I tiptoe out to the pond but the frogs sense movement and immediately stop their song. After my disastrous attempts at using strings of CDs to fend off the heron, we have now bought some bulrushes to give the frogs and fish better protection. Johnny eyes me from his favourite rock.

'Those new reeds are a lot better than those stupid CDs. Shame you didn't come up with the idea earlier.'

'We were hoping to avoid using them again. They spread so quickly.'

He stares at me. 'You all right?'

'I have a lot on my mind.'

'Yeah, right. Worrying about a coughing donkey rather than me and the lads. I saw all that new hay you carted up here the other day. Must have cost a euro or two.'

'Don't be silly. Actually, we bought it from a new distributor. It was very good value.'

He unleashes his tongue and catches a fly. 'Yum.'

'Ugh, I wish you wouldn't do that.'

'Gotta get your five a day.'

I hear the telephone ringing from the kitchen. He gives a rasping tut and plops into the slimy depths. On the other end of the line Ed is full of the joys of spring, or rather, summer.

'Scatters, I've got some fantastic news!'

'You've got even more work?'

'It's not that, although I'm having a ball at this new recruitment firm. So nice to be appreciated for a change. No, my news is... wait for it... Rela and I are getting married. We're engaged.'

I'm genuinely thrilled. At last, at the age of forty-nine, Ed has found his soulmate.

'Well you're the third couple we know of getting married. Is there something in the air?'

'You never know.'

'When is the wedding?' I trill.

'That's yet to be decided, but fairly soon.'

'I hope the MEK will be given place of honour.'

He laughs. 'Yes, I was thinking of asking it to be best man.'

When he's off the line, I share the glad tidings with the Scotsman and Ollie.

'About time too,' sighs Ollie. 'I suppose it's better late than never.'

'Who would have thought it?' smiles the Scotsman.

'Now I've been thinking,' I say. 'When I was chatting with Johnny...'

Ollie regards me impatiently. 'Oh, not your pretend friend again.'

'Go on,' says his father.

'He reminded me that we've recently bought a new supply of hay for the donkeys. I'm wondering if that could have anything to do with Della's cough, perhaps an allergic reaction?'

They both laugh. Ollie taps me on the head.

'As if a donkey can get an allergy to hay! If that's the best advice Johnny can give you, I'd find yourself a new friend.'

Much later when I'm upstairs in the office killing off a few emails before bed, I give Jacinto a call. He doesn't laugh at my suggestion of an allergy but instead agrees to discuss it with the vet. I lean out of the window and in the velvety darkness call to Johnny.

'Thanks for the tip.'

There's no reply and yet as my eyes fall on the pond, white and luminous in the light of the moon, I see a small and bulky silhouette sitting on a rock. It might be my imagination, but I'm sure he gives me a wink.

It's a hot and sticky day and the cicadas are in overdrive, rasping and calling to one another in great excitement. High in the pale-blue sky, a flight of birds offers an exquisite display of airborne acrobatics for the assembled throng who far below stroll around a beautifully tended garden in the village of Santa Maria, clutching glasses of cool cava. Perhaps the clicking cicadas and their winged friends also share in the joy of seeing two elderly people joined in holy matrimony and enjoying a celebratory and sumptuous feast with friends and family. The wedding cake has been cut and the *vino* is flowing. Sitting on a bench in her son's garden, Neus grips my hand and beams.

'We've done it! Did you enjoy the service?'

'It was wonderful, and the priest was a good sport.'

'Bernat and I have known him for years. He's in his eighties too.'

'He's amazing for his age, and you look ravishing.'

She throws her head back and laughs, then pats cautiously at her hair. 'I'll be happier when I can get back to my old clothes. I'm not used to having flowers in my hair and that stuff you put on my lashes feels very odd.'

'It's mascara. You can wipe it off when you get home, but a little make-up does suit you.'

She suddenly touches my arm. 'Didn't the bridesmaids look sweet in their white dresses arriving at the church on donkeys?'

'Adorable – and weren't the animals well-behaved?'

'More than the bridesmaids,' she quips. 'Talking of donkeys, what's the news on Della?'

'Haven't I told you? The vet confirmed that she was allergic to the dust on the new batch of hay. We soaked it and washed down the shelter and she's already much better.'

'That Jacinto's a marvel.'

'He is, and so is my…' I'm about to mention Johnny but think better of it.

Bernat comes over with the Scotsman and tops up my glass of cava. 'You know there are more than one hundred people here. Thank heavens we over-catered. We were expecting eighty.'

'You shouldn't be so popular,' Alan quips.

Ollie comes over with Angel and offers the newlyweds large slices of wedding cake. With great relish they accept the china plates proffered.

'What about us?' I joke.

Angel raises his eyebrows. 'You'll have to wait your turn like everyone else. My dad's at the front of the queue as you can imagine!'

They scamper off and a few minutes later Pep comes over nursing a huge helping of cake.

'You'd better get moving or you won't get a slice. They're already on the second tier,' he quips.

'I think I should go easy on the cake,' I reply.

He gives a snort. 'It's a bit too late for that now. I saw how much food you were tucking away earlier. The damage is done. You're one of the greediest women I know.'

Not true,' says Neus loyally. 'She's a growing girl.'

Even the Scotsman smirks. 'We'll wander over there in a while once the other gannets have had their fill.'

Pep taps Neus's bronzed, leathery arm. 'Your son's suggested I help myself to his grapes. He's got a pergola groaning with ripe fruit.'

She nods. 'Ah *si*! For your winemaking. What an excellent idea.'

'What do you say, Alan? We could double our El Toro production this summer.'

'If you think I'm crawling up a pergola in my good linen jacket, you're mistaken.'

'But I've found an old ladder and collected two big buckets from the back of my van. You can take that jacket off, for goodness' sake.'

I raise an eyebrow. 'Where is this pergola?'

He points into the distance. 'Just next to that barn. You see?'

Bernat gives the Scotsman a wary glance. 'It's quite high, so be careful.'

I watch as they trudge off. 'Do you think they know what they're doing?'

'Maybe you should supervise,' says Neus with a grin.

'Perhaps you're right.'

After draining my glass, I follow in their wake, avoiding laughing children in party dresses playing and running about on the grass and groups of guests feasting on wedding cake. As I draw near to the barn, I see that the Scotsman has removed his jacket and is piling up the grapes that Pep is busily tossing to the ground in huge bunches. On the top step of the ladder he rises on his toes as he attempts to reach the higher vines that twist about the pergola's wrought iron bars. Suddenly Judas begins ringing from my handbag. It's Greedy George.

'Wotcha, guv. Where are you?'

'At a wedding reception.'

'Well go easy on the amber nectar. Now I've got some interesting news for you.'

'You're taking up pole-dancing at Felipe's strip club?'

'Nah, don't like cold metal. It's about Ratón.'

'The bull? What of him?'

'Well, Celestina, my showroom manager in Barcelona, went all cosmic after the launch saying that Ratón was a good omen for Havana and shouldn't go back to Jerez. I thought about it and decided to take the plunge.'

'You've bought Ratón? But he must have cost a fortune.'

'You don't want to know, guv.'

'And is he in the showroom now?'

'Unfortunately he'd already been returned to Jerez so he's being transported back to Barcelona by sea.'

'By SEA? Are you mad? Remember what happened last time.'

'That got you! No, he's coming by land, don't you worry. I'm going to put him plumb in the middle of the showroom.'

There's a loud crash accompanied by moaning and cursing.

'What's that noise?' asks George.

'I'm not sure,' I reply.

I rush forward in time to see Pep swinging like a distraught gibbon from one of the wrought iron bars of the pergola, a ruffle of vines around his neck while his accomplice in crime frantically attempts to erect the overturned wooden ladder. A mass of ruby-red grapes and leaves form a scruffy pyramid at the Scotsman's side.

'Everything all right, guv?'

I look away from the chaotic scene, unable to contain my mirth. 'Yes, it's just a mad Mallorcan doing battle with a murderous vine.'

'Those islanders know how to have a good time, don't they?' he chortles.

'Well they certainly know how to live life, or should I say, how to grab life by the horns.'

Turning back, I watch as the Scotsman tries to coax the swaying Pep to step down onto the rickety ladder but he seems reluctant to prise his fingers from the iron bar. And then all of a sudden he lets go and lands on his backside right in the middle of the heap of grapes.

A LIZARD IN MY LUGGAGE

Mayfair to Mallorca in One Easy Move

Anna Nicholas

£8.99

Paperback

ISBN: 978-1-84024-565-3

Anna, a PR consultant to Mayfair's ritziest and most glamorous, had always thought Mallorca was for the disco and beer-swilling fraternity. That was until her sister hired an au pair from a rural part of the island who said it was the most beautiful place on earth. On a visit, Anna impulsively decided to buy a ruined farmhouse.

Despite her fear of flying, she kept a foot in both camps and commuted to central London to manage her PR company. But she found herself drawn away from the bustle and stress of life in the fast lane towards a more tranquil existence.

Told with piquant humour, *A Lizard in my Luggage* explores Mallorca's fiestas and traditions, as well as the ups and downs of living in a rural retreat. It is about learning to appreciate the simple things and take risks in pursuit of real happiness. Most importantly, it shows that life can be lived between two places.

'A beautifully written and highly entertaining account of the upside of downshifting.'
DAILY MIRROR

'A witty and devilishly intelligent foray into the highs and lows of a new life in Spain.'
XPAT magazine

CAT ON A HOT TILED ROOF

Mayhem in Mayfair and Mallorca

Anna Nicholas

£8.99

Paperback

ISBN: 978-1-84024-683-4

Having moved with her family to rural Mallorca to escape the stresses of London life, PR consultant Anna Nicholas continues to commute back to her glitzy Mayfair agency to earn a crust. Meanwhile she is harbouring a bizarre dream to open a luxury cattery on the island – unbeknownst to her long suffering Scottish husband, Alan, and son, Oliver.

Life in the mountains is never uneventful as the author gets to grips with phantom sheep, midnight snail hunts, Catalan lessons, ghosts, floods and flighty hens. London also has its challenges, as she juggles eccentric, rich and often neurotic clients between Mayfair and Manhattan and is hotly pursued by lucrative deals. But increasingly Anna finds herself craving the simple life of her Spanish idyll because as she discovers, you can take the girl out of Mallorca, but you can't take Mallorca out of the girl.

Wickedly irreverent, laugh out loud funny and lovingly observed, *Cat on a Hot Tiled Roof* celebrates the wonders of Mallorcan rural life.

'Anna Nicholas has a tremendous gift for descriptive writing.'

Nicholas Parsons

'Terrific'
Lucia van der Post

'Witty, evocative and heart-warming. Another Mallorcan pearl from Anna Nicholas.'
Peter Kerr

GOATS FROM A SMALL ISLAND

Grabbing Mallorcan Life by the Horns

Anna Nicholas

£8.99

Paperback

ISBN: 978-1-84024-760-2

Life on the small island of Mallorca is entertaining and fascinating for Anna Nicholas, who moved her family to a rural mountain setting for a more *mañana* existence. But it's never simple.

She pursues her dream of opening a cattery, is devastated by the abduction of her beloved toad, and becomes fixated with Myotragus, the extinct goat that roamed Mallorca in ancient times. Meanwhile, trying to cut loose from her PR agency and its clients in London and New York, she finds herself among nutty Russian models and amorous rock climbers.

Hilarious, informative and brimming with memorable characters, *Goats From A Small Island* is a delightful tribute to Mallorca's rich way of life.

'insights into Mallorcan life away from the tourist traps; the manana existence among the olive groves, fruit trees and goats... makes you want to go there yourself'   THE DORSET ECHO

'No one is more of an authority on life in Mallorca than Ms Nicholas and this title proves that down to a T.'   St Christopher's e-zine

DONKEYS ON MY DOORSTEP

Hoofing it in the Mallorcan Hills

Anna Nicholas

£8.99

Paperback

ISBN: 978-1-84953-038-5

The dream is near completion. Anna is loosening the reins on her London PR company to spend more time in Mallorca with her family, cattery, chickens and goats, and insists their menagerie will only be complete with not one donkey, but two. She attempts almond harvesting in the countryside amid summertime ant and wasp infestations in the finca, and attends a traditional wedding and the spectacular Sant Juan horse festival in Menorca. Meanwhile, she befriends an elderly poet whose love letters to his fiancé during the Spanish Civil War waft into her field, unveiling a poignant story of bravery and sacrifice.

Brimming with humorous and loveable characters, *Donkeys on my Doorstep* is a charming take on the simple and rewarding life of rural Mallorca.

'filled with humorous anecdotes... the Majorcan countryside is described in attentive, often lyrical detail'   Telegraph.co.uk

'endearing, funny and poignant. What more could one wish for'
                                                       REAL TRAVEL magazine

Have you enjoyed this book?
If so, why not write a review on your favourite website?

If you're interested in finding out more about our travel books
friend us on Facebook at **Summersdale Traveleditor**
and follow us on Twitter: **@SummersdaleGO**

Thanks very much for buying this Summersdale book.

www.summersdale.com